Dedicated with love to Carol Gimbel Loder,
whose courage and faith humble me.

MOON DANCE

"Enchanting. . . . A story filled with surprises."
—The Philadelphia Inquirer

"Stewart hits a home run out of the ballpark . . . a delightful contemporary romance."
—The Romance Reader

WONDERFUL YOU

"Compares favorably with the best of Barbara Delinsky and Belva Plain."
—Amazon.com

"*Wonderful You* is delightful—romance, laughter, suspense! Totally charming and enchanting."
—The Philadelphia Inquirer

For "spine-tingling reading for a warm summer's night" (Library Journal), don't miss Mariah Stewart's novella " 'Til Death Do Us Part" in the anthology

WAIT UNTIL DARK

"A diverse quartet . . . penned by some of the genre's more talented writers. . . . Chilling . . . eerie."
—Library Journal

"Exciting, non-stop romantic suspense."
—Harriet Klausner

Books by Mariah Stewart

Moments in Time

A Different Light

Carolina Mist

Devlin's Light

Wonderful You

Moon Dance

Priceless

Brown-Eyed Girl

Voices Carry

Published by POCKET BOOKS

MARIAH STEWART

DEVLIN'S LIGHT

POCKET BOOKS
New York London Toronto Sydney

An *Original* Publication of POCKET BOOKS

POCKET BOOKS, a division of Simon & Schuster, Inc.
1230 Avenue of the Americas, New York, NY 10020

Copyright © 1997 by Marti Robb

ISBN-13: 978-0-671-00415-6
ISBN-10:   0-671-00415-8

First Pocket Books printing August 1997

10   9   8   7   6

POCKET and colophon are registered trademarks of
Simon & Schuster, Inc.

Cover photo © Gandee Vasan/The Image Bank
Cover design by Jae Song

Manufactured in the United States of America

For information regarding special discounts for bulk purchases,
please contact Simon & Schuster Special Sales at 1-800-456-6798 or
business@simonandschuster.com.

Love and thanks to—

Patricia N. Holsten, Esquire, of the Delaware County District Attorney's office, for cheerfully researching and answering all my questions with her customary thoroughness and good humor.

Dede Frederick, who brought me Swiss chard and monkshood when mine refused to grow, and who understands what *down and dirty* really means.

Helen Egner and Nolia Scott, the real chefs in the family, for graciously contributing their recipes (Darla would be proud of both of you!).

Loretta Barrett, my agent, for taking care of business and for always being there for me.

Kate Collins, my editor, for her hard work and total commitment. Working with you is a complete pleasure—I'm privileged to have you in my corner.

DEVLIN'S
LIGHT

Chapter 1

With cool impartiality, India Devlin regarded the face of each and every mourner who stood at her brother's open grave, wondering if perhaps she were, at that moment, looking into the deceptive eyes of a killer who hid a terrible secret while at the same time offering well-rehearsed condolences.

Everyone who was *anyone* in Devlin's Light—and many who were not—had come to pay their last respects to Robert Forman Devlin. India, the only sibling of the deceased, shifted her sights first to the group gathered on the opposite side of the waiting grave, then to the large coffin, still draped and flower strewn, which rested almost at her feet. She tucked a strand of unruly blond hair behind her ear and shifted her weight, one foot to the other, all the while watching, watching, praying that someone would do something to give themselves away.

Ludicrous, she chided herself. As if Ry's killer would step forward and announce that he—or she—was the guilty one.

But who?

Ry Devlin had been the last of the male line of those same Devlins who had come south from the New England colonies in the mid-1600s and whose name was borne by both the lighthouse they had built and the settlement they had founded on the uncertain coast just west of the point where the Atlantic Ocean met the Delaware Bay. Handsome, affable, full of the Devlin charm, Ry had been well liked, admired, respected by all who knew him, and he had seemed to be without an enemy in this world.

Well, he'd had at least one.

India shook her head, incredulous that she should find herself here, in this centuries-old burying place, at so unlikely an event. Once, as a child, India had unsuccessfully attempted to count the number of Devlins whose final resting spots lay behind the small, whitewashed church that had served many generations of the town's residents. The weathered structure had gone unused for years, since long before India's birth, though it was faithfully maintained through the efforts of the Devlin Trust; for the country church, like the ancient cemetery and much of the coastal boundary of Devlin's Light, was on Devlin land.

Beyond Ry's grave, in this corner of the churchyard, lay the remains of their father, Robert Sr., their mother, Nancy, and their paternal grandparents, Benjamin and Sarah. A little farther down a well-worn path, side by side and for all eternity, lay Benjamin's parents and, a bit farther more, their parents. And so on, through more generations of Devlins all the way back to Eli, Samuel and Jonathan, the first Devlins to stand on the shores of the Delaware Bay.

And there, about six feet to the left of Ry's intended eternal home, was the marker erected but two years earlier for Maris Steele Devlin. Ry's wife of eight months, Maris had taken a rowboat out into the bay to go crabbing one summer morning and had been caught in a sudden squall. Now Maris was memorialized here, amidst the remains of a family she had never belonged to, had never really been part of.

Unconsciously India sought and found the hand of her late brother's stepdaughter and gave it a squeeze, then gathered the little girl to her in an embrace meant to comfort, all the while wondering if this child would ever know comfort again. As dismayed as India had been over Ry's choice of a wife, India had adored Maris's daughter, Corrine. Sweet, shy Corri, who had dealt with loss far too often for one so young and who now, at six, believed she faced the world alone.

Not while I have life, India promised silently, her fingers gently untangling one of Corri's strawberry-blond curls. She knew exactly how deep the little girl's grief would be, and she sought, in whatever way she could, to absorb some of it.

India bowed her head and squeezed her eyes closed against the tears welling up behind them and tried once again to swallow the lump that would not be swallowed away as the Reverend Corson cleared his throat and began the final prayers over the heavy bronze coffin. It was long and wide—"oversized," the funeral director had noted absently—to hold the body of the deceased. Ry had been a big man, tall and broad-shouldered. Agile as a cat, though, and gentle as the wishes they made when, as children, they had sat upon the rocks overlooking the inlet, waiting for the first of the evening stars to appear in the night sky.

"Go 'head, Indy, you first," Ry would coax his little sister. "And make it a *good* wish. *Good* wishes always come true. . . ."

Star light, star bright, first star I see tonight . . .

"But you can't tell anybody what you wish for. Or it won't come true," he would caution her.

I wish I may, I wish I might . . .

"'cept you, Ry, right? I can tell you?" she would ask, wanting to share the secrets of her child's heart with her much loved big brother.

Have this wish I wish tonight.

"'fraid not, Indy. Got to be a secret, even from me . . ."

Many years later, Indy could still hear Ry's voice, see the twinkle in his blue eyes as he searched the heavens for her very own wishing star and guided her eyes to it, encouraging her to dream.

Who could have done this to so good a soul as Ry?

"We gather together today in memory of our friend and brother, Robert . . ." Reverend Corson's soft voice floated with the ease of a mist across the tranquil bay even as India's eyes continued to skip from one face to another.

Surely not you, Peter Mason. You who knew Ry since nursery school, who fished the bay with him and shared the treasures of the marshes with him.

". . . and to commend his loving spirit to its everlasting rest . . ."

Nor you, Ely Townsend, who spent so many summer days on the front porch of our house on Darien Road, watching the girls saunter by in their short shorts and halter tops on their way to the small stretch of beach at the end of the street.

"and so we ask you, Father, to have mercy on his soul . . ."

Or you, Nat Tomlin, who, with Ry, built that old playhouse in the oak tree behind our garage, where you used to sneak cigarettes and girls. The playhouse Ry fell out of when he was fourteen and broke both his legs. No football, no baseball, for all his freshman year.

". . . to open the gates of heaven to your servant . . ."

The cry of a solitary gull echoed across the dunes and over the bay to her left, and India turned toward the sound. From behind an ancient stand of scrub pine, Devlin's Light rose toward a cloudless sky. Though a storm was in the forecast for later in the afternoon, no sign of it could be seen at eleven in the morning. The shadow of the lighthouse reached almost to the jetty that stretched into the deep blue-green calm of the bay. Here and there a fish leaped out of the water as if to tease the ever-present gulls. But it was the lighthouse, always, that drew the eye and held the gaze.

A three-story clapboard, Queen Anne–style house, shaped like an L, with a six-story tower at the juncture of the two parts of the structure, Devlin's Light had weathered many storms and had always survived intact. A few of the slate shingles had blown off in this storm or that, its red shutters had faded some and it sorely needed a good painting, but the lighthouse had stood on its present site since the year of its construction, 1876.

The irony of Ry being laid to rest almost in the shadow of the lighthouse that had so dominated his life was not lost on India. As a boy he had played in it. As a man he had devoted much time and energy to its restoration. There was no one spot on this earth he had loved more than he had loved the lighthouse.

The fact that someone had chosen to attack Ry in that place he loved above all others struck India as nothing less than obscene. It was merely an act of fate that he had not actually died there, but in the back of the ambulance that had sped off through the early morning hours, sirens shrieking, though they'd not pass more than five cars between Devlin's Light and Cape Hospital Emergency Room some twenty miles away.

". . . and to grant him everlasting rest and peace in the harbor of your love, O Lord . . ."

An act of fate, she recalled, and of Nicholas Enright, who, from the deck of the old crabbers cabin he had purchased from Ry, watched as the lantern's light had ascended the stairwell, then flashed a sudden and erratic descent before being extinguished at the bottom of the steep steps. It was Nicholas Enright who had called both the police and the ambulance, before setting off by rowboat across the small inlet to the lighthouse; Nicholas Enright who had found Ry at the foot of the winding stairs, who had ridden with him in the ambulance to the hospital, who had held Ry's head and heard his last words and been the last human contact her brother had known on this earth.

India's eyes wandered across the faces of the strangers in the crowd, wondering which one was Nicholas Enright, certain that he stood among them; since she'd never met the man who had moved to Devlin's Light the summer before, she could not pick him out. Ry had had so many friends—most of whom she had never met—from Bayview State College, where he had taught for the past few years, from the environmental group that had worked with him to preserve the marshes, from the historic preservation group he had joined some years before to encourage renovation of the town's many ancient structures.—Nicholas Enright could be any one of the men, young or old, who had come to pay their respects.

". . . as we commend our brother Robert unto You . . ."

Nicholas Enright had shared her brother's last breath and, from the accounts of the ambulance attendants with whom she had spoken, had done so with gentle affection and the greatest of care. She needed to meet him, to thank him. And, she reminded herself, she had questions to ask that only he, as close a witness to the events of that night as had come forward, could answer.

5

". . . in His name. Amen."

"Amen."

"What else can I do for you, Aunt August?" India asked, placing a stack of bone-china cups and saucers on the sideboard in the dining room.

"There are more plates in the kitchen, on the counter there." Augustina Devlin waved a small, deeply tanned hand in the direction of the tidy kitchen that had served generations of Devlins. "I expect half the town or better will be coming to call at any minute. Weddings and funerals. It's the same all over. Brings 'em all out. There now, what'd I tell you?"

August adjusted large round tortoise-shell eyeglasses on her no-nonsense face, which was framed by a cap of short-cropped, straight salt-and-pepper hair, and nodded toward the front window, past which seemed to drift a goodly percentage of the population of Devlin's Light. It was only a matter of seconds before the screen door opened and the first of the townsfolk appeared in the front hallway.

Come to share our grief, Indy thought as she moved with open arms toward Liddy Osborn, who had gone through school with Aunt August in the one-room brick schoolhouse at the foot of Peck's Lane. Liddy, it seemed, had been there to share all the Devlins' sorrows. She had been there to hold a weeping Indy the day they'd found Robert Sr., Indy's father and August's brother, dead of a heart attack out on the dunes off Lighthouse Road. And Liddy had been there when Nancy died, though India was just a baby when she'd lost her mother and had no firsthand recollection of that. Liddy had been August's best friend, always. A dear, giving woman, Liddy had seen her own share of sorrow but had refused to let it destroy her loving heart.

And Grant Richardson, there in the hallway, behind Liddy. A county judge, as Indy's father had been, and a friend of the Devlin family for as long as Indy could remember. Al Carpenter, the chief of police, and his wife, Patsy. Mrs. Spicer, the librarian, and Mrs. Donaldson, Indy's third-grade teacher. Todd and Wanda Fisher, who ran the general store, and Ed Beggins, Ry's first piano teacher. Bill Scott, who used to take Ry surf fishing off of

Cape May. And Liz Porter, who, as owner of the local paper, the *Beacon,* knew everything about everyone. All come to share the memories and the pain. All part of Devlin's Light, as much as she was.

India had not, until this moment, realized how much she missed it, this sense of *connecting,* though each time she came home the past few years, it took her a little longer to shake off the city and the ugliness that came from having to prosecute its dregs. As an assistant district attorney in Paloma, Pennsylvania, she had seen enough crudeness and pain and evil over the past five years to last a lifetime. Every time she returned to Devlin's Light, it became harder and harder to remember what drew her back to Paloma. Obligation, she told herself. Certainly it wasn't Ron Stillwell, the fellow assistant district attorney she had, up until about six months ago, dated pretty regularly. At one time—it embarrassed her now to recall—she had actually toyed with the idea of marrying Ron, until someone had left an anonymous note on her desk tipping her off to the fact that he was also seeing a young law clerk on a lot more regular basis than he'd been seeing her.

Suddenly there was too much loss to deal with. It hit her like a sharp blow to the head and took her breath away. She fled to the back porch, seeking refuge where she always had when things became more than she could bear. She leaned over the white wooden railing and forced deep breaths, filling her lungs with the thick humid air laden with the smell of the salt marshes and something decomposing—probably some beached horseshoe crabs, she guessed, or maybe some hapless fish—down on the beach just a short walk over the dunes.

Why did it all look the same, she wondered, when their world had changed so suddenly and so completely?

The wooden porch swing still hung at one end, its new coat of white paint giving it a clean summer look. Aunt August's prize yellow roses stretched over the trellis in full and glorious bloom. The day lilies crowded in a riotous jumble of color against the stark gray of the back fence, line-dancing like manic clowns in a sudden gust of breeze. Fat little honey bees went from blossom to blossom, like little helicopters, oblivious to everything except the promise of pollen and the effort necessary to gather it and take it home. A small brown sparrow plopped upon the ground below the railing and pecked intently in the dirt. Finding what she was seeking, she returned to her young, all plump, dun-colored and downy-feathered little bundles waiting to be fed by the base of the bird bath in the midst of the herb garden. An ever curious catbird landed on a nearby dogwood branch and began to chatter. Just like any other summer day in Devlin's Light.

So. It was true what they said: Life went on.

"Indy?" Darla Kerns leaned out the back door, her long blond hair hanging over her right shoulder like an afterthought.

"I'm here, Dar."

"Want some company?" Darla asked hesitantly.

"If the company is you." Indy smiled and patted the spot next to her on the swing. Darla sat, and for the third or fourth time that day, Indy put an arm around the shoulder of the woman who was her closest friend, and who, for the last year and a half of his life, had been Ry's lover.

And for the third or fourth time that day, Darla totally shattered into gut-wrenching sobs that seemed to hold her very soul.

"Indy, I'm so sorry." Darla wiped away mascara, which had been long since wept into a darkened patch under her eyes. "I just can't cry it away. No matter how hard I try . . ."

"It's okay, Dar. I understand."

"Every time I think about it, I just . . ."

"I know, sweetie. It took you and Ry so long to get together."

"When I think about the years we wasted . . . years I spent married to a man I never loved . . . when Ry and I could have been together . . ."

"Don't, Dar. You can't change it. Be grateful for the time you had." India heard the words roll off her tongue and wished she had something more to offer than clichés.

"Oh, I am," Darla whispered. "I am. It just wasn't enough."

"It never is." India stroked her friend's soft blond hair, much as she had earlier stroked Corri's. So many in pain. So many to be comforted. "How are your kids today?"

"Devastated. Especially Jack. He has been so withdrawn since this happened. He and Ry had become so close." She mopped at her face with a wet linen square trimmed in lace. "Corri doesn't look much better today."

"She is so filled with pain it's a miracle she can hold it all in so tiny a body."

"Well, to have lost her mother . . . such as she was . . . and now Ry, who was—let's face the truth here—the only loving parent that little girl ever knew . . ." Darla's voice held a decided and bitter edge.

"Ry told me that Maris left a lot to be desired when it came to being a mother to Corri. But you know, I just never understood why he married her. Maris was just so . . . so . . ."—India sought to be tactful—"not Ry's type."

"Maris was a hot little number and she wrapped that hot little self of hers around Ry so tight and so fast he never knew what hit him." The words snapped from Darla's mouth in an angry clip. "I swear, Indy, I never saw anything like it. I never saw a man go down for the count as quickly as Ry did for Maris Steele."

Amare et sapere vix deo conceditur. Aunt August, a retired Latin teacher whose conversations were inevitably sprinkled with Latin phrases, had muttered this when Ry announced his marriage to Maris. *Even a god finds it difficult to love and be wise at the same time.*

"Well, if nothing else, it's given Corri a family. If not for that, when Maris drowned, Corri would have been left totally alone. Ry never did find her father when he was going through the adoption proceedings last year."

They sat in silence, each lost in their own memory of that day two years ago when Maris Devlin's small boat drifted ashore without Maris in it.

India had never warmed to her sister-in-law. She had thought Maris to be an ill-mannered gold digger, and it had always been on the tip of her tongue to tell Ry so, but she could not bring herself to hurt him. It wasn't until after Maris was gone that Ry admitted he'd been sucker punched but had remained married to her for Corri's sake. Maris had not been a very good mother, Ry had confided, and Indy had feigned shock even though she'd heard tales of the woman's shortcomings from both Darla and Aunt August long before Ry had spoken of it. Then, over the past eighteen months or so, he and Darla had rediscovered each other. They had appeared so like a family at Christmas, at the Easter egg hunt at the park last spring, at Aunt August's sixty-fifth birthday party in early June.

No one had been happier than Indy when her brother began dating her best friend. Darla and India had been inseparable since their playpen days—literally. They had shared everything through school, from clothes to hairstyles to secrets. No one other than Indy had known for all those years that the love of Darla's life was Robert Devlin. It had broken Darla's heart when he ignored her as an adolescent; when, as a high-school junior, he gave his class ring to Sharon Snyder; when he took Julie Long to his senior prom; when he brought home various and sundry girlfriends over the years. Darla had eventually accepted the fact that Ry would never love her and married Kenny Kerns within six months of this truth sinking in. It may have been the biggest mistake of her life, but still, she had confessed to Indy one night several years ago, she had her son, Jack, and her daughter, Ollie—Olivia—and they had made life worth living for her. She had felt badly about leaving Kenny, hotheaded and hot-tempered though he had been, feeling a vague sense of guilt that perhaps she had gotten only what she deserved for having married a man she didn't truly love. Kenny had been a good husband over the years, Darla conceded, and she knew she had had more than a lot of women had to look forward to each morning. A husband who loved her; there had never been any doubt but that Kenny was crazy about Darla. A cozy home in her home-town. She had friends and a social life to be envied. The only thing she wanted and could not have was Ry Devlin. And for most of the time, it was okay. She had accepted this one sad fact of her life. No one knew but her and India.

And then Ry took a teaching position at nearby Bayview College and moved home to stay after several years of teaching at a university up north, and suddenly the sham that was her life shattered, and the truth threatened to overtake her and drag her down as cleanly and as swiftly as the bay's erratic current had dragged Maris out to sea.

No longer able to live with a man she didn't love, Darla

had left Kenny, but before anyone knew what had happened, Maris Steele hit Devlin's Light and snatched Ry from under her very nose.

And then Maris was gone and somehow a miracle had occurred and she and Ry had found each other. And then, just like that, Ry had died.

Darla began to weep again.

This time India wept with her.

Chapter 2

"Miss Devlin?"

Indy looked up at the man who stood in the back doorway holding the screen door in one hand and a glass of Aunt August's iced tea in the other.

"Yes?"

"You're India Devlin?"

"Yes. And you are . . ."

What he was, was *big*. Ry's size and better, she could not help but notice.

"Oh"—Darla struggled to compose herself and to rise from the seat of the swing—"Indy, this is Nick Enright. I'm sorry. I had forgotten you had not met."

Nick Enright extended a large, well-worked hand in her direction.

"Miss Devlin . . ."

"India . . ."

"India." He said her name as if measuring it against her to see if it fit. "I wanted to express my condolences."

"You were the one who found Ry," India said simply.

"Yes."

"Please, sit down." Darla gestured to the seat she had vacated. "Indy, I want to check on the kids and see if your aunt needs any help. And I'll bring you something cold to drink."

"If I'd known you needed something, I'd have brought you an iced tea," he said, with the demeanor of a man who was suddenly feeling unexpectedly awkward. India looked up into his face, unaware that her violet eyes struck at his very core and rendered him momentarily speechless.

"I didn't know that you looked so much alike, you and Darla," Nick said once he remembered how to control his tongue. He thought he sounded sort of stupid, then couldn't resist making it worse by adding, "But then again, you really don't look alike at all."

"When we were in school we used to dress alike and wear our hair alike. We're the same height and pretty much the same build. From the back, no one could tell us apart."

"Your faces are very different," he continued, wondering how much more stupid he could make himself appear. *Oh well, in for a dime, in for a dollar.*

"Once we went to a costume party as each other. I penciled in a mole next to my left eye, like the one she has." Indy cleared her throat, realizing that she was dangerously close to babbling. "I was hoping to meet you. I wanted to thank you. For what you did for Ry. I am so grateful that he wasn't alone when he died."

"So am I."

"You were his friend. It must have been hard for you."

"It was." He nodded tersely.

"Chief Carpenter said that Ry was conscious for a few minutes."

"Yes. For much of the ride to the hospital."

"And that he spoke."

"He only said one word." Nick shifted uncomfortably on the swing, almost wishing he hadn't told anyone about that.

"'Ghost.'" Spoken softly, in her lilting voice, the word held no menace.

"Or something that sounded like it. I could have been wrong, it could have been something else . . ."

"Do you believe in ghosts, Nick?"

"Never had a reason to." He shrugged.

"You know, there's a legend in the family that before a Devlin dies, he sees old Eli Devlin swinging his lantern at the very top of the lighthouse tower."

"Who was Eli?" Nick leaned against the side of the swing

and turned slightly to face her more directly. He wondered if she knew just how devastating her eyes were to a man's heart.

Ry had spoken often about his sister. Bragged about her. About how tough a prosecutor she was. About what a great swimmer she was. About how well she knew the marshes and the bay. Nick had seen photographs, here and there throughout the house, and once he had even caught a glimpse of her through a shop window. But Ry had never told Nick that India's hair spun like a soft golden cloud around her face, or that her eyes were the very color of spring violets. Given the sad circumstances of their meeting, Nick felt almost embarrassed at having noticed. Almost.

"Eli Devlin was the one who built the lighthouse. Ry didn't tell you the story?"

He had, but Nick shook his head. It was a long story, and the telling of it would take a while. A little while to sit and watch her face. A little while when neither of them would be thinking about Ry, and the fact that he now lay beneath the sandy soil in a bronze box.

"There were three Devlin brothers who were part of the whaling community that settled around New London, Connecticut. They were all single, all pretty lively fellows, so the story goes. Jonathan, Samuel and Eli. All very ambitious. When the opportunity arose to become part of a new whaling venture down in the South River area—which is what the Delaware River was called back in the 1600s—they jumped at the chance."

"Whaling? Here? On the Delaware Bay?"

"Well, it probably sounded like a good idea at the time, and whales do show up occasionally. Just not often enough for it to have grown into a lucrative endeavor. Eli stayed ashore and ran the lighthouse to guide his brothers home safely through the storms. The first lighthouse was not much more than a shack. But over the years he added to it . . . made it bigger. Taller. Then taller again, until it reached its present height."

"But the lighthouse doesn't appear to be that old."

"It isn't. The one Eli built burned down in the 1700s and

14

was rebuilt on the same spot. It burned again in 1876 and was repaired."

"It's a wonderful structure. It's obvious why Ry had been so proud of it."

"Ry considered the lighthouse almost a member of the family. Restoring it had been his life's work. His goal was for it to be a working lighthouse again. He wanted to give it back to the bay. He wanted it to be a place where people could come . . ."

Her voice broke and he took her hand, a gesture meant to comfort. Her skin was soft though a bit cool, her fingers long and slender. Her nails, streaked with remnants of pale pink polish, were bitten to the quick.

"Why would anyone want to hurt Ry?" she whispered fervently. "Why?"

"Well now, you know that the police investigation was inconclusive, India. It hasn't been proven that Ry was murdered or that there was, in fact, anyone else around the lighthouse that night."

"But everything points to there having been someone there, Nick. My brother would not have gotten out of bed in the middle of the night to go out to the lighthouse for no reason at all. *Someone* did something that gave him a reason. I just can't imagine who—or why."

"Have you discussed this with Chief Carpenter?"

"Yes. He agrees that there most likely was someone there, waiting for Ry. But there is absolutely no evidence to support a theory of murder."

"What did the coroner's report say?" Nick asked.

"That he died as the result of a blunt trauma to the head. There was blood on the bottom step of the top landing. The chief said that Ry had apparently hit his head there before going the rest of the way down the steps to the bottom, where you found him."

"There was no evidence that he had been struck with anything before he fell?"

"No. Something caused him to fall backward." She shook her head. "Someone must have pushed him down the steps."

"But there was no sign of a struggle, from what I understand."

"No. It's so strange. I can't think of anyone he even had a serious disagreement with. I mean, he told me about a group of environmentalists who were hounding him about opening the lighthouse area to tourists during the bird migrations."

"Well, they could get pretty intense at times, but I can't see any one of them becoming violent."

"That was my impression too. He did say that some of the bay men were angry with him, they felt that he hadn't supported their efforts to get the horseshoe crab off the state's restricted list."

"I don't see any of them taking it this far. In some ways, Ry was one of them."

"Couldn't that have been a motive? Maybe one of them felt he had betrayed them by not taking their part completely."

"India, I don't—"

"Or Kenny." She stood up and began to pace. "Maybe it was Kenny. Darla said that he was really upset about her seeing Ry. And he has always had a pretty short fuse when he drinks. And I heard he's been drinking a lot lately."

"Nah. Too obvious." Nick shook his head. He'd been over all this ground himself a hundred times over the past five days. "And besides, Chief Carpenter has questioned Kenny—and just about everyone else in Devlin's Light, for that matter—and he has an airtight alibi. He was on an overnight camp-out with his son's cub scout troop when Ry was killed, India. And for the record, Kenny has been on the wagon for the past five months."

"I guess the first thing we have to do is figure out why Ry was there, in the lighthouse, at that hour of the night."

"I think Chief Carpenter is still working on that." Nick thought that now would be a good time to remind India that the Devlin's Light police department had not closed the book on the investigation.

"Nick, I know that you discussed all this with the chief, but would you mind walking me through everything that happened that night? What you saw?"

"Of course not. Where would you like to start?"

"What time did you first notice that something was going on over there?"

"Um, maybe around two, two-ten."

"And you were where?" Her eyes narrowed as the interrogator in her kicked in.

Nick sighed. Her eyes took on the fervor of one who was about to begin a crusade. Well, he'd expected it. Anyone who was as adept a prosecutor as Ry had said India was would want to be involved in the investigation.

Indy had obviously chosen to begin with him.

"On the deck of the cabin." He leaned back and folded his arms across his chest. "I couldn't sleep. Something woke me up."

"Do you remember what it was? A noise? A boat out on the bay, maybe? Or maybe lightning?"

"No, there was no storm. Actually, it was a very quiet night. I turned in early—right after the eleven o'clock news—and there was nothing, not even a wave on the bay that I can recall."

He frowned then, recalling. It had been a moonless night. Totally quiet. All had been still until . . . until . . .

"A bird. Took off across the bay squawking as if someone had stepped on its tail."

"And what time was that—did you look?" She raised an eyebrow, and a smile of satisfaction tugged at the corners of her mouth. There had been no mention of a bird squawking in the police report. She knew there had to be more.

"Yes. It was about one-thirty."

"What did you do? Did you get up, turn over, what?"

"I think I was sort of half in, half out of sleep for a while. Finally, when I realized that I was not likely to fall back to sleep, I went into the kitchen and got a beer out of the cooler, took it out on the deck and pulled up a chair. Watched the stars. Breathed deeply. Felt glad to be there."

"Please"—she touched his arm—"maybe if you described it to me, maybe I could try to see what you saw that night."

"There was a light at the top of the tower. At first I thought I was mistaken, because it was bigger and brighter than a lantern like the one Ry has. And then about ten minutes later, I saw Ry's lantern light going up the steps."

"You're assuming that the second light was Ry's?"

"I am. And it was his light that I saw come backward

down the steps. The lantern was next to him on the ground when I arrived."

"When you got to the lighthouse, where was the first light—the one you first saw at the top of the tower?"

"Gone. There was no light when I got there except for Ry's."

India digested this for a moment before asking, "But you're positive there had been one?"

"Absolutely."

"You said there was maybe ten minutes between the time that you saw the first light and when you saw the second light . . . Ry's light?"

"Yes."

"I know that all of this is in the police report, but I can't help it—I have to ask, Nick. It's what I do—question people about crimes. I'm trying very hard not to sound as if I'm interrogating you."

"I understand. Ry told me you were good at what you do. He bragged about you all the time. About how many convictions you've gotten. He was very proud of you."

"I was very proud of him." India twisted the small sapphire ring she wore on the middle finger of her right hand. "It is very difficult for me to accept that he is gone, Nick. And harder still that there's no way of knowing what happened there that night. It's just so frustrating. I guess I think if I look hard enough, I'll find something."

"Indy?" A voice called from the other side of the screen door.

"Yes?" India turned toward it.

"Your cousin Blake is here. Your aunt would like you to please come in." Patsy Carpenter opened the door and stuck her broad face out. "Oh. Hello, Nick."

"Hello, Patsy."

"Indy . . ."

"I'll be right in. Thank you."

The screen door closed softly.

"I'd like to finish this conversation sometime later. That is, if it's all right with you."

"Of course." He watched her unfold from her seat on the opposite side of the porch swing and stood up as she did. "At your convenience."

"I just need to *know*, Nick."

"I understand completely, India." He watched the afternoon sun cross her cheek as she turned toward the door. "If you think it would help, you're welcome to come out to the cabin."

"That's very kind, Nick. And maybe it would help me to see it in my head. It might be easier if I'm there."

"Whatever you think is best."

"Thank you." She nodded and extended a hand to him. "Thank you, Nick. For everything."

She slipped into the cool of the house, unaware that eyes the color of honey followed her well-fitting black linen sheath as it disappeared through the doorway, or that the man leaning against the porch railing could suddenly think of nothing but the way her golden hair curled around her face.

Chapter 3

*I*ndia awoke to the sound of ill-mannered gulls squabbling over some luckless fish that, having ventured too far into shallow water, was now a sure bet to end up as breakfast for the gull that emerged victorious from the fray. She could picture it in her mind, having watched countless such seaside struggles over the years. The gull with the fish would be hounded and harassed until it swallowed the prize— often live and whole—or dropped it, leaving others to pursue the catch until one of them got lucky and managed to snatch the meal and fly off with it.

A vast change from the early morning sounds of the city. India smiled wryly as she stretched out her full five-foot-five-inch frame and pushed her toes out from under the light summer throw. There were no street noises to speak of much before noon in Devlin's Light, unless you counted the sound of the Parson boy's bike as he slowed down to toss a newspaper onto the front porch. And that wasn't till around seven or so, so it didn't really count. In the city, the first-edition newspapers landed on the front steps well before the sun came up, and you were lucky if someone hadn't lifted your copy by the time you came outside looking for it.

India squinted at the small numbers that circled the hand-painted face of the delicate porcelain clock that stood on the bedside table. Eight o'clock. India could not remember the last time she had slept till eight o'clock. On a normal workday, she'd be halfway through the documents she would need for court that day. Here in Devlin's Light, there was no courtroom, no jail beyond the single holding cell where prisoners, mostly DUIs, would be housed till they made bail or were transferred over to the county jail. The crime rate in Devlin's Light was so low it was almost nonexistent. There were exactly two unsolved crimes in the files of the Devlin's Light police. One was the theft of the Lannings' skiff the summer before. The second was the suspicious death of Ry Devlin.

India threw her legs over the side of the bed and sat up in a single motion. For a few minutes she had almost forgotten what had brought her here, to the peace and quiet of a weekday morning in the old house on Darien Road, when this hour of the day would normally find her in a flurry of activity in her busy, noisy office in Paloma. She squeezed her eyes tightly shut.

Ry.

For the first time in a week she had had almost two minutes of consciousness when she had not thought of Ry. And not thinking of Ry had given her a reason to think of him.

From down the hall she could hear the early morning sounds of a house coming to life. Aunt August, plagued by allergies this time of year, sniffled softly from the front bedroom where she had awakened almost every morning of her life, not counting those four years of college upstate many years ago. Water splashed in the sink in the bathroom next door. Corri washing her face, India guessed. The old faucet squeaked as the water was turned off—as it had squeaked for as long as Indy could remember—and the door opened softly. Corri's little feet padded lightly on the rag runner that traced the length of the hallway as she returned to her room quietly, as if afraid to disturb anyone.

Indy rose, lifting her arms toward the ceiling to stretch out the kinks. She gathered clothes from her suitcase— cutoff denim jeans and a blue and cream striped T-shirt— and headed for the shower.

By the time India had dressed and made her way downstairs, Aunt August and Corri had already finished their breakfast in the cozy little nook off the kitchen. India joined them, grateful for the cup of freshly brewed coffee awaiting her.

"It's a perfect summer day, Indy," Aunt August said purposefully as she rinsed her breakfast dishes under a stream of steaming water in the kitchen sink. "You and Corri might want to think about taking a picnic down to the beach."

"Sounds good to me," India replied. "How 'bout it, Corri?"

Corri shrugged indifferently.

"There's lots of good things left over from yesterday." August paused in the doorway and glanced at the child who was quietly beating a long, thin brown crust of her toast against the side of her plate. "I can pack up some chicken and some salad, some cookies that Liddy made . . ."

August's worried eyes caught India's from above the head of the little girl who was clearly tuning out.

"Do that, Aunt August." India nodded. "We'll be ready to go in half an hour. Soon as I finish my breakfast and take a glance at the morning paper."

Corri looked up at her with wide brown eyes from the opposite side of the table. Without speaking she rose and repeated August's activity at the sink, rinsing her plate, then her glass, before placing them both in the dishwasher that was one of August's concessions to modern living in a house whose original section was close to three hundred years old. Without a backward glance, Corri moved like a zombie through the back door into the yard. From the breakfast-room window, August and India watched her as she climbed onto the swing Ry had made for her and hung over a branch of the enormous oak that stood like a sentinel in the far corner of the yard. Pulling against the ropes and pumping her little legs, she propelled herself ever higher, toward the sky.

"I'm almost afraid that one of these days she'll try to fly right off that swing," Aunt August told India. "She is so filled with sadness, India, she doesn't know what to do with it all."

"She is a very small girl who is being asked to cope with more than most adults could handle." India stood up and looked out the window. Corri's head was tipped back as she sailed to and fro across the morning sky.

"I think she is afraid we will send her away."

"Send her away? Why would we do that?"

"We wouldn't. We won't. But I don't know that *she* knows that."

"Well, before today is over," India said, gathering her plate and her cup, "she will."

"What do you think, Corri, is this a good spot?" India shaded her eyes from the sun's glare and dropped the picnic basket on the sand.

"I guess," Corri replied without enthusiasm.

"Well then, here"—Indy tossed a corner of the old patched quilt in Corri's direction—"help me to spread this out. . . . There, that's fine. Perfect."

She placed the basket on one corner of the quilt, then knelt upon the worn, soft fabric.

"This old quilt has seen a lot of sand in its day," India told her. "It was our regular beach blanket. Mine and Ry's."

She had decided they needed to speak of him, she and Corri, the sooner the better.

"We used to have picnics just like this. Aunt August even packed us pretty near the same lunch."

Corri drew a circle in the sand with the toe of her sandal.

"Why didn't your mom?" Corri asked without looking up.

"Why didn't my mom what, sugar?"

"Why didn't your mom pack your picnic?"

"My mother died when I was just a baby."

"Did your mommy drown too?"

"No. She died in the hospital, a few days after an operation."

"Oh." Corri pondered this for a few moments, then asked, "And then Aunt August took care of you?"

"Yes. Aunt August was my father's sister, and she loved us. Just like she loves you and takes care of you."

Corri appeared to reflect on this but offered no response.

"Want to walk along the water with me?" India kicked off her sandals and took a few steps toward the bay.

"I guess so." Corri shrugged.

India set out toward the shoreline, an unenthusiastic Corri trailing behind.

"Oh, look, sea glass!" India bent to pick up the piece of wave-worn green glass. She handed it to Corri, who pocketed the offering without looking at it.

"Here's some mother of pearl." India lifted the pale, opalescent shell from the water's edge. "The inside of an oyster shell . . . they call it 'mother of pearl' because pearls grow inside of oysters."

"I know that," Corri told her impatiently. "Ry told me."

"Did Ry used to walk on the beach with you?"

Corri nodded, her face settling into a sad little mask.

"What else did he tell you about the beach?"

"Stuff." She shrugged her small shoulders under a thin pink T-shirt.

"Like what kind of stuff?" India persisted.

"About different kinds of shells. I used to find them and Ry would tell me what they were."

"I used to look for shells with Ry too, when I was little."

"You did?"

"Umm-hmm. Ry was four years older than me, and he was a good teacher."

"That's 'cause Ry knew everything about the beach. He knew everything about the bay." Corri's eyes brightened slightly.

"Yes, I believe he did. He loved it here, and he—"

Corri froze as they rounded the tip of the cove. The lighthouse rose across the inlet, silent and tall and proud.

"I want to go back." Corri turned to run, and India grabbed her gently by the arm.

Turning the little girl around as calmly and gently as she could, India told her, "It was the place he loved best, Corri. You can't run away from it. You can't hide from it if you're going to stay in Devlin's Light, sweetie."

"Am I?" The tremulous voice was barely a whisper. "Am I going to stay?"

"Of course you're going to stay." Aunt August had been right. In addition to grieving over Ry, the child was uncertain of her future. And the uncertainty had her terrified. "Corri, we are your family. Aunt August and I love you. You belong here with us, and absolutely, positively, you are staying here with us. Devlin's Light is your home."

"I . . . I . . . wasn't sure. Ry adopted me, but my mama said—" She stopped suddenly, her little face taking on a worried look.

"Your mama said what, sweetie?" India sat on the sand and tugged on Corri's hand. Corri sat down next to her and permitted India to put a loving arm around her. The child relaxed almost immediately, her slight body easing into India's side.

"Mama said that we . . . we weren't like Ry. That we never would be like real Devlins . . ." Her little voice faltered.

"Well . . ." India cleared her throat. Why was she not surprised that Maris had planted such seeds in her daughter's young mind? "You know, your mother wasn't married to Ry for a very long time, so maybe she never got to feel like a Devlin. But you've been family for two whole years now, and when Ry adopted you, your name changed to Devlin. That makes you very much a real Devlin."

"You think?"

"I'm certain of it."

Corri's face visibly relaxed.

India let out what felt like a long-held breath. Whatever it took to give this child security, to make her understand how much she was loved, she would do.

Three sandpipers landed on the sand a mere fifteen feet from where they sat. The frenetic little birds pecked at the sand, seeking favored tidbits of food. Soon several other shore birds lighted at the water's edge, looking for lunch, their little feet following the gentle ebb and flow of the waves.

"Look, Corri"—India pointed—"there are some terns."

"*Least* terns, they are called," Corri corrected her.

"Hmm. Right you are." Impressed, India smiled to herself. The child *had* spent a lot of time with Ry, who had known every variety of every shore bird on the East Coast.

"And those," said the little girl, pointing a straight little finger at a small group of chunky little birds, dark feathered above, lighter below, "are purple sandpipers. Ry called them 'rock peeps.'"

"Why, so he did." India laughed. "I had forgotten that."

"And there—look, India!" A hushed Corri rose onto one knee, whispering excitedly. "That's a plover. We don't see so many of them, 'cause they're *dangered*. Ry called them 'sand peeps.'"

"Very good, Corri." India rubbed Corri's back fondly. "Ry would have been so very proud of you."

Corri beamed at the praise. For a moment, the child was there, in her smile, for the first time in days. And in that moment individual grief became shared grief. As she burst into tears, Corri buried her face in India's chest.

"It's okay, Corri, it's okay to cry." India fought herself to speak the words she knew the child had to hear, then gave in to the tears she herself had not yet shed that day.

India rocked the weeping child in her arms until the sobs slowly subsided and eventually ceased to rack the small body. Both Darla and Aunt August had expressed alarm to India that Corri had not wept since the night Ry had died. The cork on that bottle of emotions having finally popped, Corri cried until her throat hurt.

"Feel any better?" India asked as Corri tried to dry her face with the back of her hands.

"A little." Corri's frail shoulders still trembled sporadically.

"Listen, Corri, it's okay to cry. When you hurt inside, sometimes crying is the only way to bring out some of the hurt. Do you understand?"

"I think so."

"Anytime you want someone to hold you while you cry, you come to me, hear? Or Aunt August, or Darla. We all hurt too, Corri. It helps to share it sometimes. But we all have to remember that as long as we love him, Ry will still be with us, even if we can't see him."

Together they sat on the sand, watching the gulls swoop down for a tidbit here and there. Soon Corri was pointing out the distinctions between the black-backed gulls and the herring gulls. The August sky hung hazy and cornflower-blue over the primeval beach and the flat of the bay. A scorching noonday sun beat down, and India began to swelter.

"Let's go back to the house and put our bathing suits on," India suggested, "and we'll go for a swim."

"Can we bring my tube so I can float in the bay?" Corri asked, her voice still somewhat hoarse from crying.

"Certainly."

"Okay. But can we have a drink first, before we walk back to the house?" She gestured toward the picnic basket, which, she knew, housed a small jug of Aunt August's tart lemonade and some paper cups.

"I'm a bit thirsty myself." India nodded. "I'll race you to the quilt."

Woman and child took off down the beach, sand flying. Corri slid feet first to reach the edge of the blanket before India, who had given her a slight head start.

"Why, I do believe you've done this before." India grinned, and Corri collapsed in gales of laughter as powerful and as vital as the sobs that had earlier engulfed her. She rolled onto her back on the quilt, still giggling at having outmaneuvered India. Shielding her eyes from the blazing sun, she sat halfway up and called, "Hi, Nick!"

India turned in time to see the tall, lean form of Nick Enright make its way across the sand. Cutoff jeans revealed amazingly tanned legs, and a pale yellow tank top stretched across his equally darkened shoulders and broad chest. Curly dark brown hair hunkered down beneath a red Philadelphia Phillies baseball cap worn brim-backward. Dark glasses hid his eyes, but she remembered they were light brown, the color of clover honey, of molasses. He smiled, and twin dimples punctuated the corners of his mouth. Had she been too distraught the day before to have noticed?

And why, she wondered, had Darla not told her about Nicholas Enright?

"Hi, sugar plum." Nick reached down and grabbed Corri by one of her bare toes and gave it a little shake, and she giggled.

He slid his glasses off and turned to India.

"How are you today?" he asked as if it mattered.

"Doing better." She nodded. "Little by little . . ."

"Good," he told her. "I'm happy to hear it."

"We're going to have some lemonade and then we're going to go home and put on bathing suits and come back and swim and then have a picnic," Corri announced all in one breath.

"All that in one morning?" Nick asked earnestly.

"Yup." Corri bounced on her knees to the cooler, which she struggled to open. Nick bent down and removed the cap for her.

Without asking, India poured a glass of lemonade for him and passed it to him, then poured two more. She sat down on the quilt next to Corri, who downed the cool liquid in record time. Just as quickly, Corri refilled her cup, then danced down to the water's edge to stand in the surf wash and wiggle her toes in the warm bay water.

"Corri seems a little better today," Nick noted as he lowered himself to sit on the blanket's edge.

"She finally had a good long cry," India told him, "and I think that helped her enormously."

"And you?"

"I've had more than my share of cries this past week," she said, sipping at her drink, "and none of them seemed to have helped at all."

"You know, if there's anything I can do for you, for your family . . ."

"Help us find the person who killed my brother."

"If I could do that, it would have been done already."

"Sooner or later Ry's killer will be found," India insisted. "The answer is always there if you read the evidence the right way."

"There *was* no evidence," he reminded her.

"There is always something, Nick. It just hasn't been found. Or recognized."

"You really believe that?"

"I have to." She shrugged. "There is someone who knows what happened."

"Right. The killer. And all we have to do is figure out who that person is."

"It isn't impossible."

"It becomes less and less probable every day, India, but I would guess that you, out of all of us, would best know that."

"Someone lured Ry to the lighthouse that night. There was no reason for him to have been there. You said yourself it was a beautiful, calm night. A full moon. No storms. No reason to shine a light from the tower. So someone must have called him, arranged to meet him there."

"Well, no one's been able to come up with a likely suspect, India."

"Why would someone want to meet him in the middle of the night? Someone who wouldn't want to be seen speaking with him?" She frowned as she pondered this. "Why wouldn't someone want to be seen with him?"

She stood up and began to pace unconsciously, still speaking, but it was obvious to Nick that she was thinking aloud.

"Or maybe . . . someone who had a grudge, a quarrel . . . a reason to wish him harm . . ."

"India, I've asked myself those same questions a dozen times."

"If we don't keep asking, we'll never find the answer." She stopped and studied his face. "Nick, you've lived on the bay for the past year, you must know who is making a living off the crabs, who is fishing for a living these days. And it might help to know who was opposing Ry's plans to open the beach to tourists during the bird migrations."

"I can find out." Nick nodded.

"Good. Maybe between the two of us, we'll come up with something that will help Chief Carpenter to narrow the field. And I still want to come out to the cabin."

"Anytime," Nick offered without hesitation. He had wanted to approach her, to find an excuse to get to know her better, to spend some time with her. If he had to become her personal part-time private investigator to do that, so be it.

"I think I want it to be on a night when the lighting is the same."

"Sort of to re-create the atmosphere?" he suggested.

"As much as possible." She nodded. "Of course, there won't be a full moon for almost another month. I should be back by then."

"You're leaving?" He appeared surprised, as if the thought had not occurred to him that she would leave so soon.

"I have to. I have a trial set for next week. I've done all the work on this case myself and I don't want to hand it over to anyone else." Her eyes narrowed. "This particular piece of offal needs to be put away for a very long time."

"Sounds personal."

"Anytime a man preys upon children, it's personal." Her jaw set like stone, India tossed the remaining drops of liquid from her cup onto the sand with a deliberate flick of her wrist.

"When do you think you'll be back?"

"Well, if the trial starts on schedule—which is always impossible to predict—I don't expect more than a week of testimony. Unless more witnesses crawl out of the woodwork, which can happen with a case like this one. Then I have two more trials coming up." She shrugged. "I need to sit down with my files and see how much time off I can get, and when."

"Well, if you think of anything you want me to do, you know that you only have to call."

"Thanks, Nick."

Later, she would think back on that moment and wonder if there had not been something there in his eyes. Something meant truly just for her. She would never know, however, what that something might have been, since Corri chose that moment to come flying back up the beach.

"A peregrine! There, look there, up on the dune!" Corri danced up and down in delight, whispering loudly.

She pointed a finger trembling with excitement. There, on one of the remaining posts of what had once been a fence across the crest of the dune, sat the bird, regal and lethal.

"See, Indy, that's why there're all gone," she whispered loudly. "All the birds have left the beach. That's why they're all hiding someplace, so that he can't see them."

The falcon turned toward them, bestowed an imperious glance, as if aware of their admiration, then dropped with grave elegance from the fence post. It swept over and past them as it flew toward the lighthouse and the marsh beyond.

"That's the same one Ry and I tracked last spring. I know it is." Corri's eyes shone brightly. "He always sits there and flies over to there. Isn't he beautiful?"

"Magnificent," India agreed.

"Can we get our suits now?" Corri begged. The bird, now out of sight, was in fact out of mind, and so on with the agenda.

"I was just leaving." Nick stood up, then reached a hand down to assist India. His hands were large, as she had noted on their first meeting, slightly callused, but gentle. He held on to the tips of her fingers and asked, "When do you plan on leaving?"

"Probably in the morning."

"Tomorrow?" Corri's head shot up, her eyes widening. "You're leaving tomorrow?"

"I have to go back to the city to finish a job that I started," she said softly, sensing the child's panic.

"What kind of job?" Corri was clearly on the verge of tears.

"The police arrested a very bad man who did very bad things to some very good children," India explained. "My job is to tell the judge and the jury what the bad man did, so that the jury will decide to send the man to jail for a very long time."

Corri thought this over. "Will you come back?"

"Of course. As soon as I can, sweetie."

"And you'll stay?"

"For as long as I can," India promised. "In the meantime, you'll have Aunt August."

"Aunt August doesn't like to fish." Corri shoved her hands into the pockets of her shorts.

"Hey, what about me?" Nick feigned insult. "I can't fish?"

"Would you want to take me someday?" she asked hopefully.

"Sugar plum, I would take you with me every day."

"And crabbing too? Aunt August *hates* to go crabbing. She says, it's a waste of time at her age to float around the bay waiting for the crabs to bite when she can go right down to the dock and buy them by the bushel and it only takes fifteen minutes."

"Well, I can't say that I won't feel the same as she does when I get to be her age, so maybe I should get all my crabbing in now, while I still enjoy killing a few hours just floating on the bay."

"Early in the morning is best, Ry said," Corri confided.

"Looks like you found a partner, Nick," India said, laughing, "though you might end up doing a lot more crabbing and fishing than you had bargained for."

"It's okay," he said softly. "I enjoy her company. And we're pals, right, Corri?"

"Right." Corri slapped the open palm he held out to her. "So can we go tomorrow? Aunt August will cook 'em if we catch 'em. And clean 'em, of course. That's what she always told Ry and me."

"They will be caught and cleaned and all ready for your Aunt August to cook."

"Yippee." Corri danced from the blanket onto the sand. "Ow!"

"What did you step on?" India bent down to inspect the bottom of Corri's foot.

"A sharp shell!" Corri wailed, pointing to the offending piece of clamshell.

"Well then, looks like I'll have to give you a ride back to the house." Nick swept her into the air and plopped her onto his shoulders. The small cut on her foot immediately forgotten, Corri threw her thin arms around his neck and squealed her approval.

Nick took a few steps toward the dune, then turned to call over his shoulder to India, "Are you with us?"

"Yes," she said, "I am with you."

"Good." His eyes narrowed slightly as he watched her approach. "I'm all out of shoulders, but I can offer you a hand."

He held one out to her, and she took it.

"A hand will do just fine today," she said quietly as she folded her fingers into his and walked with him across the dune.

Chapter 4

"**A**unt August, what do you know about Nick Enright?" Feigning a nonchalance that didn't fool either her or her aunt, India poured cream from a blue and white pitcher into the morning's first cup of coffee while she rummaged through the flatware drawer in search of a spoon.

"Nick?" August set her own cup down on the counter and opened the back door to allow some early morning breeze to fill the kitchen. The last bit of dawn lingered in the semidarkness, but already the birds were gathering to sing in the branches of the pines. August never seemed to get enough of their songs.

"Well, I know he was a good friend to Ry, India." August sat down on the edge of the bench forming the window seat overlooking the side yard. From there she could watch the wrens. "And that he's been a good friend to me. What exactly did you want to know?"

"Who is he?" India wished it hadn't come out in such a blurt, but there it was. "Where did he come from? Why is he in Devlin's Light?"

"Ry met Nick in graduate school at Rutgers years back. I believe they were both going for their master's in marine biology at the time. They stayed in touch afterward. Nick visited several times over the past few years." August sipped cautiously at her coffee, testing the temperature of the brew,

33

and, finding it to her satisfaction, took another sip or two before continuing. "Nick decided to go for his doctorate and began a study on the ecosystem of the bay, what species were here ten thousand years ago, five thousand years ago, a thousand, which are still present in one form or another today. How the bay has changed, and how it is likely to evolve, and so on."

"You seem to know a lot about him," India noted.

"We spent many an hour talking about the bay, Nick and Ry and I. Nick spends a lot of time here," August said, then corrected herself, "or at least he did. I hope he still will. For Corri's sake. And for mine. I'd miss his conversation and his company, I don't mind saying."

"That's why Ry talked me into agreeing to sell the old crabbers cabin to Nick."

"Yes. And I have to say that at first, there was no one more surprised than I was when Ry told me he was selling it. There hasn't been so much as a foot of Devlin land sold in over a hundred years, since your greatgrandfather sold off that parcel to the town for the park and the library. Charged 'em a whole dollar for the entire transaction. But after I got to know Nick a little better, I knew it was a good thing. He respects the bay, respects its life. He's been an asset to Devlin's Light, I don't mind saying so."

"Somehow I can't seem to picture him living in that little ramshackle cabin." India smiled, amused at the thought of the handsome Mr. Enright sharing his limited living space with a couple of raccoons.

"Oh, but you haven't seen it lately." August's eyes began to twinkle. "Nick's mother came down from someplace outside of Philadelphia and practically had it totally rebuilt."

"What?"

"The cabin. His mother sent some builders down to 'fix it up a little,' she told Ry. I can tell you that there's none of the old crabbers who'd recognize it now." August chuckled, not for the first time, at the thought of the cabin's former tenants' reactions to the new bath and kitchen, the fireplace, the deck, the Berber carpet on the newly installed hardwood floors.

"His mother did that?" Somehow, Nick Enright had not quite struck India as a "momma's boy."

"Oh, didn't you know that his mother is Delia Enright?"

"The writer?" India's eyes widened. Delia Enright, internationally acclaimed for her series of mysteries, was the only writer whose books India *always* bought on the day they were released onto the book shelves. "Delia Enright is his *mother?*"

"Indeed she is. And I can tell you that she is just so lovely."

"You've met her?"

"Oh, yes. She has visited several times." August refilled both coffee cups while India scraped a little butter onto two English muffins. "She just sort of swept right down on that little cabin and took over. But if the truth were to be told, Nick seemed amused by it all. Oh, yes, Delia definitely has *a way* about her."

"I am a huge fan of hers," India told her.

"Really?" August asked, as if she did not know. As if she did not have autographed copies of Delia's last two books tucked away under her bed as Christmas presents for Indy.

"She's a wonderful storyteller." India was oblivious to August's sly smile of pleasure at having obtained a gift she knew would delight her niece.

"Yes, that she is." August sat a crock of Liddy's homemade sour cherry preserves on the table.

India sat down and began to nibble on her muffin, trying to envision what a new kitchen might look like in the old crabbers cabin.

"Don't act as if you're not interested, India."

"Interested in what?"

"In Nick." August folded her arms across her chest. "Don't even try to pretend you haven't noticed him."

"Why, I . . ." Suddenly feeling like a fourteen-year-old again, India stammered, then blushed, then laughed out loud.

"Of course I noticed. How could I not notice?" She laughed. "How could anyone not notice a man who looks like that?"

"That's a relief." August sighed and spread some jam on

her muffin. "I was beginning to think you'd been working so hard for so long that you'd forgotten what a man looked like."

"There are times when I have done exactly that," India conceded.

"Well, Nick Enright's not a man to be soon forgotten." August met India's eyes across the table. "I don't mind saying that I don't know what I would have done without him that first day. And you know, Indy, Nick—"

"Damn, look at the time." Sparing herself her aunt's recitation of Nick's virtues, which she was certain was about to follow, India stood up and gulped down the last few remaining mouthfuls of coffee in her cup. "It normally takes me three hours to drive back, and the rain will slow me down. Do you think it will last?"

"The weather report is for thunderstorms," August replied, pleased to have confirmed that Nick had in fact caught Indy's attention.

India disappeared through the doorway, on her way to the second floor to grab her things and prepare to leave. August heard the squeaking of the third step from the bottom as India's foot fell upon it as she raced up the steps, heard the door to the third bedroom—Corri's room—open and close again softly. Corri had been permitted to stay up late the night before to help Indy pack, so it was unlikely she'd wake before Indy left. India's soft footfall was almost imperceptible, but August knew that her niece was tracing the steps to the back bedroom. Ry's room. The same room he had slept in as a child had been the room he had returned to after Maris's accident and he and August had agreed that Corri needed to be surrounded by as much family as possible. August had welcomed him home and been delighted to have Corri move in with them. It had been so long since the house had been filled with young people.

August leaned on the wide window ledge and looked out toward the bay. *Prima lux.* First light. She had never missed this favorite moment of each new day. It was hers, and she cherished it and gave thanks for it. One more morning. One more day.

One more day to be there for Corri, for India. One more day to mourn Ry, to carry the void her beloved nephew had left. One more day to anchor the Devlin family, to breathe the salt air and to hear the gulls cry, to watch for the herons, to listen for the call of the geese as they passed overhead, heralding the coming of fall.

Tempus doth indeed *fugit.* She sighed.

Twenty minutes later a red-eyed India came into the kitchen, suitcase and travel bags in hand, and kissed August goodbye before leaving. Watching her from the doorway, August said a little prayer that the trial would go quickly so that India could be back in Devlin's Light before Corri might begin to wonder if India, like her mother and Ry, had vanished from her life for good.

"Hey, Indy, welcome back." Barry Singer, a detective from the city's vice squad, greeted India as she plowed through the ever-crowded space allotted to the district attorney and his staff in the basement of City Hall.

"I told you I'd be here for the trial," she told him.

"Indy," Singer said, laying a hand on her shoulder, "we're all sorry as hell about Ry."

"I know, Barry. And I want to thank you guys for the flowers. I appreciated the thought. So did Aunt August."

"How's she taking it?" Singer, himself raised by an elderly grandmother, had been extremely solicitous to August on those few occasions when she had visited India at the office.

India paused in the doorway of her assigned workplace and reflected. "Aunt August is strong. She is the backbone of the family. Even my dad acknowledged that, that it was August who kept us all together over the years. But she adored Ry, and frankly, I am concerned about her. She is terribly sad. As we all are. And of course, now there's Corri . . ."

"Did Ry appoint you as her guardian?"

"He didn't spell it out in a will, if that's what you mean. But of course, between Aunt August and me, Corri will have all the loving family she could want. And since Ry had formally adopted her, Corri will inherit his share of the family trust. She'll be well provided for, in any event."

"Anything we can do, me and Liz"—he made reference to his wife—"we're there."

"Thanks, Singer." India acknowledged the kindness with a half smile, then turned the corner of the gray divider used to create cubicles for the assistant district attorneys in the basement of City Hall.

"So"—India plunked her pocketbook and briefcase on the floor next to her desk in the overcrowded and chaotic cubical and was suddenly all business—"did you get a statement from that kid who was hiding behind the swings when Axel scooped up the Melendez girl?"

"His mother won't let him talk to me. And Indy, I don't know that I blame her. Axel Thomas is a really nasty guy. Between you and me, I don't know that I'd want to bring my little boy to his attention."

"Maybe I could give it a try." Indy flipped through a pile of messages on her desk. "Do you have their number?"

"Yeah, I'm sure you can convince her to let her five-year-old come in to open court and make an I.D. on a child molester who may or may not go to jail. You are smooth, Devlin, but if it was my kid, I'd tell you to—"

"The number, Singer," India deadpanned, "or I'll tell everyone that 'Barry' is short for 'Bardolf.'"

"That's low, Devlin. Real low." The short, stocky detective turned pale.

"That number was . . ." She batted her eyelashes expectantly.

The detective wrote it down on a piece of paper and handed it to her. "India, I really don't think—"

"Look, Barry, it won't hurt for me to talk to her. I want this guy." She dialed, then looked up at him. "I'm not going to try to talk the parents into letting their son testify, if that's what you're worried about. I would not jeopardize a child's welfare for the sake of a conviction. I just want to talk to him, maybe get just enough information so that we won't need to have him on the stand—Hello, Mrs. Powell? This is India Devlin, Paloma district attorney's office. I'd like to stop in this afternoon to speak with you about Axel Thomas . . ."

By seven-thirty that evening, India had met with the Powells and, through careful questioning, discovered that there may have been another witness. The Powell boy had described a woman who had been leaning out the second-floor window of an apartment overlooking the park at the same time that he had seen Thomas take off with the little girl. India called Singer and asked him to try to track her down and see if he could get a statement.

Returning to her office, she read through piles of statements that had been taken while she had been in Devlin's Light pertaining to yet another case before pulling out the files on the Thomas case. She would need to refresh herself on the facts if she was going to go to trial on Monday.

Welcome back. India rotated her neck in a full circle to unkink it and glanced at the clock. Eleven-forty. The night had gone by in a blur. It was too late to call Aunt August and Corri. She would have to call them first thing the next morning. She packed three files into her already overstuffed briefcase. Frowning when she could not get the brown leather satchel to close, she pulled out one file, tucked it under her arm and hoisted her shoulder bag over her head to hang from her neck, thereby freeing up both hands for carrying.

The hallway was darkened except for the lights over the doors and the exit sign. Walking past the double doors leading to the annex housing the city morgue always gave India a severe case of goose bumps, and tonight was no exception. Her heels made muffled popping sounds on the old tiled floor as she struggled down the hallway to the elevator, where she pressed the button for the lobby with an index finger. The old lift groaned as it slowly ascended, reminding her once again that the slowest elevators in Paloma were, in fact, in City Hall.

"Can I give you a hand there, Miss Devlin?" Paul, the night guard, who pronounced her name *Dev-a-lin,* rose from his wooden chair, which stood right next to the elevator, halfway between the front and back doors of the building.

"Oh, I'll make it to the car if you can open the back door for me."

"Certainly, Miss Devlin." He nodded and walked briskly, with purpose and importance, to the back door, his heavy ring of keys clanging loudly in the silent building.

"Thank you." India smiled at him gratefully as he held the door open for her to pass through. "I'll see you in the morning."

"I'll just wait here till you get to your car." Paul stood on the top step, his right hand on his gun, as if daring some unseen felon to jump out at India. As she reached her car, he called to her across the quiet night: "Miss Devlin . . ."

"Yes?" she called back as she hit the security button on her key ring to open the car door with a "beep."

"I was sorry about what happened to your brother."

"Thank you, Paul. So was I. Thank you for remembering him." India opened the rear door on the driver's side and threw her heavy bundles onto the seat and slammed the door. She slid in behind the wheel and turned the key. Waving to Paul, the silent, shadowy sentinel who still watched from the top step, she pulled out of the parking lot and onto the rain-slicked streets of the city that had been her home for the past five years.

Paloma was a city on the mend. At one time it had been a busy manufacturing center, but the textile mills moved south and those days were long past. Concentrated efforts begun ten years ago to revitalize the downtown area, however, had met with some success. The shopping district was coming back to life, the new shops having been joined by a variety of cultural attractions and fine restaurants; a music hall built at the turn of the century today served as a popular venue for plays as well as concerts. Over the years the university had grown on the north side of the city, bringing with it a well-endowed library and a highly regarded museum of natural history.

Driving through this, the oldest part of town, India rechecked the locks to reassure herself that all the doors were secured. It was dark and it was late, and this was not the best place in the city for a young woman to be driving alone. Old City had stubbornly refused gentrification and had seemed to decline as rapidly as other parts of the city had improved. There were pockets of Paloma that resembled a war zone, where crime was so common it was rarely reported. India always felt relieved when she reached her street, which was several blocks beyond Old City and on the fringes of a section of Paloma known as the Crest, a totally renovated area that had caught the fancy of upscale buyers ten years ago and was now the fashionable place to live.

India's townhouse was narrow and three rooms deep, three stories high. She had seen similar homes in Philadelphia some years before, but there they were called "Trinities." Here in Paloma they were known as "treys." Everest Place lay as still as a sleeping child as she pulled up to the curb, grateful to find her usual parking space in front of her house empty and waiting for her return. The slamming of her car door echoed through the neighborhood, a rude interruption in the night silence. She unloaded everything at once, piling suitcases amid work files on her front steps so that, once inside, she would not have to venture back out onto the deserted street. Unlocking the front door, which swung without a sound into the small foyer, she tried to step over the mail, which had been propelled through the mail slot for the past week and now littered the entire floor of the entryway. Some pieces had made it all the way into the living room, she noted wryly.

Dumping the suitcase onto the floor at the foot of the steps that led to the second floor, she returned to the front door and retrieved the rest of her belongings, kicking envelopes, catalogs and other assorted mail out of the way. She turned on the light nearest the sofa, scooped up the mail and dropped it on the table in the entry. It could all wait until tomorrow. Tonight she was too tired to read another word.

The light on her answering machine blinked incessantly. Too many messages to listen to now. The morning would be soon enough, she decided with a shrug as she turned the key in the deadbolt lock on the front door. Dragging the suitcase up the steps, she sought the peace of her bedroom, where she had created a little getaway of sorts for herself. She turned on the overhead light and sighed. It was good to be home. Tonight she was exhausted, the emotions of the past week having taken their toll on her mind and her body. Every inch of her craving sleep, she all but crashed face first onto her bed. Tomorrow she would read her mail and listen to her messages and call Aunt August. Tonight she would, for a while, put aside her work and all it entailed, all the dirty, ugly things that people do for reasons no sane person could ever comprehend, and she would lose herself to sleep.

The rude buzzing of the alarm awakened a reluctant India at six. Through barely opened eyes, she took in her surroundings and was surprised to find herself, not in Devlin's Light, as she had been in her dreams, but in Paloma. Instead of the faded yellow daisy wallpaper of her old room on Darien Road, this room was painted white, as was the furniture. The carpet was softest plush blue, the curtains a blue and white stripe. Across the foot of the white iron bed rested a blue and white floral comforter, which coordinated perfectly with the bedskirt, pillow covers, sheets, and a lightweight summer blanket. From the small wingchair right inside the door tumbled an array of pillows, all made by August from the hand-embroidered linens India had begun collecting as a young girl.

India rolled over and looked at the clock, groaning when she realized that she did, in fact, have to obey its command. She swept her hair from her face and tottered into the bathroom across the hall and turned on the shower, hoping it would revive her. It did.

She dressed hastily for work, pulling on a somewhat casual, totally comfortable pantsuit of soft gray and white pinstriped linen, since it was not a court day and she did not need to "dress." That would come on Monday, with the start of the Thomas trial. Before closing the closet door, she checked to make certain that her favorite dark blue suit was clean. Smiling to herself when she saw that it was, she closed the door. She always wore that suit—her lucky suit—on the first day of a trial. She had never lost a case when she delivered her opening statement wearing that suit. India wasn't going to take any chances. The suit was a go for Monday.

Breakfast was a cup of coffee in the car and a bowl of fruit at her desk, lunch was less. Before she knew it, it was four o'clock and she still had two more briefs to read and respond to. Roxanne Detweiler, the inhabitant of the cubicle next to India's, stuck her curly dark head through the doorway at seven-twenty and asked, "Want Chinese? Herbie is calling in an order."

Lost in thought, India nodded affirmatively.

"What do you want?"

Not raising her head from the file spread across the top of

the desk, Indy replied absently, "Pepperoni, mushrooms, whatever you're having."

Having seen India so immersed in her work in the past, Roxanne grinned devilishly.

"You want a little sweet and sour bat wings on that, Indy? Maybe a side of frog toes and fried slugs?"

"Sure, Roxie." India waved a hand indifferently. "Whatever."

"What's she want? Herbie's waiting." Singer poked Roxanne in the back.

"Get us an order of hot and spicy chicken and an order of rice noodles with oriental vegetables and some steamed dumplings."

Roxanne folded her arms across her chest, well aware that India had no clue that someone was in her office. There was a joke circulating around the D.A.'s office that you could rob India's office of everything except the file she was working on at that moment and you'd most likely get away with it.

"India has been like that for as long as I've known her," Roxanne once told the rest of the staff. "She has the enviable ability to block out everything and totally focus on the business at hand. She did it in college, she did it all through law school, and she's still doing it. She says she tries to hear the person's voice when she's reading a statement, to see the scene as the victim did, to hear what they heard and feel what they felt."

"Spooky" was the consensus of India's colleagues, but every one of them agreed she was the best at what she did. Her uncanny ability to block out what she considered irrelevant might be responsible for a good part of that success.

It wasn't until Roxanne called over the partition to tell her that her phone was ringing that India heard it. Searching through piles of papers, she finally located it and picked up the receiver.

"Oh, hello, Aunt August." India's eyes sought the small desk clock. It was almost seven-thirty. "Oh, Aunt August, I am so sorry. I meant to call last night but it was so late when I got home, and then this morning just sort of got away from me and before I knew it . . ."

"I understand, India." Aunt August, as always, went straight to the point. "However, there is someone else to be considered now."

"Corri. Oh, damn, I meant to call her . . ." India dragged her hand through her hair and sighed deeply, berating herself for the oversight.

"She's right here, Indy." August handed the phone to Corri.

"Indy?" The sweet little girl voice poured like liquid sunshine through the wires.

"Hey, sugar." India tried to think of some excuse for not having called in the morning, as she had said she would do. "Corri, I meant to—"

"It's okay, Indy. Nick took me fishing," she announced.

"This morning?" India relaxed. Corri wouldn't have been home if she had remembered to call.

"No, this afternoon. To make me feel better."

Ouch.

"Did you feel badly because I forgot to call?"

"I just felt sad because you weren't here. But Darla said that after you put the bad guys in jail you'll come home."

"Darla is right, sugar."

"Indy . . ."

"What, Corri?"

"Do you have to put away all the bad guys, or just a few, before you can come home?"

India smiled. "Just the ones that get caught in Paloma. I doubt anyone could put away all the bad guys."

"You could," Corri said confidently. "Ry said you were the best prostitutor in Paloma."

"That's 'prosecutor,' Corri." India laughed, and through the phone line, she could hear August laughing too. "Say the word, so you'll remember it correctly."

"Posse-cutor."

"That's a little better, but you still need some practice. Maybe you'll have that down pat by the time I come home."

"When will that be? Tomorrow? It's the weekend."

"I'm afraid not, sweetie. I have to get ready for Monday. I have a lot of reading to do between now and then."

"But when the bad guy's in jail, will you come home?"

"You can bet the ranch," India told her.

Corri giggled. "We don't have a ranch."

"Oh, you're right. Well then, you can bet the dunes."

"Will it be next week?"

"Next week might be a little too soon."

"That's what Nick said. He said he thought it might take a while. He said this was a really bad man and it might take a while for everyone to come in and tell the judge just how bad he is."

"Nick is a pretty smart fellow."

"He is, Indy. Oh, he said to say hi for him when I talked to you. So hi from Nick."

"Tell him hi back."

Roxanne called over the intercom that dinner had arrived.

"Listen, Corri, I'm going to go and have some dinner." India was suddenly starving.

"We had dinner," Corri told her. "We had fish that Nick and I caught. Aunt August let him stay for dinner. And Ollie and Darla and Jack too."

"You must have caught a lot of fish," India noted somewhat wistfully, imagining them all in the Devlins' old kitchen, crowded around Aunt August as she worked miracles with an old black iron griddle and some freshly caught fish. Her mouth began to water at the thought of it. "Is he still there? Nick?"

"No. He left to drive Darla and Jack home. Ollie is sleeping over with me. Tomorrow Aunt August is taking me and Ollie to the library for the story hour."

"That sounds like fun. Call me tomorrow night and you can tell me all about the story, okay?"

"Okay. I will."

"Now put Aunt August back on the phone," India instructed.

"You did miss a lovely dinner," August told her. "Corri and Nick caught a couple of blues that would have knocked your socks off."

"I am sorry I missed it." Mentally, Indy amended her earlier fantasy. Bluefish would have been stuffed with a savory stuffing—cornbread, perhaps, or maybe sage—and wrapped in foil and baked in the oven to the perfect degree of flakiness.

"And we all missed you," August told her. "Nick asked for your phone number. I didn't think you'd mind if I gave it to him."

"Not at all," India said, playing with the cap from a Bic pen. "He promised to get me a list of Ry's acquaintances from Bayview and from the Save the Bay group."

"Well, I've no doubt if there's anything to be found, the two of you will find it," August said. "Must run. I have two little girls here who are waiting to make peach ice cream."

"Bye," Indy said, knowing that August had already moved on.

"You coming into the kitchen to eat, or are you going to eat here?" Roxanne asked from the doorway.

"I'll come in." India stood up on legs that badly needed stretching, taking in the mess of papers and files that were her professional life. One wall held her degrees: a bachelor of arts from Middlebury College, her law degree from Dickinson. Between the two hung a framed piece of embroidery, a gift from Aunt August when Indy had passed the bar exam. *Summum ius summa inuria.* The more law, the less justice.

India rubbed her back with one very tired hand and massaged her neck with the other as she followed Roxanne to the kitchen down the hall.

Nick Enright's big hands came suddenly to mind, and India could not help but speculate on what a great massage one might expect from a pair of hands like that. She brushed the image away abruptly and slid into a seat at the small table in the makeshift kitchen where her dinner awaited. Surrounded by FBI posters—Have you seen this man?—she sat down to her first real meal in forty-eight hours. Not, she silently lamented, perfect baked bluefish, caught by a winsome man with honey-colored eyes and a killer smile and his darling six-year-old assistant, prepared with love by Aunt August, and shared with friends and family in the warm, inviting Devlin kitchen, but half-cold Chinese from the corner takeout. She sighed and for the first time in a very long time questioned her sanity.

Aunt August's Baked Stuffed Bluefish

1 whole bluefish, split and cleaned (head removed unless it doesn't bother you. I personally don't like the idea of the fish watching me while I stuff it.)

Stuffing:

4 cups bread cubes
1 large onion, chopped
1 clove garlic, minced
4–5 mushrooms, sliced
1 apple, chopped
1 stalk celery, chopped
3 tablespoons butter
1/2 teaspoon salt
1/8 teaspoon pepper
1/4 teaspoon poultry seasoning
2 tablespoons chopped fresh parsley
2 tablespoons lemon juice
2 teaspoons grated lemon peel

Sauté onion, celery and garlic in butter in large skillet or Dutch oven until onion is translucent. Add mushrooms and apples and cook until the mushrooms just begin to brown and the apples begin to soften. Add seasonings, parsley, lemon juice and lemon peel, sauté for 1–2 minutes. Toss with bread cubes. If bread cubes appear too dry, add a tablespoon or two of boiling water to moisten.

After cleaning the fish and removing all bones, place the fish on a sheet of aluminum foil 2½ times the size of the fish. Place a generous amount of stuffing in the pocket. Wrap the foil around the fish and bake for 35–40 minutes, or until done. The fish is done when it flakes easily with a fork.

Chapter 5

I need to find some time to rake. India made a mental note as she kicked through the yellow and green leaves that had begun their descent from the scrawny maple standing in the small front yard and trudged to her car, half dragging the overloaded briefcase, which as always, was too full to close.

Fall had always been a favorite season. India paused on the sidewalk, momentarily lost in the memory of Ry raking leaves in the side yard at the Devlin homestead, piling lofty piebald layers of yellow, brown, red and orange into a heap for a small and eager Indy to jump into. Sitting on the front porch steps eating slices of warm, cinnamon-y apple pie from Aunt August's oven, talking about the new school year and watching the ever-hopeful Darla sneaking moonstruck peeks at the always-oblivious Ry. Seeking solitary refuge out on the dunes on an October evening, sipping from a steaming mug of cider poured from her father's old chipped thermos and trying to sort out all the twists and turns that had bent and shaped her young life this way and that. Being fifteen and angry with her mother for dying before she'd had an opportunity to know her. Watching the geese take flight over the bay on a November afternoon, wishing she could take off with them wherever they were going.

The honking of a neighbor's car horn brought her back to the present and she waved absently.

India swung the heavy satchel onto the backseat. The Thomas trial was into its third hard week. She was taking no chances on losing this one. She would put on every witness, use every piece of evidence, turn herself inside out to put him away. India remained unruffled in the courtroom, seemingly unnerved by the defendant's bold stare of defiance, meeting his taunting eyes with a cool, level gaze. She would spend hours cross-examining witnesses, shaking his alibi, smoking out the truth. In the end, she would have him. She knew just how to play it. It wasn't the easiest case she had ever tried; far from it. It was proving to be grueling, emotionally as well as physically, but in the end, she would have him. She owed it to his victims—to all such victims—to prove to the jury beyond a shadow of reasonable doubt exactly what this man was, all he had done, and to make certain that his particular evil was contained for the rest of his days on this earth.

Per ardua ad astra, Aunt August had so often reminded her. Through hardship to the stars.

The courtroom was filling rapidly. The city had become enamored of the trial, and the press had been all over her from day one. Every local newspaper and television news show featured her face, highlighting her cross-examination of this witness or that, reporting every caustic remark exchanged between India and Jim Cromwell, the city's best-known criminal defense attorney, who had drawn the unsavory court appointment to represent Thomas.

India set up her exhibits in front of her on the long pine table and stacked a pile of yellow legal pads and a score of pens where she could easily reach them. Today she planned to present physical evidence to the jury. Blood smears and DNA, strands of hair found in Thomas's car that had come from the head of his third victim, a nine-year-old girl who had played soccer and read Nancy Drew books, who walked her elderly neighbor's dog and baby-sat for her little sister. For a long moment, memory brought India face to face with another young girl who had once played soccer. Who had loved Nancy Drew. Who had played with India on the dunes of Devlin's Beach . . .

India slammed a file onto the table. *This* one would go

down, she promised, and would *stay* down. There would be no deals, no safe place for Axel Thomas.

By four-thirty in the afternoon, India was drained and frustrated, and no closer to the end of the trial than she'd been at eight o'clock that morning. Procedural arguments had dominated the entire day. The minute that court was dismissed, India gathered the exhibits that had been lost in the mire of Cromwell's rhetoric and their dueling citations of case law. Her carefully prepared charts and photographs would have to wait until court resumed on Monday morning, when, hopefully, she would have an opportunity to place them into evidence. India tucked her portfolio under her arm, pointedly ignoring the smirking defendant, who whistled an upbeat version of the theme from "The Bridge on the River Kwai" as she prepared to leave the courtroom for the weekend.

"It's time to deal, Lady Prosecutor. Deal or lose," Thomas said, sneering mockingly from twelve feet away.

She turned to snap a response, when a waving hand from the third row caught her attention.

"Indy!" Corri jumped up and down, trying to restrain herself from shouting.

"Corri, what on earth—" She started toward the child, then saw the man who stood behind her. "Nick? What are you doing here?"

"We came to take you out for your birthday." Corri clapped her hands excitedly.

"My birthday?" India repeated, then recalled the date. "It *is* my birthday. I'd forgotten."

She made her way through the thinning crowd to hug Corri to her, closing her eyes for a moment of solace as the child's thin arms wrapped tightly around her neck.

"Aunt August told me it was your birthday, so we brought you dinner and a cake." Corri beamed.

"Where is Aunt August?" India searched for her in the still-crowded courtroom.

"She couldn't come. She had a migrate," Corri announced, "but Nick said we couldn't let you celebrate your birthday alone, so he brought me."

"You mean a *migraine?*" India frowned. It seemed that

her aunt's headaches were increasing in frequency. She wondered if Dr. Noone had been consulted.

"I offered to bring Corri because she had her heart set on surprising you," Nick explained.

"Nick, this is really very sweet . . ."

"I hope that isn't a *but* I detect." Nick lowered his voice and leaned closer to her. "Corri would really be disappointed, Indy."

"No, no, of course not," she assured him. She had planned to stay up half the night to go over today's proceedings, but she would have the rest of the weekend for that. Tonight she would put it aside and be with Corri. And Nick. "I'm just so surprised, that's all. I didn't even realize it was my birthday, I've been so wrapped up in this trial. But I'm delighted, truly. Just let me get my things. And Corri, you can help me carry—"

She stopped in midsentence. Corri stood all but frozen, facing the front of the courtroom, her gaze held fast by the man in prison blues. Axel grinned meaningfully with the eyes of a son of Satan.

"Nick, take Corri out into the hallway. I'll meet you there." India practically shoved the girl into Nick's arms. "Please."

She turned and walked toward the defendant's table, too enraged to speak.

"That your little girl, Madame Prosecutor?" Axel drawled as he was pulled to his feet by the bailiff. "She's a pretty little thing."

"Don't even look at her," India hissed like a maddened viper across the defense table, "or you won't have to wait until the jury convicts you. I'll rip your heart out myself."

Axel laughed as he shuffled toward the side door, where he'd be loaded into a van and returned to his cell until Monday morning.

Shaking from head to foot with the raw terror that washed over her with all the force of an unforeseen tidal wave, India folded her arms across her chest and sought to control her breathing. She forced her feet to carry her back to the prosecutor's table, where, with trembling hands, she began to pick up stacks of paper and shove them mindlessly into folders.

"India, my God, what is it?" Herbie Caruthers took the papers from her hands. "You look as if you've seen a ghost."

"For a moment, I guess I thought I had." India dropped into a chair and rested her head in her hands.

"Here." Herbie handed her a glass of water. "Are you okay?"

She sipped at the water, which had grown tepid as the day progressed and the chips of ice melted in the warmth of a sunny, late September afternoon.

"I'm good. Thanks."

"Look, how 'bout if I take this stuff back to the office for you," Herbie said, packing up their case documents, "and I'll meet you in the conference room in an hour and we'll go over today's testimony."

"It'll have to wait until tomorrow morning," she told him, her composure slowly returning. "I have a birthday to celebrate."

"Since when has a minor detail like a birthday come between you and a big case?"

"Since now." She thought of Corri's little upturned face, so filled with the joy of having a surprise for Indy. India couldn't remember the last time anyone had offered her so great a gift. She had no intention of disappointing the child.

India gathered her things and left the courtroom, her briefcase under her arm and her shoulder bag swinging along next to her, filled with the sudden certainty that whether she worked tonight or not, Axel would not walk away with a sweet plea bargain this time, as he had done in the past. He may have dealt his way through other states, other jurisdictions, but this time he had chosen Paloma in which to play his evil games. Backed by a district attorney who had been elected on a strong anticrime platform, India had the blessing of the department to take this one all the way. Unaware of promises she had made long ago, promises she had spent her entire adult life trying to keep, Axel Thomas had made the mistake of getting caught in a city that had no interest in making deals. Had she been in any danger of forgetting those promises, the unvoiced threat to Corri had been more than enough to remind her.

Tonight she would celebrate her birthday with a child who asked only that India love her. Tomorrow she would return to the task of putting away Axel Thomas once and for all.

"Indy, can I play with your soaps?" Corri bounced into the bright kitchen, having emerged from the first-floor powder room with a basket filled with little soaps in various shapes and colors—a house-warming gift to India from a co-worker, which, until now, had been pretty much forgotten.

"Sure," India said, laughing.

"How does one play with soap?" Nick asked from the corner of his mouth, and India nodded toward the carpeted area between the kitchen and the dining room, where Corri had planted herself and proceeded to remove the soaps, one by one, from the basket. All the starfish went into one pile, the flowers into another, the little animals into yet a third. Corri then separated them by color.

"I see." Nick grinned as he hoisted a large basket onto the kitchen table.

"What's in there?" India tried to peek under the lid, but Nick closed it from her view.

"Dinner. Complements of August. She gave me strict instructions. Let's see now, where did I—oh, here they are." With a flourish, Nick removed a sheet of folded paper from the pocket of his blue and white pinstriped shirt and snapped it open. "Now, let's see what I need here . . . a long baking pan—got one of those?"

His eyes were dancing as he looked into hers, and she nodded, somewhat dumbly, that she did in fact have one of those . . . whatever it was he had asked for. It was hard to concentrate when he stared directly into her eyes like that, like they were the oldest, the very best of friends, friends who had shared so very much.

But then again, she told herself, they had shared something special. They had both been blessed with Ry's presence in their lives. It made Nick less of a stranger, more of a friend.

"And we need to set the oven to 350 degrees," Nick said, reading from her aunt's crisply printed instructions.

India rummaged around in her cupboard and emerged with a baking pan. "Will this do?"

"That'll do just fine." He smiled, and those little dimples she'd noticed that day on the beach emerged to taunt her.

She handed him the pan, wondering what she had done to deserve having a man like Nick Enright show up on her birthday to cook her dinner.

"August said to heat these up in the microwave." From the deep basket he removed a dish of rosemary potatoes in one hand and a brown bag in the other. He plopped the bag onto the counter. "These we can just steam. Green beans. The last from Liddy Osborn's garden."

"And what's in there?" She pointed to the long object wrapped in foil and packed in ice, which Nick had removed from the basket.

"That's what we need the baking pan for." Nick began to unwrap the bundle.

"Ohmygod!" India nearly melted in anticipation. "Aunt August's stuffed bluefish."

"We caught it," Corri piped up, "me and Nick. Out by Heron Cove."

"I can't believe it!" Indy all but swooned. "My favorite dinner. You don't know how I dreamed of Aunt August's stuffed and baked bluefish. Just thinking about it makes me ravenous."

"Well, you sit right down there, Birthday Girl—" Nick pulled out a kitchen chair and motioned for her to sit— "while I prepare to make your dream come true."

"And I will set the table." Corri abandoned her little zoo of soap animals and hopped on one foot into the kitchen. "I know how."

"Is that a deck I see out there?" With one finger Nick drew the curtain aside from the window overlooking the small back yard.

"Yes," Indy replied. "The previous owners had it built. I haven't used it much."

"I want to see out back," Corri told her, the table-setting assignment momentarily forgotten.

India unlocked the back door and opened it to step onto the deck, which faced an overgrown yard.

"Indy, you need to cut your *grass.*" Corri pointed toward the lawn.

"I know, sweetie," a somewhat abashed India admitted. "I just haven't had time."

"It's too tall to walk in," Corri said, frowning from the bottom of the steps.

"I'm sorry, Corri. Maybe by the next time you come I'll have gotten to it."

Nick appeared in the doorway.

"Got a lawn mower?" he asked.

"Well, yes, I do, but . . ."

"Get it out," he told her, "and I'll cut the grass. You don't have much of a yard. I'll have it done by the time the oven has heated for the fish."

"Nick, you don't have to cut my grass. I'll do it tomorrow. Or I'll try to find someone in the neighborhood—"

He had already bounded past her and down the steps. "Out here?" he asked, pointing to the small cedar-sided shed that stood near the far corner.

"Well, yes, but . . ."

He was already into the shed and had lifted the small lawn mower out before she had finished her sentence. Soon he had the mower running, and she leaned on the deck railing, watching as he left trails of grassy clumps in his wake as he crossed back and forth across the small yard, the mower humming as he attended efficiently to the task.

"You really didn't have to do all this," she told him as he finished and turned off the mower.

"It's your birthday," he said solemnly, "and it was important to Corri to be with you, to surprise you. Ry talked a lot about making a difference in her life—it was important to him to try to give her some security after she lost her mother. He said he knew just how frightening it was for a child to lose a parent. He didn't want her to feel alone."

India nodded. "Our mother died when Ry was barely four years old, just about the same age as Corri was when Maris died. I was just a baby, but Ry said many times how scared he had been, that she just seemed to have gone away, and he never saw her again."

"Maris's death was hard enough on her, but now, with Ry gone, I think it's even more important for her to feel wanted, to feel a part of something. I owe it to Ry to do what I can, when I can. Corri really wanted to celebrate your birthday with you. I needed to make sure that happened for her. And for you."

"Thank you, Nick," she said simply. "For Corri. And for me."

"And for Ry," he reminded her.

"Certainly," she said softly, "for Ry."

Of course, that was why he had made this trip, why he had brought Corri to her. Because of Ry, because of his respect and fondness for her brother. Unexpectedly, her heart was stung by the slightest trace of disappointment as she acknowledged the reason for his presence there, in her home, on her birthday.

But even knowing that, once back inside her tidy house, she watched him fill her kitchen with energy and humor and wondered if she had ever known a man quite like him.

Dinner was exquisite, lacking only Aunt August's presence to make it the perfect birthday feast. Nick lifted the bluefish from the oven and slid it onto an old platter, happily chattering with Corri, taking pains to draw India into the conversation from time to time. They talked about various personalities in Devlin's Light, about the start of the school year and who was in Corri's class, why the art teacher was great and the music teacher not so. All in all, it was a wonderful birthday. India could not remember the last one that had brought her more pleasure.

Corri bit her lip with happy anticipation as India opened the card that had been made just for her, watercolored rainbows and balloons painted on light blue construction paper.

"Aunt August helped me with some of the words," Corri announced proudly, "but I drew the pictures myself."

Happy birthday, Indy. I love you. Corri.

"Balloons and rainbows are two of my most favorite things." Indy hugged her, holding the child close for a very long minute.

"Mine too. I used blue paper so it would be like the sky. See, rainbows are in the sky, and that's where your balloons go if you don't hold on to them."

"It's a wonderful card, simply beautiful, Corri. I'll have to find a good place to keep it."

"Oh!" Corri jumped from her seat. "We forgot!" She stuck her face into the picnic basket. "Here, India." Corri handed over two small yellow and white plastic daisies.

"What are these?" India asked.

"They are magnets, silly." Corri took them from her and used them to hold the card in place on the refrigerator door.

"Why, how very clever!" India laughed. "Thank you. Now I can see my pretty card every time I come into the kitchen."

"Thank Aunt August," Corri told her brightly, "it was her idea. She said it was time we started spreading around the 'frigerator art."

"And she wasn't kidding," Nick told her as he cleared the table. "I have a few of those little collector's items myself. August does believe in sharing the wealth."

"I painted ducks for Nick. And a bird sitting on cattails."

"Which was actually quite good," Nick told her.

Corri beamed, basking in the happy moment for a split second before bouncing up and clapping her hands. "Now we can have birthday cake!"

India's favorite coconut cake with white frosting had survived the trip from Devlin's Light with little more than some mooshed frosting on one side. Corri planted the candles across the top layer and Nick lit them, and both of them sang the birthday song while Indy closed her eyes and, for a moment, was transported back to another birthday, another time.

"Make a wish Indy," Ry was saying. "Wish with your heart and blow the candles out at the same time, and whatever you wish for will come true."

She opened her eyes and looked up into the smiling faces of two people who had become, suddenly, achingly precious to her. Taking a deep breath, enough to blow out all twenty-nine candles at the same time, India looked into eyes the color of caramels and knew exactly what to wish for.

Maybe, she thought as she watched the tiny lights on the cake go out, when this trial was over, she'd have time to work on making that wish come true. For now, she just wanted to hold on to what remained of the evening, to the warmth that came, not from the candles' glow, but from the heart of a child and the eyes of a very special man.

∽∾ ∾

Great-Aunt Nola's Award-Winning Coconut Cake

Cake:

2½ cups plus 2 tablespoons flour
3 teaspoons baking powder
1/2 teaspoon salt
1½ cups sugar
3/4 cups butter
3 eggs, separated
3/4 cup milk
1/2 teaspoon vanilla extract
1/2 teaspoon coconut extract
3/4 cup flaked coconut (soak in 2 tablespoons milk)

Preheat oven to 350° and prepare 2 cake pans (grease and flour). Add vanilla and coconut extracts to milk and set aside. Sift flour, baking powder and salt together. Set aside. Cream butter with mixer for 30 seconds, then gradually add sugar and mix on medium speed for 5 minutes. Beat egg yolks and add to butter mixture. Add flour and milk alternately to butter mix, stirring after each addition, until smooth. Stir in coconut. With clean, dry beaters, beat egg whites until stiff but not dry. Gently fold into batter. Turn into pans*, baking at 25 minutes for 8-inch round or square pans. Cool in pans 10 minutes, then invert onto racks and cool completely before frosting.

Frosting (makes enough for 2 layers or one 9x13x2-inch sheet cake):

1/2 cup butter, softened
1 lb. box of 10X sugar, sifted
4 tablespoons milk

2 tablespoons coconut
1/2 teaspoon coconut extract
1/2 teaspoon vanilla extract

Soak coconut in milk. Beat butter with mixer on medium speed 30 seconds. Add 1/2 of the sugar, beat well. Drain coconut and add milk to butter mixture, beating well. Gradually add remaining sugar until desired consistency. Blend in extracts and coconut. Frost cake and cover with as much coconut as the cake will hold.

---

*Makes 2 8- or 9-inch layers or one 13x9x2-inch sheet.

Chapter 6

*T*he glow was, sadly, short lived, since first thing Monday morning found India back in court, battling with Axel Thomas's attorney on technical issues. The trial dragged on for three more very tense weeks, every day of which was war. Certainly it had been a war worth fighting, she later noted with satisfaction. Particularly since she had emerged the victor and had the pleasure of knowing that Axel's sorry butt would soon be hauled to the state prison for what would surely be a long and miserable stay.

"Indy, we saw you on television!" Corri chirped into the phone, which had been ringing even as India had unlocked her front door and stepped inside following several hours of postverdict celebrations with her colleagues. "You looked pretty."

"Thank you, sweetheart." India laughed. She had, of course, seen the film, but she hadn't noticed whether she looked pretty or not, couldn't have told with any degree of certainty what she had been wearing or who else had been framed by the camera's lens following the pronouncement of the jury's verdict.

"I'm so proud of you." Aunt August's whisper filled her ear and gladdened her heart. "I always am, India. This time especially, I applaud your efforts."

"Thank you, Aunt August." India squeezed her eyes

tightly closed, bringing back the scene in the courtroom. The hush as the judge climbed three steps to his seat, his black robes trailing slightly behind him like a nun's habit. The rustle of skirts and the *tap-tap-tap* of one juror's high-heeled shoes as they crossed the ancient pine floor to the jury box. A poorly smothered cough from somewhere behind her. The mass of apprehensive uncertainty that filled her chest, threatening to displace every bit of oxygen in her lungs, as she waited, the very picture of composure and self-assurance, while inside her intestines twisted grotesquely. Axel Thomas's stare, deliberate and unconcerned, sure of his impending freedom, as he sought to engage her eyes in one last bemused gesture of contempt.

And then the judge asked, "Has the jury reached a verdict?"

"We have, Your Honor," replied the foreman, a tall man with salt-and-pepper hair and round-framed glasses too large for his elongated and dole face.

"How do you find?"

"We find the defendant, Axel Edward Thomas, guilty on all counts, Your Honor."

There was just the barest hesitation, a heartbeat's worth of silence, before pandemonium erupted. Those members of India's staff who had gathered across the back of the courtroom holding their breaths without even realizing they were doing so shouted and applauded the jury's decision. India fought back tears as Herbie fought to control his own exaltation, as he rubbed a shaking hand across her shoulders to signal it was all right now, the weeks of traveling into the mind of a killer were over. Axel's mask of bemused certainty dissolved into contentious disbelief, then snapped into crude threats thrown aggressively in every direction. India, the judge, his own attorney, all bore the brunt of his incensed declarations over the excited chatter in the courtroom.

In the end, it all came down to this, she later reflected: She had done what no one had been sure she would be able to do. She had won a conviction on all charges—kidnap, rape, assault, and first-degree murder—for two of Axel Thomas's three victims.

And for you, Lizzie, she whispered.

"I'm asking for the death penalty," India said softly into the receiver.

"Sic semper tyrannis," replied August. Thus always to tyrants. "Well then. Corri is jumping up and down here— she wants to know if you'll be home in time for dinner."

"Not dinner tonight, but tomorrow night for sure. Tonight I'm planning on being in bed by seven. I can't remember the last time I was this tired. And I plan to sleep late."

"Will you be able to take a few vacation days?" Concern was clearly evident in August's voice. "You've been working far too hard, India, for far too long. You haven't taken any time off except when Ry died. And God knows, that was no vacation."

"I'm taking a few days, but I have to bring some work with me. I have another trial starting in about ten days." India bit the nail on her right index finger, the Mobley case starting to swirl slowly in the recesses of her mind. How to play it. How to win. "I'll bring some files home with me, but I will have a little time to relax. I want to spend some time with Corri."

"That's exactly what you need to be doing right now, India. It's a necessity." August knew of India's commitment to her work and understood better than any living soul the depth of that commitment. At the same time, August knew how desperately the child needed India—as much, August suspected, as India needed Corri.

India heard August's sigh as she hung up the phone and knew exactly what her aunt was thinking: At least India would be home for a few days, and she, August, would see that her niece was well fed, warm and surrounded by love for however long she would stay. And to India, coming off the Thomas trial and weeks of missing meals, missing sleep and living inside the head of a madman, well fed, warm and loved sounded like pure luxury. Even better, it sounded like home, and she couldn't wait to get there.

She played back the messages on her answering machine and made notes as the recorded voices broke the silence of the small house. A magazine salesman, a credit-card company whose bill she had somehow managed to overlook in the midst of the past few weeks of frenzy, her hairdresser scolding her for having missed the appointment she had scheduled weeks ago before her trial had begun and she had optimistically thought that she might have a day when she could leave the office early enough to make a 7:30 P.M. appointment. Indy hung up her jacket in the closet as the hairdresser's high-pitched voice was replaced by a husky, masculine one.

"Indy, hi, it's Nick. Sorry I missed you tonight, but I know you've been really busy. I did get the names of two people you might want to run a check on. A guy named Hap Manning and a Gene Hatfield. Both had apparently been active last summer with the environmental protests over in Lincoln's Beach, and both were seen in Devlin's Light on several occasions. Dave Shelby at the gas station said he thought that one or both of them may have been around the week or so before Ry died, so you might want to look into them. Well, good luck tomorrow, I'll be thinking about you."

Indy played it back twice, just to listen to his voice.

"I've been thinking about you too," she said aloud to the answering machine, "between briefs and arguments and rulings."

There were several more messages, mostly from tonight, to congratulate her. There was one from the D.A. himself, several from her fellow A.D.A.s, several more from members of the police force, even one from the mayor. All the local television stations, the local newspapers, all looking for interviews. She called the police department and chatted with the detectives, then asked that they run checks on Manning and Hatfield as soon as possible. She pushed the play-back button, just to hear Nick's voice one more time before she hit the pillows.

And hit them she did, hard and fast and grateful, almost joyful, to be doing so. No files to read tonight. No statements to run through, over and over in her mind, searching for exactly the right inflection to make a key point, the most apropos expression for delivering a thought she wanted the jury to recall, the correct body language for commenting without words on a statement of the defendant. Not tonight. Tonight she would sleep. Habit lifted her arm toward the alarm clock, and she smiled broadly, remembering that she would not need it. She would sleep until her exhausted body told her she could get up.

The aroma reached out to welcome India even as she climbed the back steps of the house on Darien Road. She stood in the doorway and breathed it in, certain what the dark blue enameled pot on the stove held. Dropping her suitcase and her bags, she crossed the well-worn yellow pine floor and lifted the lid.

Aunt August's New England clam chowder. Fresh chopped clams and potatoes, onions and bacon. A cholesterol-counter's nightmare of butter and cream. She peeked in the oven, where a loaf of bread was baking to golden brown perfection. On the counter a pan of fresh gingerbread, still warm and fragrant, rested upon a wire cooling rack next to a bowl of homemade applesauce. All in all, it smelled like her childhood, like comfort. The very scents had the power to refresh and restore her.

"Ah, there you are, Indy. I thought I heard your car." Aunt August came into the kitchen through the doorway leading to the back stairwell, which led from the pantry to the second floor.

India returned the firm embrace her aunt offered, holding the older woman for a second more than she had in a long time. August's hair was flattened slightly on one side, and her usually crisp white oxford shirt—sleeves, as always, rolled to the elbows—was a little wrinkled.

"Were you napping?" How unlike her aunt, she of endless energy, tireless of mind and body.

"Just a catnap, dear."

"Why?" India's eyes followed the beloved face before it dipped down to peer into the oven, checking on the progress of the bread.

"Why?" August chuckled. "Because I was tired, India. That's why most people seek rest."

India couldn't recall a single nap that August had taken in all the years they had lived under the same roof. She recalled the recurring migraines, and a tingle of fear pricked the back of her neck. "Aunt August, are you all right?"

"India, this will come as a great shock to you, I know," August said, trying not to smile, "but I'm not as young as I once was. And life is more hectic than it has been in years, with an active six-year-old to keep up with. Goodness, we have homework to deal with again. Granted, it's usually no more than a few letters of the alphabet to print in a little copybook every night, but it's still homework. And all the parents are asked to volunteer to do something with the class, so I go in once a week during story hour and read a book."

August busied herself with removing the bread from the oven while India leaned against the counter under the weight of guilt that pressed against her. She should be tending to Corri's schoolwork and volunteering in the library, not Aunt August, who had never borne a child of her own, yet had raised her brother's children with love, and who now was blessed with the task of raising the child of a woman she hadn't even liked. As much as August loved the child, raising Corri might well prove to be more than August could handle.

"I'm sorry, Aunt August," Indy said as she tossed her keys on the counter. "It shouldn't all be left up to you. I should be doing some of those things with her. I should try to be more of a . . . a *parental* figure."

"Rather difficult to do, wouldn't you say," August said, folding her arms over her chest, "since you live in Paloma and Corri lives in Devlin's Light."

"I don't know how to resolve that."

"I suggest you give it some serious thought, India. Corri needs a *younger* parental figure in her life on a permanent basis. I won't live forever."

"Of course you will. But you're right: I need to make some decisions about her future as well as about my own. I'm just not sure I know what's best." Looking out the window over the sink, India filled the glass coffeepot with water while watching a V of Canadian geese fly over the garage.

"Paloma doesn't have a lock on bad deed doers, India. And I heard that our county D.A. is looking for an experienced trial lawyer," August said softly, trying not to sound too hopeful.

"I've made a life for myself in Paloma, Aunt August."

The back door burst open and Corri flew in, a whirlwind of plaid overalls and light blue long-sleeved T-shirt, little white sneakers and enormous grin. She hesitated only slightly before flinging herself onto India's lap.

"You're home! You did come home!"

"Told you I'd be home today, silly, didn't I?"

"We're having clam chowder for dinner and gingerbread. I have homework—wanna see my copybook? And I got a red star on my color worksheet today, see?" The serene kitchen of only moments earlier disappeared in a flurry of paper.

"And look—I spelled my name . . . see? I don't make my *r* backwards anymore, and look . . ." she said, pointing a small finger, smudged with dirt, at the *C*. "Isn't that a good one?"

"That is one great *C*, Corri. I'll bet I couldn't do better than that myself." India leaned over and followed Corri's finger as she traced the letter she had earlier that day printed across the top of the yellow construction paper. "Indy, is my name still Devlin?"

"Sure." India wondered where *that* had come from.

"Good." Corri bounced off India's lap and across the kitchen to hug August. "Everyone I like best is named Devlin, 'cept for Darla and Ollie. And Nick. And Darla and Ollie would have been married to Ry if he hadn't died, and they would have been Devlins too. Nick never could be, though. Can I have some gingerbread?"

"After you wash your hands," August said, laughing.

"Is she always like this?" Indy laughed with her as the blur that was Corri flew into the powder room and turned on the water.

"Every day." August shook her head. "And yes, it's tiring, but if the truth were to be told, I don't know what I'd do without her. She's my heart, India."

She met India's eyes across the room and India got the message, every bit as clearly as if August had spoken the words aloud. Just in case Indy harbored any thoughts of taking Corri to Paloma, August had wanted to go on record to make it known that she wanted the child to remain in Devlin's Light.

"Quieta non movere," August told India pointedly as Corri emerged from the powder room, water sloshed on the front of her overalls where she had tried to remove some paint. Do not move settled things.

India got the point: Leave well enough alone.

Later, after dinner had been eaten and homework dispatched, India sat in her father's old dark blue leather chair in the den, her files spread out around her as she organized her notes and made lists of evidence and witnesses to help her organize for her next trial. At her feet, Corri mimicked Indy's procedure, stacking her school papers according to the color of the stars that her teacher had placed in the upper right-hand corner of each completed page. The child was uncommonly quiet, as if being very careful not to disturb India's concentration. August watched from the doorway, acutely aware of just how much Corri's efforts to please India cost in terms of self-control, and she marveled that the child she'd dubbed Hurricane Corri could actually sit still for close to half an hour.

Amazing. And for Corri, totally unnatural. And that was exactly what August would tell India in the morning. For now, for August, there was a bridge club waiting at Liddy's. With India home, August was spared searching for a babysitter.

Imagine, she mused, as she kissed Corri goodnight and reminded India to lock the door, *having to worry about getting a babysitter at* my *age.*

"Indy, will you tuck me in bed tonight?" Corri asked shyly.

"Sure. Is it bedtime?" Indy frowned and looked at the clock. What time do six-year-olds turn in, anyway?

"Almost. I have to be in bed by eight, but tonight . . ." Her eyebrows arched hopefully.

"Maybe tonight I could read you a story after you get in bed," India offered. "Don't you have to take a bath?"

August hadn't given her any instructions, and she wasn't sure what the routine should be.

"Umm-hmm." Corri nodded. "I usually take my bath at ten minutes A.J."

" 'A.J.'? What's 'A.J.'?" India thought about that one for a moment.

"After *Jeopardy*."

"Oh. You mean the television show?"

Corri nodded.

"Well, I think it's a little more than ten minutes A.J., so how 'bout you go up and get your nightgown ready and get your towel and I'll meet you in the big bathroom, okay?"

"Are you gonna lock the doors? Aunt August said we have to keep the doors locked."

"I will do that right now. I'll be up in a minute."

Corri went up the steps two at a time, humming the *Jeopardy* theme song. India hunted around in her purse for her keyring, then locked the back, front, and side porch doors, lamenting as she did so the loss of the Devlin's Light she had grown up in, where no one ever locked the doors. At least, not until that summer . . .

Abruptly, she pulled the curtains across the windows overlooking the yard and followed the back steps to the second floor.

Corri was already down to her yellow-flowered Carter's underpants by the time India made it to the big second-floor bathroom. Once a bedroom overlooking the back yard, it had been converted to a bathroom with the advent of indoor plumbing. Due to its considerable size, the floor was covered with several bath mats of varying shapes. Corri instructed India on how much water and how much bubble bath, then settled down in the tub, where she played with mounds of frothy bubbles and washed herself with soap shaped like colored crayons.

"India, can you come to my school?" Corri asked. "You can meet Miss Millett."

"Is she your teacher?" India sat on the floor at the side of the tub and washed Corri's back.

"Umm-hmm. She's real nice. And she's real pretty too. Not as pretty as you, but she's fun. She let me pass out snacks this morning."

"What was today's snack?"

"Pretzels and juice. I just love snacktime. It's my favorite time of the day." She yawned mightily. "That and art."

"Do you like to draw?"

"Umm-hmm. And I like to paint. I like fingerpaint best. It's creamy and thick and it mooshes in your fingers and you

don't even have to use a brush. That's why it's called
*finger*paint," she pointed out.

"I seem to recall that I liked fingerpaint when I was little
too." India smiled, suddenly recalling the way the thick cool
paint had felt between her fingers. *Mooshes,* Corri had
called it. The word seemed just right.

"Now we wash my hair." Corri pointed to a bottle of
shampoo on the window ledge.

India did her best to wash and rinse Corri's long hair with
the handheld shower attached to the spigot in the old-
fashioned tub, Corri singing a song she'd learned in school
that day—"Baby Beluga"—and chatting happily. Soon she
was dried—hair detangled, dried and brushed smooth—
and sporting a clean nightgown, ready to climb into bed and
hear a story.

"I'll pick out a good book, Indy," Corri said earnestly as
she scanned the bookshelves. "This is a very good goodnight book. It's called *Good Night Moon* and it's . . ."

Corri stopped halfway between the bookshelves and the
bed, watching horrified as Indy, who'd been plumping her
pillows, found the prize Corri'd hidden and was drawing it
out from under the pillow.

"Corri, what is this?"

Corri started to cry soundlessly, as India held up the long
green tank top with the number *14* on the front.

"I didn't steal it, Indy, not really," she sobbed.

"Sweetie, was this Ry's?" India asked gently.

Corri nodded. "But you can have it back if you want it."

"No, no, Corri, I'm sure that Ry would have wanted you
to have it." India choked back the lump in her throat and
opened her arms to the trembling child. "I'm sure there are
lots of things that were Ry's that he would have wanted you
to have. And one of these days, we'll go through some of his
things and see what else you might like. But you don't have
to cry, Corri. You were Ry's little girl, and he loved you."

"Indy, he wasn't my real daddy," she whispered, "I was
only adopted."

"Sweetie, adopted is never 'only'. When he adopted you,
he became your daddy, officially. For real." India's fingers
traced the letters spelling out *Devlin,* which marked the
shirt as Ry's. "Do you sleep with this every night?"

Corri's little hands closed around the green shirt and gathered it to her chest. "Umm-hmm. Ry used to wear it when he played basketball at school sometimes."

"Well, I think he would have been happy to know that you keep it close to you." India pulled the blanket and top sheet down and coaxed Corri, still clutching the green shirt, into bed.

Halfway through the book, India looked up to see that Corri was sound asleep with the shirt under her cheek, the fingers of one hand entangled in its folds, the other arm draped around the large stuffed Tigger Indy herself had given Corri last Christmas. Quietly, India returned the book to its place on the shelf and turned out the light. In the shadow of the hall light, she straightened the blankets and leaned over to kiss the top of the sleeping child's head. Corri's hair was soft and silky, and she smelled like Johnson's Baby Shampoo and bubble bath.

Stepping across the hall, Indy paused at the doorway to Ry's room. Illuminated by the streetlight outside the window that faced the very front of the house, it was clear that the room had changed little since Ry had moved in when he was thirteen. The art was different—gone was the poster of Farrah Fawcett that every male growing up in the seventies had hung on his wall—but the furniture was the same old maple set that had been in this room for God only knew how many years. She turned on the lamp shaped like a pirate's ship and sat on the edge of the double bed, her hands folded in her lap.

A slight breeze from an open side window carried the pungent, salty scent of the bay and moved the curtain slightly aside. India rose and drew the curtain back to look out upon the view of the water her brother had loved so dearly. Out at the edge of the inlet Devlin's Light made a tall dark shadow across the bay. Before she left to return to Paloma, she would visit the lighthouse. She had to. It was part of her, and the longer she postponed the trip, the more difficult it would be. For her own sake—and for Ry's—she had to go there, to stand where he had last stood on this earth. It wasn't just a matter of sentimentality, she reminded herself. She could not investigate his death without visiting the scene of the crime.

Maybe tomorrow, she thought, maybe while Corri was in school she would go.

She smoothed over the bedspread where she had sat and rose to leave, leaning over to turn off the lamp. As she did so, her toes banged on something under the bed. She reached down with one hand and touched a cardboard box.

"I don't believe it," she said aloud, as she slid the box out and lifted it onto the bed.

She pulled off the lid and grinned, her fingers automatically walking through the stack of old rock and roll record albums Ry had spent years collecting. Chuck Berry. Little Richard. Elvis. The Temptations. The Four Tops. Little Stevie Wonder. Diana Ross and the Supremes. Indy's personal favorite, the Shirelles. The Stones. Cream. Traffic. Ry had damn near every album that had been released in the sixties and seventies. Somewhere, there would be his old record player. Maybe before she left, she would find it and play a few of the albums. The thought made her smile.

"Ry, can I borrow some of your records?"

"Don't you have a lot of these on cassette?" he would ask, knowing full well that she did.

"Yes, but it's not the same," she would plead, and he would give in with a smile, knowing she was right, that it wasn't the same.

"Just don't scratch them, okay?" he'd remind her as he handed over whichever she had her heart set on listening to that night.

"I won't, Ry," she whispered to the night breeze. "I promise."

Aunt August's New England Clam Chowder

1/2 pound bacon, cut into small pieces
2 medium onions, chopped
2 stalks celery, finely chopped
2 8-oz bottles of clam juice
1½ cups water
2–3 pounds of potatoes, peeled and chopped
3 6½-oz cans chopped clams
1/4 teaspoon thyme
2 cups heavy cream (light cream or half and half may be substituted)
salt to taste
freshly ground pepper to taste
2 tablespoons softened butter
1/2 cup parsley, chopped

Over medium heat, sauté bacon in large Dutch oven until light brown. Drain off fat, leaving just enough to sauté the onions and celery. Add onion and celery to bacon, sauté until onions are soft (about 5 minutes). Add clam juice, water and potatoes. Bring to a boil. Simmer over low heat until the potatoes are tender (20–25 minutes). Add clams, stir in thyme and continue to simmer. Heat the cream separately, almost to the boiling point, then pour it slowly into the clam mixture. Add the salt and pepper and stir in butter. Sprinkle with parsley before serving.

Serves six.

Chapter 7

"Miss Devlin?" The pert, dark-haired young woman stuck her head into the hallway from the noisy classroom. "I'm Marilyn Millet, Corri's teacher. If you have just a minute to chat, I'll get the children started, then we can talk for a few . . ."

India watched through the open door as Miss Millet organized the class of some twenty six-year-olds into early morning independent activities and returned in a flash.

"I was hoping to meet you." The young woman smiled as she returned, stationing herself in the doorway to keep one eye on the class while seemingly giving India her undivided attention. "Corri talks about you all the time. I have, of course, met your aunt—she's a lovely woman, we all adore her, including the children—but I think it's clear that Corri is beginning to see you as her 'parent' figure."

"Corri has had a very difficult two years, Miss Millet."

"So I understand. First her mother, now her stepfather." The teacher shook her head slowly. "It's more loss than many adults could reasonably cope with. And Corri is so young."

"Is she doing well in class?"

"Scholastically? She's a wonderful student. She's bright, curious, spontaneous." She smiled and added, "Sometimes

73

maybe a bit too spontaneous. I have to remind her to watch her chattering, but all in all, she's an asset to the class. Personally, I love her dearly. She's a darling child. And she is coping well, under the circumstances."

"But . . ." India sensed there was something more the teacher wanted to say.

"But I think she is developing little habits that I think are indicative of anxiety."

"Such as?" India frowned.

"Biting her nails, going off on her own sometimes for no apparent reason—Excuse me, Miss Devlin. Courtney," she called to a child in the back row, "please get a pencil out of the box on my desk and stop pestering Allison. . . . Sorry." She turned back to India with a smile.

"Going off where by herself?"

"I've found her all by herself in the corner of the playground, just sitting quietly in the grass. Sometimes she stares out the window, and I can tell she's far away."

"Is that so unusual for a child?" India recalled many a time she herself had been caught staring out a classroom window, many a recess when she might have opted for solitude rather than a game of kickball.

"No, of course not. And first-graders have short attention spans. But sometimes it's more than just daydreaming. I guess you'd have to see her face. I think that inside, she is a scared and lonely little girl. Let me show you a drawing she did the first week of school."

Miss Millet went back into the classroom and stopped to speak to several children on her way to her desk, where she opened a drawer and removed a folder. Returning to the doorway, she passed the folder, open to the white construction paper that lay inside, into India's hands.

"I told the children to draw a picture of themselves," Miss Millet explained.

"And this is how Corri sees herself?" India's heart nearly broke at the image, the small drawing of the child, all drawn in grays and blacks, at the very center of the paper. She had drawn nothing else.

"Here are some of the other children's drawings." Miss Millet opened a second folder and extracted several sheets of paper. Wordlessly, India looked through them. Whereas

Corri's drawing held a single figure done in somber tones, the other children had drawn whole families and had dressed them in bright colors. Some had dogs or cats. Many had siblings. All had at least one parent depicted. All but Corri.

"I see," India said softly.

"I will tell you she's been different the past two days since you've been here."

"How so?"

"She's played more with the other children at recess. She's clearly more focused—just watch her for a minute." Miss Millet gestured with her head for India to observe the child, who was working diligently at her desk in the front of the third row. "I put her up front so that I could keep an eye on her. I have to reel her back so frequently. But this week she's been fine. She made a big announcement this morning, by the way. I wanted to mention it to you because I think it is very significant."

"What was that?"

"Corri has been refusing to use a last name. She's registered as Corrine Devlin, which is how your brother registered her last year. But when she returned to school last month, she refused to use a last name. When I talked to her about it, she said she didn't know how to make a capital *D* or a capital *S,* and she wasn't sure she wanted to know how to make either letter."

"D for *'Devlin,' S* for 'Steele,' her mother's name."

"So I understand." Miss Millet smiled and turned back to the classroom. "Corri, would you come here please and show us what you are working on?"

Corri beamed and bounced from her seat, a tiny munchkin in a blackwatch plaid jumper and a short-sleeved navy turtleneck shirt.

"It's my numbers, see? One, two, three . . . I'm still working on the four," she explained earnestly.

At the top of the paper, in childish scrawl, was printed her name. *Corri D.*

India's throat tightened. "You're doing a great job. Those are handsome numbers, Corri."

"You may go back to your seat now." Miss Millet patted Corri on the back.

"Looks like she's decided who she is." India cleared her throat of the obstructing lump.

"She tells me you'll be leaving in a few days," the teacher said pointedly.

"I have to get back to Paloma. I work for the district attorney's office, and I'll be starting a new trial the week after next."

"No chance of taking some time off?"

"Not right now, I'm afraid. The trial that I'm assigned to is an especially important one."

"Corri's an important child." The retort had been sharper than the teacher had intended, and she reddened quickly. "I'm sorry, I had no right . . ."

"Of course you do." India sighed. "And of course, you are right. She is very important. I will tell you very honestly I do not know the best way to resolve this, Miss Millet. I have commitments in Paloma that I have to see through right now. As far as Corri is concerned, I really don't know what's best for her in the long run. I don't know whether I should take her with me and put her in school in Paloma."

Frustrated and defensive, India's normally cool facade began to disintegrate rapidly.

"Perhaps you might work out an arrangement to spend some time with her on the weekends. If she knew she could count on that time with you, maybe it would be enough for now. And let's not lose sight of the fact that Devlin's Light is her home. She has friends here and, of course, she adores your aunt. This is all that is familiar to her. Given the fact that there has been so little security in Corri's life, I don't know that removing her from Devlin's Light would be a particularly good thing."

"So what you're saying is that she needs me and she needs the stability of her surroundings." The suggestion had a familiar ring, India noted wryly, having been proposed twice now in less than twenty-four hours.

"That pretty much sums it up." Miss Millet offered India her hand as she prepared to return to her classroom, her point having been made. "Ideally, I think the best thing for Corri would be to live with you in Devlin's Light, but of course, that's a decision only you can make."

With a smile that left no doubt in India's mind that Miss Millet clearly felt there was no real decision, she closed the door, leaving India standing alone in the hallway to contemplate her choices.

It was almost ten o'clock when India set the thermos of coffee in the bottom of the rowboat and dug her heels into the sand for that first big push toward the bay. Once she had the boat off the dune and moving, it was easier to pull it by the rope tied to the bow than to push it across the sandy beach. She reached the edge of the bay gratefully and stepped into the water, smooth stones and rough-edged pieces of shell beneath her feet, and pulled the small boat out to where the sand dropped off a few feet in depth. Maneuvering the boat around, she climbed in, her shorts heavy with bay water, her wet shirt sticking to her abdomen, and locked the oars in place. With steady and deliberate strokes, she headed toward the mouth of the inlet and the lighthouse that served as its guardian.

India and Ry had shared a love of the structure that had seemed almost inborn. Ry once joked that their love for the bay, like their love for the lighthouse, could probably be found in their DNA, along with hair color and body type. India had laughed and wondered aloud if perhaps that might be true. Now she pulled in the oars slightly, resting them across her knees, and let the rowboat drift for a few moments, riding the swells. She loved being on the bay, loved the smell of its brackish green-blue water and loved its inhabitants. Leaning slightly to one side, she watched a large lion's mane jelly fish, a translucent mass of floating goo, bobbing up and down in the gentle waves, riding the tide toward the shore, where it was certain to be stranded. She leaned a little closer, watching the long waving arms of seaweed ripple right below the surface of the water. The storm of the night before had left the bay churned up, so where on another day she would be able to see clear to the bottom, where the large blue-clawed crabs hunted for food, today she could see only seaweed.

Thinking about the crabs made her think of Maris. It was on a day much like this one, she recalled, that Maris had dragged a rowboat to the edge of the bay and pushed it in, much as India had herself done minutes earlier, and headed out past the lighthouse to crab. The storm that had sent the waves crashing and drawn the small boat out to sea had, apparently, come from nowhere. Why Maris had taken the boat into the uncertain waters beyond the lighthouse was a mystery to India. The crabbing was just as good in the inlet, maybe better, since these shallow waters allowed the crabs to be scooped up by a net, as opposed to the more tedious means of dangling a baited string over the side of the boat and waiting for a bite, a method India had never had much patience with. Ry said that Maris had often taken the boat into the bay, though everyone knew—surely everyone *told* her—that the currents were unpredictable.

I guess some people have to learn the hard way, India thought as she slid the oars back into the water and began to steer toward the lighthouse, now in view.

India never grew tired of that first view of it from the water as she rounded a bend in the cove and cleared the stand of pines that graced the dunes almost to the shoreline. She loved the structure of it, loved the way the tower rose from the little Victorian-styled house and lifted toward the clouds. The small boat rose and fell with the waves, India rocking from side to side as she drifted with the tide toward the shore. With a sigh, she dug in the oars and guided the boat to shore, careful to avoid the rocks close to the front of the lighthouse, seeking the clear passage to the deeper waters on the bay side, where she would navigate past the jetty without danger of scraping the bottom of her boat.

Once she was within ten feet of the shore, she hopped out, tugging at the rope to pull the boat along until she reached the beach, where she pushed the small vessel onto the sand. The trip across had taken her a leisurely twenty minutes, though she had on many occasions made it in much less time. How long had it taken Nick Enright to make the trip across that night, she wondered, unconsciously looking across to the opposite side of the cove where the old crabbers cabin stood facing the bay.

India climbed upon the rocks, her back to the lighthouse, to get a better view across the inlet. A new deck wrapped around the cabin, which no longer appeared as primitive as it had the last time she had been there. But that had been some years before, and Nick's mother had made "a few renovations" since then. Shielding her eyes from the mid-morning sun, India grinned. New cedar siding, light tan now but which would in time weather gray, covered the outside walls; and if she wasn't mistaken, that was a new dock right there off the deck, where a rowboat was tied to the new pilings. She watched the slow faint curl of smoke make its way from the top of the stone chimney and tried to remember if the little house had in its previous life had a fireplace. She wondered what other changes might have been made inside the dwelling. She tried to bring to mind its interior as it had appeared the last time she had been inside, but it had been too many years since she'd been there. All she could imagine when she closed her eyes was the cabin's inhabitant, and she couldn't help but wonder what he was doing on this fine Indian summer morning.

The cabin, like the morning, lay wrapped in a quiet lassitude. Nothing moved around the house, as nothing moved across the bay except for India herself, who jumped at the sound of the gull that screamed and scolded from the roof of the porch that wrapped around the lighthouse like an old woman's shawl.

India folded her arms and watched the gull as it cracked a crab shell with its beak, flinging the discarded pieces of shell to sail off the porch roof and land on the hard yellow sand upon which the lighthouse had been built so many years ago. This second version of Eli Devlin's lighthouse had incorporated the original two rooms of the structure, which had been built in the 1700s and rebuilt following a fire. Of course, local legend hinted that old Eli himself may have set that fire after drinking himself into a stupor following the wreck of a ship on the rocks that formed a natural jetty out past the point. The ship was reported to have carried Eli's wife and youngest child, who were returning to Devlin's Light after a trip to the Massachusetts colony, where Mary Devlin had paid a visit to her parents and sisters to prove to them she was well and enjoying a life of relative wealth in the wilds of the new whaling port that her husband and his brothers were helping to establish.

* * *

The wind did roar and the rain did slash
Down through the stormy night.
And come the morning, old Eli lay dead
At the foot of Devlin's Light.

The snippets of the children's rhyme rang in her head from across the years, the rhyme they had once jumped rope to and sang in the school yard from swings that spiraled skyward on long thick ropes. Every kid who grew up in Devlin's Light knew it. As a child she had been alternatively pleased and mortified by her connection with the rhyme, with old Eli.

A shiver ran up her spine as the words taunted her.

Lay dead at the foot of Devlin's Light.

The irony occurred to her for the first time. For an instant she wondered if it wasn't perhaps some obscure, albeit macabre, coincidence. Had it been someone's idea of a cruel joke? If so, it could indicate that Ry's killer had grown up in Devlin's Light or had at the very least spent enough time here to know the local legend. It wasn't much, but it could serve to narrow the field. Before India returned to Paloma, she'd make it a point to stop by the police station to run the theory past Chief Carpenter.

This new possibility could also take the killing into another realm, the realm of premeditated murder. Whether Ry's murder had been a crime of revenge or a crime born in anger or passion, if someone had plotted it out with such deliberation, it could not have been, as they had all hoped, a random killing, a matter of Ry being in the wrong place at the wrong time. The thought made her sick to her stomach and weak at the knees, and she sat down on a small patch of grass in the shadow of the lighthouse till the feeling passed.

India tilted her head back as far as it would go and, using both hands to shield her eyes from the sun, looked clear up to the top of the lighthouse, where it jutted into the sky like Rapunzel's tower. It was hard to remember that this was a place that had so recently seen death. A China-blue sky hung overhead like a giant tent, the sun a blazing ball of orange now that the clouds had all burned off. The waves lashing against the rocks and an occasional gull made the only sounds. It was still and quiet here, but it was no longer a safe refuge from the rest of the world, no longer a place where she could find peace. She cursed Ry's killer for having taken that too from her.

India stood up and brushed the sand from the back of her shorts and the soles of her feet, ever mindful that if she was ever to reclaim the feeling of ease she had once known here, it had to be now. She blew the air out of her lungs in one heavy sigh of determination, then walked around toward the front of the building, the side that faced the bay, her bare feet cautious to avoid the sharp shells and stones that littered the sand.

Ribbons of yellow pine clapboard wrapped around the lighthouse, where the old white paint had been stripped, some errant strips of which still clung to the sea grass growing near the porch footings. Ry had wanted to restore the lighthouse, every inch of it, from painting inside and out to repointing the stone foundation. A few days before his death he had called India at her office and chatted excitedly about some plans he had for its restoration and what he had referred to as its "new life." But India had been on her way to a hearing and had only half listened. She had meant to call him back later that night, but that night, like so many others, had seemed to get away from her, lost in a haze of files filled with reports from the medical examiner, with grisly photographs. She wished she had listened. It was the last thing of importance that he had wanted to share with her, and knowing that hurt her now.

India thought back to Corri's sad little drawing, the poignant self-portrait of a small, solitary figure in the middle of an otherwise blank piece of paper. Would she be able to help her to someday see herself in more complete surroundings, to fill up that small life with enough love and happiness that the paper would no longer be blank? Or would Corri too disappear behind a mound of evidence reports and witness statements?

She pushed the miserable thought from her mind. *First things first,* she told herself. *I cannot help Corri lay her demons to rest until I have dealt with my own.*

Resolved to do exactly that, India continued her walk toward the front door, passing the rocks atop which three double-crested cormorants stood like silent sentinels, their dark brown wings outspread to dry in the sun. They eyed her warily as she passed; then one by one, in rapid succession, each jumped from the rocks and, as if playing Follow the Leader, ran along the shoreline. India watched as the birds gained speed before taking off into a cloudless sky, where they soared upward, seeking a rising thermal of air to gain altitude from which they would soar, still in a straight line, across the bay.

It was, she thought as she watched them, a fitting homecoming. She took the steps three at a time and crossed the porch directly to the front door and was surprised to find it open. The door swung back, and India hesitated only for an instant before stepping inside, willing herself not to be afraid.

A lone wasp buzzed angrily at one of the windows in the front room, which at one time had been a sort of keeping room. A massive brick fireplace covered one entire wall, reminding India that at one time, long ago, her ancestor had lived in the original two rooms that formed one section of the L-shaped structure. Eli Devlin had been born with a malformed leg, a deformity that had kept him from going to sea. In the New London community, where he and his brothers had been raised, he had served as apprentice to the lightkeeper, whose daughter he would later marry. After having moved south with the West India Trading Company, Eli had built his own lighthouse and manned it himself, ever watchful for ships captained by his brothers and, in his later years, his sons and his nephews.

Legend had it that once the notorious pirate Ian Landry had been given safe passage from the open sea in a storm and had rewarded Eli's grandson, Nathaniel, by having his men hide a large cache of his ill-gotten gains amidst the rocks on the opposite side of the inlet, guided by the light that shined from the very top of the tower. If the pirate failed to return for it before twelve months had passed, so the story went, the cache would belong to Nathaniel. No one knew whether Ian or Nathaniel had retrieved it, but it was said that on nights when the moon was full, a lantern hung at the top of the lighthouse would shine directly on the treasure.

India smiled. So much local history, real or imagined,

had a Devlin at the heart of it. The fireplace was large enough for a man—several men—to walk inside. Though the furnishings were long gone, she could close her eyes and see the room as it must have looked in the 1700s, when it had served as home first to Eli, then to Nathaniel, who had inherited his grandfather's love for the light, for the bay. Whenever she had suspected that a Devlin from centuries past still lingered here, always it had been Eli or Nathaniel she thought of. Never anyone else. She wondered today if she might catch a sense of Ry in this place.

India wandered through the front room into the area where the steps descended in a wide spiral from the top of the tower. She had expected to feel . . . *something,* something of Ry standing here, in the place where he had fallen, but all she felt was sad. Almost without thinking, she began the long ascent to the top, taking each step slowly, as if inexorably tired. From the windows on either side she could see the whitecaps out on the bay as she climbed upward, upward, the stale, hot, dusty air wrapping around her head like a helmet, her feet and legs beginning to feel as if they were wrapped in lead weights by the time she reached the top. She opened the door to the platform that stood at the very top of the lighthouse and stepped out, eager for fresh air and relief from the stifling atmosphere.

India leaned on the railing and took in the welcome sight of the bay and filled her lungs with the pungent scent of salt and seaweed, of sand and decomposing sea creatures. From one vantage, she could see clear across the bay to Lewes, Delaware; from another, she could see Cape May, New Jersey. From yet another, she could see several small islands that appeared to be comprised totally of sea grass; and by looking back toward the beach, she could see the beginnings of the salt marshes. She leaned back against the railing and tilted her head back, a strong sea breeze whipping her hair around like a scarf, wrapping it around her face. Eyes closed, she could hear him. When Ry and she were kids they would sneak forbidden trips to the top of the rickety steps, to lean on the unstable railing and look out at an endless vista.

"Indy, if you lean back and close your eyes, you can kiss the sky," Ry had told her.

The railings were new, installed by Ry last spring. India leaned back and closed her eyes, trying to bring back that feeling of power, of being mighty enough to embrace the clouds.

And she would swear until her dying moment that she had, on that day, kissed the sky. And there, with none but the gulls to hear her, she cried for her brother who had given her so much, who had taught her to believe in a world where wishes came true and the rainbow's end was no farther away than the nearest wishing star.

India was eleven when she found out that there were some things in life that could not be wished away; that, try as she might that summer, things would never be the same for her again. But Ry had tried to help her believe, and for his sake, she had pretended to, because it had seemed so important to him to make things right for her, to take away the evil that had come so close and bring back her innocence. Somehow she had known, even then, that some things, once lost, could never be wished back.

The discordant hum of a boat's motor, loud and nearby, drew her back to the present, to reality. Off to her left a Bayrider was slowing down, riding the wake it had created. A skier dropped off the side of the boat, holding on to the towline and floating his skis ahead of himself. The boat maneuvered, slowly straightening the towline until it held taut like a yellow pencil line across the water. The skier held fast, securing first one ski, then the other. With a wave of his hand, he signaled the driver of the boat that he was ready. The engine whined, louder, then louder still, as the boat picked up speed and took off across the bay. India watched until the skier was but a speck bobbing on the waves.

Just another early autumn day.

As India turned toward the steps, her eyes fell on the cabin across the inlet, and she stood for a very long minute, staring at the small house.

She *was* in the neighborhood. She *should* stop in. If for no other reason than to let Nick know that she was home for a few days and maybe see how he was doing with that list they'd talked about.

After all, they were friends, weren't they?

Chapter 8

*F*rom halfway across the inlet, India could hear the music floating from the cabin. The Temptations. "Just My Imagination."

Shades of Ry Devlin. Enright was a Motown fan.

She let the tide roll her gently to the floating dock. India grinned as she stepped out of the rowboat and onto the new floating boardwalk that rode atop the water, rising and falling with the bay. Must be another of his mother's little "improvements."

India tied up the boat and started up a wide set of steps that in turn led to a deck. By the time she got to the top, he was leaning over the deck railing, sipping from a red mug and watching her with a smile that grew wider with every step she took. The smile, and the welcome it held, were genuine, she knew, and just for her. The thought warmed her. Maybe a bit too much, it occurred to her as she crossed the deck, wondering idly if the sound that suddenly filled her head was her own heart beating in her ears or the flapping of the wings of the dozen or so Canadian geese that were just at that moment taking off from the marsh behind the cabin.

"Hi," she called up to him.

"Hi," he called back.

"I was just in the neighborhood . . ." Lame, Devlin. You sound *lame*.

"And I'm delighted you stopped by." He offered her a well-worked and tanned hand as she started up the last few steps to the deck. "I heard you were home for a few days. I was hoping I'd get a chance to see you."

"I rowed over to the Light," she explained. He was still holding her hand, and the unmistakable current running back and forth between them made her blush unexpectedly.

"First time since Ry's accident?" he asked, pretending not to notice that her face was delightedly pink and her hands had gone clammy just before he let her fingers slip from his.

"Yes."

"How was it?"

"Not as hard as I thought it would be, in some ways. More difficult in others."

"I feel that way every time I go over there." He nodded in the direction of the Light.

"Do you ever feel him there?" she asked tentatively.

"All the time." He smiled. "It's one of the reasons I go. Ry was one of the best friends I ever had. I miss him."

He said it simply and without apology.

"I miss him too. I always will. You know what they say about time healing and making it better? It doesn't make it better. You just get a little more used to the feeling, that's all. But you never stop missing. You never stop wishing."

He reached over and massaged the back of her neck in the most natural of gestures.

"I'm sorry . . ." She shook her head, Ry suddenly too much with her.

"Don't be." He waved away her apology. "It's natural, India. He was a part of both our lives. It would be unnatural, I would think, if we didn't talk about him. Now come inside and let me get you something cold to drink. I was just stopping for lunch. I'd love to have some company."

He held open the door for her, and she stepped into the little screened porch at one end of the deck.

"This is so cute," she said, then laughed. "I don't know if you appreciate 'cute.' "

"It *is* cute." He laughed without a trace of self-consciousness, pointing out the rocking chairs painted white, their cushions done in navy and white stripes, the table between the two chairs bright red. "My mom's idea of *nautical* decor."

"Aunt August mentioned that your mother did some, ah, redecorating."

Nick laughed out loud.

"What my mother did was rebuild the cabin from the ground up," he told her.

"Aunt August said that Delia Enright, the writer, is your mother."

"She is."

"I'm a big fan of hers," Indy told him.

"Then that's something else we have in common." He smiled. "Want to see what else she did?"

"I'm afraid I'm wearing a bit of the bay." India gestured to her wet shorts.

"India, this is a beach house, designed to be lived in by people who wear wet clothes and occasionally bring sand in on their feet."

He opened the screen door for her and led the way into a cabin no one would ever have recognized as the place where the old crabbers had once hung their hats and their nets.

The entire cabin had been gutted and the resulting large, square room paneled in the warmest shades of honey pine. A scattering of colorful Native American rugs covered the heart-of-pine floor, and a fireplace of rough-hewn stone faced her from the opposite wall. A long sectional sofa of the softest, creamy ivory leather curved around the hearth, and a knitted afghan of fluffy tweeded wool in shades of green was flung casually over one arm of the sofa. Pillows heaped at one end of the sofa repeated the colors from the carpets, and abstract paintings hung on the walls. A large rounded table, piled high with books, occupied the space formed by the half moon of the sofa. To India's right a long wooden refractory table—an antique piece if ever she'd seen one—was placed under a wall of windows that opened onto the bay, and beyond the table, a small kitchen area was tucked into the far corner of the large room. The entire effect was homey, comfortable and, like the man who lived there, utterly charming.

"Your mother did all this?" India asked, her jaw dropping at the unexpected simple *luxury* of the room that had opened before her.

"Yes, bless her heart, she did. And no, to answer the next question before you ask, it doesn't bother me that she completely took over the entire project." He grinned.

"It doesn't?" India frowned, wondering how she would feel if someone else tried to force their taste in furnishings on her.

"Nope. I guess you'd have to know my mother to understand. First of all, I can't think of a thing I'd change here. I couldn't have done better if I'd personally picked out every item, which I had neither time nor inclination to do. Let's not even talk about the expense. Some things I did select, and some things I brought with me. Mother says she does stuff like this because she just has to feel that we still need her. She likes to feel like she's still in charge, even though we all know that when it comes to the really important things, she isn't. So she does things like this. You should see what she did in my sister Georgia's condo."

"When does your mother find time to write if she's busy organizing everyone's lives?"

"She takes her laptop with her wherever she goes—never misses a beat. And she never interferes with our lives, just our living spaces. It gives her great pleasure to spend her money on her children. So we humor her and let her do her thing when she wants to."

"I would love to have to humor someone to this extent." India waved her hands around to take in the room.

"Shhhh." He held a finger to his lips. "Don't let that get around! You'll find her on your doorstep one of these days, and your townhouse will never be the same. 'India, dear, what would you think of skylights . . . and—tell me the truth, Indy—don't you think that corner is just begging for a plump little chair?'"

"Does she speak like that? That fast?" India laughed at the characterization.

"Faster. Mom can talk you dizzy." He opened the refrigerator. "Now, what can I get for you? Iced tea, soda, beer?"

"Iced tea is fine." She watched as he took another red mug from a cabinet, filled it with ice over which he poured a pale brown liquid and handed it to her in what appeared to be one smooth movement.

India sipped at the tea, not realizing until now how dry her mouth was. Must be the salt air, she told herself. That and the heat.

"And of course she had a new bath put in." Nick gestured for India to follow him to a small hallway off to the right of the fireplace and then to a handsome, spacious bathroom where the walls and floor were lined with what looked like small Mexican tiles, all in terra-cotta and cream, with dashes of bright enamel blue and yellow. No little shells or duckys for Delia Enright. India looked overhead to the large skylight that opened up the ceiling to the sky, and to the left where the whirlpool tub stood. Wide windows overlooked the swampy marshes. An oversized shower—with room for two, India noticed—completed the room. Looked like Mom thought of everything.

"Very nice." India sipped at her tea, trying not to speculate how many doubles had showered in that Mexican grotto.

"And my bedroom." He swung open the door and she could not help but smile.

A king-size bed covered in a dark green comforter filled the room, most of the other furniture being built into the walls, which were made of what appeared to be white birch logs. All very comfortable and masculine. A manly room. Right down to the large, well-worn teddy bear sitting in the middle of the bed.

"I saw that smirk," Nick said, trying his best to look insulted. "Don't think I didn't notice."

"I can't help it, Nick." India tried to stifle a giggle behind her hand. "The whole effect here is so 'single man'—strong colors everywhere, solid, heavy furniture. And then there's . . ."

"She's laughing at us, Otto," he said, addressing the bear. "We'll pretend not to care, but deep inside, we're crushed."

"Have you been, ah, roommates for long?" India tried to adopt his serious tone.

"Since I was four. He looks pretty good for his age,

wouldn't you say?" Nick pulled the bear across the bed by one plush foot and held him up for her inspection.

"I'd say he wears the years well." She nodded.

Nick smiled and returned Otto to his place of honor. "Back this way," he said, stepping into the hall and turning to the left, as she followed, "there is an office for me and a guest room."

He opened the door to the guest room first. It was softer than the rest of the house, more feminine, with deeply piled sage-green carpet and three double-sized bird's-eye maple beds and matching dressers. The beds were dressed in peach and green stripes of a silky fabric and were piled high with decorative pillows.

"This is some guest room," India noted. "Three double beds?"

"For the queen, the duchess and the princess." Nick grinned. "My mother thought that as long as she was doing the cabin over, she might as well prepare a little spot for herself and my sisters."

"Do they come often, the three of them together?"

"Every once in a while they'll drop in and stay for a few days. It's like a slumber party for the three of them. They stay up all night and talk, take the boat out at dawn to watch the sun rise. It's great for them. Sometimes just one—my mother or one of my sisters—will come alone. Last year my sister Zoey came down for a week or so, between jobs."

"What does Zoey do?"

He laughed. "Whatever occurs to her at the time. Zoey has done a little bit of everything, from the evening news to selling perfume in high-priced boutiques. She's still looking for that 'something' to turn on all her lights, so to speak, the way Georgia and I have."

"Georgia is your other sister?"

"The baby. She's a dancer. Classical ballet, modern ballet."

"Isn't it unusual to do both?"

"Maybe. She says she needs them both. She likes the structure of classical, the 'freedom of expression' associated with modern. So she does both. Georgia is very good at what she does. And she's never wanted to do anything else."

"It sounds as if you are close," she observed.

"Very close. We always have been. Our dad left when I was ten, and we've been a team since then. When Mom first started writing, before she made any money with it, I used to have to entertain the two girls in the afternoon and after dinner so that Mom could have some time to work."

"Well, it certainly paid off. Delia Enright is one of the most widely read mystery writers in the world. Just think, if you hadn't helped her find time to write back then, we might have been deprived of Rosalyn Jacobs and Penny Jackson, not to mention Harvey Shellcroft."

India rattled off a few more of the recurring characters in one or another of the series of books Delia had written over the years.

"You really have read a lot of her work." Nick looked pleased.

"I've probably read just about everything she's written," India confessed.

"Wait till I tell her. She'll be delighted."

"Like it's something she's never heard before."

"Mother always says that fan loyalty is not something to be taken for granted or treated cavalierly. Trust me. She's always happy to hear that someone enjoys her work. That's the only reason she keeps writing at this point. Because people look forward to reading something new of hers."

That and that multimillion dollar contract I read about in People *magazine a few months back.* India suppressed a smile but said nothing. *God knows that would kick-start my creative juices.*

"And last but not least"—he pushed open the last remaining closed door—"my office."

Nick Enright's office overflowed with paper. Books. Magazines. Notebooks. Stacks of whatever it was he had printed off his computer. Research notes. And just notes, a word or phrase scribbled here and there, some impaled on a metal spike that protruded from a large smooth stone, some posted on the bulletin board that covered one wall behind the desk, which was shaped like a large C and overlooked the bay.

"Wow. Looks like you spend a lot of time here," she said diplomatically.

"I do. Probably forty percent of my waking hours."

"What exactly is it that you do?"

"Right now I'm working on the thesis for my doctorate in marine ecology. I've chosen to study the Delaware Bay, cataloging the species that are here now, comparing them to species we knew were in existence millions of years ago. To see how life here has evolved. Maybe find out what pushed some creatures into extinction while others thrived and adapted."

"Are there many species that have survived intact through all those years?" He was too close, and she felt the need to make conversation. Suddenly the room seemed very small.

"One that might surprise you." He leaned back against the desk casually and asked, "Care to take a guess?"

"Sharks?"

"Certainly there were sharks millions of years ago, though maybe not in the exact form we know them today. I was thinking of a species that goes back even farther. Try again."

She thought for a minute, then shrugged. "I have no idea."

"Old Limulus." He tossed her a black-and-white photograph of what appeared to be a pile of shiny army helmets with tails.

"The horseshoe crab?"

"Also called the king crab." He nodded. "Been around these parts for the past four hundred million years. Roughly one hundred and fifty million years before the first dinosaurs."

"Ugly little buggers," India noted.

"Ah, but they're not totally without virtue," Nick told her.

"The only thing I know they've ever been useful for is fertilizer. Except, of course, the eggs are a food source for the migrating birds in the spring."

"Over the past several years marine biologists have discovered a number of uses for these 'ugly little buggers.'"

"Like what?"

"There's a substance in the blood of the horseshoe crab—

LAL, which stands for limulus amoebocyte lysate—which is used to test medical drugs for contamination and to detect vitamin B-12 deficiencies. And lately there's been a great deal of interest in its use as a cancer inhibitor."

"All that from the blood of a horseshoe crab?"

"Yup."

"Wow. And to think that we Devlins have had unlimited access to millions of those homely things over the years."

"Not quite 'unlimited' these days. The state of New Jersey passed restrictions—I think in '93—limiting the harvest of the crabs to three nights per week. It's rankled a good number of the locals who make their living off the bay, I understand." He dropped the photograph back onto his desk. "And I don't know that there aren't some who have found a way around the limits."

"I see you've been to the beaches for the spawning." She pointed to a photograph tacked to the corkboard by one large green pin, in which the sky was blackened with swirls of indistinguishable shapes. Only one who had witnessed the phenomenon would recognize the shadowy forms as an endless flock of birds.

"It's one of the things that drew me to Devlin's Beach," he told her, sliding into his chair. "I had, of course, read about the massive migration of birds from the southern hemisphere flying north to breed in the Arctic, how they come to the Bay to feed on the eggs of the spawning horseshoe crabs. How those two events coincide perfectly."

"My father always said there were no coincidences in nature."

"I agree with him." He nodded. "But it wasn't until I actually experienced the sight: millions of birds, thick as fog, swirling around the beaches, most of them little more than bone and feather at this point in their long journey . . . gobbling up the eggs laid on and under the sand by thousands and thousands of spawning crabs. It was the most truly primitive thing I've ever witnessed. I half expected some prehistoric beasts to appear on the dunes."

"It is something to see." India recalled the countless times that she and Ry had watched, from the top of the dunes or the top of the lighthouse, while millions of birds—from Brazil and Guyana, from Tierra del Fuego and

Belize—fed like gluttons until they had regained their strength and added enough extra body fuel to take them the rest of the way north to their Arctic breeding grounds.

"It's been said that up to eighty percent of an entire species can be found here at one time," he said, twirling a paper clip around on a pencil point. "It's staggering to watch."

"Exciting, though," she added, "in a very primal way."

"Very primal." His eyes, the softest, palest brown and very flecked with gold, sparked mischief.

India backed slightly toward the door as other equally primal forces were beginning to stir within her. The room was growing smaller by the minute and was suddenly far too small to contain both her and Nick.

"I had, of course, read about the phenomenon long before I'd witnessed it," he continued, leaning back against the edge of the desk to indicate he was in no hurry to follow her to the door. "Did you know that the birds leave their southern homes at a precise time each year, navigating through the night by some internal compass, to arrive at this exact spot at the exact time when the horseshoe crabs are hauling themselves from the bay to the shore? And that the birds will continue to fly until some of them literally drop from the sky in fatigue?"

"Yes. I'd heard all that."

"It makes you wonder, doesn't it, about how many of our instincts are preprogrammed from another time, just how much is inherent in our species. And I know I for one certainly have a healthy respect for that urge to survive and to procreate."

"I'll just bet you do." She nodded.

"What?" His brows knit together.

"I mean, studying all the species here on the bay, and watching firsthand, as you do, all the adaptations that have occurred to ensure their survival . . ." She was rambling, backing into the hallway, away from those eyes that seemed to narrow and darken somewhat, as if they were teasing her and enjoying the joke.

"Hmm. Right." He rose and started toward her.

"So. I don't want to keep you from your work."

"I had just stopped for lunch when you arrived. Why

don't you join me? I make a wicked grilled-cheese sandwich."

"I, ah, promised Corri I'd pick her up at school and take her shopping this afternoon." India continued to back down the hall, hoping she didn't look like she was fleeing from him, though she knew she was. He probably knew it too, but she couldn't help it. He was too close and she was too unprepared for the likes of Nick Enright.

"How is she doing?" He took the now empty cup from her hands as they passed from the dim hallway into the large and airy great room.

"She'll be okay." India frowned. "At least I think she will be. She has a lot of adjustments to make, but overall, I think we'll be able to work it all out."

"You know, of course, that if I can do anything for you, anything for Corri, that I am always available. Anything at all, India."

"I appreciate that, Nick, I do." India had backed herself to the door and there seemed little to do at this point but open it and go right on through.

"Well, if I can't talk you into lunch, how 'bout dinner?"

"I promised Corri I'd take her to dinner when we finish shopping."

"Then how 'bout dessert and coffee afterward?"

"Well, I . . ."

"It's a full moon tonight, India. Didn't you want to come out and sit on the deck and try to re-create the scene by the light of a full moon?"

"Yes. Actually, I did." She frowned again. Who knew how long it would be before she was in Devlin's Light for another full moon? "You're on. I'll drive out after I get Corri to bed. Probably by eight-thirty or so."

"Great. I'll have the coffee on." He reached around her, his hand grazing her hip as he reached for the doorknob to open it for her.

"I'll see you then."

"Right. Thanks." She followed her feet down the steps to the bottom of the dock. As she untied the small boat and racked the oars, she made the mistake of looking back up to the cabin where he leaned against the jam of the open door, looking all too adorable with his hair falling across his forehead almost to the top of his dark glasses. All too adorable indeed.

"Indy, I can't decide." Corri frowned, looking down at her feet, where one foot wore a gray leather Buster Brown strap shoe, and the other a black-and-white oxford that tied.

"Let's get them both," India said, nodding to the saleswoman that they would take both pairs of shoes as well as the sneakers and the soft black leather dress shoes. "Tappy shoes," Corri had called them, for the sound the heels made on the tiled area of the otherwise well-carpeted floor.

"Wow. Really?"

"Really. Sure." India handed over her American Express card at the cash register and watched the sales assistant slide the four boxes into the open mouth of a shopping bag. "Now, let's see, what else do we need?"

"Nothing. Aunt August took me out right before school started and bought me some stuff."

"Are you sure you don't need anything else?"

"I'm sure." Corri fairly danced from the store opening into the mall proper. "Can we eat now?"

"Sure. Any place in particular you like?"

"The Brown Cow." Corri pointed across the mall.

"The Brown Cow it is."

"So, what was the best thing that happened at school today?" Indy asked after they had been seated in a comfy brown-and-white plaid booth and had placed their orders.

"Ummm . . . Kelly shared her cookies with me at lunch."

"What kind?"

"Chocolate cookies with white chocolate chips." Corri pulled the white paper tube from her straw and blew bubbles in her chocolate milk, sneaking a peek at India to see if she would object. India was busy squeezing a lemon into her diet Pepsi.

"Yum. That sounds very gourmet." India nodded.

"Her mom made them. She makes all kinds of neat stuff. Sometimes she bakes stuff and sells it to Mrs. Begley and she sells it in her shop with Darla's stuff." Corri leaned back to permit the waitress to place a plate holding chicken fingers and fries before her on the table.

"Oh." India bit her lip and drizzled low-fat salad dressing

on her small bowl of greens, wondering how many of the other moms sent their kids off to school with home-baked goodies.

"Kelly's mom knows how to make doughnuts," Corri told her, as if in awe of the feat.

Trying not to sound peevish, India said, "Well. It sounds as if Kelly's mom is quite the baker."

"She is, Indy." Corri nibbled on the end of a fry.

"I'm sorry that I'm not home to do things like that for you," India told her, all of a sudden feeling sad. Sad and guilty. She was not there to bake for Corri. Corri had to share other kids' homemade snacks. She was overwhelmed with guilt, was two beats away from letting the lump in her throat erupt into tears.

"It's okay, Indy. You do important stuff too." Corri nodded, seemingly unaffected by India's shortcomings. "And besides, Aunt August bakes neat stuff too."

Of course, Aunt August would. The Devlin honor was intact.

India thought back to days long past, when she and Ry would arrive home on frosty afternoons to find a freshly baked treat newly sprung from the oven and waiting for them.

"Does she still make raspberry cobbler?"

"Umm-hmmm." Corri nodded. "And peach and apple too."

"Well then, I don't feel as badly now."

"Why do you feel badly, Indy?"

"Because I don't do enough for you. Because I'm not here when you need me."

"But I like the stuff Aunt August bakes. And she shows me how to do things. Do you know how to not let pie dough crawl up your arm?"

India suppressed a laugh, as Corri's expression was so serious. "No. How?"

"You make your arms and your hands all white with flour and the doughy stuff won't stick to your skin." Corri coated her arms with imaginary flour, then added proudly, "And I know how to punch down bread dough when it's rising too."

All the things Aunt August had taught me when I was a

little girl, India mused, wondering if Corri would develop more proficiency in her domestic skills than India had.

"Well, it sounds as if you are learning very important things."

"I am. And Nick said he'd teach me how to kick a soccer ball." Corri stabbed at a circle of catsup on her plate with a fry.

"He did?"

"Yup. So I can play with the Girls Club again."

"You're only six."

"Last year I played when I was five." Corri got quiet all of a sudden. "Ry took me. And Nick said if I wanted to go again this year he would take me."

"Do you think maybe you should go with Ollie and Darla?" India frowned. Funny, Nick had not mentioned that he had joined in the group effort to raise Corri.

"All the parents pitch in to do stuff for the team. Nick thought that maybe Aunt August wouldn't want to, since practice is on her card night, so he said he would."

"That was very nice of Nick." India felt the lump returning to her throat. It seemed that everyone was taking an active part in Corri's day-to-day, except for her. "Corri, you know that if I was here all the time, that I would take you to soccer? That I would do more things with you?"

"Now I know. I wasn't so sure until this time when you came home. But I am now."

"I just wish there was some way for me to spend more time with you. Right now I am committed to following through with something I started months ago." She thought of Alberto Minchot, awaiting trial behind the steel bars of Paloma's finest accommodations.

"But if I needed you, you would come, wouldn't you? If I really did?" Corri's eyes were wide and guileless.

"Absolutely." India responded without hesitation, knowing it was as true as anything she had ever known.

"And when you're all done, doing important stuff, will you always come back to Devlin's Light?"

"Yes."

"Then I guess it's okay." Corri shrugged and went back to the cabin she was building out of leftover fries.

India pondered the situation. Aunt August had been a fine

mother substitute for her and for Ry. She was, India knew, a woman whose heart had no boundaries, who dished out love with the same generosity of spirit as she dished out cherry cobbler at the church suppers. August was a wise disciplinarian, a wonderfully pleasant companion, and she possessed a sharp sense of both humor and fair play.

But it seemed as if Corri had twice lost out on having a real mom, the first time when Maris died, the second time when Ry died and Corri's hopes of being able to share Ollie's mom vanished. Now she looked to India to fill the empty spot all the leavings had left in her little heart. Afraid to ask for too much, Corri tried to be content with whatever India saw fit to give of herself. In her heart, Indy knew it hadn't been near enough. In the coming months, she would, one way or another, find a way to change the glass from half empty to full.

Chapter 9

*T*he stones crunching rudely under the tires of India's car as it wound up the narrow lane from the main road to Nick's cabin disturbed the nocturnal marsh in the same manner in which the crackling of paper would disturb the silence of a chapel. She hadn't remembered the road being this long or this dark. Rolling down the window to let in the sounds of the night, she crept along, careful to keep the car straight on the road—if this carpet of stones could be called a road—and off the soft shoulders from which a slide into the ooze of the tidal marsh was just a poorly calculated turn of the wheel away on either side. She approached a small wooden bridge that stretched across a meandering stream, braking to avoid taking it too quickly and perhaps missing a turn up ahead and finding herself in need of a tow out of the thick black goo that lined the bottom of the swamp.

It was still warm enough that a few mosquitoes, that scourge of the New Jersey coast, made their presence heard. And felt. India slapped at an overly eager specimen that had seemingly bitten her arm immediately upon its landing there. With her index finger she flicked its crushed corpse through the open window as she reached the end of the lane. Parking behind Nick's white Pathfinder, she cut the engine and stepped into the light cast by the sensor-activated spot mounted on the back of the cabin, which served to illumine the entire flat parking area.

From the stand of pine that formed a border between the lane and the woods just to the left of her car she heard a rustling sound. Raccoons, most likely, she thought, or perhaps foxes. Off in the distance, the shrill high scream of something, caught in the talons of an owl or perhaps a night heron, protested its plight. The sound rang up her spine like a bell struck too hard. It jarred her nerves and sent her just a little more quickly on her way toward the deck, which wrapped around to the front of the house to face the bay.

"Nick," India called from the doorway.

"Come on in," he called back, and she pushed open the screen door to the small porch at the end of the deck. The interior door was open, awaiting her arrival.

"Something smells outlandishly good," she told him as she walked into the great room and dropped her sweater on the back of the sofa.

"India Devlin, you of all people should immediately recognize the aroma."

"Hmmmm." She closed her eyes and sniffed the air with purpose, then groaned with pleasure as she identified the scent. "Aunt August's deep-dish apple pie." She whispered the words as if in awe.

"Damn, you're good," he told her. "Only took you one sniff."

"When did she bake this?"

"I am truly crushed to the bone!" He laughed. "August's recipe. My pie."

"You baked that?" She peered down at the perfect crust, golden and flaky, which hid the tender slices of apples lightly tossed with raisins, sugar and cinnamon.

"With my own two hands." He grinned.

"Nick, is there anything you can't do?"

"Sure. Lots of things." He turned his back and proceeded to fill the glass coffeepot with water, giving India an opportunity to take a long hard look at the flip side.

Never had a pair of Lee Five Button jeans looked so good.

"How 'bout you?" He turned suddenly, catching her in the act of staring at his posterior.

"How 'bout me what?" She blinked innocently, all the while reddening at having been caught giving him the same once-over he had earlier in the day given her.

"I'd have thought you would have all of August's recipes down pat." He was grinning, clearly enjoying her discomfort.

"I have them all written down"—she leaned on the counter, giving her an excuse to look out the window toward the bay—"but I'm afraid I haven't cooked in weeks. Months, maybe."

"You're kidding, right?" He poured the water into the top of the coffee maker.

"Nope."

"What do you eat?"

"Whatever I can whenever I can," she told him truthfully.

"That's one hell of a schedule you have, lady." From the small dishwasher he removed the same red mugs they had used earlier in the day and set them on the counter.

"Somehow it only seems really horrendous when I get away for a few days and look at it from a distance."

"And how often is it that you get away for a few days?"

"Not very," she admitted.

"Where'd you go on your last vacation?" he asked.

"Here," she replied. "Devlin's Light."

"Now India, you know what they say about all work and no play . . ." He leaned over, close to her, and for a split second she thought he was going to kiss her. When he did not, she felt a pang of disappointment she had not anticipated.

"What about you?" She tried to turn the tables. "I'd say it would appear that you work a lot."

"All the time. Every day." He nodded. "And I love every second of it."

"I love what I do too." She wished she did not sound so defensive, so insistent.

"I take time off. I take several breaks a day, as a matter of fact. How 'bout you, Indy? How often do you get a break?"

"During the day? Are you nuts?" She frowned at the thought of it.

"That's what I thought. Don't you ever want to just lean back and put your feet up for a few minutes?"

"Nick, I don't have quite the view that you do." She gestured toward the deck.

"More's the pity. It's wonderful. Come on out for a minute and we'll take a break right now."

She laughed and followed him onto the deck, to stand next to him at the railing, where they both leaned their elbows at precisely the same time.

"See? It's instinctive," he told her. "You approach the rail, you lean the elbows and you take it all in."

Leaning her head back slightly, India inhaled the warm tidal breath of the night, thick and salty and familiar.

"I miss it," she admitted, her eyes still closed as she luxuriated in the sea air.

"What keeps you away?"

"My work."

"You know you'd be able to get a job anywhere."

"Maybe." She shrugged and looked out across the dark water.

"No *maybe*. Want to tell me what keeps you from coming back to Devlin's Light to stay? Or is that a secret you're not ready to share."

"Why would you think that I don't want to come back?" She stared straight ahead, uncomfortable with the question. And its answer.

"Well, your family is here . . . your home. And from all appearances, you love it here . . ." His voice trailed away slightly.

"I do. More than any place," she said softly, still not looking at him, knowing if she met his eyes she might want to tell him what he wanted to know, but not yet ready to share that part of herself.

"And yet you seem to put as much distance between yourself and your home as you can."

India looped her fingers together and hung them over the railing, looking out to the bay but not at Nick.

"Something tells me there's no simple answer. Maybe someday you'll want to talk about it. Right now," he said, pointing overhead, "there's a serious moon on the rise."

Silently she thanked him for not pushing her into speaking of something she did not want to speak of, something that would sully the night and take the focus from finding clues to Ry's death and place it instead upon her, on her past, on her nightmares.

A flock of geese landed noisily, feet first, somewhere across the bay, their loud honks drifting across the water as if to scold the lead bird for not having stopped sooner.

"How 'bout we get our coffee and make ourselves comfortable and we can compare notes?"

"Sounds good." She started to follow him through the door.

"Just stay and relax for a minute," he told her. "I'll bring everything out."

"You sure?"

"Absolutely."

India welcomed the few minutes alone on the deck, a few minutes to listen to the night sounds of the bay, to watch for the faint splashes as fish here and there poked through the plane of the water, to rest in the stillness of the marsh. The bay at night had always offered a peace to her she had not found anywhere else.

Nick returned with a tray upon which sat two mugs of steaming coffee, a carton of half and half bearing the logo of a nearby convenience store, two plates, two forks, a knife and the entire apple pie. "You planning on eating all that?" She laughed, pointing at the pie.

"Very possibly. When was the last time you ate only one piece of August Devlin's apple pie? Even if August herself didn't bake it, there's nothing else that even comes close, in my book."

"Good point." She grinned and sat in one of the deck chairs.

"Help yourself to coffee," he told her, "and I'll tend to the pie."

She giggled as he cut two large wedges from the pie and slid them onto the plates, then handed one to India, telling her, "It's just perfect, still warm."

"It smells too wonderful," she noted, her mouth watering at the very thought of it. "It is perfect," she told him as she took the first impatient bite. "Wonderful. Heaven."

"Agreed." He nodded as he too succumbed to the lure of the fragrance that surrounded them momentarily, before a soft land breeze began to drift the aroma toward the bay.

"Eat fast," he joked, "or we'll have every raccoon within sniffing distance prowling up here for his share."

"Corri tells me that you're taking her to soccer on Tuesday nights."

"Well, it's August's card night, you know." He shrugged it off with a grin.

"You don't have to."

"Hey, Indy, it's no big deal. Corri wants to play. Ry took her last year and she loved it. I just wanted there to be one less thing in her life that she had to do without because someone else was gone from her life." He put his plate down to pour cream into the coffee.

"It's very nice of you to do that."

"I am a very nice guy. Thank you for noticing. And besides, it's fun to watch her."

"I meant it's nice of you to care that she wants to play."

"Well, I guess I'm just passing it on."

"What's that?"

"Oh, you know, that old expression that if someone does something nice for you, the best way of thanking them is to help someone else in return." Nick leaned back and crossed a denimed leg, resting his now-empty pie plate on his knee. "When I was about eleven, I wanted to play baseball in the worst way. But the league rules required that one parent volunteer to coach. My dad was gone. And Mom was out of the question—you could fill the head of a pin with Mom's knowledge of baseball and have enough room left over for the Bill of Rights. Plus she was working during the day and trying to write at night and keep up with my sisters. She didn't have three nights each week to spare."

"So who stepped in?" she asked.

"Mr. Hamilton. Lived across the street from us. Retired gent. Signed me up and took me to every practice. Cheered me on at every game."

"Where's he now?"

"Long gone," Nick told her softly, "but I'll never forget all he gave me. All he taught me. When my mom or I would thank him, he'd just smile and say, 'Nick, you just remember to pass it on one day.' I'm grateful for the opportunity to do just that."

"I hope you tell Corri that story some day."

"Some day." He nodded. "So, how's the dessert?"

"Wonderful." She sighed contentedly.

"Another slice?"

She contemplated the possibility. When was the last time she had had two servings of dessert?

"Just a small one." She laughed.

"You look like you could use a few extra calories," he told her.

"There's a shabby excuse for gluttony if ever I heard one." She speared a slice of warm apple and it melted in her mouth. If there was in fact a heaven, they would of a certainty serve warm apple pie made from her aunt's recipe. No doubt about it.

She was just about to share this thought when Nick asked, "So, tell me, what information have you been able to dig up about Manning and Hatfield?"

"The Paloma P.D. wasn't able to find out a whole lot. Hatfield has a history as an agitator. Seems to have joined in just about every protest launched at Bayview State over the past eight years. Heavy on environmental issues. I can't tell whether he's truly committed to the causes he becomes involved with, or if he just likes the action and the rhetoric. Either way, the consensus is that he's very much nonviolent. I got pretty much the same report on Manning."

"Is Manning a tall man, salt-and-pepper beard, wears a backpack and always has a pair of binoculars around his neck?"

"That's pretty accurate from what I recall. Unfortunately, I left the reports back in Paloma, but he was described as being about six-two, about one hundred seventy pounds, brown hair, a little gray at the temples, close-cropped beard. You've met him?"

"He was around a few times there in late May, early June, then again back in late June. First he was protesting the number of people on the beaches during the bird migrations. Next he was trying to work up support for his efforts to ban the fireworks display for July Fourth. Said it spooked the birds."

"Do you know if he had any dealings with Ry?"

"I don't know that I'd call them dealings, exactly, but I know they had words on more than one occasion."

"Words?"

He nodded. "Ry had wanted to open the beach for the first two weeks in June so that people could come to watch the migrations."

"And Manning didn't like the idea?"

"Manning thought that publicizing the spawning of the horseshoe crabs and the bird migrations, to encourage people to come to watch, would frighten the birds away. He was very open—some might say hostile—about his opposition to Ry's plans."

India frowned. "I don't recall Ry wanting to do much more than make the public more aware of how important the Bay is, in an ecological sense. Where its place is in the grand scheme of things."

"A few months back, he and Darla were talking about opening a tea room in the first-floor rooms of the lighthouse. So that people coming to watch the whole horseshoe crab thing could sit out there on the point and have a light meal while they watched Mother Nature's main event. Ry thought it would remove the sightseers from the immediate area of the activity while still providing an excellent vantage spot."

"And at the same time use the Light for something constructive and permit Darla to start her own business." India put her mug down on the floor near her feet. "Manning and Hatfield don't sound promising as suspects. I'd sure like to know who Ry saw that week, what his last few days were like."

"Well, I can take a drive out to Bayview and try to reconstruct his day at school. Maybe get a list of his students."

"They won't want to give you that."

"The administration won't, but I do know a few of Ry's friends on the faculty. I'm sure one of them will help out. Maybe I can dig up some information that might prove helpful."

"You mean you'll look for clues?"

"Sweetheart, in the immortal words of Henny Youngman, a clue is what the police boast about when they can't find the criminal." He laughed. "I'm just going to see if I can re-create his day, talk to the people he talked to."

"I think Chief Carpenter already did that," she reminded him.

"Maybe he missed someone." Nick shrugged. "In any event, it can't hurt. Maybe someone will remember something. You never know. Unless you don't want me to."

"Why would I not want you to? I just hate to see you waste your time," she added.

"Well, something might turn up. And besides, it will make me feel better. Like I'm doing something for Ry."

"You are doing plenty for Ry. Stopping in to see Aunt August—"

"She's a special lady. I just stop by to give her a hand now and then."

"And Corri . . ."

"She's a special little girl. I enjoy her company."

"And Darla? Aunt August said you showed up in your four-wheel to deliver her baked goods to her customers when her road was washed out after a bad storm a few weeks back."

"Darla is working very hard to get Darla's Delectables off the ground. How could I have left her stranded with all those muffins and breads and whatever else she had spent the past two days baking? It was no big deal. A drive out to her house, a drive into town."

"And into Cape May."

"It's not that far, India. Darla needed help. She's struggled to start up this little business of hers for the past two years. She has finally established a pretty decent clientele. I hated to see her lose out because of an ill-timed storm."

"You don't have to be defensive, Nick. I think it's wonderful of you to help her out. But tell me, did Aunt August call you and tell you that Darla was stuck?"

"Actually, I believe she may have. Why?"

"Look, don't take this the wrong way, okay? But August adored Ry. He was like the son she never had. I would hate to see her transfer that to you, if you know what I mean. I'd hate to see her, even unconsciously, try to . . . to . . ."

"Fit me into Ry's place?" he suggested. "Naw, she knows I'm not Ry. And I know how dependent she was upon him to help her here and there around the house. August and Ry both went a long way to make me feel at home here in

Devlin's Light, to make me feel like—I don't know, like a part of the family. I'd do whatever I could to help her out. I'm happy to be there for her. Especially now, with Corri back in school . . . she could use a hand now and then."

"And of course we all know that hand should be mine." India stood up and paced the length of the deck slowly.

"When you can, you will."

"May not be soon enough." India related the story of how Corri had only recently decided what last name to use.

"Look, India, for the time being, Corri is fine here. She has lots of loving adults. And she's smart enough to know that what you are doing is important."

"I don't want her to think that it's more important than she is."

"Well, you are the only one who can convince her that it isn't."

"I'm still trying to decide the best way to do that."

"Well, I'm sure you'll figure it out before too long."

"I'm not sure that the best way to do that isn't to take her back to Paloma with me." There. India had said it aloud for the first time.

Nick stared at her for a long hard minute, then said calmly, "That's entirely up to you, of course. Have you discussed that possibility with your aunt?"

"Not yet. I'm still thinking about it. But you said yourself that a small child is a lot for her to handle."

"And I also said that she doesn't have to handle it all alone. It's one of the nicest things about a small town like this, India. People help each other. And are actually happy to do it. So if you're looking for an excuse to take Corri to Paloma, you're going to have to come up with something better than that." Strangely enough, Nick actually sounded agitated.

India glanced at him from the corner of her eye, but his face told her nothing.

"And you will, of course, make your decision with Corri's best interests in mind. And in keeping with what Ry would have wanted."

"Of course I will," she replied, fighting a sudden urge to snap at him.

"Well then, there's nothing more to be said about that."

He turned on his hundred-watt smile and she felt her knees twitch, protesting her expectation that they continue to hold her upright when those little dimples on either side of his mouth appeared. Even in the dim light here on the deck, she could see that little glint in his eyes, and the agitation she had so recently felt began to melt away and was replaced by the seeds of a different kind of turmoil.

India had always been a sucker for a man with a twinkle in his eyes.

"So, India Devlin"—he reached out to touch her hair— "what do we talk about now?"

She tried to not act like the wide-eyed girl she was beginning to feel like as he inched closer.

"Let's see, we've talked about Corri. And August. Darla's business. How we will proceed to investigate Ry's death. Horseshoe crabs . . . bird migrations. Have we missed anything?"

His hand was on her elbow and he guided her toward him even as he moved toward her, bridging the slight distance between them with his body until his face was inches away from hers.

"I didn't think so." He murmured the answer to his own question as he lowered his lips to hers, tentatively at first, as if giving her the opportunity to protest, just in case she wasn't sure. When she did not pull away, he pulled her closer, intensifying the pressure of his lips on hers, then parting her lips slightly with his tongue.

Nick tasted of cinnamon and apples and smelled of Old Spice and bay breezes, a combination not to be resisted. India slid her arms toward his neck, wanting his closeness and his warmth, and he was more than happy to oblige her. His hand caressed the side of her face slowly, his thumb tracing the line of her jaw. She wondered if it was possible to pass out from the sheer pleasure of a kiss and hoped that she wasn't about to humiliate herself by finding out the hard way.

"There." He broke away suddenly and turned in the direction of the bay. "Listen. Did you hear that?"

"Hear what?" Her heart had been pounding half out of her chest. What could she possibly have heard in the midst of *that* racket?

"Listen." Without relinquishing his hold on her, he turned her body slightly toward the right, then stood stock still, as if waiting.

A sharp call, akin to a bark, pierced through the silence of the night.

"What?"

"It's an owl," he said softly, still not moving.

"Sounded more like a bark than a *whooooo.*"

"There's a short-eared owl that has been nesting in the marsh since midsummer—I've seen it several times. When it's disturbed, it makes a snarling, barking sound."

She turned her head to one side, listening.

"There it is again," she whispered. "Funny, all the years I lived in Devlin's Light, I never identified the sound."

"You lived over on the beach side," he said, smiling faintly in the dark, "this bird nests in the marshes, among the cattails—There, there it is again."

"I never would have thought that was an owl . . not from that sound."

"I might have missed that too, except that this one decided to make his home relatively close to mine. I've sat on the deck many a night and watched him hunt. He goes off at dusk, mostly hunting mice, voles. He's brought home his occasional songbird or two over the summer."

Nick's open palm was slowly stroking her back, leaving a warm river of skin beneath her sweater as it trailed across her shoulders. India was beginning to care less and less about the bird.

"But the significant thing about *that* bird," he told her, his breath soft against the side of her face, "is that the last time I heard it scream like that was the night Ry died."

"And you think it was that same owl?"

"Yeah, I do. Once you've heard that sound, you don't forget it. The first time I heard it was early in the summer. A group of kids, probably high-school kids, were out on the bay at night in small boats, a whole flotilla of them."

"Senior night." India smiled. "It's been a tradition forever in Devlin's Light. The night before high-school graduation, everyone in the class piles into boats and rows from the beach at the end of Darien Road out to the Light and back."

"Well, some of these kids apparently decided to take a shortcut through the marsh."

"Kids have been doing that for years too." She laughed. "This cabin, and one farther down toward the swamp, used to be empty from time to time. Kids used to come here to . . . hang out."

"Hang out, or make out?"

"Both."

"Did you used to, ah, hang out here?"

"From time to time I may have." She grinned as his forehead creased in a frown. "In any event, I suspect some of the kids who headed this way back in June may not have known that someone was living here."

"Quite possibly. They may also not have known that a short-eared owl had decided to build a nest in the ground out there." He pointed toward the marshy area between the cabin and the bay. "Apparently they came too close that night, because it was shrieking to beat the band. Just like tonight. Just like the night that Ry died."

As they stood pondering the possibilities, a small boat rounded the point and made a big, looping, lazy turn in the bay before heading back toward the beach at the opposite end of the cove. The shadowy forms of the two occupants of the boat appeared as little more than silhouettes against the moonlit water, and the sound of light, young laughter drifted across the bay.

"I don't recall ever seeing anyone out on the bay much later than this," Nick said, glancing at his watch, "and it's just after ten o'clock."

"But the night Ry was killed you said you woke up around two."

"What would anyone be doing out here at that hour?"

"Luring Ry to the Light."

"You think he knew someone was there?"

"Very likely. Why else would he have gone? And it was unlikely that anyone had called. Aunt August would have heard the phone."

"Can you see the Light from August's house?"

"Yes. From several of the bedrooms on the second floor, and from all the windows across the back on the third floor. You can definitely see it from Ry's bedroom."

"So if someone was in the Light, with a lantern or something, Ry could conceivably have seen them from the house?"

"Sure, Ry and I used to do it all the time."

"Do what all the time?"

"Go out to the Light, then signal home with a flashlight if we were there after dark." She grinned. "It used to spook some of the little kids in the neighborhood. Especially around Halloween. They all thought it was Eli Devlin."

"But why would Ry be up, looking out the window, at two in the morning?"

"Got me. Unless something woke him up that night too."

"Wouldn't have been the owl. It's too far from August's house."

"Well, it couldn't have been much of a noise. Aunt August said that she hadn't even known he had left the house that night."

"So whatever it was . . ."

". . . might have been meant to awaken only Ry," she finished the sentence for him.

The list of new information began to tick off in her head.

Could someone have been in the marsh near Nick's cabin that night?

Had someone, somehow, gotten Ry's attention at the house and managed to send him to the Light and to his death?

Who? How? And why?

Could the same person who disturbed the owl have awakened Ry? If not, then that could mean that more than one person had wanted Ry dead.

She shook her head. She could not think of one single person who would have wanted him dead, and two were out of the question.

"I should be going," she said. "It's late."

Nick sighed deeply but did not protest. Sliding his hands the length of her arms until they encircled her wrists, he tugged gently in the direction of the house.

"I'll get your things," he told her, freeing her arms reluctantly.

For several long moments, India was totally lost in thought.

The sound of the screen door rubbing slightly against its wood frame brought her attention back to the immediate here and now. She watched Nick step out onto the deck, and not for the first time she admired the sight of him, tall, broad-shouldered, handsome, with a tumble of dark curls and a devastating smile.

Conscience prodded her, reminding her that she had come to the cabin in the hopes of learning more about her brother's death, not to make time with his best friend.

She tried to keep this thought in mind as he draped first her sweater, then his arm, around her shoulders and walked with her toward the side of the cabin, following the wooden path to the steps and down to where her car was parked. Whistling, all the while, in her ear.

The Temptations. "My Girl."

Ry would've loved it.

∽∾ ∾∽

Aunt August's Deep-Dish Apple Pie

dough for double-crust pie (prepared, refrigerated dough works fine)

8–10 apples, peeled, cored and sliced
1 cup sugar
1/4 cup flour
3 teaspoons ground cinnamon
1/4 teaspoon salt
4 teaspoons fresh lemon juice
1/2 cup raisins
3 tablespoons butter, cut into small pieces

Prepare crust according to package (or your recipe) for a filled, double-crust pie. Roll out dough, transfer to a deep, 10-inch pie plate. Press into place, leaving a little overhang.

Combine apples, sugar, flour, cinnamon, salt, lemon juice and raisins, mixing well. Pour into pie crust. Dot with butter. Roll out second crust, place over pie. Pinch edges of the two crusts, then trim excess. Cut several slashes into the top crust.

Bake in a 350° oven for 45 minutes, checking crust to see if edges are browning too rapidly. If so, cover edges with foil and bake until filling is bubbling and the crust is golden.

Chapter 10

*T*he song was still in her head as she took the steps to the second floor of the old Devlin house two at a time. How could that man have known that "My Girl" was one of her all-time favorite songs, guaranteed to turn her knees to water every time?

August had left on the small lamp next to India's bed, and its low-watt bulb cast a faint and eerie glow into the hall. India closed the bedroom door behind her with a concentrated hush, not wanting to awaken August or Corri. It was after eleven, and the house lay in what passes for silence in an old house, with its mix of the occasional creaking pipe and the settling of old floorboards. The branch of a maple tree grazed against the window and made a slight rubbing sound. All else was quiet.

Rummaging in her suitcase, India found a nightshirt and set off for the bathroom at the end of the hall, the farthest from where her aunt and Corri lay sleeping. She wanted a quick shower to rinse the salt from the heavy marsh air from her arms and her hair. Then she would sit up in bed and make notes of all the information she had learned tonight. As the hot water pelted her skin, she began to compile a short list of possible suspects. Manning, certainly, needed to be talked to. Hatfield, possibly. And there were still some

116

who thought that Kenny Kerns belonged at the top of that list.

It was no secret that Kenny has a trigger-quick temper, she reminded herself as she turned off the hot water and stepped onto the nubby dark green bath mat that lay across the cool white tile. She pulled two towels from the rack and wrapped one around her head before wrapping the other around her body. Drying her legs and her feet, she opened the door quietly, releasing steam and heavy warm air into the cool of the hallway.

Kenny may have been hotheaded, but she'd never heard of him being violent. Had the thought of Darla marrying Ry pushed him over the line? Indy grabbed her robe from the foot of the bed where she'd left it. As she did so, something rolled past her feet. She jumped back in surprise, then bent down to pick up a small round black vinyl disc.

Funny, she hadn't noticed it earlier.

She turned the 45 RPM record over and looked at the label. An old Jackson Five hit.

Corri must have been going through Ry's record collection and for some reason picked this one out to play and forgotten to put it back.

India shrugged and placed it on the desk, then returned to the bathroom to towel-dry her hair. There was a lot to think about tonight. Starting with the man out beyond the marshes who was very slowly beginning to turn her inside out. She certainly hadn't planned for it to happen, but Nick Enright was simply too much to ignore. Too kind. Too thoughtful.

Too adorable.

Too much man.

That was the bottom line here. How much longer could she pretend that Nick was nothing more than her brother's best friend? Kissing him tonight had certainly made it abundantly clear that he was not a man to walk away from. Indy tried to recall the last time a man had taken her breath away with his kisses, or had lit a spark so deep inside her that it seemed the glow had found and warmed her very core. She wasn't sure that she had ever felt what she'd felt when Nick Enright had begun to nibble on her lower lip, but she sure as hell hoped she'd get to feel it again.

India hung the damp towel over a metal bar, then turned off the bathroom light and slipped back across the hall to her room. Too tired now, her written list of suspects and other pertinent information would have to wait until tomorrow. Turning off the light, she tried to settle in for the night but was distracted by the images running at full tilt behind her eyes.

Nick as he looked when she arrived at his cabin, his easy smile and soft eyes watching, welcoming her. Almost as if he'd been waiting for her. As if he'd wished her there.

Corri's pert little face, watching India from across the dinner table, studying the way Indy had absentmindedly stirred her iced tea before mimicking the motions.

Darla's efforts to start her own business, encouraged by Ry to take her incredible baked goods on the road, so to speak, and begin to market her craft.

Ry's plans to renovate the Light, to provide a space for Darla to have a home for the business she had always dreamed of.

India bit her lip and stared at the ceiling. She owed it to both of them—her brother and her best friend—to try her best to make that happen. It had obviously been important to Ry that he give Darla this freedom. She, India, could do no less. How to make that happen from Paloma? The weekends were short enough as it was, with trials coming up and Corri to think about. And Nick.

India turned over and punched her pillow. Life was complicated enough right now, she told herself sternly, without getting tangled up with Nick Enright.

She could have laughed out loud. If she wasn't well on her way to tangling with him, what exactly would she call it? Her fingers traced the path his lips had made along the side of her face. She could almost feel his tongue teasing at the corners of her mouth.

Yeah, that was *tangling,* all right.

With a sigh, India threw back the covers and stood up in the cool of the night. Grabbing a fuzzy blue mohair afghan from a nearby chair, she wrapped it around her shoulders and eased onto the window seat that her father, years earlier, had built for her with his own hands. She smiled at the memory of her white-haired, scholarly father, his glasses perched upon his nose as he meticulously measured the space beneath the window and drew a corresponding diagram upon a sheet of blue-lined notebook paper. He had approached the project as he researched points of law, all his tools lined up ahead of time, in order of their anticipated usage. India had never before nor after seen her father work with his hands to cut wood and hammer it into place. He had done it for her, and he had felt that had been enough to prove he could—if he wanted to. He had simply never wanted to again.

India had spent so many hours curled up just so, she mused. Weeping over school-girl crushes or planning her career. For years she had sent her prayers off, heaven bound, from this very spot. And for years she had come to this very window to look out at the night, when the nightmares came and refused to give her peace.

India shivered and shook her head as if to clear it. With a sigh of exasperation, she pulled the afghan more closely around her and sank back against the wall, alone with the night and with her thoughts.

"What do you think, Indy?" Darla passed a small white plate upon which sat a plump, fragrant muffin into India's waiting hands.

"I think it smells incredible." India lifted the plate to her nose for a closer whiff. "What kind is this one?"

"Raisin pumpkin. And these," she said, removing a muffin tin from the oven and placing it upon a rack on the counter, "are raspberry cream."

"Heaven!" India all but swooned. "Sheer heaven. Don't wrap them all up. I may eat one of those too."

"Wow. A two-muffin morning. You must have heavy doings on your mind." Darla tucked a loose strand of blond hair behind her ear and watched Indy's face for subtle changes, those little telltale signs of trouble or stress. There, there it was. Barely imperceptible, but to one who knew India as well as Darla did, the shadow that had crossed Indy's face was unmistakable.

India shrugged and reached for the butter dish.

"How's your new case going?" Darla tried to sound casual.

"Umm, okay. I think we have enough to get a conviction."

"When does that trial start?"

"Two more weeks." India nibbled at the edge of the muffin. It was dribbly with butter and tasted the way an early fall morning should taste. "Dar, I love these. These are my favorites."

"I thought the strawberry cheesecake were your favorites."

"Them too." India licked crumbs off her fingers.

"Then what about the chocolate mocha?"

"Umm, right. Those."

Darla laughed. "I wish you'd come home more often, Indy. I need your enthusiasm."

"Oh, come on, Dar. I can't believe that you'd need anyone to tell you that you bake like no one else. I'll bet there'd be an endless stream of volunteers to taste-test your experiments."

"Yeah, but I need that Devlin palate to do it right." Darla sat down and rested her chin in her hand. "I miss Ry, Indy. I miss him more and more, not less and less."

"Me too." India sat her coffee mug down quietly on the table.

"We had the best plans, Indy. We had it all worked out. We were getting the Light all fixed up, repaired and painted and restored. We were going to do a sort of café in the two rooms downstairs, just simple fare that would be appropriate for a little morning munch or an afternoon tea. It was going to be so much fun. It was Ry's idea that I sell my muffins and breads and stuff. He had a great advertising campaign all worked out and a marketing strategy." Darla sighed and shook her head.

"I've been meaning to talk to you about all that. I think we should proceed just as you and Ry had planned."

"It won't be the same."

"Of course it won't be the same. Dar, nothing will ever be the same again. But that doesn't mean that we shouldn't follow through with it. We both know that Ry would have wanted you to do this. That he did want you to have this. We'll just finish the job ourselves. It may take a little longer, but I want to do it. I want the Light restored, Dar, if for no other reason than because Ry wanted it restored. That was his dream, and we will do it for him." India closed a hand over Darla's, which were clasped as if in prayer before her on the table.

"India, are you sure you don't want to think this over? This was not an inexpensive project."

"What's to think over?" India shrugged. "It's Devlin trust money, anyway. Ry's and mine. I can't think of a better way to spend it."

"Would you want to see the plans Ry had drawn up?"

"Sure." India nodded enthusiastically. "There's no time like the present."

"I'll be right back." Darla stood up, her shoulders still sagging from the weight of her sadness.

"We'll fix it, Ry," India whispered aloud as she poured herself another cup of coffee. "I can't bring you back, but maybe I can help bring the life back into Darla's eyes. Maybe we can get her business going so that she can support herself and the kids and maybe someday she'll even be happy again. Maybe, with your help, we can make it happen for her."

"Here's Ry's briefcase." Darla swung the black leather satchel onto the kitchen table and unsnapped the closure. She opened the lid and swung it around so that it stood open to India's scrutiny.

Inside lay folders, dark brown heavy cardboard secured with black elastic to keep the contents in. Each was named, the inch-high letters printed in Ry's neat hand, in black felt-tipped pen. India's fingers walked through the stack, scrolling the files.

Her brother had been meticulous in his research into the restoration of the Light. One file held paint chips and paint charts from several manufacturers of historic colors. India smiled. It was exactly Ry's style to try to match both the exterior and interior shades as closely as possible.

Another file held a diagram of the massive fireplace that stood between the two main rooms of the Light's first floor, as well as detailed photographs of every aspect of the structure. Several business cards of masons who specialized in brick restoration were paper-clipped to one side of the folder. A hand-printed list of books relating to historic fireplaces was included in the file, as were Ry's sketches of how he saw the rooms once the renovations had been completed.

Ry's optimism, his plans for his life with Darla lay before India's eyes in the thin, penciled lines hastily sketched upon white construction paper. It pulled at her heart, which she had thought to be beyond breaking any further. In Ry's hand, the rooms had become beautiful again in their simplicity, with small round tables and mismatched wooden chairs. Those same windows, which had not, to her knowledge, been opened in more than a hundred years, stood open to the sun and the soft salty breezes off the bay. She saw the Light through her brother's eyes and knew that it was all exactly right, exactly the way it should be. The way it had to be.

India slid the sketches back into the folder and replaced the elastic before carefully opening the next folder. Ry's plans for the Light itself. Restored and opened for small tours, from spring through November. Another folder held his budget for the projects. Darla had not exaggerated. Ry was preparing to spend a lot of money on the restoration and to start up Darla's business. India tapped her fingers on the table as she studied the figures. More than she had thought. Mentally she shrugged, knowing Darla was watching her face. It was Ry's money, his portion of the trust. If that's how he had wanted to spend it, that's how it would be.

"Was anyone working with Ry on this?" India asked Darla.

"Just me." Darla sat blotting soft tears from her face. "And sometimes Nick."

A flicker crossed India's face at the mention of Nick's name, a fact that was not lost upon Darla.

"Maybe we should ask him to help us," Darla suggested.

"I think Nick has his own work to do."

"Oh, I don't know. He likes a nice diversion now and again. And he's been working on that thesis for quite some time, you know. He can't spend all his time working. And besides, Ry trusted him. They were like two sides of the same coin sometimes," Darla said softly, then smiled and added, "Sort of like the way you and I are, Indy. Nick and Ry were best friends in the truest sense. They liked and respected each other. They helped each other. I do not know what I would do without Nick, Indy."

India looked up at her friend, questioning without meaning to.

"He just always seems to know when one of us is hurting. He stops at August's several times a week, did you know? He has tea with her in the afternoon sometimes. He stops here to see if I need help getting my orders out. To see if Jack wants to throw a ball around or go down to the beach and talk. He never stays too long and he never asks anything from anyone. He's just there and lends a hand and then goes about his business. Like he's taken us all under his wing and watches out for us."

"He seems to be a very good man." India measured her words carefully.

"A very good man," Darla repeated evenly, then after a moment's silence between the two of them, she burst out laughing.

"India, Nick Enright is a hunk. He is sexy, he is smart. He is thoughtful. He is fun to be around. You are probably the only woman in Devlin's Light who has *ever* described him simply as a very good man. Now, I do not recall you ever having been totally blind as far as handsome men are concerned. So stop being so coy. Would you please admit that you are interested in the man as something more than a source of information?"

"I'm interested in the man as something more than a source of information," India repeated.

"Why didn't you say so?"

"I guess I feel awkward," India said, searching for words.

"Why should you feel awkward?"

"Well, on the one hand, it feels odd to be lusting after anyone at the same time that I still feel as if I'm grieving over Ry. And on the other hand, there just seems to be so much going on right now, and I don't feel capable of handling it all."

"The lust and grief we'll deal with in a minute." Darla pushed the briefcase aside and sat back down at the table.

"Right now I want you to tell me what you think you can't handle."

"My job and Corrie. Paloma and Devlin's Light. Ruthless prosecutor totally focused on her job and dedicated, parent figure-guardian to a darling little girl who needs and totally deserves a dedicated and loving parental figure." India leaned back against her chair, turning her head partway in Darla's direction. "It's as if I have two separate lives and I don't know how to make them work together."

"Maybe they can't work together, not as things are now," Darla said tentatively. "Maybe you need to make some changes if it's all going to work."

"I can't make any changes right now. I have cases to finish up. I have—"

"I know, bad guys to put away, dragons to slay."

India had gotten up and was now pacing slightly. To Darla, she looked like a spring ready to pop out of control.

"India, how many dragons before it's all put to rest?" Darla asked softly.

"Dar, please . . ."

"Indy, you know and I know that the best thing, the most obvious solution is for you to come back to Devlin's Light. You can raise Corri here and still work—you know you'll be able to find a job without any problem at all."

"I keep thinking about everything I've done over the past few years. The cases I tried. The people I've worked with. The life I tried to make for myself away from Devlin's Light." India leaned back in her chair and fixed her gaze on a spot on the ceiling. "All I wanted to do was to be a really good prosecutor."

"And that's exactly what you are, Indy. Everyone in Devlin's Light has followed your career, and we're all proud of you. If that is all you want from your life—to have done your job well—then you have already succeeded." Darla stood up and rubbed India's shoulders. "I just think that maybe you've had a taste of something else, and maybe just doing your job isn't going to be enough for you now. Sorta like that old song: 'How ya gonna keep 'em down on the farm, after they've seen Paree?'"

India laughed.

"You want to know what I think?" Darla asked.

"I am not certain that I do, but I am certain that you will tell me."

"I think that in spite of yourself, in spite of everything that has happened over the years, I think your heart is in Devlin's Light. And I think you'll never be truly happy anywhere else."

India dismissed Darla's comments with a wave of her hand. "What makes you think I'm not happy in Paloma?"

"Oh, well, if working sixteen-hour days seven days a week makes you happy," Darla said, folding her arms across her chest, "and if looking into the souls of the lowest, the sickest members of society makes you happy, then I guess you must be one happy girl. Can you tell me you are, in fact, one happy girl?"

Before India could open her mouth, Darla said, "Don't bother trying to con me, India, because I have known you too well for too long. And it might surprise you to know that your brother felt the same way I do."

"Well, he was wrong and so are you. I have a good life in Paloma."

"What do you do, besides work?"

"I belong to a book-discussion group."

"When was the last time you went? What was the last book they discussed? Let me guess. It was something like *The Barn Burners,* right?" Darla named a bestseller from almost two years ago, and India laughed in spite of her best efforts not to.

"Actually, it was. But it wasn't that long ago."

"What else?" Darla gestured for India to continue.

"Well, I still go to the gym and box."

"Last time?"

"Two months ago."

"Well, that beats the book club." Darla grinned, then leaned forward and asked slyly, "But when was your last really hot date?"

"About six months ago," India admitted.

"Not that Ron guy, the guy from your office?" Darla's eyes widened in horror.

India nodded her head somewhat sheepishly.

"Well, there you are!" Darla told her triumphantly. "You name one man you've met in Paloma who is, pound for pound, dollar for dollar, a better prospect than Nick Enright. And he's right here, India. Right in your own back yard."

"You make it sound as if he's pining away for me," India scoffed.

"Who's to say he isn't?"

"This is silly. Nick doesn't need to pine after any woman." India stood up to put distance between herself and Darla. "He is handsome and sexy and smart and—"

She stopped and looked at Darla.

"And everything else you said he was. And no," she said more softly, "there is no one in Paloma quite like Nick."

"I'll bet there's no one anywhere quite like Nick," Darla said. "He's one of a kind. Like Ry was. And I can tell you with absolute certainty that there will never be anyone quite like him again."

They shared a silence, deep but not uncomfortable, till Darla spoke up. "I really loved Ry with all my heart. I would give anything—anything—to have just a little more time with him. To hear his voice. Touch him. Laugh with him. It hurts me more than I can say to know that that whole part of my life is done forever."

"You don't think you'll ever find anyone else?"

"Could anyone fill Ry's shoes?" Darla smiled a crooked half smile. "No, sweetie, I can't imagine that there could be anyone else. Ry was the love of my life. Anything else would just be pretending. I spent enough years pretending when I was married to Kenny. I have my kids, and I have my work. And I have my memories."

"Memories may not be enough as time passes. Ry's only been gone a few months, Dar. Things can change."

"I don't know that I can believe that things could ever change that much. But you," she said, wagging a finger at India, "you have it all still ahead of you. If the chance is there for that kind of love, take it and cherish it for as long as you have it. If I've learned anything over the past few years, it's that life can be very fickle. If you know what you want, India, go after it with everything you've got."

"Maybe I don't know for sure what I want."

"Well, I sure hope that Nick is still around by the time

you make up your mind, sweetie." Darla shook her head slowly. "And before someone else comes along and swoops him up."

India tried to make light of it, but the thought of Nick kissing someone else—of him making her dessert, of him bringing her a birthday cake or mowing her lawn—taunted her all the way back to Darien Road.

Darla's Strawberry Cheesecake Muffins
(makes 12 muffins)

Preheat oven to 400°
Generously butter muffin tin and set aside.

Cheese filling:

3 oz cream cheese, softened
1 tablespoon sour cream
2 tablespoons sugar
1/8 teaspoon vanilla
3 tablespoons best-quality strawberry jam

Muffins:

1½ cups sifted all purpose flour
2 tablespoons double-acting baking powder
1/2 teaspoon salt
1/2 cup sugar
1 egg
2 tablespoons unsalted butter, melted
1/2 cup milk
1 tablespoon sugar for sprinkling over muffin tops.

Beat together the first 4 ingredients of the cheese filling until smooth and creamy. Swirl in the jam and set aside.

Sift together the flour, baking powder, sugar, salt and sugar in a large mixing bowl. In another mixing bowl, lightly beat the egg with a whisk or fork. Mix in melted butter, then milk. Stir in the cheese mixture just to combine. Add the liquid ingredients to the dry and fold with a rubber spatula just enough to moisten the flour mix.

Spoon into the muffin pan, filling two-thirds full. Bake 25–30 minutes until golden brown. Cool in the pan for 2–3 minutes and remove from pan.

Chapter 11

"Can I put it on right now and see if Aunt August recognizes me?" Corrie whispered hopefully as she hopped out of India's car, the bag holding her Halloween costume clutched tightly to her chest.

"Absolutely." India laughed, recalling a Halloween long ago when she had done that very thing. "Go in through the kitchen door and up the back steps. I'll try to keep her occupied. Now, are you sure you can get into that costume all by yourself?"

"Pretty sure." Corri nodded confidently.

"Oh, Corri, before I forget." India closed her car door and stuck the keys in the pocket of her blazer. "The next time you take one of Ry's records out to play, please try to remember to put it back, okay?"

Corri looked at Indy blankly.

"The record that you left on my bed last night fell off onto the floor," Indy explained, "and I almost stepped on it. I'd hate to see any of them get broken. We've had them forever."

Corri took slow steps toward the back porch.

"Corri?" India asked, puzzled at the lack of response.

"I didn't have any of Ry's records last night, Indy."

"Honey, it's okay." Indy smoothed Corri's hair as she fell

in step with her. "I don't mind that you play them. I would just like you to put them back so that they don't get broken."

"Indy, I always put Ry's records back. Always. Just like he showed me. But I didn't have one out last night," Corri insisted.

"Maybe the night before then."

"No." Corri shook her head.

"Then how did one get on my bed?" India asked, wondering why Corri would hesitate to tell the truth about something like that.

"I don't know." Corri shrugged. "Maybe the ghost put it there."

"Ghost?" India laughed. "Corri, there's no such thing as ghosts. And there're certainly no ghosts here."

Corri glanced over her shoulder as she went up the porch steps, still holding her precious bag tightly, an anxious look upon her face. India had thought she was about to say something, but instead she simply disappeared into the house.

India stood at the end of the drive, wondering where Corri would get such fanciful ideas. Did she imagine that she saw Ry? Or perhaps it was another Devlin that Corri imagined, Indy mused, recalling how the many old photographs and family portraits throughout the house had once played tricks with India's mind. Had these same images worked on Corri's imagination too?

Indy strolled to the front of the house, swinging her shoulder bag like a pendulum as she walked. The pines had grown tall and unwieldy over the past few years, giving the house a closed and sinister look. At least a young child might think it so. Had Corri's classmates been teasing her about living in a haunted house?

India stepped back to study the overall facade and decided they could live with a few less trees out front. She'd speak with Aunt August in the morning, before she left to go back to Paloma and what she was beginning to think of as her other life.

"Aunt August," India called from the hallway.

"In here, dear," came the response from the front sitting room.

India hung up her blazer and crossed the hall to let her aunt know that Corri's search for the perfect costume had come to a successful conclusion.

The smell of burning logs struck just the right chord on this frosty night, she was thinking as she entered the room.

"Umm, that smells good," she told her aunt.

"Thank Nick." August gestured to the chair behind India.

"Hi." He stood up to greet her, his smile as warm and inviting as the fire.

"I'm sorry," she said, turning toward him, "I didn't see you there."

"Nick brought me some firewood," August explained.

"That's very thoughtful," she noted.

"Well, Ry helped me take a few trees down last spring," he explained, "and I'd promised him half the wood. I thought with the chill in the air tonight, it might be a good time to bring a partial load over."

"Coffee, Indy?" Aunt August rose from the cozy wing-chair.

"I'll get it," she said, but her aunt was already into the hallway, her heels clicking on the hardwood floors as she went.

"So." India pulled a large rectangular hassock covered in a green and oyster checkered fabric closer to the fire. It was as close to Nick as she felt she could trust herself tonight; he'd been too much on her mind.

"So," he replied, looking mildly amused.

"I took Corri to get her Halloween costume today after school," India mentioned.

"So August said. What is she going to be?"

"You'll see. She'll be down in a minute. She's putting it on. She wants to see if she is recognizable or not."

"The best costume I ever had was Rocky the Squirrel," he told her. "I loved the goggles. It made the costume. My sister Zoey was Boris, and Georgia was Natasha. Mom was Bullwinkle the Moose. It was the best Halloween we ever had. What was yours?"

"My favorite costume?" She frowned, trying to remember. "Umm, I guess the year that I had a hula costume and it was a balmy seventy-two degrees that night so I didn't have to wear a jacket over it. I was so worried about that, that I'd have to cover up my costume with a coat and the entire effect would be lost."

"Why did you buy it, then?"

"Because I liked the way the skirt rustled. And I wanted to play the ukulele." She laughed, remembering. "Ry was a pirate that year."

"Oh, my, India, do you remember how mad he was when Mrs. Daley across the street wouldn't let him borrow her parrot to ride on his shoulder?" Aunt August brought in a tray laden with coffee paraphernalia for three.

India laughed again. "I do. He picked that costume with that very parrot in mind."

"He was just fit to be tied, that boy was." August shook her head as she went back toward the kitchen. "I'll just be but a minute."

"Halloween was a big thing when we were growing up."

"Us too. I used to take my sisters trick-or-treating. Of course, that was before the days when parents were afraid to send their children out for Halloween without an armed guard."

"It is sad, isn't it?" India poured coffee for him, being careful not to touch his fingers when she handed him the cup.

His eyes twinkled as if he knew that she was taking extraordinary pains to avoid touching him, and as if he knew why.

"Indy?" Corri called from the top of the steps.

"Do you need help?" India leaned forward, craning her neck to look up the stairs.

"Umm, I think so," Corri said softly. "My tail won't stay on."

"Oh, dear." August scooted into the room with a plate of homemade spice cookies and cast a solemn glance in Indy's direction. "We certainly can't have that."

"Heaven forbid." Indy chuckled and excused herself from the room after liberating a cookie from the plate. She knew they had been baked with her in mind and knew too that if she looked in the kitchen she'd find a whole batch of the fragrant treats all packed up for her to take back to Paloma.

The stairwell felt chilly after the warmth of the little sitting room. India's hands, so recently cozied by the fire, were cooling rapidly. She found the problem with the tail and took Corri by the hand as they walked down the steps.

"She'll know it's me." Corri shifted the mask on her face, trying to line up her eyes with the slits in the heavy fabric.

"Well, I think that's unavoidable, don't you? I mean, sooner or later, she'd figure it out."

"Umm . . ." Corri poked her face into the room from the doorway.

"Eeek!" August shrieked. "It's a giant mouse!"

Corri giggled and flew into the room, holding her tail in one hand and peeling the mask off with the other.

"Oh, it's a mouse child!" August laughed and held her arms open to the child who bounced into those arms and filled them.

"Do you like it?" Corri asked. "Indy bought it for me."

"I love it." August beamed. "And you're the most adorable mouse I've ever seen. Don't you agree, Nick?"

"She certainly is." Nick nodded.

"I didn't know you were here." Corri frowned. "Now I won't be able to trick-or-treat at your house. You already saw my costume."

"Hmmm. That is a problem." Nick pretended to ponder this. "Tell you what. No one is likely to come all the way out to the cabin, so how 'bout if I bring your treat to you, since you already tricked me tonight?"

"Really?" Corri's face brightened. "Were you surprised it was me?"

She pulled the mask down over her face, once again twisting it this way and that, trying to line up eyes, nose and mouth.

"Corri, that mask is cute, but you're really having problems with it, aren't you?" August frowned.

"Maybe we should forget the mask and use face paint instead," suggested India.

"Ollie has face paint." Corri remembered. "She is going to be an Egyptian queen and she has face paint."

"We could do whiskers and do something with your eyes." Indy nodded.

"But you won't be here," Corri reminded her, her little face darkening in spite of herself. "You won't be here on Halloween night to paint my face or take me trick-or-treating."

"You're right, sweetie." India sighed, feeling an unexpected sting of disappointment. "Maybe Darla can do your face."

"Nonsense," August told them. "I can paint whiskers with the best of them."

"And I'd be happy to take you out," Nick said. "I can't remember how long it's been since I went out on Halloween. But you might have to share a treat or two."

"Okay. Except for the peppermint patties." As if lecturing, Corri pointed with her index finger, her face turning solemn once again.

"That's a deal." Nick nodded. "Peppermint patties for you, Snickers for me."

"Sure." Corri grinned. "I don't like peanuts anyway."

"Okay, mouse child," August told her, "go up and take that off and leave it in the sewing room so that I can put an extra stitch or two in that tail."

"Can I have cocoa before I go to bed?" Corri asked from the doorway.

"It's almost bedtime now," August reminded her, "so if you can get ready quickly, there might be a half cup of something for you."

Corri scurried out of the room and up the steps.

"It's like living with a baby tornado, having that child around." August chuckled. "And yet I don't know what I'd do without her. She keeps me young and fit and sharp. It's not possible to feel like an old lady when there's such youthful energy in the house."

"Doesn't it get to be a bit much sometimes?" India turned her face from the fire to study her aunt's expression. "Don't you get tired?"

"Oh, sometimes a bit, maybe. But I'd not be without her, Indy. Not for the world. There's eternity to rest, if rest is what you seek. I'm not in a hurry for it. Well, if you'll excuse me, I have cocoa to make."

August scooped up the tray as she passed by

"I really can't thank you enough for offering to take Corri," India started.

He held up one hand. "We've already talked about this. You don't have to thank me."

"I just didn't feel I could leave without saying it again."

"When are you leaving?" His eyes narrowed and seemed to darken.

"In the morning," she told him. "I need to get back to the city. I have a trial slated to begin the end of next week. I have a lot of work to do."

"When were you planning on telling me?" he asked.

"What?"

"That you were leaving. When were you going to tell me?" He stood up, obviously agitated.

She looked up at him, somewhat confused.

"You were just going to go, weren't you?"

Numbly, she nodded.

"Why?"

"I guess because I'm just used to coming and going on my own," she told him.

"Didn't it occur to you that maybe I'd want to say goodbye?"

She shook her head.

"Or that maybe I'd be interested in when you were coming back?"

She was wide-eyed, watching him try to control his growing anger.

"Nick, I'm sorry that you're angry. I just didn't know how to call and say 'So. I'm leaving tomorrow, I'll be back in a few weeks.'"

"You just said it. You just said all you had to say."

"I'm just not used to having anyone to say goodbye to," she said quietly. "I didn't know how."

"You want to know how to say goodbye?" He stood in the doorway, his hands on his hips. "I'll show you how to say goodbye."

He crossed the room in two strides and drew her to him, his mouth seeking hers before she could so much as squeak. He kissed her, long and hard, before drawing back and telling her, "And *that* is how you say goodbye, India."

135

By the time she came to her senses, he was already out the front door.

"Oh no, you don't," she sputtered, and she took off down the steps.

"Nick Enright, don't you think you can come into my house, and . . . and . . ." She stood on the sidewalk, hands fisted in anger set menacingly on her hips.

In spite of his own pique, Nick laughed.

"What is so funny?" she demanded.

"You are," he told her. "You come racing out the front door like some hundred-pound avenging angel, hissing and sputtering." He cleared his throat and leaned back against his car. "I'm sorry, India, you were saying something. Don't think I can come into your house and . . . and do what?"

She paused, wondering how anyone ever stayed angry with this man.

"Don't think you can come into my house and kiss me senseless and then walk away."

"Well then, I believe we're beginning to understand each other. Yes, that is exactly my point."

She walked toward him slowly, her arms crossed in front of her.

"Were you? Senseless, I mean?" She raised a questioning eyebrow.

"Totally."

"Good." She grinned.

He reached out to her and drew her close, uncrossing her arms and wrapping them around his neck. "Wanna say goodbye again?"

She did—his way, not with words but with kisses that would burn into her and make her giddy with their warmth.

"Do you realize that we are standing right under a streetlamp?" She pulled her lips from his long enough to get the words out.

"Umm-hmm," he murmured. "Guess that's why Mrs. Ellis there across the street is hanging out her second-floor window."

"She's not!" India jumped and peeked over his shoulder. "Oh, for crying out loud," she said with a grimace, "she was looking out the window!"

Nick laughed.

"Well, I guess that by tomorrow morning, everyone in Devlin's Light will know that something was going on outside the Devlin house."

"Oh, brother. Just like when I was in high school."

"The joys of small-town living." Nick laughed. "Come back more often and stay longer, so we'd have time to really give them something to talk about."

He leaned down and kissed her again, whispering, "Don't ever do that again, India. Don't think for a minute that it doesn't matter to me that you're leaving."

"Nick, I'm sorry. It's no excuse, but I just wasn't thinking. And no, I wasn't sure that it would matter to you. My mind is on this trial that's coming up. I'm nervous about it; some of the witness statements aren't as strong as I would like them to be."

"Do you know that your face changes when you start talking about your work?"

"What do you mean?"

"You lose the softness. Your eyes narrow and your jaw sets differently, and your face develops an attitude all its own."

She shrugged off the comment.

"When you're with Corri, you lose that edge. And I like to think that when you're with me, you don't need the attitude. It's almost as if you are two different women."

"Well, maybe in a sense, I am. My life in Paloma is very different from life here in Devlin's Light."

"Must be hard, having your life split in two like that," he said, all too perceptively.

India watched him warily.

"Have you been talking to Darla?" she asked suspiciously.

"Not for a few days." He shook his head. "Why?"

"No reason."

"You know, I don't know that I could do that." He opened the car door slowly, his brows closing in on each other as if he was considering an impossible task.

"Do what?"

"Have part of me in one place and part of me someplace

else," he said over his shoulder as he got in and slammed the door of the Pathfinder. "I like my head and my heart to be in the same place."

He started the ignition and rolled down the window.

"Good luck with your case, India." Nick reached through the open window with an outstretched hand to touch the side of her face with his fingertips. "I'll be in touch."

She saluted him with her right hand as he pulled away from the curb, then stood in the middle of the street and watched the white car disappear into the fog at the corner.

India had stopped at her office—just to pick up the mail, she told herself—on her way through Paloma. It was almost eight o'clock at night before she finally left, two files and a week's worth of mail under her right arm. By the time she arrived at the townhouse and unloaded the car, it was nearing eight-thirty. Just in time to call Corri and say goodnight if she hurried. Ignoring the blinking light on the answering machine, which seemed to be counting out a week's worth of messages, she dialed the number and waited for Aunt August's cheery hello. Flipping through the mail, which had slid onto the foyer floor from the mail slot, she kicked off her shoes while Corri was called to the phone, using the time to separate bills from junk mail from magazines from letters, of which there were few. An envelope with a Texas postmark went into the read-me-first pile. It was, she knew, from a woman whose only son had been murdered by a man who now rested more comfortably than he deserved behind bars that should forever separate him from the rest of society. Every year, on the anniversary of the boy's death, his mother sent India a card, thanking her for her relentless prosecution of the animal who had taken her son's life. That was how the mother had always referred to the defendant. *That animal.* India wondered if the woman had ever bothered to learn the man's name.

India remembered.

Billy Kidman.

He was nineteen years old, hard-faced and smart-mouthed, when he was caught attempting to hide the corpse of a young boy—his third in as many weeks—in the storage bin of a basement apartment on the outskirts of Paloma.

India went after him like a hound on the heels of a fox. Kidman never had a chance. He was Indy's first big case. She won with a combination of preparation and information, and by keeping her promise to the jury that she would prove, beyond doubt, that the defendant had in fact committed the dreadful acts of which he had been accused. Once convicted in Pennsylvania, he was extradited to Texas, where he would eventually stand trial for similar crimes for which he could possibly be given the death penalty. He still, she knew, awaited his fate—death by lethal injection—which he had successfully managed to avoid by filing appeal after appeal. India took no pleasure in knowing that eventually his appeals would be exhausted.

Kidman's mother, a too young, too pale, too timid, too tired woman who had aged long before her time, had been at the trial for the first two days before returning to Houston, where her job as a janitress and her three younger children awaited her. She seemed unmoved by her son's crimes as much as by his fate. India hadn't been able to decide which bothered her more. No, India had not forgotten Billy Kidman.

Corri's girlish giggles on the phone brought her back to the present. India made Corri promise to have lots of pictures taken in her mouse costume, and in return she promised Corri a weekend in Paloma, just the two of them. They talked about what they might do, what movie they might see, what exhibit might be at the museum that weekend, what clothes Corri should pack. By the time she hung up the phone, Corri was squealing with anticipation, prompting August to thank India for getting Corri "all wound up just before bedtime."

India locked up the house and carried her stack of mail upstairs to her second-floor office, her bare feet sinking silently into the plush blue carpet. She turned on the light and dumped the junk mail into the trash and the real mail in the middle of her desk. She wanted a hot shower and a quick dinner before surrendering the rest of the night to reading over the investigative reports on a new case that had opened and been assigned to her while she had been home.

She headed back downstairs for her suitcases, which had been dropped unceremoniously inside the front hall. She passed the second bedroom, the small one with the two windows that faced the back yard, and turned on the light. The room was empty. She'd always planned to make it into a guest room, for Aunt August or Darla, but since neither of them had ever expressed an interest in staying overnight in Paloma, she hadn't bothered.

It would make a cute room for Corri, though.

India tried to envision the room in perhaps a pale yellow, or maybe a very light pink. A striped wallpaper, maybe, or a floral. She snapped the light off. Corri should decide for herself. It would, after all, be her room.

And maybe, if she likes it well enough, just maybe, someday, she'll want to stay.

Chapter 12

Waking to a Paloma morning was never quite the same as waking in Devlin's Light, India conceded after she had slapped the alarm clock silly, hoping to silence its uncivil buzz. For one thing, her bedroom in the city, while pretty and bright and comfortable, overlooked a city street, with all its attendant noises and bustle. For another, she missed the smell of the bay sifting through the windows. In Devlin's Light, one awoke with an awareness of the sea. In Paloma, one's awareness centered more on traffic reports and alarm clocks and the sounds coming through the common wall she shared with her next-door neighbors. A retired army officer, Colonel Danvers was nearly deaf and a devotee of John Philip Sousa. India looked at the clock next to the bed and held her breath. It was almost time for the cymbals to meet and greet the dawn with a thunderous welcome.

There! The marching band had gathered to send the good captain to his shower with an invigorated step. India shook her head and laughed goodnaturedly. He was a dear, the colonel was, as was his lady. They were well into their seventies, and India figured if it took a good Sousa march to get them moving in the morning, then they were entitled to it. She always awoke before them anyway, so other than the first week, when she had been unprepared and therefore a bit disconcerted, she figured a little wall-rattling crescendo in the morning never hurt anyone. And besides, it was still preferable to the previous owner of the house on her other side, who had watched horror movies late into the night. For months, she'd spent evening after evening listening to Freddy Krueger's victims shrieking on the other side of the wall. Given the choice, she'd take the marching bands any day.

While her morning coffee brewed, she played the messages on her answering machine. Shirley, the secretary she shared with Roxie and two other A.D.A.s, reminding her about a department meeting on Monday morning at nine; a woman she'd met at the library last month telling her about a new mystery book club that was just forming; a neighbor across the street who was putting together a petition regarding the need for a stop sign at the end of the next block; Gif, her boxing coach, wanting to know "where ya bin"; and three hang-ups. She poured her coffee and stepped out onto the deck, her inquisitive nose seeking the scent of autumn in the crisp morning air. It was there, but barely. No matter how hard she tried, October simply did not smell the same in Paloma as it did in Devlin's Light.

Oh, there were oak leaves, orange and yellow and brown, from a tree in the colonel's yard, and the leaves from the sugar maple that stood back behind the small shed. But they didn't seem to hold the scent of the season as they did back on Darien Road. And they didn't seem to crunch underfoot with the same decisiveness, the peremptory crackle, as those that plumped up like feather beds on the sidewalk in front of the old Devlin place. The acorns were smaller too, little gumballs compared to the rocks that fell from the tree in front of the library in Devlin's Light. And here, in Paloma, one might see an occasional formation of Canadian geese winging south, whereas a day couldn't pass on the beach without dozens of honkers passing overhead. For years she and Ry had staged their own Christmas Day bird count out on the point where the Light stood, keeping record of the sightings of the migratory flocks and the occasional strays. The trees around the townhouse seemed to hold little other than pigeons, crows, grackles and various members of the sparrow family.

India leaned over the deck and watched a small finch try

to coax a last bit of seed out of the bird feeder she'd nailed to the tree last winter. She'd have to remember to pick up some bird seed when she went to the store.

And some India feed might be a good idea, she mused. She couldn't remember when she'd last been to the supermarket. She probably needed everything. Her coffee was cooling rapidly in the frosty morning air, and she wrapped her sweater around her. Days like this called for a plate of Aunt August's waffles. Bowls of warm applesauce. Or, better yet, warm apple pie, like the one Aunt August made. Or the one Nick had made to share with her.

Sighing, she thought back to the night they'd sat on the deck overlooking the bay, watching the moon and listening to the sounds of the night. It had been romantic, and that had made it scary; she could admit that now that there was more than a mile's distance between them. Nick Enright was everything a man should be. Everything she needed a man to be. And it scared the hell out of her. It was hard enough to take on Corri, bringing a child into a life that had been, up until now, pretty much unencumbered, without taking on Nick too, hard enough to learn to parent the one without worrying about becoming lovers with the other. Learning to love one at a time would be enough. Surely Corri needed her more than Nick did.

But still the question nagged at her: Which did she, India, need more, the child or the man?

Both, she acknowledged. She needed them both. Nick and Corri. But one step at a time. Walk before you run, she cautioned herself. Her life was here now, Nick's was in Devlin's Light for however long his research might take, and then who knew? Better to be cautious. Why set herself up for a fall—set Corri up for a fall—if she didn't have to? They could be friends. They could keep their relationship platonic.

Who was she kidding?

India poured the cooled coffee over the railing and sighed. It had never been platonic, right from Ry's funeral when he had sought her out and found her on the swing on Aunt August's back porch. It had only been a matter of time.

And what to do now, she wondered. She had a child to

raise, a child she was still getting to know. And a job to do. Alvin Fletcher was coming to trial in two weeks, and she had to be ready for him. She had looked into the eyes of a shell-shocked father and promised him that she would do whatever it took to put Alvin Fletcher away for the maximum number of years permitted by law. She owed that much to the young girl who had been the victim of a brutal rape and beating at Fletcher's hands. How could she keep her promises if she couldn't keep her mind on the facts of the case?

Maybe it would be better to put distance between herself and Nick than to watch an Alvin Fletcher walk, better to lose Nick than to lose a conviction. It was more important—wasn't it?—that she put the bad guys away? Someone's life could depend upon it, the life of his next victim, should she fail.

But what about her life?

All this early morning deliberation was giving her a headache, and she rubbed her eyes behind her fisted hands.

India sighed and pushed it all away, choosing to leave it all outside on the deck with the fallen leaves and the half-eaten acorns discarded by the neighborhood squirrels. She'd deal with it later. Right now she had work to do.

At ten o'clock on the following Saturday morning, India was preparing to leave the house to drive to the train station to pick up Corri, who was to be accompanied on her travels by Amelia Johnston, a friend of Aunt August's, who was coming into the city to visit a sickly sister. She stepped out onto the small front porch, thinking about how much she had missed the little girl. She was just imagining how Corri's tender face would light up when she spied India in the station when she turned on the top step to see Corri pop out of the passenger seat of a white utility vehicle.

"What on earth . . ."

"Nick was coming to see his sister. She's a dancer and her name is Georgia." Corri made a beeline for India, her mouth moving as quickly as her feet.

"What about Mrs. Johnston?"

"Oh. Her sister died. So they shipped her to Buffalo. Isn't that a funny name for a place, 'Buffalo'? If I was naming a city I'd never call it 'Buffalo.'" Corri hugged India, wrapping her arms around her neck.

"Well then, what would you call it?"

"I'd call it 'Zebra.' Or 'Antelope.'" Corri giggled and squirmed to get down, her feet already itching to get on with the day. "Can we have lunch?"

India watched as Nick approached her uncertainly, as if measuring the distance and finding it too far but not sure of the best way to breach it.

"How did you get roped into a trip to Paloma?" She raised her eyebrows, following his every step, watching him as he watched her, his pale brown eyes seeming to drink her in.

"Well, I had told August I'd be coming in this weekend," he said, swinging Corri's bag over his shoulder, "since Georgia's in town and I promised my mother I'd make it to at least one performance. So when Mrs. Johnston changed her travel plans, I offered to bring Corri."

"She talk you to death in the car?"

"Nearly. Not as bad as Halloween, however. She had plenty to talk about that night, I can assure you."

India laughed and unlocked the front door, swinging it open for him to enter behind Corri.

"Old Mrs. Leamy gave quarters instead of candy," Nick told her as he passed into the warmth of her house.

"So I heard."

"But the Andersons gave out caramel apples, which made up for it."

"Heard about that too."

"I really missed you, India," he said softly, and he stopped her in her tracks by placing a feather of a kiss right below her left ear before whispering, "Don't tell me you heard that from anyone else."

Grinning, she closed the door behind her.

"You don't mind, do you?" he asked when he reached the living room. "If I'm intruding into your plans . . ."

"Not at all. I'm grateful that you brought Corri. To tell the truth, I was worried about her taking the train with Amelia Johnston. She takes her knitting everywhere she goes, but as soon as she starts clicking those needles together, she falls asleep."

"Are you afraid that someone would snatch Corri from the train?" He stopped in midsentence, her face having darkened suddenly and her eyes for the briefest second turning wild.

"Things can happen when no one's watching," she told him, brushing past him to follow Corri into the kitchen.

"Can we have pancakes? Are we going to the museum? Nick said we could go to the ballet tonight to see his sister dance. Can we, India?" Corri propped herself up on her knees on the edge of a kitchen chair. "I never went to a real ballet."

"Corri, I said you should see if India had plans for tonight," Nick reminded her. "Maybe she has made other plans to do something else."

"Actually, I had plans for today but not for tonight," India said, leaning back against the counter.

"Coffee?" Nick pointed to the carafe which rested on a hot plate.

"Help yourself." She handed him a purple mug with "Paloma Jazz Festival '96" written on one side in pale pink letters. To Corri she said, "The Museum of Natural History has an exhibit based on an archeological dig from central Asia."

India searched through papers on her kitchen counter to find the brochure she had received some weeks earlier and had held on to in the event that a break should occur in her schedule that would permit her a free day.

"Here." She waved the buff-colored flyer in her right hand before smoothing it out and skimming the text. "The exhibit features fossil exposures of the Gobi Desert. Dinosaur bones. Apparently the Gobi had been a nesting site for dinosaurs called protoceratops." She looked up from her reading to explain, "This says that protoceratops were dinosaurs that were six to seven feet long and had claws, a wicked-looking beak . . ."

Nick nodded. "The American Museum of Natural History sponsored an expedition to the Gobi back in the twenties that resulted in a huge find. When the photographs of the protoceratops fossils were published, some scientists actually thought that they were the remains of griffins."

"Really?" India poured herself another cup of coffee.

146

"What are griffins?" Corri asked.

"Mythical creatures with heads and talons—claws—like eagles and bodies like lions."

"Are they real?" Corri made a face.

"No, sweetie. That's what *mythical* means. Something made up, out of stories from long ago. But not real."

"Ummm, is there anything else at that museum?" Corri asked warily.

"Maybe it doesn't sound as interesting as I think it might actually be." India smiled apologetically at Corri, mentally berating herself for forgetting that she was, speaking to a six-year-old. She should have made the subject matter sound as appealing as she suspected it really would be once they got there to view the exhibit. "I really think you will like it, Corri. Are you willing to give it a try?"

"Okay." Corri did not sound convinced. "Can Nick come too?"

"That's up to Nick." India turned her back to rinse out her cup. "Maybe he has other plans for the afternoon."

"None." He smiled, and India realized that he had intended on accompanying them all along. "And since you're kind enough to let me tag along, lunch will be on me." He turned to India. "Does the museum have a restaurant?"

"Actually, it does. And it's quite good, but you don't really have to—"

He dismissed her protests and took her arm. "My pleasure. Are we ready to go?"

"I'm ready." Corri bounced off her chair.

"Do you have a sweater, Corri?" India frowned. The child was wearing only a long-sleeved T-shirt.

"In my bag." Corri took off in search of her overnight bag, which she found in the front hallway, where Nick had left it at the foot of the steps. She unzipped it and began to rummage through it until she found the dark blue sweater with green stripes across the front. Pulling it over her head in one motion, she announced, "I'm ready."

India chuckled and smoothed the child's hair where it had become mussed from the sweater dragging over it. She turned to grab her purse from a nearby chair and caught Nick staring at her, the corners of his mouth upturned in just enough amusement to free the killer dimples that lurked in the hollows of his cheeks.

Corri had opened the door and sped down the steps.

"Okay." Searching her pockets for her house key to lock up behind them, India motioned for Nick to follow Corri out. "What's so funny?"

"Just observing you with Corri." Nick flashed a heart-warming smile. "You are just naturally maternal."

"Me? Maternal? I think you have me confused with someone else, sir."

"Making sure she understands what you're talking about without talking down to her. Making sure she has her sweater. Fixing her hair before she goes out. Worrying about her safety on the train."

She lowered her eyes and brushed past him without a response.

He caught up with her at the car.

"Indy, did I say something that upset you?"

"Let's just drop it and go." How to explain to him that a child was never really safe?

He unlocked the car and she got into the front seat after just the slightest hesitation.

"Corri, can you get your seat belt?" She turned to the child, who was situating herself in the backseat.

"Sure."

Corri chatted nonstop for the entire twenty-minute drive to the museum, much to India's relief, since it spared her from having to make small talk, which she didn't feel up to all of a sudden.

Soon they were on the steps of the museum, Nick and India arguing over who would pay for the admissions. India won, since Nick had already committed to buying lunch.

The exhibit was every bit as enthralling as India had suspected it might be. Corri asked a million questions of no one in particular, and, much to Corri's delight, Nick responded nearly as often as the guide, revealing an extensive knowledge of dinosaurs and fossils and prehistoric times. Corri's curiosity led her to continue her questions right through lunch.

"But what did they eat? What did their babies eat? Why did they all die in their nests like that?" She trailed behind Nick, through the cafeteria-style line that was the order of the day on weekend afternoons, due to the number of families that visited on Saturdays.

Nick turned his attention from the steam tables to answer her as India's eye was caught by their reflection in the long mirror on the wall next to the cash register.

We look like any other family here, she thought, awed by it. *We look like a normal mom, dad, daughter, out for an afternoon together. There's no difference between the three of us and that family sitting at the table right there.*

India studied the mother, a good-looking woman in her midthirties, as she caught her daughter's jacket as it started to fall from the back of the chair onto the floor. The girl was older than Corri, maybe ten or so, and appeared to be at that brief but fragile place where childhood and adolescence met, where doing something on a Saturday afternoon with your mother and father is still fun but totally uncool. She was torn between having a good time and not wanting to, and it showed in her face. Dad was obviously amused by it; Mom had clearly had all the amusement she could take from that quarter for one day. Dad lowered his head and began to talk, perhaps about something they had seen there that morning, and slowly the girl began to respond, her face becoming more animated, the you-people-bore-me-to-tears-and-God-forbid-that-I-don't-see-anyone-I-know look beginning to fade as she spoke.

India smiled weakly at the mother, who had caught her staring, glancing at Corri and smiling back at India, as if to warn that the day would in fact come when Indy too would join the ranks of women who, by simple virtue of their motherhood, knew absolutely nothing about anything. Sighing, the woman turned back to her husband and child.

"India, I asked you what you wanted to drink." Nick had touched her arm.

"Oh. Iced tea is fine," she told him absently.

"Nick, I see a table. It's over there." Corri pointed across the room. "Can I go get it for us?"

"Sure." He nodded. "Good idea."

He slid the tray holding his lunch and Corri's toward the

cash register with one hand while the other dug into his back pocket for his wallet. India craned her neck to watch Corri weave through the crowd, unaware that Nick was watching her.

"Nick, you shouldn't have let her go by herself," she told him.

"India, she's going fifty feet away in a crowded room. What are you afraid of?"

She continued to watch Corri but did not answer.

"Someone's talking to her. Why is that man talking to her?" The deep creases of a frown dug into her forehead. She shoved the tray toward him and took off briskly toward the table where Corri was arranging paper napkins at each of three places and chatting to a man in his forties who appeared to be very interested in what she was saying.

"Excuse me." India placed herself between Corri and the man.

He smiled at her and was about to speak, when he glanced at her face and backed off a step or two.

"I was just discussing the dinosaur exhibit with your little girl," he said softly. "I write children's books. I've been working on a book about dinosaurs and I just wanted to know what she found most interesting about the exhibit."

"And I'm certain she was more than happy to tell you." Nick came up behind India, deposited the trays on the table and placed a steadying hand on her shoulder.

"Actually, she was."

Before I came up and near blew him off his feet, ready to call security and Paloma's finest and the FBI. India inwardly grimaced.

"I'm sorry," she told him, "but she's been taught not to speak to strangers."

"I understand." The man nodded, backing away as if he'd been slapped.

An awkward silence hung over the table, until finally Nick pulled out the chairs and directed everyone to sit. He slid India's tray across the table to her, then turned to Corri and asked, "Do you need help in opening that soda bottle?"

Corri nodded her head, her eyes downcast toward her lunch. Slowly, quietly, she began to unwrap her sandwich from the cellophane wrapper, as if afraid to make noise, afraid to call attention to herself.

"Corri," India began, "you do know not to talk to strangers, don't you?"

"I didn't think Mr. Carson was a stranger." Corri looked up at her with doleful eyes.

"How do you know his name was Mr. Carson?"

"Because I asked him. He was in our group when we were upstairs with the guide. And he writes books. I read the one about the grasshopper. Kimmie gave it to me for my birthday last year."

India held her breath, torn between embarrassment and fear. It was so easy to get to a child, to earn their trust, to make them believe you were anyone you told them you were.

"If Mr. Carson had asked you to come back to the exhibit with him, what would you have said?" India tried to force a calm into her voice.

Corri looked at her as if she had two heads.

"I would have said I had to ask you first."

"What if he had said he had already asked me and I said it was okay?"

Without the slightest hesitation, Corri said, "I would say that *you* didn't tell *me* I could go, and I couldn't, unless *you* told *me.*"

"You are a very smart young lady." Nick patted her on the back with great affection, all the while watching India's eyes. "India was just concerned that maybe you didn't know to do that."

"I know. Aunt August told me. And so did Ry. Ry told me that no matter what anyone said, if he didn't tell me okay, or Aunt August or Darla, it was not okay."

"Well, I think India just needed to know that you knew, isn't that right, India?" His eyes bored through her. "She didn't mean to scare you, Corri, and you didn't do anything wrong. She just didn't know that you know not to let anyone talk you into going off with them."

"Nick's right, and I am sorry, Corri. I'm not used to being"—she paused, not knowing how to phrase it—*"responsible* for little girls. I am trying, Corri, so please bear with me. I'm sorry if I embarrassed you in front of Mr. Carson. I had no way of knowing who he was or why he was speaking to you."

Corri just nodded.

"In all fairness to India, Corri, we really have no way of knowing if Mr. Carson was who he said he was, do we?" Nick stirred some sugar into his coffee.

"You mean maybe he wasn't writing a dinosaur book?" Her eyes widened at the prospect. "Maybe he didn't write the grasshopper book?"

"I don't know if he did or not," Nick told her.

"Boy!" Corri's breath came out in one long steady stream of exasperation, her face clouded over with disgust.

"It's a very sad thing, Corri, but there are a lot of people who can't be trusted." Nick put his fork down and nodded to her that it was, in fact, sad but true.

"You mean bad guys?" Corri asked. "Like the bad guys India sends to jail?"

"Exactly." He turned to India now and leveled those brown eyes at her, as if understanding was beginning to dawn.

"Exactly," she repeated.

"India, if a bad guy got me, would you send him to jail?" Corri asked innocently, waving a french fry through a puddle of catsup on her plate.

India froze momentarily. "Of course I would," she told Corri.

"I thought so." Corri reached for another fry, oblivious to the panic that had welled up inside of India, or the concern that was beginning to fill Nick. She simply began to chatter again.

"Would you like something for dessert?" Nick asked when they had finished their sandwiches. "I think they have ice cream. They also had some cakes and brownies."

"The baked goods looked pretty sad to me," India told him, then turned to Corri. "But they serve a good brand of ice cream here."

"Ice cream." Corri nodded.

"Come on then." Nick rose, taking the two trays in one hand. "We'll see what flavors they have."

They were back in moments, Corri carrying a bowl

crowded with two large scoops of chocolate ice cream and three spoons.

"We got you a spoon," Corri told her, "in case you wanted some."

"Thank you, sweetie, but no."

She watched both Nick and Corri dig in. Watching the two of them chased the dragons from her soul and brought the warmth back into her heart. When Nick left them in search of napkins, India picked up the extra spoon and took a swipe off one side of the chocolate mound.

Corri giggled.

"What's so funny?" India asked.

"Nick said you wouldn't be able to resist."

"He did, did he?" India reached across the table and smoothed her hair.

"You know, they could really use some of Darla's Delectables here," Nick said as he placed a pile of napkins on the table. "Given the quality of the rest of the food—my roast beef sandwich was excellent—you'd think they'd have something better to offer in the way of desserts."

"Maybe I should mention that to her."

"She does have an excellent product, and the clientele here seems to be pretty much upscale." His eyes wandered over the sea of well-dressed urban types who filled the room, stopping on the figure of Mr. Carson, who stood talking to a young boy, who appeared engrossed in what the man was telling him.

"Can I throw this stuff away?" Corri held up the bowl holding the spoons and the napkins, now streaked with brown where she had dabbed at the chocolate lump, which had landed on her T-shirt.

"Sure." India watched the child bounce off in search of a trash can, then followed Nick's stare. He was still watching Carson.

"You never really know, Nick," she told him. "He might well be a writer of children's books just talking to his young readers. Then again, he might be something more."

"I understand that your work would make you more sensitive to this than some others of us might be," he said, turning his gaze to her, "but I can't help but think this goes a lot deeper than that."

She ignored him, choosing to stand up as Corri returned, asking, "Are we ready? Can we go see the big dinosaur upstairs again? Did you know there are Indian houses upstairs? Can we see them too?"

Indy heard Nick sigh as he rose and followed them through the crowd.

Chapter 13

"**I**s that Georgia?" Corri would whisper every time a new dancer appeared upon the broad wooden stage that formed the focal point of the Paloma Center for the Performing Arts.

"No," Nick would answer, "I'll tell you when I see her."

It soon became apparent, however, that with all the dancers in this modern ballet being costumed in identical short flame-red dresses and white powdered wigs, their faces stark white with vivid colors at the eyes and lips, the chances of picking Nick's sister out in this crowd were slim to none. He told Corri so when intermission had arrived and he still wasn't certain he had seen his youngest sibling on the big stage.

"But we'll go backstage afterward and meet her," he promised, hoping that he'd be able to find her.

India was quiet throughout the performance, her mind too restless on this night to indulge herself in the intricacies and tension of the dance. She had brought tensions of her own, and it was increasingly difficult to stay in her seat, to keep her mind on the stage and the story that the dancers were bringing to life.

I should be home, reading deposition transcripts, she told herself. *The trial starts on Tuesday, and here I sit at the ballet.*

One glance at Corri's pert little face, so enraptured by the music and the costumes and the choreography, and Indy sighed aloud. It was worth a night away from her work, she decided, to share this evening with Corri. Enjoy it, she told herself, and she tried to force the scripting of her opening arguments from her mind.

She felt Nick's fingers seek her own and his hand close around hers.

And spending time with Nick was good too.

He must think I'm crazy, the way I went after Carson in the restaurant today. She shifted uncomfortably at the memory. The man's stricken face had stayed with her through dinner—hamburgers and salad, which India had prepared for the three of them—and all the while she dressed for the evening. Thinking back to it had only brought back the rush of fear, and she shivered at the reminder. She had reacted like a mother wolf sensing danger to one of her cubs. And yet what reason did she have to suspect there had in fact been any danger?

The resounding applause brought her back. The dancers now crossed the stage, two by two, taking their bows and acknowledging the approval of the audience. She rose as did the others, offering an ovation to the troupe.

"Oh, goody, do we get to meet Georgia now?" Corri asked over the noise, and Nick nodded that they would.

Following the crowd as the lines from each row snaked into the aisle, they headed first to the lobby, then sought the backstage area. It was a full twenty minutes after the performance before they finally found the dressing room.

"Uh-oh." Nick's eyes darted around the crowded backstage lobby, where an entire troupe of women, all in white powdered wigs, identical costumes and makeup, had gathered to sign autographs and chat with friends and relatives.

"Oh, no," Corri groaned. "They *still* all look alike."

"India," Nick said, laughing, "one of these women is my sister. Unfortunately, she could be that one, or that one, maybe the one over in the corner."

"Or perhaps the one right behind you." A slender, red-garbed woman in Kabuki makeup tapped him on the shoulder.

"Georgia"—he embraced her—"I was about to give up."

"You really didn't think I'd let you sneak out without giving me a hug, did you?" Georgia Enright wrapped her arms around her brother's neck and gave him a squeeze.

"Georgia, this is Corri." He put an arm around the child's shoulders.

"Corri, Nicky has told me so much about you." Georgia bent down and offered her hand to the little girl, who took it tentatively in her own. "I'm so happy to meet you."

"Hi," whispered a star-struck Corri, who could barely believe that she was really *there,* backstage among the dancers, those larger-than-life figures who had so recently floated and flown across the stage for all to admire. To have one speak to her made her giddy.

To India's surprise, Georgia turned to her and said, "And of course, you're India." Georgia seemed to be sizing her up. "We were all very sorry about Ry."

"You knew my brother?" How had all the Enrights met her family without her having met any of them?

"We met twice, when I was staying at Nicky's with my mother and sister. He was a good friend to Nicky. We were all saddened to hear of his loss."

"I appreciate your saying so."

Georgia leaned over and whispered in India's ear, "And of course, Mother has told me about you."

"She has?" India's eyes rose halfway to her hairline. "Why?"

"It seems Nicky has mentioned your name more than twice in the same conversation. A dead giveaway." Georgia winked.

"Dead giveaway of what?"

"That my big brother's smitten. I couldn't wait to meet you, and now that I have, I can't wait to tell Mother." Georgia's eyes danced, bright blue sparks in her stark white face. "And for once I actually got the scoop before Zoey. Yes!"

And what exactly, India wondered, would Georgia pass on to Zoey?

"Sibling rivalry can be *such* a bitch." Georgia grinned gleefully. "She'll be so jealous. And if she's nice to me, I'll even tell her that you're as pretty as Nicky said."

"Who will be jealous?" Nick leaned over his diminutive sister.

"Zoey. You know how she always has to be first. I can't wait to tell her that I met India."

To India's total amazement, Nick blushed.

"What makes the feathers stay in your hair, Georgia? How come everyone is wearing wigs?" Corri's interrogation began. "How come you're not wearing a fluffy pink skirt and a little crown? Why is your face so white?"

And why is your face so red, Nicky? India mused, thinking how charming, how adorable he looked, with the faint flush of color still fading from his cheeks. The palms of her hands still bore the delicate pressure from his callused fingers, and a hot rush passed through her, as unexpected to her as Nick's blush had been.

Better be careful, she cautioned herself, watching Nick as he made fond small talk, family talk, with his sister. *This could become very complicated.*

Nick turned to her as if he had read her mind and flashed his very devastating smile in her direction.

Very complicated indeed.

And the complications had only begun, she discovered when they arrived back at the townhouse. After tucking Corri in to India's own bed for the night, she came back downstairs to find Nick very cozy in the living room, making a fire in her fireplace, and a pot of tea sitting atop a magazine on the table in front of the sofa.

"I hope you don't mind." He looked up from the hearth where he knelt, bellows in hand. "I thought a little soothing herb tea might be more restful than coffee."

India nodded, thinking that the thought of a soothing hot beverage was exactly what had prompted her to buy that box of tea months ago. She had brought it home and promptly plunked it in the cupboard, where it had sat, unopened and forgotten, ever since.

"I'll, ah, go get some cups." She felt a sudden urge to flee to safety.

"It's done." He grinned and pointed to the mantel, where two mugs of tea were already cooling.

"Well, I guess you thought of everything," she said, feeling all at once more like the guest than the hostess.

"Well, almost everything." Nick stood up and replaced the black iron poker in the stand resting next to the hearth. "I didn't think to make hotel reservations for tonight. I was wondering if maybe you'd let me sleep on your sofa."

India looked up at him, wondering if he really expected her to fall for that one.

"Nick, I have heard some pretty clever lines, but I haven't heard 'I don't have a place to stay' since I was in college and a boy from Dartmouth had hitched out to see me, hoping to get lucky."

Nick laughed goodnaturedly. "I know how it looks. I promise you that I will not make any attempt to climb into your bed. I swear it. At least not tonight. Especially since I think it's going to be crowded enough, with Corri sleeping there."

He sat down next to her and looked into her eyes. How could anyone think straight while looking into those dreamy, warm brown eyes?

"We have a long way to go, you and I," he said softly. "There are too many things working on your mind right now. I'll fight your demons with you, Indy, and then we'll deal with us. But tonight you can relax, because I have no intention of pushing you somewhere you're not ready to go."

It was a full minute before her brain had fully processed his words. Finally, when she found her voice, she said, "It could take a very long time, Nick, to put it all away. You don't know what I'm up against."

"I have all the time in the world, Indy." His face closed slowly with hers, his lips brushing the side of her jaw, tracing the line to her chin, then in little nibbles to her mouth, which was aching for his. She felt as if she was falling, falling, into a deep warm place where there were no bad guys and there was only warmth and peace.

It terrified her to feel so safe. She was torn between losing herself in him, letting his kisses take her further and further away, and regaining her firm footing in the present, in reality. And yet was this not reality, this warmth spreading through her like molasses?

His thumbs caressed her face on either side and she slid her hands to the collar of his shirt and pulled him closer, needed him closer. She parted her lips slightly and drew him in, the taste of him turning her inside out and making her want only more. When she arched to him he lowered her down onto the sofa and covered her with his long body, his tongue running along the back of her front teeth, making her gasp softly, filling her with a heat she had read about but wasn't sure really existed until she had met him. A large hand on her hip caressed her through her silky dress, and she knew it was itching to move one way or the other, up or down. She couldn't decide which she'd prefer; she wanted his hands on her everywhere at once.

From somewhere through the fog of need that had wrapped around her, she heard a voice whispering, "I think this is not a very good idea."

Opening one eye, she focused on what was closest— Nick's face—and raised an eyebrow.

"As much as I would just about kill right now to slide that silk over your head and do what comes naturally, I think it would be a very bad idea."

"Excuse me?" she squeaked.

Surely she had not heard him clearly.

"Something tells me that you will not be happy in the morning if you let yourself get carried away tonight. You will, I suspect, back off me as if I am diseased and retreat behind your trial list, and any hope I'll ever have of keeping you will be lost."

She made a face and tried to make a protest at the same time, but she knew he was right and wondered how he got so smart.

"I need you for more than one night, India, and I want all of you. I'm not going to let things happen too soon and make you turn away from me." His voice was as sweet and soft as his kisses, and she leaned back to watch his eyes. "There are things eating away at your heart, and we are going to resolve them. But I don't know if you're ready to talk about those things, and until you feel close enough to me to show me where it hurts, we're going to go step by step. And that means I will sleep on the sofa, and you will sleep upstairs with Corri. And tomorrow I'll make you both a big breakfast. But right now, we're going to sit up and you're going to tell me about the case you're trying this week."

"You are not like any man I have ever known," she whispered.

"Good. That's a good start, Indy." He grinned. "A very good start. Now, tell me about the case."

He retrieved the mugs of tea he had made and she told him about Alvin Fletcher. And about his victims, and their families, and the pain this evil man had spread through so many good people. He watched her face, watched her eyes, and listened to the passion in her voice. By the time she had finished, Nick Enright had a very good idea of the nature of the beast he would have to slay in order to win the heart of India Devlin.

He was ready to do whatever it took.

The morning unmarred by the good colonel's rousing early-morning march, it being Sunday, and the wonderful aromas drifting up the stairwell made India believe, for a moment, that she was waking up in heaven. Or at the very least in Devlin's Light. She stretched her legs and hit a lump—a tiny lump, but a lump all the same—twisted up in the blankets at the end of the bed. Corri.

India sat up and looked at the sleeping child, then crawled to the end of the bed to look at her. Sweet Corri. So trusting and so vulnerable. So many heartaches for one so small. Overwhelmed by the need to protect her, to make things right for her, Indy sighed. Nick had been right last night. It had been too soon for them. All things in their own good time. How clever he was to have sensed that, to understand.

And how desirable. Kissable. Hugable. Lovable.

She turned her head at the soft sound in the doorway, where the kissable, hugable, lovable one stood, a soft smile on his face, brown hair tumbled over his forehead. He leaned back against the doorframe, the sleeves of his light gray sweatshirt pulled up to the elbows, his long bare feet, still lightly tanned from a summer spent in the sun, sticking out from his faded blue jeans.

A Sunday morning mirage if ever there was one, she couldn't help but think.

"Are you two going to get up, or do I have to come in there and get you up?"

"Corri's still asleep," she whispered.

"No she's not." The child stretched, her thin arms reaching out from under the blue and white blanket.

"Are you ready for waffles?"

Corri's head shot up.

"With warm syrup?" she asked hopefully.

"And blueberries," Nick told her.

"Yum!" The blankets fairly flew from the end of the bed, and Corri's little feet hit the ground running. "My favorite breakfast. My very favorite breakfast."

She was down the steps before India had a chance to sit up. When she did, Nick was leaning over her, his lips seeking hers.

"I cannot resist a tousled woman," he told her, kissing her softly at first, then with more persistence than she had expected. "Maybe I was a little too gallant last night. Maybe I need my head examined."

"Maybe we should eat those waffles before Corri does," she said, smoothing the hair back from his face.

"Hmmm." He grunted. "It's the story of my life: 'You're cute, Nicky, but given the choice between you and your waffles, well, it's, Please pass the syrup.'"

"Somehow I doubt that very much." She laughed and emerged from the cocoon she had made from blankets and sheets.

"You really are adorable in the morning, you know that?" He took two steps toward her and she hesitated just long enough for him to catch her by the arms and kiss her again. The same three alarms that had gone off between her ears the night before began to whine.

"Nick . . ."

"Hey you guys, the syrup is all bubbly all over the stove," Corri called up the steps.

"Stay away from it, Corri. I'll be right there." He kissed India's nose and frowned. "I'm beginning to wonder if this kid is a blessing or a curse."

India laughed and watched his handsome form trot down the steps.

"Hey, you guys both have sweatshirts and jeans on," Corri observed as India strolled into the kitchen ten minutes later. "I'm going to wear a sweatshirt and jeans too."

She hopped from her chair and sped up the steps.

"How were the waffles?" India touched Corri's shoulder fondly as the child passed by.

"Dee-licious."

"Brush your teeth," India called up the steps as Corri's small figure disappeared around the corner of the bedroom door.

"Those are cold." Nick pointed to the two waffles remaining on the plate in the middle of the kitchen table. "I'll make a few more."

"These are fine," she told him. "I'll put them in the microwave."

"Won't they get soggy?" He frowned.

"Nah, they'll be fine." She opened the glass door to the small appliance, slid the plate in and set the timer. "I take it you ate with Corri?"

"There are some things a man cannot wait for." He grinned. "Waffles are one of those things."

He poured her a cup of coffee and placed it before her on the table and she smiled her thanks. The microwave beeped that it had completed its task. She removed the plate and poured syrup over the waffles.

"I see you're not a butterer," he observed.

"What?"

"You don't butter your waffles before you pour on the syrup."

"Which are you?"

"Oh, I'm a butterer." He nodded as if they were discussing something of great importance. "Corri is a butterer too, just for future reference."

"These are great," she told him. "Wonderful. But where did you find stuff to make waffles with? I haven't shopped in weeks, except to grab the hamburger and salad things from the food market on my way home Friday night."

"I found all this"—he waved his arm across the counter—"in the market at the corner two blocks away."

"Thank you, Nick." She put her fork down and watched him as he picked up his plate and began to rinse it off. "Has anyone ever told you that you are one amazing man?"

"Certainly. But darlin', when I decide that it's time to amaze you, you won't believe your—"

"See? Now we all are dressed alike," Corri said brightly as she dashed into the room.

"We see," India said, both she and Nick laughing at the child's timing.

"Can I play in the leaves outside?" Corri peered through the kitchen window. The day was clear and crisp, and an overnight wind had dotted the back yard with a carpet of colors, which could be raked into a pile just right for jumping into.

"Sure," India told her, "there's a rake in the shed. Just stay in the back yard, Corri. Don't go out front."

"Okay." Corri tugged at the back door and Nick unlocked it for her.

"Is the shed open?" he asked.

"I don't remember." India frowned and started to rise.

"I'll do it. Stay and finish eating before your waffles get cold again."

As the door closed behind him, India took her plate and fork and went to the window, watching Nick stride across the yard.

Admit it, you like his rear view, she chuckled. *And the front view ain't bad either.*

By the time he had returned to the kitchen she was seated at the table, polishing off the last of the waffles.

"This was wonderful." She sighed. "You didn't have to do this."

"Hey, what kind of a man would accept a night's lodging without earning his keep?" He grinned. "Besides, I wanted to impress you with my many talents. I'm a very good cook."

"Do you do everything as well as you cook?" She grinned back.

"Most things. Of course, there are some things I do even better."

"Hmmm. I guess it's up to me to figure out what those things might be."

"And one of these fine days you will, Miss India. Now pour yourself another cup of coffee and turn those teasing eyes away from me or young Corri will get the shock of her life when she comes back through that door and finds us both on the kitchen floor, you up to your ears in my talents."

India laughed again, wondering when she had ever laughed this much in one single morning. It must have been a very long time ago. The thought sobered her and she spun the spoon around and around in her coffee until the swirls resembled a tiny mocha-colored whirlpool. She felt younger today than she had in a very long time. It felt wonderful.

"What did you say?" She tuned back in at the sound of his voice.

"I asked you why you freaked out on that man, Carson, yesterday at the museum."

"I don't know." She turned her face from him abruptly.

"Of course you do." Nick sat down next to her at the table. "What did you think he would do to Corri?"

"Hurt her," whispered Indy.

"Why?"

"Because it happens. Because children are hurt by strangers who look every bit as respectable as Mr. Carson looked. Child molesters are ministers and they are teachers and librarians, and you can't trust anyone with a child." She was unaware that her voice had risen until Nick took her hands. "I have to protect her, Nick. I can't let anything happen to her."

"Nothing will happen to her, Indy. We will take care of her. Nothing will happen to Corri." There was a sureness about him that made her almost believe him. "But I would like you to tell me why you are so afraid for her."

India struggled to get a sound out, but nothing would come.

"India, come here." Nick turned his chair around and pulled her onto his lap, holding her like a child. He put his big arms around her and she felt safe, really safe. "Do you trust me enough to tell me about it?"

She sat listening to his heart for what seemed to be a very long time. When she realized that she could finally speak of the unspeakable, she began in a very soft small voice.

"It was such a hot day that you couldn't walk barefoot on the beach, the sand burned your feet. Lizzie and I had played all day, but not on our beach." She gestured as if sitting on the back porch of August's house, pointing in the direction of the beach at the end of Darien Road. "It was the beach over off Longview. It's right on the bay, and there're better shells there. And more driftwood. We collected driftwood and pretended we were pioneers, gathered around the campfire. We took seaweed that had washed up on the shore and pretended it was logs for our cabin. We laid out a cabin on the sand, outlined with seaweed. We played house all afternoon. Several times I went home and got popsicles for us. The last time Aunt August said we'd had enough, that we'd spoil our dinners. But we wanted just one last one anyway. Lizzie wanted to come with me, but I told her to wait for me on the beach, since it would be easier for me to sneak into the kitchen alone. And I left her there, left Lizzie on the beach and went back to the house. I waited on the back porch until I heard Aunt August go upstairs, and I snuck in and took two more popsicles out of the freezer and ran back to the beach. Lizzie wasn't there. I called and called, but she wasn't there. I figured maybe her brother had come to get her. So I sat down on the dune and I ate both popsicles. Mine and Lizzie's. Then I washed my hands off in the bay—they were sticky and red from the popsicles—and I went home. I ate dinner and I caught lightning bugs in the back yard with Ry."

She leaned back in his arms and sighed. Her voice was steady, but it had a dreamy sort of quality, as if she was telling of something she could see through a haze.

"Lizzie's brother came over around seven-thirty. He'd come to get Lizzie to walk her home. Lizzie hadn't gone home."

She stopped again and sat up, her breath coming a little faster now, though she was clearly striving for control.

"When she hadn't gotten home by eight, all the grownups were worried, and one by one, all the parents sort of drifted out to look for her. I stayed home with Ry and we watched TV. I remembered feeling very, very scared. I had no idea where Lizzie had gone, but I knew—I KNEW—that something very bad had happened. They didn't find her that night. I don't think anyone in Devlin's Light got a wink of sleep. All the parents went out again in the morning to look."

India swallowed hard, and Nick knew that the hardest part was just ahead. He stroked her arm gently with a big open hand and waited until she could go on.

"They found her in the marsh over by the fishing pier at the other end of town." Her voice had gone flat and had a hollow sound to it, as if to distance herself as much as possible from the very words she uttered. "She had been raped and stabbed to death. While I sat on the dunes, eating her popsicle, someone was raping and murdering my friend."

Her voice faded to a whimper, and she began to cry, silently at first, then huge, painful sobs that racked her chest and tore at her throat. Nick held on, steady and sure, while it swept through her, waiting patiently for it to subside, and knew that he had found the key to India Devlin. The child's guilt had become the woman's obsession.

When the sobbing stopped, he asked gently, "How many will you have to convict, sweetheart, how many will you have to put away, before you can forgive yourself?"

Chapter 14

Corri stood in the doorway, ashen, her eyes wide with terror.

"Did Aunt August die?" she asked solemnly, her bottom lip trembling like tall grasses set dancing by a stiff wind.

"No, sweetie, Aunt August didn't die." Poor baby, India thought, that the sight of someone crying could only mean the death of someone important in her life. India opened her arms and the child walked slowly into them.

"Then why are you crying?"

"Because I was thinking about a friend I lost, long ago, and it made me feel sad."

"Did your friend die?"

"Yes. Yes, she did." Indy helped Corri climb onto her lap.

"Why did she die?"

"Because a very bad man hurt her."

"Like the bad men you send to jail?"

"Exactly like them."

Corri twirled a strand of hair around her index finger, then watched it unwind.

"That's why you have to be in Paloma? Because that's where all the bad men are?"

"No, not exactly. There are bad men everywhere."

"Even in Devlin's Light?"

"I suppose there could be."

"Why do you have to send the bad men from Paloma to jail but not the bad men from Devlin's Light? Who sends them to jail?"

"The county district attorney."

Corri's eyes brightened. "I think you should come back to Devlin's Light and make sure that all of the bad guys are in jail. You could help the distant attorney—"

"*District* attorney."

"You could help him so that there would be no more bad guys in Devlin's Light."

"Keep going, Corri. You're doing a fine job," Nick stage-whispered conspiratorially.

"I guess you wouldn't want to move to Paloma and live here with me." India ran her fingers through Corri's hair.

Corri sat up like a shot, studying India's face for a sign that she was teasing her.

"I can see that's an idea that has no future." India tried to smile.

"What would Aunt August do without me?" the child asked earnestly, with no hint of conceit. "She always says she doesn't know what she'd do without me, Indy."

"Well, there is that." India pondered the situation. The look of sheer panic that had crossed Corri's face put an end to any thoughts India might have had of bringing her to Paloma to stay. "Maybe I should just do the smart thing here."

"Which is . . ." Nick asked, wondering what would quali-fy as a smart thing in India's present state of mind.

"Maybe I should finish up this case, then take a leave of absence when it's over. What do you think?" She turned to Nick.

"I think it's a wonderful idea." Nick grinned broadly.

"I don't know what it means." Corri shrugged.

"It means that instead of staying here in Paloma, I would take some time off and not work for a while."

"Like a vacation?"

"A very long vacation."

"How long?" Corri asked cautiously.

"Pretty long. Maybe three months or so."

"That sounds like a long time." Corri thought this over.

"You mean you'd be in Devlin's Light with me and Aunt August, for a long time?"

"Umm-hmm." India nodded.

"That would be very good." Corri tried to contain herself.

"Very good," Nick whispered in India's ear.

The three of them snuggled for a long moment, India on Nick's lap, Corri on India's.

"We're like a little family," Corri observed innocently, "only we're not."

"Family is where you find it," Nick reminded her.

"Like I found Indy and Aunt August after Ry," Corri said.

"Right."

"That would be very good," Corri repeated.

"How long do you think the trial will last?" Nick asked.

"Depends on how many witnesses actually show up."

"You sound worried."

"I'm always worried about someone like Alvin Fletcher slipping through my fingers." She sighed. "He's smart and he's rich and he's resourceful. He has to be watched like a hawk. He's been arrested before and has always managed to wiggle away. I don't want that to happen this time."

"Then I guess that we should get out of your way and let you prepare for tomorrow."

"I like you being in my way." She turned her face to him slightly. "I could get used to having you in my way."

"Do we have to leave now?" Corri frowned.

"What did you have in mind?"

"I wanted Nick to help me build the biggest pile of leaves in the world so I could jump in them."

"Well, you could do that while I work for a while." India wasn't ready to have them leave. It felt too good. Her house felt too good with them there. She felt too good with them there.

"Sounds like fun to me." Nick placed his hands on Indy's hips to propel her forward and off his lap.

"Only Indy has to jump in it too," Corri told them. "Me and Nick will build it, but everyone has to jump in it."

"Deal." India stood up, taking a giggling Corri with her. Setting up her files on the dining-room table, India organized her work into piles. Statements from witnesses. Forensic evidence. Photographs. Copies of files from other jurisdictions where Fletcher had been arrested over the past eight years. As she read through, file to file, she took notes on a yellow legal pad, notes that would later become her opening statement. She was totally immersed when Nick came in to tell her that the pile was ready for her jump.

He leaned over her right shoulder and placed a kiss on her temple, then froze.

"That's a pretty nasty photograph," he said, noting the top picture on the pile.

"Alvin Fletcher's last victim," India told him. Searching through a pile of photos, she found the one she sought and held it up. "This is what Barbara McKay looked like before he got his hands on her."

He did not reply. No words were necessary. The smile of the bright-eyed teenager spoke of a girl who was confident, happy, pretty.

"And this is what she looks like today." The third photo depicted a young woman with frightened eyes and no expression whatsoever.

"Wow," was all he could say.

"Right. Wow." India shook her head. "Alvin Fletcher ruined this girl's life. *Ruined* her life. Destroyed everything she had been before the night she had the unfortunate luck to have crossed his path."

Her jaw hardened as she spoke, her shoulders squared, as if setting off for battle. She looked up at him and watched his face as he looked at the three photographs of the young woman. She thought that maybe he was beginning to understand.

"Do you have time for a jump in the leaves?"

"Is that anything like a roll in the hay?" She tried to smile as she slid the photos back into their protective sleeve.

"When I roll you in the hay, you'll know you've been rolled, woman." He pulled her out of her chair and propelled her toward the back door.

India giggled and allowed herself to be led outside. Corri had insisted that all the leaves from the entire yard be piled right off the deck, making an enormous mound, so that they could jump from the top step right into the leaves.

"You go first, Indy." Corri jumped up and down with gleeful anticipation.

"Well, I haven't done this in a long time, so maybe we should go together." India took Corri's hand and they counted together, jumping at three into the crunchy mattress, sending leaves flying. After two or three jumps, they made Nick jump too. India spent the next twenty minutes combing dead leaves out of her hair and Corri's while Nick made a small fire for her in the living room.

"You can set up your files here"—he pointed to the table—"and sit on the sofa to read. It might be more comfortable."

"It might be too comfortable," she said, though she was terribly pleased by the thoughtful gesture.

"When will you be coming home, Indy?" Corri asked as she strapped herself into the seat of Nick's car.

"May not be for a few weeks." She frowned. "Depends on how long this trial lasts. And how it goes."

"I'll miss you." Corri held her arms out to her and India's heart nearly melted. She leaned into the car to kiss the little girl goodbye.

"I'll miss you too." India straightened Corri's seat belt and looked over to the driver's side, where Nick was already strapping himself in. "I'll miss both of you."

"Good." Nick nodded cheerfully. "That's a very good thing, as Corri would say. Now come around here to my side of the car and kiss me goodbye."

"You should, Indy," Corri noted. "Nick made you waffles. And a fire."

"Corri, you don't ever have to kiss anyone because they do something nice for you." *Let's get rid of that notion right here and now,* India mused. "You kiss people because you want to."

"Don't you want to kiss me?" Nick frowned.

"Actually, I think I do." India leaned over and kissed him on the mouth, not near the way she wanted to, with Corri sitting there giggling, but it would have to do.

"Keep in touch," Nick whispered. "Let me know how things are going. And call me if you need to talk."

"Thank you," she said. "Thank you for everything this weekend. You've given me a lot to think about."

"That's just the start of it, sweetheart." He winked, and she stepped back from the car as he prepared to drive off.

"Indy?" Corri called from the backseat. "What about with, like, Mrs. Cummings?"

"What about Mrs. Cummings?"

"Sometimes she kisses me on the cheek and I don't want to kiss her back."

"Hmmm. Better talk to Aunt August about that one." India laughed as the car pulled away, Corri waving furiously out the window.

"Found yourself a nice widower with a little girl, did you?"

India turned to see the colonel and his wife coming down the sidewalk, dressed in their Sunday best.

"Ah, no." India felt herself blush.

"A divorced fellow, then?" The colonel seemed to frown slightly. Apparently widowers outranked divorced fellows.

"Neither, actually." India tried to smile.

"Now Henry, it's none of our business," the wife, a tiny, birdlike lady, chastised him.

"Actually, he's a friend of the family, and the little girl is my brother's stepdaughter."

"Oh." The colonel and his wife spoke in unison, clearly disappointed.

"Cute little girl, though," the colonel told her. "Watched her in your yard this morning. She sure seemed happy."

"Yes. Yes, she did, didn't she?" India smiled and made her way back to her front door.

Corri was happy. I was happy. Nick seemed happy too. For a fleeting minute she thought that they had, as Corri had observed, seemed like a family. *Don't,* she told herself. *Just because Nick is sweet and obviously interested . . . okay, make that more than interested.*

He likes me. He likes me a lot.

She dragged some files into the living room and cozied up on the sofa, enjoying the warmth of the fire he had prepared for her. She spread open a file on the table before her and spilled photographs out in a long line, trying to concentrate on Barbara McKay, but her mind kept wandering back to Nick. She could almost smell that aftershave he wore, a light, herbal scent.

He had turned her insides to butter and made her breakfast. He had made time in his life for a little girl who needed him and took them to the ballet. He checked in on Aunt August several times a week, bringing her firewood and books from his mother.

He could have made love to her last night but he didn't because he thought the time wasn't right, in spite of the fact that India had been *this close* to totally losing her head.

He had found her deepest hurt, had seen her most secret wound, and had not been appalled by it.

He had wrapped around her like a favorite blanket and held her while she cried.

He had made her feel safe.

He had made her feel the way a man is supposed to make a woman feel.

She toyed with a pen, clicking it on and off, over and over. How could she walk away from a man like that?

She could not. She knew without even acknowledging the fact that the leave of absence had everything to do with Nick as much as with Corri, as much as having an opportunity to investigate Ry's death. She wasn't accustomed to making impulsive decisions, but as soon as the words had slipped out of her mouth, she had known it was right. Corri had had more than enough life changes. Forcing her to come to live in Paloma now was a stupid idea, a truly terrible idea. The child would be totally miserable. What would she do all day while India worked? What about those nights when she worked until midnight or better? Who would watch Corri? The colonel and his missus?

And, India knew, Corri had been absolutely right on the money about Aunt August. She'd be heartbroken to lose Corri. They had held together, these past few months, because they had each other. How selfish of her to expect everyone else to restructure their lives to suit her. No, a leave of absence was exactly the right thing to do, for everyone involved. India could be there for Corri while she was still adjusting to losing Ry, and maybe at the end of her leave she'd have a clearer idea of what was best in the long run. She'd be there to give Aunt August some help with Corri. It would give India a chance to focus on investigating Ry's death.

And it would also give India some time with Nick.

"Nicky," his sister had called him. It suited him, she thought. "Nick" was so adult, so cool. "Nicky" was boyish and sexy.

And he was sexy, no way around that. Eyes to die for, ditto the dimples. She recalled his lanky frame, the long hard arms and legs, strong shoulders, capable hands, clever mouth, all of which had been so very close to her the night before. And she sighed.

Yeah. Nick was *definitely* on her list of things to do in Devlin's Light.

Warm all over, inside and out, she turned her attention to the work before her.

If she needed something to bring her back to reality, *The Commonwealth of Pennsylvania v. Alvin Fletcher* would sure enough do the job.

The courtroom was stuffy, the judge having ordered the windows closed to keep out the steady rain that had fallen since dawn. Too cool for air conditioning, too warm for heat, the air lay heavy and uncirculated, lending a stifling atmosphere to an already tense situation. The defendant had not yet been brought into the room; the prison van had reported a flat tire, delaying the proceedings and keeping everyone on the edge of their seats, like runners held too long at the starting line.

India smoothed her hair for about the fifteenth time and tapped her fingers anxiously upon the table. She had been ready to take him on, Alvin Fletcher and that hotshot lawyer from Philadelphia that the Fletcher money had bought and paid for. She pulled up the sleeves of her black knit dress that skimmed her body to the knee—no too-short skirts for this attorney, not in Judge Swain's court, anyway. Her fingers toyed with the heavy gold chain that lay at the hollow of her neck. For Gentleman Jim Swain's courtroom, classic clothes, classic jewelry, always understated, were the rule of thumb. Women were expected to look and act like ladies, the men like gentlemen. In old Jim's opinion, there were few things more tasteless than a member of the bar dressing inappropriately for court, using foul language or exhibiting bad manners in public. No such behavior was tolerated in the lawyers who came before him.

India's eyes shifted to the defense attorney who sat waiting impatiently at the next table, noting that he sighed loudly, with exaggerated exasperation, every so often. He tapped a pen noisily on the desk. He had declined pointedly to take India's hand when she'd offered it to him earlier that morning.

Bad manners, all.

Gentleman Jim was watching.

India smiled to herself. She needed any extra help she could get. The Philadelphia lawyer, Andres, had the reputation of being next to impossible to beat. He was cocky and he was arrogant, so rumor had it, but he won. He took cases that no one else would touch, charged a king's ransom for his time, ate up the prosecutor's case and spent the next month on a beach somewhere.

That would account for the tan. And the attitude.

Well, Mr. Tanner-than-thou, we'll see what Gentleman Jim thinks of you.

She heard a slight rustle behind her and turned to see Barbara McKay and her parents enter the courtroom. Barbara looked terrified, her father looked murderous. Andres glanced over his shoulder, looked Barbara up and down, then turned away, as if to dismiss her. Inside, India began to seethe. How dare he treat this young woman with such blatant disrespect.

India helped the McKays to their seats immediately behind the railing that separated the prosecutor's table from the general seating area in the old-fashioned courtroom. Judge Roy Bean—or Judge Robert Devlin, for that matter—would have been right at home. Since the defendant had not yet arrived, India sat and talked with the victim and her family, trying to calm their nerves, going over yet again how the proceedings would run.

It was almost ten o'clock when Alvin Fletcher was led

into the courtroom. In his brown tweed jacket and his well-tailored tan wool slacks, he looked like anything but a man who got his kicks hurting women. A "wolf in sheep's clothing" so accurately fit. Fletcher sat in the chair that his lawyer held out for him, seated himself, and immediately bent his head close to Andres's, deep in conversation.

Birds of a feather, Aunt August would say.

Gentleman Jim called both prosecuting and defense counsel to him. *The People v. Alvin Fletcher* was about to begin.

It had taken one and a half days to pick a jury, one and a half days that Barbara McKay had to sit and watch Alvin Fletcher as he played it so very cool. Outside the courtroom, Barbara had broken down, and India worried about her ability to hold up on the stand, despite Barbara's assurance that when the time came she would be there.

India spent the next two days arguing points of law, trading case law back and forth, another full day of arguing motions. Court adjourned early on Friday, sending India home with a briefcase full of statements and a list of witnesses—newly disclosed to the court by the defendant—whom she wanted to interview.

No time off with Nick and Corri this weekend, she told herself wearily as she dragged the heavy leather case up the front steps of the townhouse.

No cozying up in front of the fire with an irresistible man, she lamented, turning the key in the lock and pushing open the front door.

No wonderful breakfast. She scooped up a hefty pile of mail and plopped it onto a chair in the living room.

No pile of leaves to share with a happy six-year-old. She tossed her coat wearily onto a chair in the living room.

India glanced at the clock. Corri would be getting ready for her bath right about now. Aunt August would have just finished the dinner dishes. And Nick?

She could all but see him. He'd be standing on the deck outside his cabin, wearing a heavy sweater and softly worn corduroy pants. He'd be leaning on the railing, his after-dinner cup of coffee in his hands, and he'd be looking out across the bay. From the deck, if the evening was clear enough, he'd be able to see a faint glow of lights from Cape May. He'd swirl the last bit of coffee around in the bottom of the cup. He'd be thinking . . .

He'd be thinking about me.

Smiling, knowing for certain it was true, she kicked off her shoes and padded into the living room. The evening's workload suddenly seemed a little lighter.

Chapter 15

The intricacies of the human mind never failed to captivate India's imagination, and it was with total fascination that on Monday morning she watched Alvin as he studied his fingernails and awaited the court's ruling on yet another motion. Here, she thought, was a perfect example of nature gone wrong for no apparent reason. No childhood trauma, à la Ted Bundy, to use as an excuse. From all reports, even his own, Alvin's parents had been loving, caring individuals, totally involved with all their children, an older daughter, a daughter younger than Alvin, then yet another younger brother. Even now they sat together, in the back of the courtroom, a tightly knit unit, as still and emotionless as mannequins, as if stunned to find themselves where they were, not really comprehending the circumstances that had caused them to gather there.

One of Alvin's sisters sat next to their mother, holding her hand motionlessly. Just a few more victims of Alvin's twisted mind, India thought, watching them, huddled along the last row. She studied them one by one, feeling their pain from across the length of the room. It was then that the younger sister, a pretty girl of maybe nineteen or so, entered the courtroom and made her way to her seat at the end of the row, next to her father. As India began to shift her gaze back to the front of the room, she became aware that Alvin too had turned his eyes to his family, and for the first time since being led into the courtroom, a blush of something—could it have been fear?—crossed his face. India turned back once again, seeking the source of his alarm.

There, she thought, her eyes pausing on the face of the younger sister.

She is not surprised. She knows. India's breath caught in her throat.

The girl's face wore a harder veneer than the other members of her family, but beneath it, India recognized the look of triumph, of justice. Of having watched the beast caged and secretly rejoicing in its capture. Wondering what the girl might have suffered at the hands of her older brother, India's eyes shifted from brother to sister, then back again, watching the silent interplay between them.

And in that instant, India knew that she had him.

At the earliest opportunity, India caught Alvin's gaze and, with total deliberation, looked down the rows of spectators to the last row, then back at Alvin. India then crossed her arms over her chest, sat down, leaned back in her chair and smiled broadly. Alvin blanched, nervous eyes darting from his sister, who was whispering something to her father, and back to India, who continued to smile knowingly. When the judge called her and Andres to the bench to discuss a ruling, India strode to the front of the courtroom with all the confidence of a sure winner. Alvin shifted uneasily in his seat and fiddled with his cufflinks.

Damn, I should have been an actress, India mused.

Call Kosieki and tell him I want him to come into court and sit in the back row next to the youngest Fletcher girl. I want him to talk to her, even if it's only about the weather, India wrote on a notepad, adding *and make sure Alvin sees him.* She passed the pad to the young policewoman who sat behind her in the front row, waiting her turn to testify as to her findings at the crime scene. She nodded, then grinned at India and went off in search of a telephone to call the detective India had requested.

Dave Kosieki was big, blond and handsome, very Ivy League. Just the type of guy, India guessed, that the younger

Fletcher woman was accustomed to, the type she'd smile at when he sat next to her in the back of the courtroom. The type she'd engage in conversation. Alvin would have no way of knowing it was all small talk. Chances were his guilty conscience would assume it was something more. Especially after a day or two of watching Kosieki with his sister. And especially after India added the girl's name to the list of witnesses she'd be calling. It was unlikely that the girl would, in fact, tell them anything; the family unit looked too tight, too close. But Alvin wouldn't know that for sure.

I'm going to smoke you out, brother. She smiled at him again as she prepared to leave as court was dismissed for the day. She made a point of walking briskly to the back of the court, of giving the impression of pausing at the end of the back row on the end where the sister sat. Alvin stretched his neck to watch her as he was being led through the door.

There's a little something to think about while you're laying in your cell tonight, bucko.

After two days of watching his younger sister getting cozy with the lead detective, Alvin tried to plea bargain. India smiled and gave the appearance of considering his offer before refusing to make a deal. She had him rattled now, she knew it. If he took the stand to testify, he would crack. She could see it in his face. She knew the look of a coward. And Alvin Fletcher was, above all else, a coward. India could smell his fear, and she knew she had him.

He broke two days before Thanksgiving. Against the advice of his counsel—Andres made it perfectly clear to Judge Swain that he had vehemently opposed his client's action—Fletcher entered a guilty plea. It was all over but the sentencing, which would come weeks later.

India stood at the side of the prosecutor's table and held hands with the victim and her family while they offered their thanks and asked a special blessing for India, who had helped them take the first step toward making things right again.

"You taking off this weekend?" India asked Roxie as she returned from court, her cheeks still flush with exuberance.

"Going to Tom's parents in Harrisburg," she said, rolling her eyes, "where there will be a cast of thousands gathered, each of them waiting to grill me on when we'll be adding to the population. Great going, India. I heard you had Fletcher peeing himself. What did you do to him, anyway?"

"Fed him his worst fear." India grinned, accepting a congratulatory hug from Herbie, who himself was on his way to court on a DUI. "Then I watched him choke on it."

The roadside stands that had in the summer months sold wooden baskets of corn and tomatoes and squash were all boarded up as India drove the last country mile to Devlin's Light. She was grateful for the good timing on Alvin's part, entering his plea when he did, which served to extend the long Thanksgiving weekend, thus giving everyone a little something extra to be thankful for. This year India would have time to help Aunt August prepare for the traditional Thanksgiving feast, which would bring Devlins from far and wide back to the family homestead. For the second time that year, they would all gather, August's elderly cousins and their spouses and children and their children's children. They would count heads and count their blessings, pausing to remember those who had passed on during the year. This year Ry's name, along with that of an elderly greataunt, would be entered in the Devlin family Bible. It would be a hard moment for Aunt August, India knew, when the time came for her on Thursday to write his name there, below their father's.

India drove past the edge of the marsh where red-winged blackbirds perched territorially on cattails that slumped at varying angles above the tidal pools. She opened her car windows to drink in the scent of it, her nostrils seeking the smell of salt and bay. Pleased when she was able to fill her lungs with the brisk sea air, she relaxed against the car seat. She was home.

Passing by the lane leading to Nick's she paused a split second, then fought off the urge to take that left up the drive of stone and crushed shell to the cabin. Later, she decided. *I'll stop in later.* In her mind's eye, she could see the look on his face as he would watch her climb the stairs leading to his back door. He'd be looking out the kitchen window toward the bay. Or maybe he'd be sitting on the deck, watching the mallards land feet first out past his floating dock. Maybe when he saw her, he'd—

"Hey, stranger, you're home early!"

The blast from the horn of the small red car that had pulled next to her at the one stoplight in the center of town shook India abruptly from her fantasy.

"Darla, hi! I was going to call you tonight."

"I heard this incredible rumor." Darla leaned over the seat, her eyes dancing. "I heard on good authority that you are coming home for a while. Could that be possible?"

"It could." India nodded.

"When?"

"Well, I still have to talk to my boss, but I'd like to do it as soon as possible."

"Strictly for Corri's sake, of course." Darla's eyes glistened with mischief.

"Of course, for Corri." India frowned.

"And the presence of a certain handsome man having taken up residence in Devlin's Light would have nothing to do with your decision."

"Darla, how do you know?"

"Corri told us at dinner the other night that she and Nick spent the weekend with you in Paloma a few weeks back. In your house. Both of them."

"Anything else she piped into the neighborhood hotline?"

"Only that Nick made you breakfast on Sunday morning." Darla laughed.

"Well, I'd say she didn't miss much," India grumbled. "I think Miss Corri and I are going to have to have a talk."

"Too late," Darla told her cheerfully. "Everyone in Devlin's Light has already heard about it."

"I don't suppose she bothered to tell anyone that Nick slept on the sofa and that she slept with me."

"Nope. Don't remember having heard that part. Okay, okay, I'm going," Darla called over her shoulder to the driver of the car that had pulled behind her at the light and was now blowing the horn, anxious to proceed.

"I'll catch up with you tomorrow. August invited us to join you for dessert." Darla waved as she sped off.

India pulled all the way up the driveway to park in the

shadow of an ancient pine. The slamming of the car door startled a squirrel, which had been foraging at the base of the tree, seeking acorns that might have been previously overlooked. From a branch halfway up a jay scolded, and across the yard finches and chickadees chatted at the bird feeder Ry had given to Aunt August for her birthday three years ago. The perennial bed that ran the length of the back fence, so lush with color just months earlier, now displayed little more than dried stalks that had once held glorious day lilies. The remains of what had been tall, nodding heads of red and white phlox, even through October, now sagged toward the cushion of leaves discarded by the elm, maple and sassafras trees that lined the way leading out toward the dunes.

A lone herring gull circled overhead, its summer-white head feathers beginning to streak brown, signaling, her father would have said, a harsh and early winter. India shielded her eyes against the sun with one hand while she watched it glide and dip closer to the beach, calling to its compadres of some impending danger with a sharp *ga ga ga ga*. Stepping around the fence to the back of the dune, she walked to its crest, her feet sinking slightly into the sand, and scanned the sky. Nothing. Motion from the top of a nearby telephone pole at the back of the Kesslers' property several hundred feet away caught her eye. Indy held her breath and watched as the bald eagle took flight across the marsh. It was a sight that had never failed to thrill her, to fill her with wonder. The massive bird soared on flat wings toward the densely wooded area beyond the marsh.

She wondered how many were nesting now in and around Devlin's Light and thought back over the years, to Christmases when she and Ry had accompanied their father on the annual bird count, which recorded the birds seen on that one day at the Light. The first few years she had been less than a gracious participant, wanting only to play with her dolls and read her new books so early on the long awaited day, but over the years her interest had grown, until she and Ry had become rivals in their search for the largest number of recorded species. She remembered clearly the first bald eagle she had ever seen. It had soared from the top of the lighthouse the Christmas India had been nine and left her breathless in the wake of its majestic flight. She had never forgotten the sight of that bird as it winged its way across the inlet, and never again had she complained about having to count birds on Christmas morning. Determined to keep the tradition alive, she thought perhaps she'd take Corri with her this year. And maybe Nick, if he was free.

Maybe she'd drive over to see him later, she was thinking as she walked toward the house. Less than twenty feet from the back door, the smells of holiday baking seeped out to greet her.

"Ah, Aunt August." India sighed with pleasure, knowing the sight that awaited her on the other side of the back-porch door. "It's good to know that some things never change."

She stood in the doorway and inhaled, grinning broadly. That little Dorothy girl with the ruby slippers had gotten it right, all right. There was no place like home.

Mince pies and pumpkin, apple and cherry stood side by side with a row of peach cobblers across the counters.

"Now don't stand there with that back door open," August scolded as she wiped flour from her hands onto her apron.

"Sorry, Aunt August." India leaned to sniff the cobbler as she passed by on her way to hug her aunt. "Ah, glorious."

"India Devlin, I swear you have stuck your face in every peach cobbler I have baked for the past twenty-nine years."

"A record I pride myself on." India winked. "Oh, it's so good to be home. What can I do to help?"

"You can keep out from underfoot," August told her as she cut butter into a bowl for the crust of what would become yet another pie. Apple crumb, India guessed, judging from the pile of thinly sliced apples mounded in the old mixing bowl. "By the way, we saw you on the news this morning."

"Saw me on the news?" India frowned and opened the cupboard. She needed coffee to go with the smidge of cobbler she planned to talk her aunt out of.

"They showed you coming out of the courtroom the other day after that rapist changed his plea to guilty. Such a nice-looking young man and such a lovely family." August *tsk-tsked* as she floured her pastry board.

"Why would they show that today? The trial was over on Monday."

"His attorney read a statement he made—get that spoon away from that cobbler, India Devlin—about why he had confessed to the crime." August paused to point toward the coffeepot. "That coffee's been sitting there since around seven this morning. Make a new pot and I'll join you in a cup as soon as I finish this pie."

"What did he say?" India asked, curious now.

"He said that he had to confess because the prosecutor had worked voodoo on him."

India burst out laughing.

"He what?"

"He said you put some sort of spell on him and he had to tell the truth." August looked up and grinned. "Oh. And the newspaper reporter referred to you as 'Voodoo Devlin.' "

"Oh, for crying out loud." India banged her cup on the counter. "Are you serious?"

"Umm-hmm." August nodded. "Most unprofessional, I thought."

"Oh, brother." India groaned.

"Now, can his lawyer go back to the judge and ask that the case be tried again?"

"He would have to prove that I somehow did something illegal or underhanded, which of course I did not do." India could almost hear the razzing she would get when she returned to her office. Suddenly she wished she had already put in for her leave.

"I'm thinking about taking a leave of absence."

"So I heard."

"Corri."

"She is so happy. All she talks about is when Indy comes home to stay." August flattened a mound of dough with the same wooden rolling pin that had been used by her mother. "Just make sure she understands that a leave is *temporary*, India. She has to understand that it doesn't mean you're coming home for good."

"I know." India nodded.

"Three months will seem like a much longer time to her than it will to you, so don't lose sight of that."

"Okay."

"India, I don't want that child hurt by one more leaving."

"Neither do I."

"She seems to have it in her head that you might stay."

"I told her it would only be like a long vacation for me. I'll talk to her again."

"Why?" August turned to her niece. "Why does it have to be only that? Why can't you come home for good, India?"

"Maybe I can, Aunt August. Maybe that's one of the things we'll find out over the course of the next few months."

August turned the crust into the pie plate and fit it close to the sides with sure fingers.

"Not that you're not doing a wonderful job with Corri, Aunt August. I don't for a second mean to imply that I think—"

"Please." August held up one hand. "For heaven's sake, India, I'm sixty-five years old. Too old to do a lot of things with her that need to be done. Darla has kindly lent a hand, and Nick is always there for us, but what if something happened to me, India? What would she do?"

"Aunt August, nothing is going to happen—"

"India, I'm not being negative, I'm simply being practical."

"I thought about taking Corri to Paloma with me," India said softly, waiting for a reaction.

"I was afraid you would, sooner or later."

"I don't think it's the best thing for her."

"You won't get an argument from me."

"I think she belongs in Devlin's Light," India told her. "I guess I just need to know if I belong here or not."

"Well, I guess by the time your three months are up, we should have a pretty good idea, won't we?" August dumped the apples into the crust with one swift motion.

"I guess." India nodded and poured water into the coffee maker she and Ry had bought for August several Christmases back. "This thing is slow as molasses," she noted, "and it's making a funny noise."

"Just needs cleaning. You can do it after dinner."

"Is the entire clan gathering tomorrow?"

"Of course. Dan and Mabel Jane will be here by noon, as always, with their families." August ran down the list of cousins and when they were expected to arrive. "Claire and Bonnie will be in around two. Dinner is set for four, as always, and dessert will be at seven."

"Why so late?"

"Because Gordon and Evie were going to their grandson's for dinner but they did want to stop by. Christine and Andrew were having guests, but they wanted to stop by. So I decided to have a dessert buffet this year. So that everyone could come for the memorial if they wanted to."

"That's a lovely idea." India nodded, thinking it would extend the holiday, which would be nice for Corri. And good for her and Aunt August to be very busy on this first holiday without Ry.

"And I invited some other folks." August waved her hand vaguely. "I left a message on Nick's answering machine and told him he was welcome to stop by and join us."

"Did he call back and say he would?" India asked with all the nonchalance she could muster.

"I didn't ask him to. India, get that phone for me, will you?"

One of the ladies from Aunt August's card club, wanting to know what time the dessert buffet would be. With a chuckle, India turned the telephone over to her aunt and, pouring herself a cup of coffee, walked back outside and followed the lane to its end, where it met the beach.

It was beautiful on this cool November afternoon. India sunk back into her fisherman's knit sweater and sat on the back of the overturned rowboat that sat on the beach. Ry's boat. She wondered what to do with it, since she couldn't drag it back to the house by herself.

On a whim, she rolled it on its side and slid it across the sand to a point where the bay was deepest, the bottom falling off about a foot offshore. Tucking the oars inside, she climbed in and pushed off, first on one side, then on the other, until the bottom of the small boat cleared. Her face into the wind, she rowed toward the end of the inlet. She had missed him terribly, she admitted, and wanted to see him. She would surprise him. She smiled to herself as she rowed with a solid stroke to where the marsh began. Following the line of cattails and marsh grasses, she rowed quietly, stopping sometimes to let the current take her. It was such a clear day, so perfect, cloudless and sunny. It was wonderful to be here. The sounds of the marsh, the smell of the bay, the warmth of the sun filled her with a joy she had not experienced in years.

Still reveling, she floated around the tip of the inlet, fifty feet from Nick's floating dock. Her heart leapt at the sound of the screen door slamming, and she looked up, seeking his form at the railing.

She had not been prepared for the woman who stood next to him on the deck. Tall and lean, with waves of black hair swirling in the wind around what even from a distance was clearly a perfect face. The woman's light laughter rang out as Nick appeared and draped an arm over her shoulder in a clear and casual sign of affection. India sat down in her little boat, momentarily stunned, a hole the size of Nebraska opening in her chest.

Her heart pounding, India rowed as quietly as possible to the edge of the marsh, hoping that the tall grasses would hide her presence and permit her to flee unseen, back to the inlet, not quite certain that she was ready to know who the woman was or how she fit into his life.

Cranberry-Cherry Crisp

Topping:

1 cup flour
1 cup old-fashioned oats (not instant)
2/3 cup packed brown sugar
1/2 cup (1 stick) butter at room temperature

Mix flour, oats and brown sugar in bowl. Cut butter into pieces. Combine butter with the flour/oat mix, until the mixture resembles coarse meal.

Filling:

1 large jar cherry pie filling
1 bag fresh cranberries
2/3 cup sugar
1/2 tablespoon grated orange peel

Wash cranberries and sort through, discarding berries that are mushy or white. Put cranberries into a pot with just enough water to cover, add sugar and heat through till boiling, about 10 minutes. Drain berries, combine in a large bowl with the cherry pie mixture, grated orange peel and sugar.

Butter the bottom of a 13x9x2-inch glass baking dish. Pour fruit mixture into dish and crumble topping over fruit. Bake in a preheated 350° oven for 25–30 minutes, or until the fruit is bubbly and the topping has browned.

Chapter 16

*T*hanksgiving at the Devlin homestead varied little from one year to the next. At some point or another during the day, all of the Devlin cousins made an appearance. If not for dinner, then for brunch or later in the evening for dessert. But sooner or later, they all arrived at August's front door, where they would be welcomed with open arms.

As a child, India had passed through the crowded rooms with canapés and candies on serving plates, or silver trays of spice cookies and tiny fruit tarts, depending on the time of day. Corri, being the youngest in the house these days, had inherited those duties, and having cut her teeth on passing small plates of peppermints two years earlier and trays of scones at last year's brunch, she was ready for full duty this year, much to her pride.

August had cooked and baked and bustled since six that morning. India performed what she called the "accessory tasks"—chopping celery, cutting bread rounds for canapés, peeling potatoes and carrots, making sure that there was always fresh coffee and hot water for tea, cleaning the counters and rinsing bowls—while August took center stage in preparing the turkeys that would grace the dining-room table and serve as the focal points of the buffet to serve however many would show up that day. They were age-old rituals that, August liked to say, were being observed in countless homes all across the country in much the same way as in Devlin's Light. It was what she liked to refer to as a "connecting cord," one of those common threads that wound through the fabric of so many folks from different backgrounds and ethnic groups in cities and suburbs, farms and penthouses, from one coast to the other. It was part of what made Thanksgiving a uniquely American holiday, she had often reminded India, and part of the reason for celebration. Every year, while India worked side by side with her aunt, August would recite what India had come to think of as the "whos and the whats" of the Devlin clan.

"Now, look for Lil—she's first cousin to your dad and me—to be the first to arrive, usually by eleven. She'll have a basket of pumpkin muffins on her arm and one of her granddaughters in tow. The rest of her group will arrive later, but Lil likes to be first. Her kids will stay for brunch, but they'll leave to take the grandkids to the in-laws for dinner. Then Lil's sister, Rachel, will be next, with all her brood. Children and grandchildren. Rachel will bring the biggest already cooked, already sliced ham she can find, along with her homemade rolls and that cranberry relish of hers that won, oh, more blue ribbons than I can recall at the state fair several years running."

India would be thinking about Aunt Lil's fragrant pumpkin muffins and those puffy, golden brown rolls of Aunt Rachel's, and her mouth would be watering from early in the morning until dinner.

"Then of course, Jenny Devlin will come after brunch with several bottles of her elderberry wine—the same elderberry wine that has, over the years, been responsible for more than one Devlin embarrassing him- or herself before the day is over." August chuckled.

Jenny Devlin—who, like August, had never married—would take charge of the dinner table, keeping the diners moving around the buffet, making sure that a bowl or platter was refilled the very second it was emptied, keeping a steady supply of clean plates and utensils flowing from the kitchen. To accomplish this particular feat, she commandeered members of the younger generations to wash, dry and restock the dishes so that there was never a shortage.

Everyone helped out, everyone ate well and everyone left swearing that next year they wouldn't eat quite so much.

And it had all gone exactly as August had predicted. The brunch group had barely departed when the first of the dinner crowd arrived. The pace had kept India on her feet and moving, and it had given her something to focus on besides the pain that had taken up residence under her ribs when the tall, raven-haired beauty had walked onto Nick's deck as if she belonged there. It had stung more than India had thought possible.

India had barely recovered from the dinner shift when August announced that dessert would be forthcoming shortly, an event that would be marked by a seemingly endless parade of pies and cobblers as well as Jenny's Lady Baltimore cake, a trifle prepared by one of Claire's daughters and several cheesecakes by one of Mae's, a crème brûlée, which had seemed to appear from nowhere, and a very elegant-looking sacher torte. The doorbell rang constantly as those August had invited only for dessert began to crowd through the front hallway into the parlor.

Over the heads of August's card-playing buddies India could see Darla enter the dining room, accompanied by Jack and Ollie, both of whom disappeared into the kitchen with Corri, only to emerge minutes later with small trays of chocolates that the girls passed to the guests, Jack following behind to snitch first one, then another of the homemade truffles brought by who knew whom. India hugged Darla in the doorway and pulled her into the kitchen for a breather.

"I am dead on my feet," India told her, as she sank gratefully into a nearby chair, seeking a comfort that she knew would be only temporary. "And my aunt barely looks winded."

"She's a breed apart from the likes of us." Darla laughed. "How many people have come through that door today?"

"I have no idea. All of Aunt August's cousins and at some point during the day most of their families. Then she invited several people that she knew from town who had noplace to go today for dinner, her card club, various and sundry others, so that swelled the ranks. She thrives on all this, I swear she does."

"Well, you'd best be taking notes, honey, because someday all of this will be yours." Darla waved her hand toward the dining room, and India groaned.

"I heard that, Darla Kerns," August said, entering the kitchen with a silver pot from the ornate service that stood upon the sideboard. "And I'll have you know that I'm not ready to throw in my apron just yet."

August hugged her in passing, then handed India the coffeepot. "India, refill this, please, and check to see that the creamer is full."

"I'll hit the creamer, you fill the pot," Darla told India, who was rising slowly from her chair. "It will give me an excuse to nab a slice of the sacher torte before it's all gone."

A newcomer appeared in the kitchen doorway, a handsome woman in her midfifties, simply dressed in a heather-gray cashmere sweater set and matching skirt that closely matched her hair. Her eyes were lively and her smile bright. She was familiar, somehow, though India knew she'd never met her before. She would have remembered. The woman wore a sure and casual presence the way some women wore perfume.

"Is August here?" she asked India.

"Yes, I'm . . ." August poked out from the butler's pantry where she had been dusting a tray of cream puffs with powdered sugar. "Delia! Why I'm so pleased to see you!"

"I was hoping you wouldn't mind." The elegant woman beamed and pecked a kiss on August's cheek, placing a beautiful gift basket on the counter as she did so. "Nicky said you'd invited him to stop over this evening. I didn't expect to still be here tonight, but we had a rather full house at Nicky's for dinner."

"I'm delighted that you've joined us." August patted her arm.

India tried to sneak past her aunt's back to escape up the back steps while she tried to talk her heart into beating at a normal rate.

"Delia, I'd like you to meet my niece, India." August grabbed her with one hand as she started for the doorway. "India, this is Delia Enright. Our favorite author. And Nick's mother, of course."

"India. I'm so pleased to meet you." Delia held out a hand that was impeccably manicured and beautifully jeweled. A fat diamond in a wide gold band. A tennis bracelet set with rubies. Diamond studs. A wide shimmer of gold at her neckline.

"It's my pleasure, Mrs. Enright," India said, forcing her best manners into play. "And my aunt is correct, you are my favorite author."

"Really?" Delia laughed. "Then everything I've heard about you is obviously true. And please, call me 'Delia.'"

India was just about to ask what Delia had heard, and from whom, when Nick appeared, dragging the dark-haired beauty past the dessert table and into the kitchen. The young woman was even more beautiful close up, with flawless ivory skin and laughing sapphire-blue eyes. India searched the deepest recesses of her memory to try to recall if she had ever felt such a stab of jealousy the likes of which she experienced at that very moment. It seemed to rip at her insides and burn all the way to her throat.

"India." Nick smiled at her and reached for her hand, and that only made things worse. She felt weak-kneed and confused that he would bring this woman into her house, into her family gathering.

"Oh!" the young woman said. "So you're India. Nicky has told me so much about you. I'm Zoey."

Zoey?

"Nicky's sister." She offered a slender hand to India, who could not seem to react quickly enough to take it.

"Nicky's sister," India repeated dumbly.

His sister. You idiot, she's his sister! Yes! His sister!

"India," August said pointedly. *What has addled that girl?*

India looked down at the hand that was still stretched out and waiting.

"Oh. Oh, I'm sorry." India, relieved to the point where she fought the urge to kick her heels together and dance, attempted to recover. "I . . . um . . . I have something sticky on my hands . . . that's why I didn't . . ."

August turned her head to look at her as if she was daft. Delia looked down at her own hand, as if searching for some sticky residue India might have left there. Not finding any, she shrugged.

Nick folded his arms and leaned against the doorway,

terribly amused by India's totally uncharacteristic bumbling.

"I was just telling Mother that this is how I always pictured a proper Thanksgiving. We always have just us. Though this year we had Georgia and a few of her friends from her dance troupe." Zoey's voice was pure honey over whiskey, sexy and sure.

"Is Georgia here?" India attempted to redeem herself by speaking coherently.

"No, they all went back to Baltimore. She's doing the Nutcracker starting tomorrow evening. Mother invited her and all her friends to Nicky's for dinner."

"And did Nicky cook dinner?" India directed the question to Nick.

"Now, do I detect a bit of sarcasm there, Miss Devlin?" Nick frowned, reaching out to snag her arm and pull her toward him. "I'd be willing to bet that I did more cooking today than you did."

"Don't let him con you, India," Zoey stage-whispered. "Mother's *cook* cooked dinner."

"Hey, who heated everything up, huh?" Nick pretended to be wounded that his sister had seemingly belittled his efforts.

"You did, Nicky." Zoey patted him on the back affectionately and pretended to be contrite. "And you did a damned fine job too."

"Well then, now that Nick is here, I think we can start, India." August tapped her on the arm. "Will you please get the family Bible and call everyone into the front parlor for the memorial?"

India's throat tightened. She had tried not to think about this part of the Thanksgiving ritual. Every year, the names of those who had departed this world over the past twelve months would be entered into the old family Bible, and those who had something to say about—or to—the deceased would have a chance to do so. It was a beautiful tradition, a fine way of remembering those whose presence would be missed at future family gatherings.

"Nick, could I impose upon you to help my nephew Adam pass the champagne for the toast?"

August handed Nick two bottles of well-chilled champagne and led him off in search of Adam, calling over her shoulder, "India, go out on the back porch and tell the children it's time."

Within minutes, the entire group was crowded into the front parlor, many of them spilling into the hallway. A hush had fallen upon them, their voices lowering to a whisper one might reserve for church.

August lit the candles that were clustered atop the baby-grand piano in the corner, upon which rested the Devlin family Bible and a gold fountain pen.

"Jeremy." August nodded to her cousin, the oldest of the male Devlins gathered.

"Tonight we will record the names of those we have lost since the last time we gathered here." The elderly man's voice was low but steady. "August, if you will do the honor of adding the name of Evelyn Devlin Boone. Is there anyone who would like to say a word about Evie?"

"I remember the summer Evie and I were sixteen." Cousin Berry—Barbara—spoke up, her old woman's voice strong despite her eighty-five years. "It was 1927, and all the girls were bobbing their hair. Evie was the first one in Devlin's Light to sneak off to the hairdresser's down on Hoolihan's Lane and get her hair cut short and curled. Oh, my, what a scandal she caused in church the next morning." Berry chuckled, then paused for just a moment before adding, "I always thought Evie had more fun than anyone I knew. I always wished that I could have been as bold as Evie."

The silence in the room was expectant, respectful. August's cousin Jeremy looked around the group to see if anyone else had memories to share of cousin Evie. Evie's children spoke up, one by one, each recalling an anecdote that demonstrated a cherished aspect of their mother's character. When the last tribute had been spoken, Jeremy raised his glass and said, "To Evelyn," to which the others responded, "May she rest in peace."

"Robert Forman Devlin." Jeremy announced the name slowly, and August nodded, making the letters with a firm hand upon the page.

There was a very long, heavy silence before Elena Carney, a contemporary of India's, spoke up.

"When I was little and afraid of the water, Ry took me in the bay and taught me how to swim." Elena stopped, overcome and unable to continue.

"The year my dad died, Ry went on my Cub Scout camping trip with me," Bill Devlin recalled, then smiled a shaky half smile. "He taught me how to mark a trail, how to make a fire, how to catch crabs with your hands. He was like a big brother to me." Bill's voice faltered and he shrugged his shoulders, adding, "He was the best."

And so it went, everyone in the room adding a little something. India thought she could almost feel him there, could imagine his smile, which would be humble and grateful for the accolades. It was the closest she had permitted herself to feel toward him since the morning they buried his body up on the little rise overlooking the bay. Finally, when it was her turn to speak, she said simply, "Ry was a very special man who left us long before he should have. I get angry every time I think about all of the sunsets he'll never see, all of the birdsongs he'll never hear. Ry loved Devlin's Light, and he loved this family, and we are all a little better for having been loved by him. I miss him terribly."

She swallowed the hard, tennis ball of a lump in her throat. "Darla?" she said softly, offering her a chance to speak.

"I can't." She shook her head.

India nodded to Jeremy to indicate she was finished, and he looked around the room. When it appeared that all the tributes had been made, he raised his glass. Before he could speak, however, Corri tugged on India's skirt and said, "Can I tell about Ry too?"

"Of course you may, sweetie." India lifted the child in her arms so that she could be seen by the rest of the family. "What would you like to say?"

"That Ry wanted to be my daddy, and he read good stories to me. He played soccer with me." Her tiny fingers twisted a button on the front of her dress. "And he told me all about birds and shells. He took me fishing. Sometimes he called me 'Amber,' 'cause he said that sometimes my hair looked like amber." Her fingers tugged at a curl. "He was so fun. And I wish he didn't die."

"Thank you, Corri. I sincerely doubt that anyone in this room could have paid a more eloquent tribute to Ry than you just did." Jeremy smiled, and, glancing around the room to insure that there were no more comments, he raised his glass. "To Robert."

"May he rest in peace."

"That's quite an interesting tradition you have there," Nick said as he added a log to the fire and gathered some empty glasses from the mantel in the sitting room.

"It's a Devlin thing." India shrugged as she picked up the dessert plates from the tables. "Passed down for two hundred plus years."

"Really?"

"Yup. We're on our fourth Bible."

"Every single Devlin?"

"Every single Devlin who died since 1738. That's when Jonathan died. His death was the first one recorded. One of his nephews—the son of one of his sisters, that is—died in 1703, the year they built the first lighthouse, but it isn't recorded here."

"That's amazing."

"I guess it is when you stop and think about it. Which I don't usually do. The oldest Bibles are in a safe-deposit box. The entries are very tiny," she told him. "My dad always used to say that whoever wrote them had excellent vision."

"What else is left in here, India?" August poked a weary head into the sitting room, the guests all having long since departed except for the Enrights.

"Very little, Aunt August. I'll wash up everything. You go relax."

"I am tired." August appeared to be surprised by the admission, even though she had been up since the first light of day. She had spent the entire day on her feet, and it was now nearing eleven.

"I would think so." India placed a fond kiss on August's temple and led her back to the kitchen. "Tea and a comfortable chair for you, Aunt August."

"Tea it is." Darla poured a hot cup of mandarin orange tea and placed it on the table.

At India's prompting, Nick brought in a rocking chair from the front room and directed August to sit in it.

"Is there another dry dish towel?" Zoey asked. "This one just about drank its fill."

India went through two drawers before she found another towel, which she passed to Zoey.

Funny, India thought, *just last night I dreaded finding out who this woman was, and tonight, here she is, in our kitchen, drying dishes like a member of the family, well on the way to becoming a friend. Of course, last night, I hadn't known that she was Nick's sister.*

India shivered, recalling how the hot pangs of jealousy had ripped through her as she rowed the boat back to the beach.

"Penny for them." Nick caught up with her in the butler's pantry and trapped her in his arms.

"I don't think you really want to know," she said, laughing ruefully.

"What is it?"

She shook her head.

"Okay. Then I'll ask why you didn't let me know when you got home yesterday."

"I tried to."

"What does that mean?" He frowned.

"I rowed out to the cabin in the afternoon."

"I didn't see you."

"Well, that was pretty much the idea," she said with a sigh, "after I saw you."

"I don't get it."

"I saw you on the deck with Zoey."

"Why didn't you join us? She was dying to meet you."

"I didn't know she was your sister, Nick."

He stared at her blankly.

"I still don't get it."

"I thought she was maybe your . . . your girlfriend, a house guest . . . whatever," India told him sheepishly.

"Zoey?" He laughed. "You thought Zoey was my girlfriend?"

"Nick, I had no way of knowing. All I knew was that I saw an absolutely beautiful young woman on your deck and you had your arm around her."

"Well, how 'bout that?" He rubbed his chin. "And here I was, all put out because you didn't let me know you were here, and there you were, all . . . all . . . what would you say you were?"

"Jealous," she told him. "Sick with envy."

"You weren't."

She nodded and could almost feel the knot well up in her, just thinking back to it. He put his arms around her and held her very close to him.

"There is no girlfriend, Indy. There isn't anyone I care about, except you. No one I'd care to have as a house guest—family excluded, of course—except you." He wrapped her up close to his face, rubbing his cheek against hers. "There isn't anyone I want in my life except you. Got that, Indy?"

"Got it, Nick," she whispered.

"Well, well." Darla's eyebrows were raised in surprise as she stepped inside the doorway and bumped into the embracing couple.

Nick groaned.

"Could've been worse, honey." She winked as she stacked dishes on the shelf. "I could have been Corri. That'd be just like having everyone in Devlin's Light pass through."

Zoey stuck her head in through the doorway. "Oh. So that's where the plates go. Here, Nicky, put these away."

"Do you people care that you're interrupting a moment here?" Nick complained as he reluctantly disengaged himself from India and took the stack of plates from his sister.

"Oh." Zoey looked from Nick to India, then back to Nick. "Sorry."

"Come on, Zoey." Darla grabbed Nick's sister by the arm. "Let's go find some dishes to wash."

"Talk about a mood breaker," Nick muttered. "Now, where were we?"

"You were put out and I was jealous," India reminded him. "And I was right about here." She tucked his arms around her and lifted her face to his.

"Right. Oh, right, I remember." He nodded. "I think I was just beginning to do this"—he nibbled lightly on her bottom lip—"sort of as a prelude to this." His tongue parted her lips and slid into her mouth, and she tasted wine and raspberries and knew that if he didn't stop immediately, they would very shortly embarrass themselves in front of both their families.

India struggled slightly to pull herself away, fighting off the mental image of her dragging him to the floor of the butler's pantry and having her way with him.

"I think we'd best join the others," she whispered.

"In just a minute." He sought her mouth again, still hungrily and insistently. "I haven't quite finished giving thanks."

∽∾ ∽∾

Cousin Rachel's Cranberry Relish

1 package (16 oz) fresh cranberries
1/2 cup water
2 oranges, unpeeled, quartered
1 cup sugar
2 tablespoons fresh lemon juice

Wash and pick over cranberries. Mix berries with sugar, water and lemon juice in large, heavy saucepan. Over medium heat, cook berries until they begin to pop (5–7 minutes). Using off/on turns, chop oranges in food processor, gradually add cooked cranberries to processor and chop until berries are coarse. Cover and refrigerate until ready to use.

Chapter 17

"Indy, there's a man at the door to talk to you." Corri bounced into the laundry room and, having made her announcement, was preparing to bounce right on out.

"What man?" India frowned as she sorted darks from lights, heavy fabrics from delicates, and yesterday's table linens from everything else.

"I don't know." Corri shrugged. "A man."

"Where's Aunt August?"

"She went to the library to return some books."

"Ask him to wait." India flipped the last handful of yesterday's dish towels into the gaping mouth of the washing machine and closed the lid. "You didn't let him in, did you?"

"Of course not." Corri drew back, stung by the very suggestion that she would not know better than to let a total stranger into the house. "He's waiting outside."

"I'll be right down," India told her. She turned to see Corri pulling a brightly knit wool cap down over her strawberry curls. "Are you going out to play?"

"Me and Ollie are going to roller skate."

"Be careful." India eased up the zipper on Corri's jacket, smoothed the flat brim of the hat and kissed the tip of the child's nose. Corri had already made a dash to the steps to join her friend by the time India realized she had done what every mother does before sending her child out to play on a chilly late fall day. Zip the jacket. Straighten the hat. Kiss the kid and always remind them to be careful.

"I'm India Devlin," she announced as she opened the front door. A well-dressed man in his late thirties stood patiently on the porch, hands respectfully folded in front of him, military style.

"I'm sorry." He smiled, not unpleasantly. "It was *Maris* Devlin I was looking for."

"Maris?" India's eyebrows were raised nearly to her hairline.

"Yes. Is she available?"

"Ah, Mr. . . ."

"Byers. Lucien Byers." His voice held a gentle trace of the South.

"Mr. Byers, Maris Devlin is dead."

"Oh," he exclaimed, clearly taken aback by the news. "Oh, I had no idea. I'm so sorry. And she was . . . your sister?"

"No. My brother's wife."

"Well then, perhaps I should speak to your brother."

"Mr. Byers, my brother is also deceased."

"Oh, dear. I really am so sorry." He seemed to digest this latest bit uneasily.

"Is there something I can help you with?"

"Actually, Miss Devlin, I'm not sure. You see, I—that is, my company, Byers World—purchased some land from Mrs. Devlin several years ago."

"I wasn't aware that Maris owned any land."

"Well, actually, I believe it may have belonged jointly to her and her husband."

"Mr. Byers, any land that my brother owned was part of a family trust. Since I am the only other party to the trust, I can tell you with all certainty that there has been only one parcel of Devlin land sold in the past hundred or so years. And it was not to Byers World."

"Miss Devlin, I have a deed, I have an agreement of sale for the property that we purchased." Byers looked confused.

"With you?" India raised a skeptical eyebrow.

"Not the deed, but I think there may be a copy of the

204

agreement of sale in the file." He patted the side of a plush chocolate-leather briefcase.

"Mr. Byers, perhaps you should come in." India opened the door all the way to permit him to enter.

"May I?" he asked, holding up the briefcase.

India nodded, gesturing to the mahogany table at the bottom of the steps.

Byers slid a pair of tortoise-shell glasses onto his well-tanned face and opened the leather case, from which he removed a carefully drawn map.

"This"—the index finger of his right hand traced a bright yellow line on the map—"marks the boundary of the land we purchased two years ago."

India peered over his shoulder. "Why, that's the land on either side of the river."

"Yes."

"Mr. Byers—"

" 'Lucien.' "

"Lucien, I think there's been a terrible mistake here. We—the Devlin family, that is, the Devlin trust—own that land. We have not *sold* that land."

"Ah, but you have." He searched through his files, opened one up and said, "Yes, this one. Here. Right here."

He handed her an agreement of sale. Her eyes quickly scanned the page until resting on the signature and date at the bottom of the document.

Maris Steele Devlin. June 21, 1994. Right next to a very poorly forged version of Ry's signature.

India half laughed. "Mr. Byers—Lucien . . . I hate to have to tell you this, but this agreement of sale is worthless."

"Worthless? How can you say that? It's notarized, I paid Mrs. Devlin."

"Lucien . . . here, come sit down." She led a shaken Byers into the sitting room and offered him a chair. "Lucien, I don't know what Maris told you, but she couldn't have sold that property to you. She didn't own it. Her signature is worthless, and the signature purported to be my brother's is a very obvious forgery."

"What!"

"That land belongs to the Devlin trust. The trust was

controlled by my brother and me. If both our signatures are not on that document—or at the very least my brother's and my aunt's, since she has power of attorney in my absence—it's totally worthless."

"You mean I've been . . ."

"Duped. Yes. I'm so sorry."

"Oh, this is terrible. Absolutely terrible." He rose and began to pace. "Miss Devlin, I purchased that land in good faith on behalf of my shareholders. We have spent considerable money on surveys and development plans. We have entered into an agreement with a builder to construct little cottages on those lots. The whole purpose of my visit today was to see if I could persuade Mr. and Mrs. Devlin to sell me just a small additional piece, which would give the future owners of these cabins access to the beach."

"Lucien, I'm afraid I do not know what to tell you." India suddenly felt very sick to her stomach.

"Miss Devlin . . ."

" 'India.' " She gestured for him to sit back down.

"India, I paid Mrs. Devlin a great deal of money for that land."

"How much, might I ask?"

"Two hundred and fifty thousand dollars, as you can see." He pointed to the line where the cash part of the transaction was indicated.

"Oh," India exclaimed. "Oh," was all she could say.

"Oh, indeed." Lucien sank back onto the sofa, looking every bit as miserable as he must have felt.

"I think perhaps you'd better start from the beginning."

"A little more than two years ago, I started to look for some undeveloped land around the Delaware Bay. A place where I could build a new community of small, relatively inexpensive beach homes. I found Devlin's Light, and of course, when I saw that entire stretch of undeveloped land running along an unspoiled beach, well of course, I had to find out who owned it. It wasn't difficult to get in touch with your brother. I made him an offer—a very generous offer, I should tell you—right there on the spot. And on that very same spot, your brother flat out turned down my very generous offer and told me in no uncertain terms that the beach was not for sale. There seemed to be no reason to even attempt to negotiate. I thanked him for his time and that was that."

"Lucien, if you approached Ry to buy land and he refused to sell it to you, why would you have called his wife to sell it to you?"

"Oh, I didn't," he told her. "Mrs. Devlin called me."

"Maris called you?"

"Yes. She said that her husband didn't want to sell the beach property but that he had some property along the river that I might be interested in."

"You obviously did not speak with my brother about this."

"Well, I believe that all of our dealings may have been strictly with her from that point on."

" 'We'?"

"I personally was not involved other than to speak with your brother that first time, and to speak with Mrs. Devlin when she called back. Will Shuman, our then-vice president of development and special projects, handled this transaction for Byers World." Lucien's eyes knit together pensively.

"Then perhaps you should discuss this with your employee."

"My *ex*-employee." Byers sighed heavily.

"Where is he now?"

"I haven't the faintest idea." He shook his head. "I should have known there was something . . ."

Byers rose and began to pace again.

"How long ago did he leave your employ?"

"He resigned about two years ago. Said he was moving to Atlanta to be closer to his family."

"Lucien, Maris has been dead for two years."

"May I ask how she died?"

"She drowned in the bay." India told him the story, then added, "Her body was never recovered, though we did find a few things that had been hers. One of her sandals. Her sunglasses. A hat she always wore while she was crabbing."

"Hmmm. An accidental death." He gazed out the window. "Now that I think back on it, I think this may have been the last piece of business Shuman worked on for us."

Lucien sat back down on the chair and exhaled loudly. "You know, I had heard rumors, but I never for a minute suspected that he could have been so desperate."

"What are you talking about?"

"There had been some rumblings that Shuman had a gambling problem. That he had run up a sizable tab at one of the casinos in Atlantic City." Lucien tapped his pen in the palm of his left hand. "Since his departure, some small irregularities have appeared in several of his expense accountings, a few minor shortages involving several of the deals he was working on, but nothing of this magnitude."

"You think he worked with Maris to defraud you?"

"Actually, I'm thinking perhaps he defrauded both Byers World and Mrs. Devlin." Byers looked at her, his eyes heavy with speculation.

"You mean he worked with Maris to take your money, then disappeared with it all himself?"

He nodded.

"Maris was not one to go quietly, Lucien. If Shuman had defrauded you and cut her out, you can bet your bottom dollar that she'd have come straight to you about it."

"Not if Shuman killed her first." He spoke the words softly, his voice fraught with a quiet horror.

"Killed?" Her eyebrows raised at the thought of it. "You think Shuman may have killed Maris?"

"I think we have to consider that possibility, don't you? How difficult would it be to overturn a boat? To take the body out to sea?"

Maris murdered? A chill ran though her. Ry had definitely been murdered, but the thought that Maris had met with foul play had never occurred to her.

"Lucien, it's no secret that the circumstances surrounding my brother's death are still being investigated. Now you're suggesting that his wife had been murdered? If Maris had been killed by this Shuman, why would Ry have been killed? Shuman would have already had the money. And it was more than two years between the time that Maris died and the time that Ry died. It doesn't make sense to me."

Byers pondered this. "Maybe Shuman hid the money somewhere around Devlin's Light, then came back looking for it. Maybe your brother caught him."

"I guess that's possible." India frowned, her arms crossed against her chest.

"The other possibility is that the two deaths, while unfortunate, were unrelated."

"Let's think this through. Who else was there when your company went to settlement on this property?"

Byers sorted through the papers in his briefcase. "There was Mrs. Devlin and a lawyer named Patricia Sweeney. A representative of the title company named Peter Hales. Shuman . . ."

"Lucien, we need to talk to these other people." India looked over the papers.

"My thoughts exactly." Byers nodded. "And first thing Monday morning, I will personally do that very thing. May I call you next week?"

"Let me get one of my cards for you," she said as she left the room. "I'll be right back."

Once in the dining room, where she'd left her pocketbook earlier that morning, she searched through her wallet with shaking hands until she found a card. Returning to the sitting room, she found Lucien Byers looking out the front window to where Corri and Ollie were trying to maneuver over the cracked pieces of sidewalk on roller skates without falling. Corri made it through the worst of it, but Ollie did not. India grimaced as the child fell half onto the sidewalk, half onto the grass.

"Ollie, are you all right?" India called from the front door.

The child picked herself up and brushed the leaves and pine needles from her denimed bottom, nodding that nothing much was damaged but her pride.

"Is she hurt?" Byers asked with apparent concern as India handed over her business card.

"No, just embarrassed. I'll have to have that sidewalk repaired, though, before someone does get hurt. It's the sort of thing that my brother used to take care of." She smiled wanly.

"It's obvious that you miss him terribly. I'm so very sorry."

"We all are." She shrugged, then turned her attention back to the card. "I'll be at this number on Monday."

"Assistant district attorney, city of Paloma, Pennsylvania," he read. "Quite impressive. I suppose you could look into the whereabouts of some of the players." He raised the sheaf of papers and shook them slightly.

"Absolutely. As a matter of fact, if you fax copies of those documents over to my office, I'll get someone working on it first thing this week."

"Excellent. And I will start to gather what information I can on Shuman. I know a very fine private investigator."

"Maybe I can help locate Shuman. I'll see what's in the computer banks on him."

"Wonderful. Maybe if we work together we can get to the bottom of this. And perhaps, eventually, reach some sort of agreement on that tract of land."

"An agreement?"

"India, regardless of what our combined efforts find, I—my company, that is—is still out a quarter of a million dollars. Money that was paid to your sister-in-law."

India stiffened. "Lucien, I am not responsible for Maris's actions, nor do I have any responsibility to you or your company. Certainly I feel terrible that this has happened, but I don't believe I have any obligations here, even if I had two hundred and fifty thousand dollars to pay you back."

"I wouldn't expect you to. It isn't the money I want. We have invested a good deal of money into the development of that land—land that our records show we purchased. I would like to think we could work out something that would permit me to proceed with those plans."

"I think we both need to speak with our lawyers and see where this all stands." She frowned.

"India, I hope you don't take this personally, but I have an obligation to my company. If there is any recourse, I will have to pursue it."

"I understand. I'm sure I'd do the same thing. I just feel so terrible about this."

"I appreciate that." He snapped the briefcase closed briskly. "I'm only sorry that we had to meet under such unpleasant circumstances."

India walked him to the door and shook his hand when it was offered. He gave her a card, which she placed upon the table just inside the doorway.

"I'll talk to you on Monday," he told her as he walked across the porch and down the steps, pausing to look up the street to where Corri and Ollie were skating toward the corner. He waved as August pulled the Buick into the driveway.

Business couldn't be too bad, India noted as he drove off in his brand-spanking-new Mercedes. *But if he makes any more deals like the one he made with Maris, his next trip will be on a Raleigh ten-speed.*

"Who was that slick-looking fellow?" August came into the kitchen through the back door and set a bag on the counter. "Someone from Paloma?"

"No, why would you think he was from Paloma?" India frowned, in search of a fresh cup of coffee to replace the one she had left in the laundry room.

"He just had *city* all over him." August slid out of her winter coat. *"Ad unguem factus homo.* A man polished to the nail."

India paused, then poured a second cup of coffee and handed it to her aunt, gesturing her toward the window seat.

"Aunt August, I think you'd better sit down for this one."

It took a while, but by two o'clock that afternoon, India's temper, initially suppressd by shock, was about ready to blow. How dare Maris even attempt to sell off Devlin land! How dare she involve this family in a fraudulent scheme! Was she really so stupid she could have believed that the truth would never see the light of day? Madder than she'd been in longer than she could remember, India decided to do what she always did when her cork was about to pop. She went running.

Dressed in a long-forgotten pair of sweatpants and heavy socks she found in the bottom drawer of her dresser, a turtleneck from her suitcase and one of Ry's old sweatshirts, India rummaged in her closet until she found the old sneakers she'd been certain she had left there. How did any of us ever manage to run wearing nothing but plain old *sneakers?* India smiled as she tied the laces of the old white tennis shoes, envisioning the array of athletic shoes she had recently seen in a specialty store in the mall. Walking shoes. Running shoes. Cross-trainers. Tennis shoes. Basketball shoes. As she went through the motions of a too-brief warmup, she compared the old white canvas sneakers to the fancy, high-priced numbers sitting neatly on the floor of her closet back in Paloma. She could not in all honesty say that she missed them.

Corri and Ollie were in the attic playing dress-up with the old clothes set aside for just that purpose, and Aunt August was in the sitting room, cozy in her favorite chair nearest the fire when India set out. August had been totally unprepared for the news India had had to share that morning, but she was not shocked to learn that Maris had been involved with underhanded dealings.

"I cannot say that I'm surprised, India." August's chin set and her mouth was drawn into a tight, straight line. "There was something about Maris. . . . I do not mind telling you it near broke my heart when Ry brought her home. I never understood it even for a second. Except for Corri, there was nothing good to be said for that woman. And sometimes it was hard for me to believe that she was really that child's mother, she was so indifferent to her. But that's another matter. For her to involve the Devlin name in a dishonest scheme . . ."

August shook her head as she reached for the phone to call the family lawyer to alert him to this latest bit of news, pausing to add, "God forgive me for my lack of charity, India, but the woman only got what she deserved."

A chill from the east blew through Devlin's Light, and the sky, pale gray earlier that morning, had deepened to the color of gun metal, the clouds falling so low that they all but dropped into the bay. A snow sky, India thought as she headed out through the town in the hopes of running off her anger. The first mile was arduous; it had taken her that long to find her rhythm again. The second mile was better, and she slowed as she looked through the high black wrought-iron fencing that marked off the grounds of Captain Jonathan Devlin's mansion. The property took up the whole block, but it was only a small portion of what had once been the holdings of the oldest of the three original Devlins. Long ago given to the town, and used by the local historical society for a variety of fundraisers, the house stood tall and white, black shuttered and handsome, built to prove to the captain's in-laws, prominent Quakers from Philadelphia, that their beloved daughter Salem—short for "Jerusalem"—had married well. Which was all the consolation Jonathan could offer them, since Salem, by marrying a non-Quaker, had not been welcomed into the homes of her family.

It had been said that Salem Devlin lacked a proper Quaker spirit, having become overly fond of the exotic fabrics and fine jewelry that her seafaring husband brought to her from foreign ports. India wondered if the portrait of Salem still hung over the fireplace in the grand front hall. In a pastel done by a leading artist of the day brought all the way from Philadelphia solely for the purpose, Salem appeared boldly elegant in a white lace shawl over bare shoulders, her pale pink satin dress scooping low to display a long neck and creamy skin. Delicate fingers, one sporting a ring of blood-red rubies, tucked a dogwood blossom behind one ear, while her wrist was encircled with a double strand of pearls held fast by a clasp of rubies. Salem had not been a classic beauty, but her eyes sparkled and teased, even across the centuries. Clearly, there had been nothing plain about the captain's lady.

India made a promise to herself that, while she was on her leave, she would visit the mansion, walk the worn floors and maybe take the time to read Salem's letters to her beloved Jonathan and the journal her ancestor had kept while her captain was at sea. As she turned toward the beach end of town, India noted the flurry of activity near the front door of the big house; cars were parked in the circular drive and several of the townspeople had gathered on the front porch. Members of one committee or another, meeting to discuss some project, she mused.

The wind blew colder on the open expanse of beach, whipping India's hair around her face, into her mouth and her eyes. She slowed her pace but did not stop as she drew up the hood of the old sweatshirt around her head, tucking her hair under it as best she could. Her face burned with exertion and cold, and she resolved to begin running on a more regular schedule and to call the gym as soon as she got back to Paloma. She missed her sessions at the gym as much as she missed Gif, a crusty old soul who for years had appeared on the regular card at the Blue Horizon in Philadelphia and who now gave boxing lessons to youths he pulled off street corners in Paloma and tried to give them a place to work off their aggression. India had met him when he appeared as a character witness for a young man who was accused of beating up a schoolteacher in an alley on Paloma's dark side. Gif had testified that the young man had been at the gym, boxing at the time of the attack, and had invited a skeptical India to check out his facilities. She did, and, having been goaded into getting into the ring for a quick lesson, India discovered a new love. Gif, with his totally flattened nose and four o'clock shadow twenty-four hours a day, was a wonderful teacher, and before long a stop at the gym had become a necessary diversion whenever India's schedule permitted.

Unconsciously she slowed her pace, jabbing the air with her fists clenched from rage and cold, her body twisting with every punch thrown at an imaginary opponent.

Maris.

Just one shot, that's all I want. Just one swing. Just one chance for one good shot at that LYING [punch], *DECEITFUL* [punch], *SWINDLING* [punch], *NO GOOD* [punch punch punch], *THIEVING . . .*

"Hey, India, slow down!" someone called from the top of the dune.

She turned to see Zoey Enright making her way across the hard-packed sand.

"Sheesh, I'd hate to be on the receiving end of those blows. Where'd you learn to throw a punch like that?" Zoey's face was red as if she too had been too long in the afternoon cold.

"A gym in Paloma." India grinned. "I'm terribly out of shape."

"Looked just fine from where I stood."

"Maybe boxing is like riding a bicycle." India laughed. "Maybe you never forget how, once you've learned."

"Looked like fun." Zoey threw an unskilled punch into the air.

"It is. I was just thinking it was time to start taking lessons on a regular basis again. It's great exercise."

"Something I haven't had in a while. After yesterday's

dinner, I thought perhaps a little fresh air and exercise should go back on the agenda. But I'm afraid I didn't dress well enough and I'm chilled to the bone and craving some of the hot chocolate that I saw advertised at the little shop back there on the dock. Can I talk you into joining me?"

"With very little effort. I've already gone a few miles, and to tell you the truth, my hands and feet are numb. Hot chocolate sounds great."

"Which way is fastest?" Zoey asked.

"Straight down the beach." India pointed over her shoulder.

"Lead on, then." Zoey fell in step with India and they headed back up the beach.

"Were you headed anyplace in particular?" India asked.

"No, just exploring. Every time I visit Nicky, I try to see a little more of the town."

"For a small town, there's actually a lot to see. Starting right here." India pointed to an osprey that had sailed out of nowhere to hover over the choppy water before diving down and grabbing a fish with its talons and soaring off. "The osprey population had been in a decline around here, but the ban on DDT some years back appears to have resulted in a recovery. The birds are more plentiful now across southern New Jersey. They nest in high places, and the electric towers along the coast have become favorite nesting spots."

"What's that one?" Zoey pointed upward to their right to a large, light-colored bird whose wide wingspread showed off dark patches on the wings and tale.

"That's a rough-legged hawk. Actually, it's a light morph. I haven't seen one of those in years."

"What's a, er, morph?"

"It's a variation of coloration that occurs regularly, though less commonly than others. Like more people having dark hair than red. Rough-legged hawks are more commonly dark-feathered. But there are some that are light, like that one."

"It's beautiful." Zoey watched it soar back along the edge of the bay on its way toward the marsh and the woods beyond.

"They're not frequent visitors here in the late fall. You

have good eyes. We should take you on our bird count this year."

"I might be interested in going," Zoey told her. "When is it?"

"Ry and I used to do it on Christmas Day. I don't know when we'll do it this year. Look, there's Captain Pete's."

"Not a moment too soon."

Zoey followed India into the dimly lit wooden structure that, in the summer months, served as bait shack and dockside café, as well as a place to rent small boats and crabbing nets. Now, in November, Pete sold newspapers, binoculars, duck decoys and hot drinks.

"Hey, Pete," India called into the back room.

"Who's that?"

"India Devlin."

"Well, 'bout time." The old gent limped out, leaning on a thick wooden cane. He thumped India on the back with the palm of his hand. "Good to see you, girl. How's Augustina?"

"She's well. I'll tell her you were asking for her."

"Saw you on television a few months back." He nodded as he walked to the counter. "Philadelphia station."

"After the Thomas trial?"

"One of them." Pete grunted and swung himself onto a stool. "Proud of you, we all were. Mighty proud."

"Thank you, Pete." India nodded appreciatively. "I was sorry to hear about your wife, Pete."

"Appreciate it, India. Appreciate the card you sent." Pete cleared his throat. "Well then. What brings you out to the docks on such a cold day?"

"I didn't want my friend here to leave Devlin's Light without having some of that remarkable hot chocolate of yours, Pete." She grinned. "This is Zoey Enright, by the way."

"Enright. You related to Nick?"

"He's my brother."

Another grunt from Pete as he rose to fill two tall Styrofoam cups with steaming dark brown liquid. On the top of each he smacked a dollop of whipped cream.

"Whoa, go easy on the whipped cream." India laughed.

"You look like you could use a little extra there, girl. Both of you could, for that matter." He passed the cups across the counter one at a time. India patted her pockets, then realized she had no money.

"Oops." Her face reddened. "I don't have my wallet."

"I do." Zoey reached into the deep pocket of her jacket.

"No, no." Pete waved her away. "My treat. Been a quiet day. Glad you girls stopped by. Miss seeing those boys around here, I don't mind saying it."

"What boys would that be, Pete?" India asked, grabbing a napkin from the metal container on the counter's edge and passing a few to Zoey.

"Ry and Nick. They spent some good days out here with me, the two of them did. Broke my heart when Ry died, just like I told Augustina. But I'm glad Nick stayed around. Boy like that belongs on the bay. Got it in his blood, just like Ry did."

"I'll tell him you said so, Pete." Zoey nodded, acknowledging the compliment to her brother.

Pete turned on his cane and walked toward the back of the cluttered shop. "Don't seem right without a young Devlin in town. You think about that, India, hear?"

"Wow. What a character he is! Handsome, in a rough sort of way, but all he needs is an eyepatch and he'd fit every child's idea of the perfect pirate." Zoey giggled once they had gone back outside and closed the door. "Tell me a shark gave him that limp."

India laughed. "I'd be lying if I did. He took a bad fall coming out of Roslyn's—that's the local tavern—a few years ago and hurt his back. The doctors said he needs surgery, but he doesn't want to hear it. Personally, I think he likes the limp and the cane."

"India, how many years have you done the bird thing on Christmas?" Zoey leaned back against one of the thick round pilings and opened the lid of her hot chocolate to allow it to cool.

"Since I was a child, why?"

"I don't know. I was just wondering." She shrugged. "Seems like a shame to stop something you've always done."

"It was always sort of Ry's thing." India sat on an overturned boat that was huddled up against the building in much the same manner as the gulls huddled together out on the jetty.

"Well, if you decide to go this year, count me in."

"Oh, then you'll be here for Christmas?"

"That would be my guess. We always spend the holidays together. Mother insists on it. She doesn't care who or how many guests we bring, but we have to be together. Usually we are at Mother's, but this year I have the feeling that Nicky is planning on staying in Devlin's Light." Her dark blue eyes danced.

"Oh?" India sipped at her chocolate and ignored the fact that it was still just slightly too hot.

A sharp, clean wind blew in off the bay, and Zoey openly shivered.

"Want to walk to my car? It's only a block or two that way." Zoey pointed toward town.

"That sounds very good." India eased herself from her seat on the boat's bottom. "I think I've had all the fresh air I can take for one day."

"India, it may be none of my business, but . . ." Zoey appeared to be debating with herself momentarily. "Well, Nicky is very special. Not just because he's my brother, but because he's, well, he's just *Nicky.* I like you a lot, India. You're smart and fun and great company . . . everything that Nicky said you were."

"Nick said those things about me?" India's head shot up. "That I was smart and fun and good company?"

"Along with a list too long to repeat." Zoey sighed and rolled her eyes. "The thing is, if you hurt him, I will track you down." It appeared that perhaps Zoey was only half kidding.

"I wouldn't hurt Nick. And he is special. More special than any man I've ever known," India admitted.

"He misses your brother so much. Ry was one of the two best friends Nicky ever had. And he lost them both." They had reached Zoey's car. She stood in the street and searched in her pockets for the keys.

"What happened to the other one?"

"We don't know where he is. He disappeared from our lives a long time ago." Zoey opened both doors and the two freezing women slid gratefully into the car.

"Who was he?"

"Ben Pierce. His mother worked for our mother. Maureen was Mom's right hand. She was in charge of Mom's life, and so of ours." Zoey turned the key and started the engine. A blast of cold air blew out the heating vents, and she turned off the heater. "After our dad left, Mother worked in a doctor's office during the day and started writing at night. She did very well in a relatively very short period of time. She had started out writing a detective series—"

"Harve Shellcroft." India smiled.

"Yes! You've read the Harves?"

"Every one of them."

"I personally like the Penny Jackson series better, but Harve is a classic." Zoey turned the heater back on to see if the temperature had warmed up.

"Anyway, old Harve was such an instant hit, her publisher wanted more, the sooner the better. Now, Mother was smart enough to know that if two Harves were good, four Harves were better, but there were only so many hours in the day. So as soon as she started to make serious money, she hired someone—Maureen—to do all those things that kept her from writing. Drive us kids around. Food shop. Cook. Take us shopping. And Mother just stayed home and wrote."

"You make it sound as if you never saw her."

"Oh, no, it wasn't like that. Maureen did the things that would have taken up Mother's time when she wasn't writing, so that she could spend time with us." Zoey leaned back against the seat. "She was great, Maureen was. Younger than Mom and sassy as the day is long. Supposedly she was the only child of very wealthy parents. She had incurred their wrath by insisting upon marrying someone they felt was totally unsuitable. She thought they'd come around, in time, to accept her husband, who apparently proved to be every bit as much of a gold digger as her parents said he was. He left her, and she and Ben never heard from him again."

"So what happened? She tried to go home but her parents wouldn't take her back?"

"No. Mother thought that Maureen felt so guilty that her mother had died while she was out trailing around with this reprobate she'd married that she couldn't face her father. Anyway, she came to work for Mother. Her son, Ben, was Nicky's age. They were inseparable."

Zoey's eyes took on a faraway glow, a fact that was not lost on India.

"I had a terrible crush on Ben, from the day he came to stay until the day he left. And then some, maybe." She tried to shrug it off, but the wistful look lingered on her face. "All the time I was growing up, when I was in high school and I was so gangly and odd looking, I always dreamed that Ben would come back and take me to the prom and slay my dragons. Too much, huh?"

"I can't imagine you not being gorgeous, Zoey."

Zoey laughed. "For most of my life, I looked like a puzzle whose pieces had been put together just slightly off. I couldn't even look at myself in the mirror without cringing until I was eighteen or nineteen years old." Zoey's face softened, remembering. "Nothing like Georgia, who is so perfectly pink and golden and always has been. Or like Mother, who is, well, you saw what my mother is like. Even when we were poor as church mice, those first two years after Dad left, my mother always had that air of elegance around her."

She sighed. "And now you know probably more than you'd ever want to know about the Enrights."

"What happened to Ben?" India asked.

"Maureen got sick, very sick. The doctors told her she was dying. She wanted to go home to die. Her father came and took her and Ben back to Massachusetts."

"And you never saw him again?"

"Once. After his mother died, he ran away from his grandfather and came to my mother. Who, of course, had to call his grandfather and let him know where Ben was. His grandfather came and took him back. We never heard from him again." Zoey leaned against the steering wheel and stared out the front window as if looking back through time. "Ben was so different. He was so angry. Even his eyes were angry. I cried for days."

"Maybe someday your paths will cross again."

"I've never stopped hoping that they will." Zoey forced a

wistful smile as she pulled away from the curb. "Do you believe in fairy tales, India?"

"I guess a little." India smiled.

"Well, I don't know whether Ben grew up to be a prince or a toad, but I've never stopped wishing that he'd come back."

"Zoey, I do believe that if anyone could *will* something to happen, it would be you."

Zoey flashed the Enright mega-watt smile, and India laughed.

Wherever he was, Ben Pierce didn't know what he was missing.

Chapter 18

"Where have you been, dear?" August called from the dining room when she heard the soft fall of India's stockinged feet in the hallway.

"I ran into Zoey Enright out on the beach. We went to Pete's for some hot chocolate," India told her. "Pete sends you his regards."

"Hmm." August shrugged off Pete's sentiments as casually as she might shrug off an idle remark.

In another life, Pete had been among the many young men in Devlin's Light whose heads were turned by a saucy Augustina Devlin. In those days of youthful arrogance, she had been a woman who liked a man to dance to her tune. Pete, however, preferred a tune of his own and so had sought out a woman more willing to dance along with him. No one knew for certain whether or not August had ever regretted having turned her back on Captain Pete Moreland, but there were those in town who had their suspicions.

"Coincidentally, India, while you were gone, Nick called. They have two extra tickets to see the *Nutcracker* in Baltimore and asked if the two of us might be available to join them."

"I would love to go, but I can't." India shook her head. "You and Corri should definitely go, though."

"India, what do you mean you can't go?" Aunt August wore her stern face, her fists resting on her hips.

"I have to be back in Paloma early on Sunday. I have a lot of work to catch up on, and I need some time to make some phone calls within the department on Monday to follow up on the information I got from Lucien." India sat upon the bottom step. "As much as I would love to go to Baltimore, Aunt August, it's time I simply don't have to spare this weekend."

"Well, perhaps if you . . ." August frowned, and India recognized her aunt's where-there's-a-will-there's-a-way face.

"Aunt August, I want to take a leave of absence. I cannot ask my boss to grant that while I have so much work pending. It wouldn't be fair. Plus I need to start looking into this land deal that dear Maris pulled off right before she died."

"It does seem coincidental, doesn't it? Maris gets mixed up with this . . . this *bamboozler* Shuman, together they bamboozle Byers, then she drowns." August's eyes narrowed. "Shuman, Maris, and the money all disappear at the same time." She shook her head as if shaking off a chill. "And to think that my boy *married* such a woman."

August blustered into the kitchen. India sighed and followed her.

"Let's call Nick back and tell him that you and Corri will go. It'll be a real treat for Corri as well as for you. You haven't been to the ballet in almost a year, and I know you dearly want to go. And you'll have a wonderful time, August. Just think of how much fun it will be on Tuesday night, telling your card club about going to Baltimore with Delia Enright."

"You know me entirely too well, India." August laughed. "And you're right, I do want to go."

"Go where, Aunt August?" Corri sailed into the kitchen on her roller skates.

"Uh-uh," India pointed to the skates. "Not in the house."

"Where is Aunt August going?" Corri sat down and without argument began to remove her skates.

"To see Georgia dance in the *Nutcracker* tomorrow night in Baltimore," India told her grandly.

"Oh, oh,"—Corri jumped up, the left skate still tied on her foot—"can I go too, please, please? I heard the *Nutcracker* music on television this morning. It's so floaty!"

Corri twirled around.

"Well, we were considering that very possibility." India tried to look pensive.

"Really? I really could? Is Zoey going too? And Nick?"

"I think all of the Enrights are going," August told her, "but they could only get two extra seats."

Corri visibly counted. "But there are three of us," she pointed out.

"I can't go, sweetie," India told her. "Even if there were three tickets, I couldn't go. I have tons of work to do between now and Monday morning."

"Oh, but Indy—"

"Sorry, sweetie. Maybe another time. But if I want to take lots of time off, I have to put in lots of time now. Understand?"

The phone rang and August answered it.

"Why, we were just discussing that very thing, Nick." August's clever eyes did not miss the way India's color deepened at the sound of his name, or the little smile that played across her lips and that her niece thought no one else could see.

Good. Just as August had hoped.

Very good.

"She's right here, Nick." August tapped India on the shoulder and handed her the telephone.

"What's this I hear about you passing on the ballet?" he asked.

"Aside from my normal work schedule, something has come up that I need to look into."

"Now what could have come up so quickly?"

She paused. Corri was in the room, working hard to get a knot out of her skates' laces, well near enough to hear every word India said. India did not want to discuss the shady dealings of the mother with the child so close at hand.

"India?" Nick questioned the unexpected and overly long pause.

"Ah . . ." She sought the words.

"Why don't you let me take you out to dinner tonight and you can tell me all about it."

"Aren't your mother and sister still there?"

"Yup. But they have their own plans for this evening. Some parlor concert at Captain Jon's."

"Oh, I passed by there today. I saw the activity but forgot about the concert." India smiled at his use of the locals' name for the Devlin mansion in town. "And now that you mention it, I believe Aunt August is going also."

They agreed upon a time for dinner, and India fled to the shower, taking the steps her usual two at a time. August sighed with true satisfaction and hummed as she rinsed out the coffeepot in the kitchen sink. Things were moving along quite nicely. Quite nicely indeed.

Casual dress, Nick had told her, which was, India thought, fortunate, since casual was about all she had brought home, other than the dress she had worn on Thanksgiving Day. Shaking the extra water from her hair, India brushed it from underneath with one hand and blow-dried it with the other, hoping to give it volume. She pulled on a pair of khaki pants and a sweater the color of ripe plums, popped shiny silver shells on her ears and slid her grandmother's large silver filigree ring set with amethysts onto her middle finger. She was ready long before Nick rang the doorbell.

"Hey." He grinned and leaned down to brush his lips across hers when she opened the front door. "I'm happy to see you."

"Hey, I'm happy to see you too."

"And I'm happy to see my niece getting out for a change." August came into the hallway from the back of the house. "Now, where are you going tonight?"

"I thought maybe we'd have dinner at Carol's," Nick said.

"Ummm, Carol's crabcakes," India's eyes lit up at the thought of the plump little cushions of chunky white crabmeat, expertly seasoned and browned.

"Carol's it is, then."

"Will you be home late, dear?" August watched Nick help India into her suede jacket. Watched him straighten her collar. Watched India smile up into his face.

"I doubt it," India called over her shoulder as Nick took her hand and led her through the front door.

"Where's Corri tonight?" He took her hand and they strolled, unhurried, down the sidewalk. "Umm. You smell as good as you look. What is that scent?"

"Freesia," she told him. "And Corri is at a birthday party at a friend's house. Darla will bring her home."

"Then we have, oh, a whole few hours to spend together." He looked pleased at the prospect. "Walk or drive?"

"Walk. It's only a few blocks. I could use the exercise."

"According to my sister, you had plenty this afternoon."

"Not nearly enough to make up for all I ate yesterday," she said, laughing.

"I'm glad you had a little time to spend with Zoey. Besides being my sister, she's one of my all-time favorite people."

"I enjoyed her company. But you know, I never did get around to asking her what she's doing these days," India noted.

"I believe she may be gainfully unemployed once again," Nick mused. "Though I think she is considering several options. I told you, I believe, that Zoey has had many jobs over the past few years. She just hasn't found her calling yet."

"Would you call Zoey a bit of a rolling stone?" India asked.

"Not really. Mother says it's not that Zoey's *flighty* so much as she just hasn't *landed* yet. But we all know that when she does, it will be with both feet. She'll make an enormous splash and she'll live happily ever after."

"Does believing in fairy tales run in your family?" India looked up at him as they passed under a streetlight. The halo of pale yellow obscured his features for a brief instant, rendering him faceless in the foggy night.

"Maybe." He laughed and passed out of the light, his eyes and nose and mouth returning to their appointed places. "Must have something to do with having a mother who writes fiction, who always makes certain there's a happy ending. Why do you ask?"

"Oh, just something Zoey said today." India and Nick stepped sideways to permit a group of noisy teenagers to pass by. "She was talking about an old friend of yours that she had a crush on."

"Ben Pierce."

"That's it."

"Why was she talking about him?"

"She said he had been your friend, like Ry had been. And that she was sorry that you had lost both of them."

They had reached Carol's, the small restaurant that occupied the first floor of a rambling Queen Anne–style house on Bond Street in the "newer" section of town. "New," in Devlin's Light, referred to houses built after the Civil War, as so many of the structures had been built before 1800. There would be a fifteen-minute wait for their table, they were told, so they opted to wait at the bar, which occupied what had once been the music room in the century-old house.

"India Devlin, I haven't seen your face in here in, well, I can't remember how long." Jake the bartender dried his hands on a towel and reached them across the mahogany plank that served as the bar top. "Hey, and Nick too. How's it going?"

"Going well," Nick told him.

"Hello, Jake." India smiled.

"Let's see, a glass of zinfandel for India and a beer for Nick, right?"

"You've got a great memory, Jake." India nodded.

"How's your aunt doing, Indy?" Jake set the wineglass on the bar in front of her.

"She's doing just fine."

"Gotta be tough on you guys this year with Ry gone." Jake shook his head sadly. "Hell of a guy, Ry Devlin was. *Hell* of a guy."

"Thank you, Jake. I appreciate your remembering him," India said softly.

"Aw, how could you forget a guy like that?" Jake shook his head again and took a few steps to the left to fill another order.

India sipped at her wine and Nick stared into his beer, his fingers slowly turning the glass around in his hand.

India broke the silence. "It's hard to lose a friend. It's

good when people remember him, when they talk about him."

She thought back to Lucien Byer's visit that morning.

"Someone stopped by the house this morning," she told him. "A real-estate developer named Lucien Byers. He said he is the president of Byers World. He was looking for Maris."

"Maris?" Nick's eyes widened. "Did you tell him he was about two years too late?"

She nodded. "It seems that not long before her accident, Maris had 'sold' Byers some of the Devlin land—about seventeen acres or so down along the river. He had the agreement of sale with him, with Maris's signature and a very poor forgery of Ry's on the bottom."

"What?"

"Of course, it's not worth the paper it's printed on, but Mr. Byers wasn't happy to learn he'd been tricked out of two hundred and fifty thousand dollars."

Nick slammed his glass on the bar. "Start from the beginning, and tell me everything."

She did.

"Wait a minute," he said when she had concluded. "You think there may be some connection between Maris's death and Ry's?"

"It's beginning to look that way. Suppose for a minute that Maris did take this cashier's check and cash it—"

"She'd have been walking around with a quarter of a million dollars. Where would she have stashed that?"

"I think that's exactly what this Shuman wanted to know. So maybe she didn't tell him."

"And he killed her? Or maybe she did tell him and he killed her anyway, then hid the money and disappeared before Byers could figure out the fraud."

"Then he came back looking for the money in Devlin's Light."

"Where else could she have hidden it? The house, the Light, or someplace in between?" India rationalized. "Maybe Ry caught him, and he killed Ry."

"Hmmmm." Nick pondered this. "I guess it makes as much sense as anything else. Ry really didn't seem to have any enemies. I spent several days out at Bayview last week. I couldn't find one person who said one thing against him, India. From the faculty to the administrators, he was well liked, highly respected. Even the students I spoke with had nothing but good things to say about him. But didn't you say that you thought there might have been two people involved in his death?"

"That's a possibility. Someone to get his attention, to draw him out to the lighthouse. Someone waiting there to kill him."

"Then there was someone else working with Shuman."

"There were several names on the settlement papers. A lawyer, a settlement clerk, someone from the title company. At the very least, one of those persons would have had to be involved in order to have lent a sense of authenticity to the sale. Byers promised to fax me copies of all the documents first thing on Monday morning. Once I have the names of the players we can start to track them down."

"That's why you need to be back in Paloma early on Sunday?"

India nodded. "That's part of it. I need to get my ducks in a row if I'm going to ask for a leave. The Man won't be happy."

"'The Man?'"

"The D.A. My boss."

"You're really going to do it, then? Take time off?" His eyes watched her face.

"I am. I owe it to Corri to be here. I owe it to Aunt August to be here."

"I think the person you most owe it to is India," he said as the waitress tapped his arm to let him know their table was ready.

They were seated at a small round table in the dining room next to a window overlooking the side yard.

"There used to be a goldfish pond out there." India pointed toward the darkness outside. "Ry and I used to bring bread crumbs and feed the koi. Some of them were as big as catfish. That was before this was a restaurant."

"What did it used to be?" he asked, knowing that her face would light with the telling of it and loving the look on her face as she drew up a memory to share with him.

"It used to be Mrs. Mason's place. Her husband was a

pharmacist. He died in the sixties, but she stayed on here until she died, maybe ten years or so after he did. Carol is their granddaughter." India laughed then as she told him, "Now, understand that *Mr.* Mason's family was *new* to Devlin's Light. His family built this house in '87; that's *1887*. Mrs. Mason, however, was from an old Devlin's Light family. She was a Whitlock, one of the yeoman whaler families that settled here in the late 1600s."

"'Yeoman whalers?'" Nick looked amused. "There's a new term."

"There were thirty-five families—whalers—that came to the Cape May peninsula from New England and Long Island in the late 1600s. By purchasing large parcels of land—several hundred acres or so each—they were able to build modest plantations. They had come to hunt whales but stayed to work the land and become respected members of the community. In those days a yeoman occupied the rank just below that of gentleman. So 'yeoman whaler' refers to not only their occupation but their social standing in the community as well. Descendants of some members of those families ended up over time in Devlin's Light. The Whitlocks were one of the families that sailed with the Devlins."

"So Mrs. Mason outranked the old man, eh?"

"By several centuries." She grinned.

The young waitress stopped by their table to recite the dinner specials, prompted by a card she had tucked into the palm of her hand. Nick stopped her midway through to order crabcakes for both of them, thus sparing the young girl from peeking at her cheat sheet.

"I've had dreams about these things," India told Nick when the golden brown bundles of crabmeat were placed before them.

"Well, since my goal in this life is to make your dreams come true, I guess it's a good start." India blushed and smiled that half smile he was beginning to know well, and he grinned. "This is, after all, only our first real date."

"What about that weekend in Paloma? We went to the museum, to the ballet . . ." she reminded him.

"That was a play date for Corri. This is a play date for you." He smiled into her eyes and her heart flipped over in her chest. "Now, tell me, what would you like to do after dinner?"

She looked across the table at his face, handsome as an autumn sky, his eyes warm and lush as honey, his dark hair a tumble across his forehead.

If she told him what she really wanted he'd fall off his chair.

Respectable, she told herself sternly. Keep it *respectable*.

"Well, it might be fun to stop in at the parlor concert. Aunt August said the singer, Margarite Cosgrove, is truly wonderful."

"You know, I might enjoy that." He nodded. "I'm beginning to get suckered in to all this small-town stuff. All these Devlin things."

India laughed.

"The concert's for a good cause. All the money they raise during the year goes to maintenance of the good captain's property. Then at the end of the Christmas season, they have the Twelfth Night Ball and everyone gets to come and see how their money was spent that year."

"Would you like to go?" he asked.

"Go . . . to the concert?"

"To the Twelfth Night Ball."

"Really? You'd go?"

"I've heard people talking about it since I moved to Devlin's Light. It sounds like it might be fun."

"Oh, Nick, it is!" She laughed, her eyes brightening. "It's fancy dress, costume-y clothes, with the men in velvet waistcoats and the women in ball gowns. The fun part is that the dress can be from any time period from the 1600s to the present, because there has been a Twelfth Night Ball in that house every year except during wartimes. So the house has seen colonial-style gowns as well as Empire and Victorian. It's wonderful. And there are dances from each time period—" She stopped and frowned. "I don't suppose you know too many of them."

"I know how to waltz."

"Hah!" She leaned back in her chair. "The waltz is just the start of it. Actually, the ball begins every year with the Grand March."

"Lost me," he told her.

She took his hand and pretended to study his palm. "I see music in your future," she said, lowering her voice dramatically. "And dancing. Lots of dancing. Dancing *lessons,* to be more exact."

"I didn't know you were part gypsy."

"Everyone has a touch of gypsy." She laughed. "Would you be up for dancing lessons if anyone is giving them this year? I'd hate to see you miss out on all the fun."

"I don't mind, but who will I be learning with?"

"I'll go with you." *Anywhere. I'd go with you anywhere.*

"Will you be home in time?"

"I'd like to be home by the weekend before Christmas. I'd like to go to Corri's Christmas play and the Olsons' Christmas Eve open house. I want to go caroling and I want to go on the House Tour."

"Why, India Devlin, you sound homesick."

"I didn't even realize how much I missed it all. I had a chance to do this all last year with Ry and Darla. And I stayed in Paloma and worked. No one remembers the name of the case I worked on, whether I won it or lost it, whether there was an appeal or a retrial." India swallowed hard. "But Darla remembers every minute of the last holiday season she spent with my brother."

Nick's hand reached over, his fingers tracing tiny circles on the inside of her wrist. "I'm glad you'll be home. I want you to be home. I want to share the holidays with you this year." *And every year,* he could have added. Instead, he raised her hand to his lips and kissed the very spot where the invisible circles had wound around her wrist.

"Dessert?" The waitress appeared from nowhere and broke the spell his voice was weaving around India.

"You know, there's a lot of dessert-type things left over from last night," India told him pointedly. "We could skip the parlor concert and have dessert at home. You could build a fire."

He got the picture. Corri out. Aunt August out.

Nick and Indy would stay in.

"Aunt August?" India called from the foot of the steps. "I thought she went to the concert?"

"Just checking," India said innocently.

"Hmmm." Nick nodded. "Well, how 'bout if I get that fire going? It's chilly in here. And you can make us some coffee and get us dessert, and we can have it right here."

India went to make coffee and to cut slices of cranberry apple tart with hands that were just slightly shaking. Hands that wanted to be touching his warm skin, fingers that wanted to run through that dark hair.

Keep it together, Devlin. Maintain a little dignity.

India managed to do just that for roughly thirty seconds after she set the tray on the coffee table in the sitting room and he pulled her down to the floor in front of the fire. He sought her mouth before she had a chance to seek his and together they plummeted into a swirl of sensation, of warm hands that sought warmer skin, of tongues seeking tongues and bodies needing bodies. His lips led a long slow trail followed by his all too clever tongue, down her throat from chin to collar bone, to where the neck of her sweater kept him from the rest of her. Her breath came in hot little bursts and she began to undo the buttons, his mouth following behind her fingers to tease every inch of her skin. He moaned softly when he reached her breasts, and he cupped each one in his hands while she caressed the sides of his face. She was too soft, her skin too delicious, his hands too wise. Her lips parted and a soft gasp escaped when he eased her breasts free and sought them with his mouth. She tugged him to her, fitting him to her body, wanting more of him, wanting all of him. Wanting—

"What was that?"

"What?" She opened her eyes but barely.

"It sounded like a car door." He rose up on one arm.

A car door? Now?

"Yup. That's a car, all right." Nick forced a cheerfulness he did not feel into his voice. "Darla's car."

"Darla?" India squeaked. "Oh, she's bringing Corri home from the party."

Nick bent down to kiss her swollen lips. "The child needs a lesson in timing." He sat up and pulled her by the arms until she was seated next to him. "Why don't you button yourself up while I let her in."

"Do we have to let her in?" India teased.

"I'm afraid so."

"Maybe we should send her right to bed. It is late for a little girl to be up."

"Good thinking, sweetheart." Nick laughed as goodnaturedly as one could under the circumstances and stood up. "And you're right, it's almost eight o'clock. Much too late for a six-year-old to be up on a Friday night."

India stuck out her tongue at him and he laughed again.

Looking out the window, he said, "Oh, and there's more good news. Darla and Ollie are coming in too."

India sighed and began fumbling with the buttons on her sweater.

"Faster, sweetheart," he told her. "I hear the pitter-patter of little feet on the porch."

"You might as well go and let them in then, since they aren't likely to go away."

"Nick's here!" Corri squealed from the door. "I won a prize at the party. In the scavenger hunt. And look at my balloon, it's a Pilgrim. Ollie got the turkey, see? Get it, for Thanksgiving? Where's Indy?"

"You make my head spin sometimes, Corri." He laughed. "India's in by the fire."

Corri and Ollie flew in to show off their balloons and their party favors, little cornucopia baskets filled with candy.

"Just what you need." India sat Indian-style, her back to the fire.

"Can we have milk?"

"Sure. Help yourselves. Darla, can we get you some coffee?"

"Sure," Darla replied brightly.

"I'll get it, Dar," Nick told her, gesturing for her to sit in a chair near India's feet.

"So, Indy. How was dinner?" Darla asked.

"It was fine. Great."

"Umm. I see you decided to have your dessert and coffee back here. Nothing good on Carol's menu tonight?"

"We just had so much left over from last night, we thought . . ."

Darla reached over and took a sip from India's cup. "Well, your selection of desserts may be better, but I'll bet Carol serves her coffee hot."

India stood up and put her hand out for the cup.

"I was just on my way into the kitchen," India said, avoiding Darla's eyes, "to warm that up."

"India . . ." Darla grinned meaningfully.

"What?"

"This." Darla tried unsuccessfully to stifle a laugh as she tugged on the front of India's sweater.

The buttons, hastily fastened, were done up out of sequence, making a bulge here and a gap there.

India reddened and cleared her throat. "I . . . ahem . . . well, you see, Dar . . .."

"Oh, I see." Darla laughed as she rebuttoned India's sweater for her. "I see perfectly well. And I think it's about time."

∽∾ ∾∽

Carol's Crabcakes
(makes 8–10 crabcakes)

1 tablespoon butter
1 clove garlic, minced
1 onion, finely chopped
2 teaspoons sweet red, yellow or green pepper
1½ tablespoons flour
1/3 cup whipping cream
1 pound fresh lump crabmeat (carefully picked over for shells)
1⅓ cups finely ground bread crumbs (divided in half)
1 egg
1 tablespoon finely chopped fresh parsley
2 teaspoons dry mustard
1 teaspoon lemon juice
1/2 teaspoon salt
1/4 teaspoon freshly ground pepper
1 teaspoon grated lemon peel
2 tablespoons butter

Melt 1 tablespoon butter in a large, heavy skillet over medium heat. Add garlic, chopped sweet peppers and onions. Cook 3–5 minutes, stirring frequently. Stir in flour, cooking 4 minutes more, then gradually add whipping cream. Cook until thickened, stirring constantly.

Stir in crabmeat, 1/4 cup of the bread crumbs, egg, mustard, lemon juice and peel, salt and pepper. Mix well, remove from heat. Cover and refrigerate for 4 hours.

When mixture has chilled, shape into 2-inch patties. Coat with remaining bread crumbs. Melt 2 tablespoons butter in large skillet. Cook crabcakes over medium heat until golden.

Chapter 19

"Are you sure we can't talk you into coming with us, India?" Delia Enright, elegant in a cashmere coat that floated around her tall frame like a sigh, stepped into the hallway ahead of her son. "I'm sure that we could find a seat for you somewhere in the theater."

"I'm certain, but thank you," India assured her.

"Well, maybe you'd like me to stay home with you then." Nick followed India through the doorway of the sitting room.

She laughed. "Then I'd be guaranteed not to get a damned bit of work accomplished."

"Oh, but you'd enjoy every minute of every page you did not read." He leaned closer and kissed the tip of her chin.

"No doubt I would. But I really have to—"

He silenced her with a kiss and she drank him in. Kissing Nick was like nothing she had ever experienced before, and it was becoming a very addictive habit.

"Nick," she reminded him, "your mother is in the hallway."

"Umm-hmm." He nodded. "With your aunt. And Corri."

He bent down as if to kiss her again when Delia called him from the hall. "Nicky, dear, we're all waiting. Please don't make me embarrass India by asking you what you're doing."

He laughed and hugged India to him, asking, "Are you sure you don't want me to stay home with you?"

"Nick, I'm a big girl. I can stay home alone. Honest. I'll be fine." She followed him into the hall. "You all have a wonderful time, and tell Georgia I said hello."

"We will, Indy. We're going backstage, like we did in Paloma." Corri chatted excitedly and stood still barely long enough for India to button up her coat and kiss her cheek. "And we are going all the way to Baltimore in a *limousine!*"

"That in itself is a treat," India told her as the child flew out the door toward the waiting car.

Nick tucked a kiss right below her left ear on his way out.

"Have fun," she called from the doorway, where she stood and watched as Delia's long silver limo pulled down the street.

India crossed her arms against the chill and looked into the night sky. The clouds were low, snow clouds, and she hoped the weather would hold until she returned to Paloma. Part of her wished she was in the long sleek car, setting off for Baltimore to see a wonderful performance in a beautiful theater, to share the night with Nick and his mother, Aunt August and Corri. Had she not only last night said she wanted to make more time for her family this holiday?

And I will, she promised herself. *As soon as this trial is over, as soon as I finish up this last bit of work.*

There's never going to be a last bit of work, she told herself. *There's always going to be another case. Another victim. Another trial.*

She sighed as she checked the locks on the back door, on the cellar door, on the side-porch door. She remembered a time when no one in Devlin's Light locked their doors, winter or summer. There had never been a reason to. Not until that summer that had changed everything.

How many bad guys do you have to convict, how many do you have to put away, before you can forgive yourself? Nick had asked.

India knelt in front of the fireplace and stacked a few more logs onto the fire, watching until the flames inched upward to the top of the stack.

How many bad guys, India?

Tossing a file onto the sofa, she spread its contents out before her and began to separate the work into her customary piles. Statements. Photographs. Diagrams. Forensic reports. Police reports. Medical reports.

How many, India?

She stared into the fire, Nick's face rising before her in the flames, looking as he had when she walked into the hall tonight. The same look he had when he kissed her wrist in Carol's the night before. The flames flickered just as the candlelight had danced across his face when he blessed her with his full and easy smile. She closed her eyes and felt his hands on her skin, his lips trailing down her throat. The memory of it sent a tingle down her spine all the way to the tips of her toes.

How many, India?

Maybe—just maybe—not as many as she had once thought.

She sighed and went to work.

It was almost seven-thirty when it occurred to her that she had not eaten since noon. Putting aside her notes, she padded into the kitchen on feet cushioned by thick woolen socks. The refrigerator was stocked with Thanksgiving leftovers, and India opened containers and foil-wrapped packages until she had a little of this and a little of that on her plate. A turkey sandwich on homemade whole wheat bread, a little mayonnaise, a little lettuce, a dollop of cranberry relish. Some black olives, celery stuffed with cream cheese. She made a nest of sorts on the floor in front of the fire with several throw pillows from the sofa and a soft crocheted afghan, and it was there that she curled up to eat her dinner. The house was so quiet, quiet enough to hear the ticking of the hall clock and the hum of the refrigerator's motor when she went into the kitchen to rinse off her plate. She poked into the pantry and found one small slice of cranberry pear tart left, and it called to her. Leaving it on the small chipped china plate, she grabbed a fork out of the dishwasher and went back to sit by the fire.

I probably did not need that dessert, she told herself. *I feel like a total glutton.*

She leaned back against the sofa, but the fancy hardwood

carvings on the arms dug into her back. An elegant little settee, it had not been designed for comfort. She piled some cushions closer to the fire and pulled the afghan up to her chin and snuggled under it.

Just for a minute or two, she promised. She'd go back to work in just a few minutes . . .

India opened her eyes with a start. There was a whisper of movement, of some soft uncertain sound, a sense of a presence there in the house. She sat up slowly, cautiously. The charred end of a log fell and hit the brick firebox with a thud, causing her to jump nearly out of her skin. She tilted her head to listen. No, whatever had awakened her was more subtle than the falling log. The hairs on the back of her neck stood straight up as she strained to listen. Something—some *hushed* something—there in the hall-way, there on the steps leading to the second floor, no louder than the sound made by furtive eyes watching in the dark.

As quietly as possible, India stood up and backed to the fireplace, reaching behind her to grab the black wrought-iron poker. A vague bump from overhead, an indistinct but dull sense of *disquiet* from the second floor sent her skin to gooseflesh. Her fingers tightened on the cold metal, and she took small, muted steps toward the stairwell. One by one, holding her breath, she took the steps upward, leaning into the dark, all of her senses on total alert. The muscles in her neck and shoulders soon began to protest the prolonged tension, burning to remind her she had stood motionless for far too long.

Taking a deep breath, she turned on the hall light and listened. Nothing.

Slowly, as quietly as possible, India went from one bedroom to the next, turning on the lights, looking in the corners. Nothing.

She locked the attic door from the outside and checked the bathrooms. Nothing.

There was nothing. No sound. No longer any sense of anyone in the house except herself.

With an unconvinced sigh, she went back down the steps to return the poker to its place, wondering if she had just experienced what Corri had referred to as a ghost. She paused on the landing to study the faces of several generations of Devlins who were immortalized there in paintings and in photographs.

"Okay, folks," she said aloud, "which one of you was it?"

None, she knew. All the years she had lived in that house, surrounded by the spirits of her ancestors, she had never once sensed anything even remotely sinister. The feeling she'd had tonight had caused her skin to crawl.

When, she wondered, had a less than benign spirit taken up residence on Darien Road?

"Is Corri awake yet?" India dropped her suitcase, already neatly packed, near the back door.

"I don't expect her to wake up until ten," August told her. "So much excitement last night, you know. She slept all the way home in the car—as did I part of the way—but it was such a big night for her."

"Was the ballet wonderful?" India searched in the refrigerator for cream for her coffee.

"Always." August sighed. "The *Nutcracker* always enchants. The music always enthralls."

"'Floaty' music, Corri called it." India smiled.

"And 'floaty' it was. Georgia made a wonderful Snow Fairy. She's just lovely, as are all of Delia's children."

"Speaking of which, Nick asked me to the Twelfth Night Ball." India tried to sound as casual as possible.

"Really?" August attempted to match her niece's nonchalant tone, but it wasn't easy.

"Umm-hmmm."

"Well, it's been a few years since you showed up at that affair." August turned her back to hide her little smile of satisfaction.

"More than a few. I haven't gone since high school. It is still costume, isn't it?"

"Of course."

"I'll have to find a dress."

"Well, start by looking in the attic. There're all sorts of things stored away up there. Darla wore one of your great-great-aunt Priscilla's gowns last year. Fit her like it was made for her. She looked so beautiful." August turned and smiled. "There's a picture on my dresser, if you haven't already seen it, of Darla and Ry standing on the verandah of the captain's house. Touched by moonlight, they were."

"Maybe we should talk Darla into going with us this year."

"That's a lovely thought, dear. If it wouldn't be too painful for her, it would be lovely."

"Didn't Priscilla have a twin sister?"

"Yes, Prudence."

"Maybe Darla and I can go as Priscilla and Prudence. We could do our hair the same way, just like we did when we were in high school." India smiled, thinking back to those days that, in retrospect, seemed so simple.

"And flirted with all the same boys, making them all crazy." August chuckled. "Don't think I didn't hear about it. It seems like years since those days."

"Aunt August, it *has* been years since we were in high school."

"Sometimes it seems like only yesterday that your father came back and brought his babies home. After Nancy died." August shook her head. "Things were never quite the same for anyone after your mother died."

"You know, I don't remember her at all," India told her. "Even when I look at her picture, it's almost the same as looking at the pictures of Gramma Logan. I never knew her either."

"I always thought you must have missed her so, growing up."

"I guess in some ways I missed *knowing* her, but I had you."

"Not quite the same as having your mother, India."

"I don't know that I knew the difference," India said softly.

"Thank you, India. Those may be the most loving words I have ever heard." August's eyes unwittingly filled with tears, and she brushed them away with the back of her hand.

"You were always there for Ry and me." India found her own throat constricting with emotion, and she knew no further words were necessary.

India cleared her throat and sought less poignant ground. "Do they still do all of those dances?"

"Yes, certainly. It's a *ball,* India."

"Do the Websters still give lessons?"

"Yes, I believe so. Were you thinking about brushing up on your fancy steps?"

"Yes. Nick said he'd go too, so that we could dance."

August closed her eyes and saw India swirling around the dance floor in Nick's arms. The vision was so real to her, so vivid, she could almost hear the orchestra, almost smell the gardenia tucked into India's hair, right there behind her ear.

"Well, I'm glad to hear that you will attend. It would have been the first time in, oh, I don't know how many years that there was no young Devlin to lead the grand march."

"Ry went every year," India recalled.

"I can't remember one year that he missed. Even the year that Maris died. He took me as his date." August's face softened, remembering. "He was so handsome, my boy. He wore a Victorian-era dinner jacket he found in the attic. Every lady in Devlin's Light lined up to dance with Ry that night. Oh, they all said it was so that he wouldn't be without a partner—him being a young widower and all, that was their excuse—but not a one of them fooled me. You could see it in their faces when they danced with him, young and old, they all looked the same way."

"What way was that, Aunt August?"

"Beautiful," she said simply. "As if waltzing with a beautiful man made them beautiful too."

She was lost for a moment, remembering.

"Even me." She smiled.

"Was that the year he took Darla home?"

"Yes. And they were inseparable from that night on." August shook her head sadly. "It was Darla he had belonged with all those years. He was never meant to be with anyone else. Destiny *shifts* when you try to change it."

"What's that supposed to mean?"

"There are some things that are meant to be, India, in order for things to be right. Pretending that *you know better,* trying to rearrange the natural order of things, throws it all off." August turned her back and began to fuss with the toast. "It's important to recognize who you are and where you belong, and with whom."

"What if you don't know where you belong?" India asked softly.

"Everyone *knows,* India. Deep inside, it's there, though some choose to ignore or, worse, think they can outsmart fate. Well, you can't." August's chin squared and she rattled a drawer for a knife and proceeded to butter her toast. "Only thing worse than dodging it when you're young is wanting it when you're old, when it's too late to call it all back."

August poured her coffee and looked out the back window, and her eyes clouded with what might have been regret, as if seeking a glimpse of those wasted years. India wondered what it was that her aunt had let slip through her fingers so long ago that she sorrowed for now.

India sat on the edge of the dark blue leather chair in the big bright office of the district attorney of the city of Paloma, across the desk from the Man himself, and watched as the first glimmer of understanding crossed his well-worn face.

"It's out of the question, India." He leaned back in his chair. "I can't do without you for three months."

"Then I'm afraid that you'll need to begin looking for my replacement," she said gently.

"Now, hold up there." He waved a navy blue and gold ballpoint pen loosely in her direction. "What's this all about, India?"

"I need to be home for a while," she told him, "home in Devlin's Light."

"This has to do with your brother's unfortunate death, I am assuming."

"Partly, yes. But there are other considerations."

He tapped the pen on the desk with beefy, well-manicured hands.

"What guarantee do I have that you'll be back in three months?"

"None I'm afraid," she replied.

"Let me see if I understand this." His head moved slightly from side to side as he appeared to ponder the situation, a habit that fooled neither of them. They both knew he understood perfectly. "I have a choice between letting you take your leave and *maybe* coming back in three months, or I could know *definitely,* right now, that you will not be back at all."

"That pretty much sums it up." India did her best not to blink.

He shook his head. "What's that saying, 'What goes around, comes around'?"

"Pardon?"

He stood up and paced to the window. "For five years now, I've been bragging about how tough you are. I even encouraged you, went so far as to feed your tenacity to the press to make that reputation stick. But I never thought I'd have that 'no deals' attitude turned on me."

"I'm sorry."

"No, you're not, India." He sighed. "You're not sorry at all. When did you plan on leaving?"

"I'd like to be in Devlin's Light by the eighteenth of this month."

"That gives me roughly three weeks to go through your caseload, figure out what can be postponed, what needs to be reassigned."

"That's done."

"Hmm. And it would be nice to have your input."

"There will be a summary in every file before I leave."

"Looks like you've thought of everything." He crossed his arms over his chest, signaling that the conversation was over. She had been dismissed.

"I tried to. Thank you." She extended her hand and he took it with both of his, holding it for just a second.

"India," he called to her as she reached the door. "Keep in touch."

Chapter 20

*P*acking up her office had been easier, and somewhat less painful, than India had anticipated. With Roxie's help, she was able to clear her space in a little under two hours.

"Have you lost your mind? India, you're on the top of the damned heap. The Man almost *likes* you." Roxie had utterly gaped when India first announced her plans.

"Roxie, there's a little girl in Devlin's Light who not only likes me but needs me," India replied.

"I don't believe this." Roxie stood in the doorway to India's office with her hands on her hips. "There has to be something else to this. You don't walk away from what you have done here just to play mommy. You don't leave behind four years worth of work and your whole career for . . . Wait a minute, India, there's a man in this equation, isn't there?"

India just smiled and continued to clean out her bottom desk drawer.

"That's it. Little girl *plus* man. That's the combination that did it, isn't it? Now, who would ever have thought that India Devlin's head could be turned?"

"What is that supposed to mean?"

"It means that I have watched you stare down the devil in open court. I have seen you better the best. But I have never seen you fall in love, India."

"First time for everything." India shrugged.

"She admits it." Roxie grinned. "I'll be damned, the rumor's true."

"What rumor might that be?"

"The one going around the detectives' lounge. Someone suspected that underneath it all, you might be human. Now Herby, he said he couldn't see it, but I said I was still on the fence."

India laughed.

"You want me to follow up with trying to track down the Byers World scam?" Roxie opened a file box and held it open for India to throw in some copies of the transcripts from a case she had tried two years earlier.

"I would really appreciate it, Roxie. We've just run into one dead end after another. The attorney who represented Maris at settlement, this Patricia Sweeney, is not a member of the New Jersey, Pennsylvania, Delaware, Maryland or New York bars. The title company that issued the report and passed clear title on to Byers World doesn't even exist. Lucien Byers has had a P.I. trying to track down this Shuman for the past couple of weeks and hasn't been able to get so much as a cold trail. I just don't get it."

"Well, we both know that if someone doesn't want to be found, there are ways to not be found."

"I guess that's true. Still, you'd think something would turn up."

"Something will. Sooner or later, one of these birds will slip up." Roxie bent to pick up a poorly tossed wad of paper that hit the floor instead of the trash can. "I guess, all kidding aside, you'll use the time off to track your brother's killer."

"If we don't resolve it now, it's not likely that it will ever be resolved. I need to know, Roxie." India pulled up the sleeves of her gray sweater as she prepared to tackle the last desk drawer.

"I understand. In a way, I'm surprised that it took you so long."

"I really have been torn between going back and just doing what I'm doing." India pitched a pile of old notebooks toward the trash.

"Hold up there, Indy, are those your notes on the Elliott trial?"

When India nodded, Roxie retrieved them from the trash, saying, "That was one of the best summations I ever heard. Unless you have serious objections, I'd like to keep those. You never know when they'll come in handy."

"Help yourself."

"So, who is he?" Roxie asked.

"He?" India frowned as she poked through a file drawer. Why had she kept so much paper?

"The guy responsible for you finally going home."

"It's not just him, Roxie. There's Corri."

"India, you could have left here any time since August. There were some people around here who were surprised that you even came back at all after the funeral. Now all of a sudden, you're hot to trot your buns back to Devlin's Light. I'm just curious about the man who is special enough to take you away from all this."

"It wasn't really 'all of a sudden.' I've been fighting going back since Ry died. It's just taken me a while to realize that I should, and can, go back. But I'd be lying if I said that Nick had nothing to do with the decision."

"Well, it's good news and bad news as far as I'm concerned. I'll miss you a lot. You've been a good friend, India. And from a professional standpoint, I'd have to go a very long way to meet someone else as good at this game as you are. On the other hand, I'm not sorry to see you go back home. I think we all knew—all but the Man, anyway—that that was where you belonged."

India smiled, recalling Aunt August's words. *Know where you belong, and with whom.*

"It's taken me a while, but I may have come to the same conclusion. I figure I'll know for sure before the three months are up whether I'll stay or come back."

"Oh, there's a pool on that too," Roxie told her. "Odds are five to one."

"On what?"

"On you staying in Devlin's Light." Roxie lifted the box that India was taking with her and set it near the door next to the stack of diplomas, personal photographs and Aunt August's needlepoint that they had removed from the walls.

India looked around the office, now stripped of everything that had made it hers. It looked much the way it had that day, now almost five years ago, that she had first arrived, nervous and unsure of herself. How had that untested lawyer, fresh from passing the bar, developed into what many criminal defense attorneys in Paloma feared as their toughest adversary?

Lizzie, she told herself. It was love for a lost friend that had brought her here, to do this job. But it was love of another kind that would take her home.

Maybe Nick was right. Maybe the woman had atoned for the sins of the child. Maybe she could finally forgive herself.

Maybe she could go home, and stay home.

Only time would tell.

"India, you're just in time." August, having heard India's car pull into the gravel driveway, had opened the back door and stepped onto the porch to greet her niece. "I was hoping you'd be here earlier, but we still have time."

"Time for what?" India frowned.

"Time to get you dressed and over to Captain Jon's." August held the door open as India passed through to the kitchen with two suitcases full of winter clothing. Having emptied her closets in the townhouse, her car was now full of boxes and bags.

"Why?"

"India, you signed up to hostess for the Christmas tea." August stepped into the warmth of the house and closed the door. "And it starts at three o'clock."

"Today?" India dropped her bags.

"Today."

"Oh, damn, I forgot." India shed her winter jacket and disappeared briefly into the hallway to hang it up, calling back to ask, "What should I wear?"

"Well, you have a choice of things I brought down from the attic," August told her. "I left several dresses on your bed. Something of Jerusalem's, something of Felicity's, something of Sarah's."

The names rolled off August's tongue as if she spoke of contemporaries rather than ancestors long departed.

"Eat some lunch first, then run up and see what fits best.

249

We may have time for a rudimentary alteration here and there, if necessary."

"What are you wearing?" India lifted a lid from a pot that simmered on the stove and sniffed. "Umm. Yankee pot roast."

"That's dinner. There's soup for lunch. I'll heat some up while you look over the options." August lifted a large earthenware bowl of chicken corn chowder from the top shelf of the refrigerator. "And I'm wearing the same afternoon dress of dark green wool that I wear every year. It still fits quite handsomely, if I may say so. I'm not certain who wore this one first; most likely it belonged to my grandmother Kearney, though."

"And I'm wearing a pretty white dress with hollies on it." Corri bounced into the kitchen and threw her arms around India's waist. "And Aunt August said I could help, that I'm big enough."

"I think I was just about your age the first time I served at the holiday tea. Maybe a little older, but then, you're a very grown-up girl."

"And I did a fine job on Thanksgiving," Corri reminded her, holding up an index finger as if to make a point.

"Yes, you did." India laughed and hugged the child. "You most certainly did."

"Come upstairs and see the dresses you could wear. I could help you choose." Corri tugged at India's arm.

"Go ahead, India, I'll call when the soup is ready."

India followed a gleeful Corri up the steps to her room. Across her bed an array of colors, fabrics and textures fanned out like a faded rainbow.

"Look, India, this is my favorite." Corri pointed to a dark blue dress of fine wool.

"Hmmm, that is lovely," India held the dress up to her body and stood before the mirror. It was perfect, from the lace-trimmed neckline to the trim waist and the full skirt, to the tightly fitted sleeves that ended in more lace. It was simple but beautiful. She could easily overlook the tiny moth hole here and there if it fit.

Carefully replacing the dress on the bed, she lifted each of the other two dresses her aunt had brought out of storage for her to try. A black silk Victorian-style dress, high-necked and mutton-sleeved, with green and white embroidery on the bodice, looked too hot. The dark cranberry-red satin looked too formal. The blue would be just right for today.

August called from the foot of the steps to announce that their soup was ready.

"Yeah! Aunt August said I could get dressed after lunch!" Corri shouted gleefully as she fled down the steps.

Laughing, India followed behind, pausing in the hallway where the old black telephone stood on its table. Lifting the receiver, she dialed the number she had committed to memory and waited while it rang. Disappointed to get a recorded voice urging her to leave a message, she did as she was told.

"Nick, hi, it's Indy. I'm at Aunt August's—actually, I'll be going to Captain Jon's for the Christmas tea at three today. Maybe you can stop by. If not, well . . . I just wanted to let you know that I'm home."

She replaced the receiver quietly, then trailed behind Corri's loud rendition of "Jingle Bells" to the kitchen.

At two, all three of the Devlin ladies had dressed and made a hurried stop at Darla's to pick up some of the tea goodies that would be served that day to the ladies and gentlemen—and the occasional child—who had purchased tickets for the event that was a holiday tradition in Devlin's Light. Generations before, attendance at the tea had been one of the *musts* of the town's social season. Ten years ago, the tradition had been revived as a means of raising money for maintenance of the property, and it had proven to be so popular an event that every available seat in the mansion was sold well before the end of November.

"Oh, it's like a palace!" a wide-eyed Corri exclaimed upon entering the wide front door to stand in the massive entry hall. "A Christmas palace."

Fresh garlands of white pine bedecked with ivy, sprayed gold, and huge burgundy satin bows draped the magnificent stairway, which curved from the top of the second-floor landing thirteen feet above. At the foot of the steps stood a massive fir tree, which reached all the way to the top of the open stairwell and sported sparkling diamonds of white and gold lights, burgundy and gold ornaments of angels and spun glass. The entire effect was that of a crystal wonderland. Not a soul entered who did not gasp, much as Corri did, when they saw the tree.

"Wonderful, this year!" August's friends would tap her on the arm as they passed by on their way to whichever room they were to be seated in.

"The best ever." India heard the pronouncement over and over throughout the day.

"Exquisite."

"Just perfect."

"The committee has outdone itself once again."

August would agree, ushering the arrivals through the hallway lest traffic back up, leaving guests stranded on the front porch in the cold. "Wait till you see the dining room," she would say to coax them forward.

Taking a cue from her aunt, India would gently ease an elbow toward the library or the conservatory, the sitting room or the music room, saying, "The table decorations are just delightful this year." Or "I just can't wait to show you what they did with this mantel."

By three-fifteen, all but the stragglers had been seated, and the hustle of serving began. Stealing an occasional peek toward the door whenever it opened, India realized that she was, in fact, looking for Nick. Waiting for him. As if her casual mention of where she'd be would be enough to draw him there, make him drop whatever he was doing and abandon his plans for the day.

In her heart, she had known that it would be so.

"I wouldn't stand so long under the mistletoe if I were you, Miss Devlin. I might have to take advantage of the situation and start the tongues wagging." He had come out of nowhere to whisper in her ear.

"It might be worth it," she whispered back over her shoulder as she placed a delicate china plate of watercress, cucumber and onion, and ham-salad tea sandwiches in front of a blue-haired lady seated just inside the doorway of the library.

"Then come back into the kitchen with me and we'll take our chances."

"Nick, have you noticed we're always sneaking into the pantry, into the kitchen?"

He silenced her with a kiss of welcome and the promise of more kisses before the day was through.

"That's because it's the holiday season and the holidays mean celebrations. And celebrations mean food. Of course, it also means a total lack of privacy," he said pointedly as Darla bustled back in with an empty tray.

"What do you expect?" Darla laughed. "This is one of the two biggest social events of the season in Devlin's Light." She quickly and efficiently replaced the tray's doily of paper lace and restacked the sandwiches, then handed it to Nick. "Here. Go be gracious and charming in the dining room.

"And you, India, take this one to the conservatory. And tell your aunt that I have two more silver teapots ready to go."

"Give some people a little authority and look what they do with it," India muttered, purposely loud enough for Darla to hear. "Napoleon had nothing on you."

"Flattery will get you nowhere." Darla held open the wide swinging door to the hallway for India to pass through.

By the time the last tea drinker had passed back through the festive entry on their way to the front door, hundreds of scones, tiny sandwiches, fruit tarts, petit fours and truffles had been served and happily consumed. Two full tables of first-timers, up from Cape May for the day, upon hearing that the mansion would be open for the Twelfth Night Ball, had eagerly asked to purchase tickets to that gala as well. All in all, the tea had once again been a rousing success, having raised equal amounts of money and civic pride.

"Nick, have you ever had a tour of the captain's manse?" August asked as the clean-up crew—those members of the committee who had not dressed in period clothing for the event—arrived to take over.

"No, I haven't, but I'd love one. Are you offering?"

"I'm old and I've been on my feet for hours," she told him, "but India will take you."

"Right this way, sir." India beckoned him back toward the front of the house. "You're familiar with the first floor, so I'll take you upstairs."

Her long dress trailed behind her, sweeping on the

parquet floor like a wide and elegant broom. She unfastened the velvet rope that blocked off the foot of the steps.

"I'm sorry," a voice called to her from a doorway, "but no one's permitted on the second—Oh, India, it's you."

"Aunt August suggested that I give Nick a tour," India explained to Linda Forrester, the president of the historical society and self-designated keeper of the gate.

"Well, I guess it would be okay." She frowned in a way that made it obvious that if India's name had not been Devlin it would *not* have been okay. "As long as you don't touch anything."

"I hope that doesn't include the guide," Nick whispered, and India giggled, taking his hand and leading him into the first room on the left.

She snapped on the light switch, and twin chandeliers illuminated the cavernous bedchamber, dominated by a massive canopy bed.

"All of the furnishings are original," she told him, "right down to the sheets on the bed. This is the room Captain Jonathan shared with his wife, Jerusalem. 'Salem,' he called her. That's her portrait down in the front hall over the fireplace, and there, on the wall behind the captain's desk."

"She was an interesting-looking lady," he noted, studying the features of the woman who seemed to look down upon them somewhat imperiously.

"Not a true beauty, in the classic sense," India agreed, "but a strong and handsome woman. She was the absolute center of Jonathan's life, and he was hers. Here, sit here"—India pointed to a window seat where dark green cushions were piled high with gold silk pillows of various shapes and sizes—"and I'll show you something."

"Sit?" he stage-whispered, his eyebrows raised in mock horror at the suggestion. "What if Mrs. Forrester catches me?"

"We'll tell her you were feeling faint." India opened the center drawer of a delicately gilded lady's desk that stood off in an alcove by itself and removed a small white leather book. "This was the journal that Salem kept while Jonathan was at sea."

India sat next to him, leaning slightly toward the right and holding the small book at an angle to catch the light.

"Sunday, 12th September, 1701. It being the Sabbath, I spent the day in prayer for my beloved Captain. The storm that raged for two days, it is said, now spreads its fury at sea. I dare not sleep, lest he come home and think I prayed not, but rested while his ship faced such fearsome dangers. How could I sleep, knowing that this evil storm could take him from me? That the last time I kissed him may have, indeed, been the last time I would taste of his lips, that the last time we lay together could have planted a child that might never look upon his father's face? Oh, beloved, thou art my very heart, and my heart beats only to count the minutes until thou art in my arms again."

Sensing Nick's smile, India looked up at him and asked, "What?"

"I was wondering what it would take for a man to inspire such love in a woman." His eyes darkened, from honey to whiskey, as he watched her face. "What would it take, India?"

She closed the journal softly, without looking at it, and placed it beside her on the seat. Turning to him, she wrapped her arms around his neck to draw him close to her.

"I'd have to say that old Captain Jon had nothing on you, Nicholas Enright." She eased his face down toward the kind of kiss that the captain and his lady had probably shared a hundred times, right there on that very same window seat.

"I'd say you were doing just fine."

"India?" August's voice floated down the hall from the top of the steps.

With a reluctant sigh, India called back, "Here, Aunt August."

"Ah, there you are." August entered the grand room with all the grace and authority of its first occupants. "We're all cleaned up downstairs, and everyone is leaving. All the doors are locked, except for the front door, which I will lock on my way out. Here's a key—you'll need it to get out and to relock the front entry behind you when you leave."

"Does Mrs. Forrester know you have that key?" Nick asked with just the right note of suspicion.

"Pooh. Linda Forrester knows better than to take me on. India will leave when she's ready to leave. Just secure the house before you go. Corri and I are taking some things to

Darla's, then Darla and Ollie and Jack will be having dinner with us. As you know, it's pot roast, so it'll be there when you are."

"Thanks, Aunt August." India kissed the woman on the cheek, as did Nick.

"So, here we are," India said as August's shoes tapped softly on the worn carpet and then on the stairwell.

"Yes, so we are."

"I guess I could show you some of the other rooms."

"You could," Nick agreed.

"Although this room has a certain ambience, don't you think?"

The front door slammed shut with a muffled thud.

"Good thing you have that key," he noted. "We might have been stuck here all night."

"Umm." India backed slowly across the room, watching his face, the captain's canopy bed behind her.

His eyebrows raised just a tiny bit more with each step she took.

"Are you thinking what I think you're thinking?" His mouth was suddenly dry.

India grinned.

"What would Mrs. Forrester say?" He grinned back at her, a slow, lazy smile that promised good things.

"What she won't know won't hurt her." India stood at the foot of the bed, and in a heartbeat he was there with her, filling her arms and her mouth, kissing her until she was boneless, leaving her wanting only more of him.

"This dress is only one step up the evolution ladder from the chastity belt," he muttered, the row of tiny buttons seemingly endless in their march from the low neckline to her hips.

"One at a time, Nicky," she whispered, "just take them one at a time."

And one small button at a time was the way he took them, from top to bottom, until her skin felt the cool of the drafty room and the heat from his breath.

She pulled him back onto the bed and he groaned softly, his hands seeking the softness of her, all of her, needing to feel flesh upon flesh, filled with the terrible need of her. Only her. Only India.

She slid the dress from her shoulders and pulled him closer to feast upon her softness, moaning softly as he did so with a mouth that was wet and warm and dark and that drew her toward places she had never been before.

"More," she insisted, and he gave her more of what she demanded. His mouth filled with her, making her cry out.

"More," she told him yet again, and he obeyed, slipping into her warmth and turning the room and the night upside down, and setting it all spinning out of control.

"I love you, India." She heard him say the words just as the dense fog that had swirled around her had finally come to claim them both.

"I love you, India."

There. She heard it again.

She half opened drowsy eyes and sought his face in the darkness. Nick lay still, wrapped around her like a quilt, his head under her chin. Her fingers played with the curly brown hair that tickled her chin. She gazed upward, to find the top of the canopy where she expected the ceiling to be, and began to giggle.

"Why is that funny?" he asked, turning to shift himself onto one elbow. "I confess my love for you and you *giggle?*"

"It's just that where we are."

"Oh, that." He laughed with her. "I tried to tell you that this was inappropriate, India. I did try to remind you that this was a shrine of sorts here in Devlin's Light, but you were so hell-bent on having your way with me that my words of protest fell on deaf ears."

"Words of protest?" India's eyebrows raised. "And which protests were they?"

" 'No, India, we shouldn't, not here, not in the captain's own bed.' "

India shook her head. "Nice try."

"Are you denying that you lured me up here for the sole purpose of seducing me?"

"Actually, it didn't occur to me until I realized that we were alone in this grand old house, in this wonderful room, with this romantic bed."

"The former occupants of which are probably watching." He looked over his shoulder at the portrait of proud

Jerusalem, whose eyes seemed to meet his from across the room. "What do you suppose she would have to say?"

"Salem?" India laughed and drew Nick back to her. "Salem would say, 'Again.'"

∽∾ ∾∽

Darla's Cranberry Walnut Scones
(makes 16 scones)

Preheat oven to 425° and butter a baking sheet and set aside.

2 cups all-purpose flour
1/4 cup brown sugar (plus 1 tablespoon extra for sprinkling on tops)
2 teaspoons baking powder
1/2 teaspoon salt
2 teaspoons unsalted butter
1/2 cup fresh or dried cranberries
1/4 cup chopped walnuts
1 cup buttermilk (plus extra for brushing tops of scones)

In a large bowl, sift flour, brown sugar, baking powder and salt. With a pastry blender or with fingers, cut in butter until the mixture resembles coarse crumbs. Stir in cranberries and walnuts. Make a well in the center and gradually add buttermilk to form a ball. Knead lightly. Do not overwork (dough will be sticky).

Divide dough in half. On a lightly floured board, par or roll each half into an 8-inch round about 1/2-inch thick. Cut each round into 8 triangles. Place the triangles onto baking sheet. Brush tops with buttermilk and sprinkle with remaining 1 tablespoon brown sugar. Bake until golden.

Chapter 21

*T*he hard, raw wind off the bay chilled India to the bone, and she pulled her wool hat down farther, to cover not only her ears but part of her neck as well. She kicked along the wrack line, where debris had washed up following the morning's storm, treading the hard sand cautiously, looking for the clamshells Corri had come in search of while at the same time keeping her eyes peeled for an especially nice piece of driftwood or two to add to Aunt August's collection.

Only an odd gull made an appearance to soar above the frigid beach in search of an early dinner. India called to Corri, who, bundled to the teeth, seemed to almost roll across the dune. Corri pretended not to hear, having not yet gathered a sufficient number of shells to complete her latest project. India bent down and with a gloved hand dug a shell from the sand. Only a partial, it would not do. She tossed it into the bay and walked on down the beach. Across the bay the fog had stalled at the Light like a big gray bus. Soon the bus would head for shore and envelop the entire town.

India called to Corri again, and this time the child responded with a wave. India beckoned her to come, and Corri held up one hand, indicating she would be there in a minute. India turned her face into the keen bay air and inhaled deep shafts of icy breath into her lungs.

He loves me. Nicholas Enright loves me.

She dug her hands deeply into her pockets and repeated the words aloud.

"Nick Enright loves me."

In spite of the cold, she was warmed with the knowledge, blushing at the memory of how she had so shamelessly pursued him the night before. Then she laughed, in spite of herself.

Nick Enright is in love with me.

The joy of it began to flood through her. This incredible man, this wonderful man, loved her. She wished she could share it with Ry, this delight. In an instant, the sadness pulled at the sides of her mouth, and for a long moment, the pain tugged at her. There was nothing to be shared with Ry, not the joy of her falling in love with his best friend, not the wonders of the holiday season.

She drew a shell from her pocket and bent down to write her brother's name in the sand. The slow, shallow waves crept toward it, eating away slowly until the letters had disappeared. It was no more certain than *that,* she thought, watching the water lap at the shore.

Corri ran toward her, calling her name, and India turned to watch the child fly across the beach—in spite of her overabundance of clothing—her pockets bulging with shells. The child's mission had been accomplished. She had found shells perfect enough to be turned into Christmas presents for the people she loved. All in all, in spite of life's uncertainties, was its mystery really any more complicated than the simple delight of a child?

Ry was gone, but the season held wonders to be shared, traditions that India, in her obsession to convict over the past few years, had simply ignored. This year, she would make up for it. There would be a night of caroling, and she would take Corri just as Aunt August had taken her and Ry. There were Christmas cookies to be baked, and presents to be selected and wrapped with equal care. There was so much she had pushed from her life over the past few years that she desperately wanted now. It was too late to share it all with Ry except in memories, but there was Corri and there was Aunt August. And there was Nick.

And there were new memories to be made. India hugged

Corri to her and, against a frigid wind, turned back toward the dune and the warmth of the house on Darien Road.

"Do you think they're dry enough yet, India?" Corri peered anxiously at the counter where her clamshells were lined up after a good scrubbing.

"I think maybe." India nodded. "Now, tell me again what you are going to do with them."

"I am going to glue these little flowers onto them. Then I will paint 'Merry Christmas' *here*"—she pointed to the bowl of the shell—"and tie a ribbon on them so people can hang them on their tree."

"They will be very pretty ornaments, but how will you get the ribbon through the shell?" India asked.

Not having worked out this little detail yet, Corri stared hard at the shells, as if the solution would come to her if she stared long enough and hard enough.

"Ry had a little drill," Corri announced. "It made little holes in things."

"Do you know where it is?" India asked.

"Downstairs, in the basement."

"Okay, then it's down to the basement we go."

After cracking the first three shells she attempted, India got the hang of the drill and managed to make proper round holes just large enough for thin satin ribbon to slip through. Corri gleefully scooped up the shells and raced up the steps to the kitchen to begin her project. India watched as Corri slid a long opaque stick into a sort of gun.

"What is that?" she asked.

"Glue gun." Corri responded without looking up.

"Are you allowed to use that?"

"Umm-hmm. Aunt August lets me help her."

"But does she allow you to use it by yourself?"

Corri hesitated, not wanting to lie. "Do you know how, Indy?"

"I can learn. Let's get these done so we can clean up and start baking."

With India's help, Corri made a dozen shell ornaments, then put them aside on the window sill while both paint and glue dried.

"These really are lovely, Corri," India told her. "Tell me who they are for."

"My teacher. My piano teacher. Mrs. Hart at the library 'cause she always saves special books for me. Mrs. Osborn. Darla's mom." Corri went right down the row, naming the recipients of each shell. "This one's for Zoey, this one's for Georgia and this one is for Mrs. Enright."

"You have two left over," India pointed out. "Are you sure there's no one else?"

"I guess I just made too many."

"Could I have them," India asked, "to send to friends in Paloma?"

"Sure."

India searched through Corri's jars of paint until she found the red. With a careful hand she printed "Season's Greetings from Devlin's Light, NJ" across each of the two shells. She planned on sending one to Roxie and one to the colonel and his wife, who were keeping an eye on her townhouse while she was gone.

"Indy, I don't have a present for Nick." Corri bit her lip.

"Hmm. What might he like?"

"Something special. It has to be special."

"How about a goodie basket?" Aunt August suggested, sweeping into the kitchen in her long black woolen cape, which covered her to her ankles.

"What's a goodie basket?" Corri frowned.

"A basket of goodies, of course." India laughed. "What a great idea."

"Now Corri, you know that Nick has a real sweet tooth," August told her. "You could fill a basket with cookies and homemade fudge and little fruitcakes and nuts and such."

"And a gingerbread man with his name on it?" Corri asked.

"Exactly."

"Yeah. Nick would like that." Corri beamed. "Let's do gingerbread now."

"I guess there's no time like the present. Corri, run and answer the door, sweetie. I think it's the mailman. India, get the butter out to soften and check to make sure we have enough flour. Good grief, here we are, a scant week until Christmas, and the baking's not even done yet." August disappeared into the front hall briefly to hang up her cape. "You were a long time on the beach this morning for such a cold day, India."

"Corri wanted to look for shells. She made tree decorations." India pointed to the counter where the shells lay.

"You were gone long before she joined you." August poured herself a cup of coffee from the pot on the counter and sipped at it. Frowning when she found it to be cold, she popped the cup into the microwave and set it for thirty-five seconds. "India, you know I try never to interfere with your life, but if there's anything you need to talk about, I'm here to listen."

"Thank you, Aunt August. I know that you're there for me. I appreciate it."

"Nick called while you were out," August told her. "He said he'd stop over."

When India didn't comment, August said, "I remember when you were younger, every time you had something on your mind, you headed out to the dunes alone."

"I always seem to think better when I'm by myself." India nodded.

"I was wondering if it was Nick who sent you out to the dunes this morning."

"I guess he was part of it. Nick and Ry were both on my mind."

"Two very fine young men." August put her glasses on to set the oven temperature for the cookies she and Corri would be baking.

"I was thinking about how it would have pleased Ry. About me and Nick. I was wishing that Ry could know."

"Why, child, what makes you think he doesn't know?" August chuckled. "And I think he'd have been more than pleased that you and Nick are"—she glanced at India from behind her dark lenses—"finding each other. Ry wanted you to find someone special and fall in love."

India opened her mouth and was about to speak when August waved her hand at her niece and laughed, saying, "Please don't insult us both by refusing to admit that you're in love with Nick, India."

"I don't know what I am." India sighed.

"Of course you do, dear." August patted her on the back.

"And no one's happier than I am. It's time you settled down."

"Like you did, Aunt August?" India reminded her aunt of the obvious.

"Like perhaps the way I should have," August replied, a shade more sharply than she should have.

"I'm sorry." India softened. "I never stopped to think that maybe you would have rather done something other than take care of Ry and me."

"I never regretted for a minute the days I spent with the two of you. My own children could not have been more dear to me. I could not have been more proud of either of you, could not have loved you more than I did."

"Aunt August, I feel a large *but* hanging in the air," India said.

"But . . ." August sighed and sat in her seat near the window and looked out at the now desolate garden.

"What happened?" India asked.

"India, you may not have noticed, but I have a very broad streak of independence."

"Really?" India dead-panned.

"And when I was younger, I was a little too full of myself. When I left Devlin's Light to go to college, I was certain I'd never come back. What could a little town like this offer to the likes of me? Why, once I got my degree, I'd move on to better things. I would find the love of my life. Oh, I knew exactly who he'd be, India."

"Who?"

"He'd be a scholar, perhaps of Latin or Greek. Perhaps ancient history. Not at all like . . ." A name seemed to catch on her tongue, but she swallowed it back. "Well, like the boys here in Devlin's Light who were on their way to being bay men like their fathers were. Oh no, August Devlin was not going to settle for anything less than a romantic hero who sat with her by the fireside and read Browning's sonnets."

"Did you never find him?"

"Oh, I found him all right." August smiled ruefully. "A classics professor from Princeton, if you will."

"What happened? Why didn't you marry your hero and live happily ever after?"

"It took me a while to realize it, India, but he was a man who was more in love with the image he created of himself than he could ever have loved someone else. He loved the idea of being a man who dressed in tweeds and drank sherry. He loved the idea of reciting poetry to a breathless young woman. He loved the idea of being passionately in love. But he never loved *me*. Not the way I needed to be loved. Not the way . . . some others might have loved me."

Not daring to ask who those "some others" might have been, India watched her aunt take a small sip from her cup.

"Well, by the time I realized just what it was that I really did need, it was too late." August tapped her fingers on the table in front of her. "By the time I had returned to Devlin's Light, it was simply too late."

"Too late for what?"

"Too late to do what I should have been doing all those years I was chasing the fancies of a young and very foolish girl."

"Why was it too late?"

"Because while I was sipping sherry with the man in tweeds, the man I should have married had done exactly what I had told him to do when I left Devlin's Light. He found someone else and married her."

A shocked India watched her aunt walk to the cupboard where she kept her baking supplies and begin to take down what she would need that afternoon.

"Aunt August . . ."

"Don't bother asking who, or why," August told her without turning back to face her. "Just learn from my mistake. Don't think there's anything better waiting for you anyplace else, India, because men like . . . like *Nick* don't come along but once in a lifetime."

"Know where you belong, and with whom," India repeated the sentiments August had expressed.

"My words, all right." August nodded. "And don't think I haven't choked on them."

"What made you choke, Aunt August?" Corri asked, concerned, as she carried the mail into the kitchen. The stack of magazines, catalogs and Christmas cards filled her arms. "Can I help open the cards?"

"You may open all the cards," August told her. "But you

must show them to India and me, so that we know who to thank."

As Corri carefully opened each envelope and read each card aloud, asking for India's help when confronted with a word she did not know and could not sound out phonetically, India watched her aunt putter efficiently in the kitchen and pondered this new information. Aunt August had had a beau, one from Devlin's Light, whom she had scorned in favor of a great unknown world that had beckoned her. She had told him to find someone else, and in time, he had. What had become of him?

And no, in her heart, India knew that she would not make the mistake August had. If nothing else, last night with Nick had confirmed what she herself had begun to suspect. There had never been a man like Nick Enright in her life, and there would never be another. She now knew *who,* and she was pretty sure she knew where.

She was wondering if it was too soon to tell Nick when his face appeared in the glass panel of the back door. He rapped twice before letting himself in.

"Hi," he called in.

"Hi," all three Devlin women answered back.

"I was just down at Lolly's and she was telling me that tonight was Christmas caroling night." He stood in the back doorway, his hands in the pockets of his brown leather jacket, his face ruddy from the cold.

"Well, if you want to know what's going on in Devlin's Light, Lolly's coffee shop is the place to go." August smiled and took down a big yellow earthenware bowl and set it on the table. "So, Nick, what did you think of the captain's house?"

"It's wonderful." He looked over August's head to meet India's eyes. "I hope I don't have to wait a whole year to go back."

India blushed and Nick laughed. August pretended not to notice.

"We're baking stuff," Corri announced. "Christmas stuff, 'cause Christmas will be here before you know it."

"Hmm." He looked over August's shoulder at the recipe she was scanning. "Looks pretty good. Want some help?"

"India, is he allowed?" Corri asked, pointing to the

basket she had hauled in from the pantry to serve as the repository of Nick's goodies.

"Sure." India nodded, then leaned over and whispered in Corri's ear, "He won't know that some things will find their way into his basket."

"Okay," Corri whispered back.

"And then," Corri said, "you can go caroling with us. And drink cocoa at Mrs. Osborn's house."

"That sounds like a great plan. I haven't gone caroling in years."

"Neither have I," India admitted.

"You're kidding, right?" Nick took off his jacket and hung it over the back of a kitchen chair. "How could you be in Devlin's Light at Christmas and not do all the Devlin's Light Christmas stuff?"

"Because for the past few years I haven't been home except for Christmas Eve and Christmas Day."

"Where were you?"

"Chasing dragons, Nick."

He nodded, understanding.

"And how 'bout you, Nick? What do you usually do on Christmas?"

"I usually go to Mother's. This year I told her I wanted to be here."

"Does she mind?"

"No. Not at all. She's looking forward to spending the holiday in Devlin's Light. She thinks it's time I started making my own traditions."

"She does, does she?"

"Umm-hmm. I think we did exactly that last night, don't you?" His face was close enough to touch, and she did, the fingers of both hands trailing the outline of his jaw.

"You are referring to serving at the holiday tea, of course?"

"Of course." He grinned. "Now tell me what I've been missing besides caroling."

"Mrs. Carpenter's wassail party," Corri piped up. "The house tour—that's where people decorate their houses real special and everyone else comes in to see. And there's a living manger down at the church down the street with real animals. And . . ."

Corri chatted away, giving Nick the full holiday rundown. In her mind's eye, India saw it all, as it had been for all of her holiday seasons for so many years of her growing up, not realizing until that very minute just how much she had missed the simple joys of a small-town holiday season. This year would be different. This year she would do it all, and share it all with Nick and Corri and Aunt August, and along the way, maybe she'd establish a new tradition or two.

She smiled to herself, wondering how, in an effort to maintain tradition, they would manage to sneak into Captain Jon's bed again next year.

Chapter 22

*I*t had been the best holiday ever, filled with so much love and joy that India could not believe she had stayed away so long. With old friends and neighbors, she had wandered through the wide streets of Devlin's Light, singing traditional carols and holding hands—Corri on one side, Nick on the other—stopping at this house or that throughout the night for hot drinks and nibbles of holiday treats, their faces stinging from the cold air that blew off the bay. Once back at the big house on Darien Road, Nick had built a fire and they warmed themselves at the hearth, sipping herbal tea, which Aunt August insisted would chase away any chill they may have caught along the way. Nick had hung mistletoe right inside the front door, and he kissed India senseless before he left the warmth of the old house to set off for his own later that night.

India had forgotten what an event it was to trim a Christmas tree until the Sunday before Christmas, when Aunt August announced that *today was the day* and the three Devlins headed toward Captain Pete's, where trees were offered for sale in the parking lot right off the dock.

"I want a really big tree," Corri sang as they got out of Aunt August's Buick and danced across the parking lot.

"Corri, wrap that scarf around your neck, child," August

called after her. "You'll catch your death. India, where are your mittens? That wind is biting cold."

"Aunt August, relax." India laughed. "We're bundled. We're warm. We're fine."

Grumbling under her breath, August trailed behind India, seemingly nonchalant, yet somehow, suddenly, plagued by a bad case of the fidgets at the same time.

Curious, India thought. *She's jumpy as a cat.*

"I found one!" Corri zipped around a row of Scotch pines. "Oh, India, wait till you see!"

The excited child dragged India to the first row of trees, those largest ones that stood apart and lined up along the edge of Captain Pete's dock.

"Here, here, look!" Corri jumped up and down and pointed to a large blue spruce that lay stretched out along the wooden boards for ten feet running.

"Oh, it's enormous!" India laughed.

"How on earth would we get such a tree home?" August took a step back and squinted skyward as a young man in a dark blue parka hoisted the tree and turned it slowly to show off its perfection.

"Nick said he'd meet us here," India told her. "He'll get it home for us."

"Oh, can't you just see it in the sitting room?" Corri closed her eyes and smiled joyously, envisioning this king of trees gaily bedecked and suitably bedazzled.

"Well, you know that we always put a tree in the dining room as well. I doubt Nick will be able to get both that monster tree and another tree on top of that four-wheel-drive of his."

"Well then, I suppose I could arrange to deliver one for you." Captain Pete leaned on his cane and surveyed the scene. Was it India's imagination, or did he appear to be looking at everyone except her aunt?

"That won't be necessary, Pete," August told him, not looking at him either. "India said Nick would take it home for us."

"Suit yourself, August." Pete stiffened slightly and turned toward the door of his shop.

"Wait, Captain Pete," India called after him. "Maybe you

could have someone deliver the big tree and Nick can take the smaller one."

"That's what I said," Pete told her.

"That would be fine." India smiled and patted the older man on the arm. "We would appreciate it. And I'm sure that Nick will be happy to have only one tree to strap on to the roof of his car."

"Nick already has one strapped on the roof of his car," Nick said, emerging from the pine forest that rose temporarily between the boardwalk and the parking lot, "but there's room for one more."

"Oh, Nick!" Corri clapped her gloved hands. "Wait till you see. There. There it is! Isn't it the best tree *ever?*"

"Wow!" Nick whistled. "Now that's what I call a *tree.* Makes that little six-footer I just bought look like a twig."

"Won't it be wonderful?" Corri danced.

"What does India say?" Nick asked, putting an arm around India's shoulders and pulling her to him.

"Wonderful." She smiled into his eyes, a smile of welcome, of promise. "It will be wonderful."

"We still need a tree for the dining room," August spoke up, her voice flat and devoid of her usual enthusiasm.

"One more tree for Miss August." Nick took her by the arm. "How big?"

"Five, six feet or so."

"Fat or thin?"

"Whatever." August shrugged, and India turned to stare. Whatever was going on?

"Show us what you've got, Pete." Nick turned to the captain, whose eyes seemed to follow August's back as Nick led her down the path toward the smaller trees.

Pete coughed and scratched his head when he realized that both India and Nick had caught him staring at August.

"I'm sure Pete has someone who can help us." August marched on without turning back.

"Oh, but no one knows trees like Pete." India, determined to get to the bottom of whatever it was between the good captain and her aunt, gestured to Pete to accompany her to the six-footers.

"Well, what kind would you be wanting?" Pete nodded,

falling into step next to India. "We've got some nice **white** pines."

"White pine needles are too soft. The ornaments fall right off. If all you've got is white pine, then we're wasting our time," August called over her shoulder.

"You know I carry more than one kind of tree, August. But if you want to take your business out to the highway to one of those places where they sell half-dead trees out of the back of a truck, don't let me stop you," Pete called back, leaning on India so that he could wave his cane at August's back.

"I saw some great Scotch pines and some beautiful firs," Nick said. He dropped back to whisper in India's ear, "What do you suppose that's all about?"

"Beats me." India shrugged. "I have never seen my aunt act like that to anyone."

"You'd almost think they were . . ." Nick stopped on the path and grabbed India's elbow. "It's almost as if there is something there."

"Aunt August and Captain Pete?" India asked, wide-eyed.

"You have to admit, they're circling each other like a couple of wary cats. Let's just watch this play out." Nick grinned.

The captain and August were still at it when Nick and India caught up to them right around the five-foot firs.

"It's as fresh a cut tree as you'll find," Pete said, leaning forward on his cane, "unless of course you cut it yourself."

"Hmmm. There's a thought."

"That's a perfectly lovely tree, Aunt August," India interjected. "I think it's perfect for the dining room."

"If you say so, India." August shrugged, as if it was all the same to her.

"Well, then." Nick held his hands out to take the tree. "Let's get these babies bound up for travel. Let's see, we can put this one on top of the Pathfinder with my tree, and Pete can have the big one dropped off later."

Before August could protest, India had paid for the two trees and Nick had tied the fir on top of his car with his Scotch pine. Anxious to get home and start decorating, India found Corri chasing a schoolmate through the aisles, then set about to look for her aunt. She found her at the end of the dock, facing the Light.

"Our first Christmas without our boy," August said softly, recognizing India's footfall on the wooden planks.

"I miss him too." India put an arm around her aunt and hugged her.

"It'll never be the same." August cleared her throat.

"No, it won't," India agreed, "but it can still be good."

"I suppose so." August nodded.

A languid land breeze bore the scent of pine, and India's nostrils sought out the underlying salt smell of the bay. Pine plus salt equaled Devlin's Light at Christmas, she thought, clinging to the smell of both land and sea. It smelled like home to her. She sighed deeply and, with her arm still around her aunt, walked back to the car, knowing full well that the eyes of the old captain followed every step they took.

"We are going to be decorating trees all day!" Corri crowed as the car pulled into the driveway on Darien Road.

"It's a dirty job, but somebody has to do it." India nodded.

"It's not dirty at all," Corri told her, "'cept maybe in the attic when you go to get the boxes out."

"I'll do the dirty work this year," Nick told her as he swung their tree off the roof of his car. "But in return, you have to keep me plied with snacks and warm drinks."

"We have lots of good snacks," Corri assured him. "We made tons of cookies and good stuff to eat. And we can make hot chocolate."

"There you go then." He leaned the tree up alongside the back of the house. "Tree stands?" he asked India.

"In the attic. With the dusty boxes."

"Lead the way." He stood back while August unlocked the back door.

"Follow me, sir." India pulled off her red wide-brimmed wool hat and shook her curls loose, fluffing her hair with her hands. "I hate hat-head."

"Hat-head?" Nick went up the steps behind her, thoroughly enjoying the view.

"When you wear a hat and your hair gets flattened down." She grinned. "Hat-head."

"Here, let me help you with that," he murmured, stopping her halfway through the attic door and running his fingers through her hair, from her scalp to the end of the silky strands. "I have the cure for hat-head," he told her, lowering his lips to hers.

"Nick," she said, after kisses that left her breathless, "what has this got to do with my hair?"

"Nothing." He shrugged and kissed her again. "Absolutely nothing."

"Save it." She giggled and tugged on his sleeve, leading him up the steps to the large, well-lit attic. "We have work to do."

They found the boxes of Christmas ornaments stacked in one corner and, after dusting off the lids, began the job of carrying them all to the first floor, where Corri poked in every one, exclaiming over its contents. Nick found the tree stands and, under August's guidance, set up the tree in exactly the right spot in the dining room.

"Now, this tree gets the angels," August told them. "So Corri, you find the box with the angels. First, of course, we need to get the lights on."

"I'll do that," Nick volunteered, "and India, you can get me some of those wonderful spice cookies."

"It's almost noon," August told them. "We'll have some chowder first, then you can have some cookies."

"Why do I feel like an eight-year-old all of a sudden?" Nick laughed and set about the task of getting all the lights on the tree, arguing all the while with India over whether the proper progression was from left to right or right to left.

Corri found the angels, and after lunch Nick sat back and watched Corri and India decorate the tree. There were finely spun glass angels, delicate as wishes on the wind, and cross-eyed angels made of bright construction paper by India as a first-grader, angels made of papier-mâché and painted with pale, heavenly shades of pink and blue and yellow, and angels made of porcelain, their wings touched with gold. Nick quietly watched the interplay between woman and child, his heart aching with love, a song of thanks singing somewhere in his consciousness. Not able to wait until Christmas morning to give Aunt August her special gift, Corri proudly showed off the angel she had made of shells, and she could not contain her joy when August pronounced that it was the very angel that should sit at the top of the tree that year and look over all the other angels. Nick lifted the child to the top of the tree to place her angel there, and he felt a lump in his throat at her delight in the simple act of having her gift acknowledged for the treasure it truly was.

"Auctor pretiosa facit," August murmured. "The giver makes the gift precious."

It was near four when a white panel truck pulled into the driveway and stopped near the end. Corri peeked through the curtains and shouted, "It's Captain Pete with the big tree!"

India opened the front door, and Nick went out to assist in bringing the tree inside. The captain, obviously cold and tired after standing in the wind all day but still gallant, in his own peculiar way, started slowly up the front steps of the house to greet India.

"For heaven's sake, come in, Captain Pete." India showed him into the front hall. "You look like you're frozen."

"Well, I admit it's been a long day, India."

"Come in by the fire," she insisted.

"Maybe just till they get the tree in." He let her take his arm and lead him into the sitting room, where he looked around slowly, as if taking it all in. "Funny how some things change so little over the years."

"What's that?" India asked.

"Oh, this room." He waved his cane in a one-eighty turn. "The smell of this house at the holidays. Brings back memories."

Really, India mused.

"Why don't you sit right here on the settee and let me get you something hot to drink." India gestured to the small red love seat.

"Well now, India, I'm only here to deliver a tree."

"From the looks of things it'll take a few minutes for Nick and your son to get that tree in here. You just sit right down and relax for a few minutes. What would you like to drink?" she asked from the doorway.

"What?" His eyes had wandered around the room again, as if searching for something that was no longer there. "Oh. Coffee would be appreciated, India. Very much, it would be. I've had enough hot chocolate today to turn my blood to sugar water."

"I'll be right back," India promised.

Crossing the threshold into the kitchen, India saw her aunt gazing out the back door.

"Aunt August, Captain Pete is here."

"Is he now?" August turned back to the stove and lifted the lid on a pot of chili. Without looking at India, she slid a pan of cornbread into the oven.

"Yes, he's in the sitting room." India took down a mug and filled it with fresh coffee. "I should have asked him what he wanted in this."

"Black," August muttered without turning around. "The captain always took his coffee black."

"Oh." India's eyebrows raised slightly. *So. She knows how he takes his coffee, does she?*

"Aunt August said you took your coffee black," India said as she handed the cup to Captain Pete.

"Oh, she remembered now, did she?" He smiled softly and spoke as if only to himself. "Fancy that."

Nick and young Pete brought the tree in, then struggled with the stand, which was not inclined to hold so tall a tree. After forty minutes of effort, they finally had it in the stand, albeit tied to the mantel on one side and the bookcase on the other. India refilled the captain's cup twice, the second time just as his son was ready to leave.

"Oh, stay and finish that." India smiled as she placed a plate of cookies on the table in front of the settee and gave Nick a tap on the shin with the toe of her shoe. "We'll drive you home, won't we, Nick?"

"Uh, sure we will." He nodded. "Be happy to."

"Hmmph." August stood in the doorway, her hands on her hips, surveying the jerry-rigged technique used to secure the tree. "I hope no one gives that rope a good tug."

"How are you planning to get an angel to the top of that tree, young miss?" Pete asked Corri, pointing to the topmost tip of the tree, which brushed up against the ceiling.

"Someone will have to help me," she said. "But first we

have to decide what to put on the top of this tree. We have all angels in the dining room."

"Is that a fact?"

"It is. Want to see?"

"I'd be pleased to see your angels." Pete pushed himself up off the settee with the use of his cane. "You don't mind, do you, August?"

"Of course not, why should I mind?"

"Good." He brushed past her.

"That is one ornery man," August muttered, plumping the pillows on the love seat to give herself something to do.

"Really?" India snickered.

"And what is so funny, miss?" August's eyes narrowed, seeming to challenge India to answer.

"Nothing, Aunt August." India shrugged innocently.

Corri's girlish laughter floated from the dining room.

"Sounds as if Corri doesn't find him ornery at all," Nick noted.

"Corri is six years old. She'll laugh at anything." August sniffed and swept back to her kitchen, pausing in the doorway to the dining room, where Corri saw her and called her in. The woman hesitated a moment before joining them.

"Let's go to my place," Nick whispered in India's ear.

"Now? But we just said we'd take Pete . . ." She paused, then smiled. ". . . home."

"I guess he could wait till we got back." Nick nibbled on her earlobe. "Or perhaps August could drive him."

"I should tell her that we're leaving," India said.

"Let's put our coats on first so she doesn't have time to stop us."

"Good idea." India nodded.

As quietly as humanly possible, India and Nick tiptoed into the hall and retrieved their jackets, sliding their arms into sleeves and fingers into gloves without making a sound.

"We'll ambush 'em," Nick deadpanned, "then bolt for the door, got it?"

India giggled, and he steered her into the dining room.

"We'll be back," Nick announced. "We're just going to run my tree out to the cabin."

"Won't be long." India waved and backed out of the room.

"But . . ." August's protests were lost as, even as she rose to speak, Nick and India were out the front door and closing it behind them.

"Nick?" India asked as he was backing out of the driveway.

"Hmmm?" Nick had turned on the radio and was searching for a song to sing along with.

"Are we really driving all the way out to your place just to drop off your tree?"

"Of course not." He looked at her as if she was daft.

"Are you planning on seducing me?"

"Yup."

"Nick?"

"Yes?"

"Drive faster."

Chapter 23

A mean fog had rolled in off the bay and spread like a down quilt through the marsh. Nick had slowed to a crawl on his way up the lane. The sensor lights on the back of the cabin were barely visible as anything other than a dim, opaque glow at the end of the drive.

"This is so spooky," India whispered as she opened her car door and hopped out. The crushed white stones crunched slightly under her weight, the soft grinding of stone on stone the only sound in the dense night.

"No, no, sweetheart." Nick draped an arm over her shoulder and ambled gently to the steps leading to the wraparound deck. "Think of it as a low-lying cloud come to wrap us inside. It's much more romantic."

Unconvinced, India glanced uneasily behind them as they reached the front of the cabin, their shoes an echoing *tap tap tap* on the wooden walk, giving her the feeling of being followed. Nick unlocked the back door and held it open for her to pass through, and she did so gratefully.

"It's cool in here," he noted, glancing at the thermostat. "Would you like me to build a fire for you?"

"Not in the fireplace."

She could hear his chuckle in the dark as he relocked the back door. Dropping her jacket on the nearest chair and kicking quietly out of her shoes, she slipped into the hallway and down two doors to where she remembered his room to be. A scarce minute later he followed her.

"Hand over old Otto," he told her, and from the opposite side of the bed she tossed the bear.

"Careful with the old boy," Nick said, pretending to scold her. "You know, my mom and dad gave me this bear when I was three. Best Christmas present I ever got."

She pitched her sweatshirt across the bed and hit him in the chest with it.

"Until this year," he mumbled, and she laughed, her jeans following the sweatshirt. He met her halfway across the king-sized bed and pulled her down and under him.

"Kiss me, Nicky," she demanded, drawing his face to hers.

"That's the very least I plan to do to you tonight," he promised.

"I will hold you to that." She sighed as his lips skimmed the tip of her chin to the hollow of her neck. She arched slightly beneath him, inviting him to feast, and he accepted the gift of herself hungrily.

By the time they were sated, the fog had started to recede across the bay, and a moon of majestic proportions had just begun to push its face through the clouds.

"Is it still Sunday?" India asked, opening heavy eyelids and searching for a clock in the unfamiliar room.

"Only barely." Nick sat on the edge of the bed and placed a tray between them. "Sit up."

"What is that?" she asked sleepily.

"Dinner."

"Dinner?"

"Nothing elaborate." He gestured for her to sit and handed her a plate upon which sat a perfectly golden grilled cheese sandwich and some chips.

"You'd make a great short-order cook." She wrapped the soft flannel sheet around her chest and sat up a little higher on the pillows. "Nick, this is heaven. It's wonderful." She took the tall glass he handed her and sipped at the sparkling water. "You are spoiling me. No one ever served me dinner in bed at midnight."

"Good. You deserve to be spoiled." He grinned. "And we should have dinner at midnight in bed often."

"Oh my gosh! Midnight. I should call Aunt August. She might be worried, with the fog."

"Relax. I already did."

"You called my aunt?" India laughed. "What did you tell her? Where did she think I was while you were calling her?"

"She didn't ask where you were, and she didn't seem overly surprised that you would be staying. She said she knew the fog was bad, since she had driven the captain home around eight."

"Aunt August drove the captain home?" Wrapping the sheet more tightly around her, she leaned forward and said, as if to herself, "I'll bet he's the one."

"He's the one who what?" he asked.

"I'll bet Captain Pete is the man she left behind when she left Devlin's Light in search of her romantic scholar."

"Sounds like there's a story there."

"There is. If you give me some of your chips, I might even tell you about it."

"August and Old Pete, eh?" He plunked a few more potato chips on her plate.

"I wonder if it's too late to get them back together again."

"I think they're probably old enough to decide that for themselves," he told her, taking the plates and stacking them one on the other on the tray. "You ready for dessert?"

"Umm. I am." She slid sure fingers under his robe to tangle in the brown curls on his chest.

"On the other hand, this can probably wait." He passed the tray to a nearby dresser.

"What was that?" She peered over his shoulder at the two bowls, each of which was covered by a white porcelain saucer.

"Ice cream with chocolate sauce." He nibbled on her bottom lip. "Of course, by the time we get back to it, it will be chocolate soup."

"Chocolate soup sounds just fine."

Nick slid under the sheet to join her and he leaned on one elbow to gaze down into her face. "I never wanted anyone the way I want you. And I knew it the first time I saw you."

"After Ry's funeral?"

"I think it might have been before that."

"I never met you before that."

"I saw you, though. I saw you when you were home one time last spring. You were walking down the street, just sashaying along."

"I don't sashay." she protested.

"Well, you did this day. And your hair was blowing around your face, and I stopped dead in my tracks. I was at Potter's market looking out the window, and you walked by and I asked who you were. I couldn't believe you were Ry's sister."

"Why not?"

"Because I'd seen pictures of you in your aunt's house," he said, caressing her shoulder with a gentle hand, "and they just didn't do you justice. The camera doesn't seem able to catch that light in your smile, or the exact color of your eyes, like rain-washed lilacs. Or the way you bite your bottom lip when you think I'm going to kiss you."

"Like now?" she asked.

"Exactly so."

"Do it, Nick." She snuggled against him. "I've never been naked in your bed before, and I want to take full advantage of the situation."

The early morning sun had burned off the remnants of fog, and with the sun came the aroma of something totally wonderful. Tantalized by the smell, India slipped into the soft robe that Nick had left over the bottom of the bed and went into the great room. Nick stood at the stove, his back to her.

"Can't resist my omelets, can you?" he said without turning around.

"Hmmm." She wound around him to sniff. "No. I can't."

He turned the omelet expertly with one hand and handed her a cup of coffee with the other. She leaned her elbows on the window sill and looked out across the bay.

"I love waking up right on the water," she told him.

"Then we should make it a regular part of your routine." He grinned and slid the smooth omelets onto two plates, which he placed on the small table near the window.

"Come eat your breakfast." His hands slid around her waist and he nuzzled the side of her face.

"Nick, do you realize that all we do is eat and make love?" She sat down and lifted her fork.

"What? Are you sure? Damn. And here I thought we were engaged in something meaningful. Something with *merit*. And now you tell me that all we've been doing is making love and eating. Why didn't you stop me before this got out of hand?"

"Nick"—she laughed—"have you done any work in the last week?"

"Actually, I have. I spent part of yesterday morning making sketches from some slides."

"Sketches of what?"

"Tiny multicelled animals called rotifers. They look like minuscule hairy pears under the microscope. I'll show you after breakfast if you like."

"Where were they?"

"Before they were on my slide? In the marsh. I collected them during the summer, but I'm just getting around to doing the sketches."

"Ah, yes, life on the bay, seen and unseen."

"It's all part of the whole."

"Ry used to do that when we were little. He used to get a jar of water from the bay or the swamp and put tiny drops on slides."

"We talked about that. I used to do the same thing when I was little, only I used pond water. It fascinated me. All these things were living in the water—like a secret world—and you couldn't even *see* them without a microscope. It was just one of the many things we had in common, Ry and I."

"I miss him." India felt the sudden lump rise to swell her throat. "I'm almost dreading Christmas Day. It will be so quiet."

"Don't you have a big group on Christmas?"

"No. Thanksgiving is the day we all gather. Christmas is always just the immediate family."

"India, what would you think of us spending Christmas together? I mean all of us, my mother and sisters and you and August and Corri?"

"I'd love it. I'll have to ask Aunt August, but I'll bet she'd be delighted."

"We could go out to the Light for the bird count and then have dinner. Even Zoey said she was interested in going."

"I hope she does. I like Zoey," she told him as she stirred her coffee. "I hope she can make it."

"She'll be here. Mother will insist on it. Of course, last week she was thinking about handling show dogs that belong to one of my mother's neighbors, but that's subject to change. This week I think Zoey may just be working on being Zoey."

"I would think she could do just about anything," India told him. "She's beautiful enough to be an actress or a model. She seems to have a bit of a dramatic streak. And I'd bet the camera just loves her face."

"Modeling bored her. And she's tried acting. It seems that our Zoey has a problem with memorized lines. She thinks the stage should be a little more spontaneous. I'm afraid she ad-libbed a few times too many. Mother keeps insisting that it's all going to come together in the new year."

"I'm with your mother." India stood up and stretched. "I can't remember when I've been this lazy. The last time I was still undressed at ten in the morning."

"It's good for you to relax." He pushed back from the table and patted his thighs, motioning for her to sit on his lap. "Tell me what you'd like to do today."

"I need to finish my Christmas shopping and help Aunt August finish the decorating. Christmas is in two days. How 'bout you?"

"Guess I'll do a few more sketches, maybe see if Darla needs help making her deliveries."

"That's sweet, Nicky." India tucked a curl behind her ear. "Do you think she could go with us to the Twelfth Night Ball? I'd hate to think about her home alone with nothing to think about except the great time she and Ry had there last year."

"If she'd like to go, I think it's a wonderful idea."

"We could dress alike. Like my twin great-great-aunts. And we'll do our hair alike, like we did when we were in high school." She envisioned it in her mind, she and Darla befuddling the boys at the sophomore dance. "It used to drive people crazy. From the back no one could tell us apart."

"I'll remember to be very careful. I could end up embarrassing myself terribly." To make his point, he patted her rear as she stood up. "Where are you going?"

"I thought I'd take a shower, if that's okay."

"It's okay, if I get to supervise."

"Nobody supervises when I shower. If you come in, I'll put you to work." She twirled the end of the robe's sash.

"What exactly did you have in mind?"

"You'll have to wash my back," she told him, backing toward the hall. "Or something."

"It's that 'something' that gets my attention every time." He sighed and followed her.

"Indy, Indy!" Corri's little face, puffed from sleep and glowing with anticipation, hung over India's own. "I think he was here!"

"Who was here, sweetie?" India yawned, reluctant to leave the dream she had been having before she'd felt little fingers shaking her shoulder.

"Santa! He was here! I peeked from the top of the steps and the lights are on the tree and it looks like lots of things are under it."

"Hmm, well then"—India stretched and sat up—"Merry Christmas, sweetie."

"Merry Christmas, India."

"Merry Christmas, you two," August called from the bedroom doorway. "Corri, I was just downstairs and it looks like there are a lot of presents under that tree with your name on them. I think you'd better get down there and see what's what."

"Yea!" She whooped and sped down the steps.

"Was I that anxious on Christmas morning?" India pushed the covers aside and stood up.

"Worse. You and your brother used to set an alarm clock for four A.M. and wake me and your father up to open presents. At least Corri let me sleep until six."

India went into the bathroom to splash water on her face and to slip into an Irish knit sweater the color of clotted cream and a pair of soft olive corduroy jeans. She dug a pair of big black and white tweedy socks out of her dresser and pulled them on over chilly toes. From the stereo in the sitting room the *Messiah* was just beginning. The aroma of freshly brewed coffee and cinnamon met her halfway down the stairs. Christmas in the Devlin house on Darien Road always smelled exactly the same. At the thought of Aunt August's sinfully good cinnamon raisin buns, India's mouth began to water and she quickened her step, following her nose into the kitchen. As quietly as possible, she opened the oven door to peek in.

"India Devlin, get your nose out of that oven," August scolded from the front of the house, and India laughed out loud. Pouring herself a cup of coffee, she went into the sitting room, where billows of discarded wrapping paper spread across the old oriental carpet like bubbles blown from a magical pipe.

"Indy, wait till you see what I got." Corri rushed to her. "Look, look! She's real!"

"Why, yes, I believe she is." India's eyes sparkled as Corri gingerly held out the tiny orange tabby kitten.

"I can name her anything I want, Aunt August said so. She's my very own kitty. My very own pet."

"Well, you know that having your very own pet is a very big responsibility." India smoothed back the child's hair, recalling a Christmas long ago when a similar kitten had waited under the tree for her.

"I will take wonderful, excellent good care of her, I promise."

"I know that you will, sweetie."

"Want to hold her?"

"I would love to hold her." India sat on the floor and looked into the deep blue eyes of the kitten. "I used to have a kitty that looked just like her. Remember, Aunt August?"

"Oh, I do indeed."

"What was her name?"

"Mary Francis."

"You named your kitty 'Mary Francis'?" Corri eyed her strangely, clearly wondering whatever would possess one to do so.

"Yes." India laughed. "It is an odd name for a kitty, I agree, and for the life of me I can't remember why I chose that name."

"Is that what you called her?" Corri tried to picture India

standing at the back door and calling "Here, Mary Francis!" but could not.

"No, I called her 'Francie.' She used to sleep on my bed and bring me mice that she caught in the attic."

"Real live mice?" Corri's little nose wrinkled up.

"Well, they were real enough, though not so live by the time Francie was finished with them." August shook her head. "She had the most endearing habit of leaving their little mouse bodies in my shoes. It got so that I had to close my shoes into the closet at night so she couldn't leave those furry little gifts for me."

"She was so proud of herself," India mused.

"Oh, that she was. Francie was an excellent little mouser."

"What happened to her?"

"She died when I was in high school," India told her. "Ry said it was because she knew I'd miss her too much when I left for college, but it was just old age. She was fourteen that year, and that's a pretty good age for a kitty."

"What did you do with her?"

"We buried her out back, all the way at the end of the yard, where the dune comes in. Where she could hear the birds and smell the sea and rest in the warm sun." India's voice caught, remembering.

"I will take very good care of my kitty, India. And if she ever dies, I will bury her with Francie, and they can be together." Corri, sensing India's sudden sadness, assured her that Francie wouldn't always rest alone.

"Well, I hope we have . . . whatever you decide to call her . . . for a long time. She's a dear little thing."

"I'm going to call her 'Amber,'" Corri announced a while later, "'cause that's what Ry used to call me sometimes and I like that name. He said when I grew up my hair would be the color of amber."

"Well then, 'Amber' it is," August said softly, taking her own memories of past Christmases with her into the kitchen.

India had just settled down by the fire to read a line or two from one of the books August had given her when the sound of car doors caught her attention. Rising to look out the window, she laughed out loud. Who but Delia Enright would arrive in Devlin's Light for Christmas dinner in a Mercedes sedan, her driver at the wheel? India sought shoes amidst the wrappings and boxes and slipped into them.

"Merry Christmas!" she called from the doorway, and Delia waved heartily.

"Come give me a hand," Delia called back, and India bounced off the porch and down the sidewalk.

"Nicky is driving his four-wheel and Zoey is with him, but I have most of the gifts here." Delia paused to kiss India's cheek at just about the same time she gestured to her driver to take some of the packages from the long white car.

"Delia, for heaven's sake!" India gasped at the number of brightly colored shopping bags lined up, waiting to be carried into the house. "Who are all these presents for?"

"Hmmm? Oh, mostly for Corri." Delia's eyes sparkled. "I was in New York last week, and I passed F.A.O. Schwarz and I thought, why not? It's been so many years since I had a little one to buy for. I hope you don't mind, India, I just couldn't help myself."

India laughed, recalling Nick's descriptions of his mother's generosity.

"I don't mind, Delia, and I'm sure that Corri will be overwhelmed."

"Wonderful!" Delia smiled happily as she removed several more bags from the car and piled them into India's arms. "Every child should be overwhelmed on Christmas morning at least once in their life."

The driver, having delivered the packages to the porch, opened the trunk and began taking out more packages. India raised an eyebrow, but before she could say anything, Delia waved a hand and told her, "Those are a few things for Georgia. Randall here is on his way to Baltimore to pick her up and bring her back. I'm afraid she took a bad turn on her ankle this week and is off it for a few days."

"Wasn't she performing in the *Nutcracker* this week?"

"Was. And while I'm sick over her being hurt and disappointed, I'd be lying if I said I didn't want her here with us for the day, India."

Nick's Pathfinder pulled into the driveway, Zoey popping out of the passenger-side door before the vehicle had completely stopped.

"Merry Christmas!" Zoey danced across the lawn to hug India. "This is so wonderful of you to share your Christmas with us, India. It'll be such fun. What time does the bird count start? I'm all ready."

"You had me fooled." India laughed, pointing to the fine, soft woolen dress and butter-soft leather boots that Zoey wore.

"Not to worry, I brought stuff to change into."

"Merry Christmas, India." Nick, loaded down with packages from his car, bent to catch her lips in passing.

There were holiday hugs all around in the hallway, and the happy chatter seemed to expand on its own to fill every corner of the house. Corri, eager to show off Amber, gave Delia patient instructions on the proper way to hold a kitten and permitted Delia to do so while she opened this newest round of gifts. As the mantel clock chimed two o'clock, India suggested that it was time to leave for the Light for the bird count.

"I want to go." Corri shot up and ran for her jacket.

"So do I." Zoey yawned. "All this comfort and joy is doing me in. I need fresh air. I need to get moving."

"Go change, duchess," Nick told her. "You have exactly five minutes."

"I'll be down in less," Zoey told him, and India watched, amused, as brother and sister synchronized their watches and counted seconds.

"Go," Nick told her, and Zoey took off up the stairs while India gave her directions to her room.

"Oh! I almost forgot!" India ducked under the tree and retrieved a present wrapped in gold-foil paper. "This is probably the best time to give this to you."

She handed the box to Nick and tugged on his sleeve, indicating for him to sit beside her on the sofa.

With a happy grin he accepted the gift and proceeded to tear the wrappings off with all the flair earlier exhibited by Corri.

"India, these are perfect! Wonderful! Thank you, sweetheart." Clearly pleased with her choice, Nick lifted the new Minolta field glasses to his eyes and adjusted the lenses. He rose and walked to the window, focusing on something in a tree across the street. "These are fabulous, so much better than the old ones I have at the cabin. They don't have nearly the range nor the clarity that these have." He leaned over and kissed her on the mouth.

"Four minutes, forty-seven seconds!" Zoey panted as she plopped on the bottom step to tie her sneakers.

"You're not done, you're still tying," Nick observed.

Zoey stuck her tongue out and grabbed her down jacket from a chair in the front hall.

"Do you think we should wait for Georgia? Do you think she would want to go with us?"

"The closest Georgia's ever gotten to the great outdoors is the L. L. Bean catalog." Zoey laughed. "I don't think we have to worry about not waiting for Georgia."

"Are you dressed warmly enough, sugar?" India asked Corri. "Where's your scarf? And your gloves?"

"You sound amazingly like your aunt." Nick chuckled, taking India's hand as they walked to the Pathfinder.

"I admit I do hear a touch of her every now and then."

The foursome loaded into Nick's car and headed out to the cabin, where they would take his rowboat across the bay to the Light.

"We're lucky it's not really too cold today," India told them as they piled into the small boat, she and Nick on the one seat, Zoey and Corri on the other. "One year my dad and Ry and I had to row back in a snowstorm."

She grabbed her oar and closed her eyes, remembering how immutable the Light had looked, rising from the beach with swirls of snow streaking around it. The water had been choppy and dark and the snow had stung her face sharply as they rowed across the inlet. She had never felt colder than she had on that day, when the wicked storm had hit hours earlier than predicted and brought with it a bad-tempered wind from the north. The frigid waters had sloshed into the boat and numbed their feet and legs. Her father had carried the two frozen children into the sitting room to deposit them in front of the fire, and August had stripped them of their wet clothes and wrapped them in blankets and made them all drink hot lemonade laced with honey. By the time the week had ended, August was nursing both Roberts through pneumonia.

This year a more benevolent breeze blew around the

small craft, chilling their hands without cutting to the bone. India rowed hard against the slightly agitated waters, her eyes on the Light ahead, her heart beating curtly under her sweater. It was hard to come here, to be here on this day, to face the place where her brother had died, when he should be here with them to share the traditions, to count and record the birds, and later to kiss Darla under the mistletoe and help Aunt August to lift the holiday goose from the oven.

As if reading her mind, Corri asked softly, "Indy, do you think Ry knows we're here?"

"I'm certain of it." She nodded.

"Good. He can help us find birds." Corri hopped out of the boat onto the hard sand.

Chapter 24

"Here, Zoey," India said, as she drew a notebook from the inside pocket of her down jacket and handed it over, "since this is your first time, you can be the official recorder. There's a pen clipped inside the cover."

"Great." Zoey opened the notebook to the first blank page. "What do I do first?"

"Enter the date," India told her. "Let's start out on the jetty. That way we'll have a good view of land and sea."

"Right." Zoey took Corri's hand and marched behind India and Nick. "Look. There's a bird." She paused to enter "One seagull."

"Ah, Zoey, we try to be just a little more specific than that," an amused India told her.

"Oh. Sure." Zoey nodded and amended her original entry. "One white seagull."

Corri giggled and Zoey shot her what was supposed to pass for a dirty look.

"With gray wings," Zoey added pointedly.

Corri laughed.

"What was wrong with that?" Zoey asked, pretending to be insulted.

"We have to record the bird by name, Zoey," India told her gently.

"The bird's *name*? You're kidding, right? How do you

know what his name is?" Zoey's brows knit together and she called to the bird. "Excuse me, Edward? Stephen? Jonathan Livingston?"

"Tell her, Corri." Nick grinned and sat on the nearest rock.

"It's a laughing gull."

"A laughing gull?" Zoey frowned. "It doesn't look all that happy to me."

"That's what it's called." Corri shrugged. "That's what kind of gull it is."

"Okay." Zoey sighed and sat down beside her brother and bent her head to write. "One laughing gull. Oh, there's another. We'll make that *two* laughing gulls. Nothing to this bird-counting stuff, once you get the hang of it. What? India, are you laughing at me?"

"I'm sorry, Zoey, the second one there is a Bonaparte's gull. It's smaller and has kind of pinkish legs," India pointed out.

"And what, dare I ask, is that one?" Zoey pointed to a third gull that flew overhead.

"What do you notice about it that's different from the other two?" Nick asked from his casual perch.

Zoey watched the bird as it swooped toward the lighthouse.

"Well, it seems to be much bigger." She cast a wary eye at her brother, who nodded and gestured for her to go on. "I don't know, Nicky, it's a seagull, for cripe's sake."

Having gone through the same instructional period with her father, India handed Zoey the field glasses and sat down next to Nick.

"Oh, all right. Let's see." Zoey raised the glasses to her eyes and went from one bird to the other, adjusting the focus as the distance varied. "Ha!"

She lowered the glasses triumphantly. "That one has a yellow beak!"

"Very good, duchess." Nick grinned. "You have just correctly identified a herring gull."

"Yes!" She crowed gleefully and entered the name into the book. "One herring gull. How many kinds of gulls are there, anyway?"

"Lots," India told her. "Now, write down an old-squaw. A male."

"Where, Indy?" Corri whispered, and India pointed toward the inlet side of the jetty, where a brown duck with a white head had landed.

"Old-squaw?" Zoey asked.

"Right. One word, hyphenated. It's a kind of sea duck. A male. And there's the female. And a harlequin duck. Corri, count the mallards for Zoey so she can write them down."

Corri used her finger to count the ducks with the green heads. "Five."

"Do I want to know how many kinds of ducks there might be around here?"

"Lots and lots," Corri told her solemnly.

"I figured as much. And I'll bet you know every last mother-loving one of them, don't you, Miss I-Know-More-Birds-Than-You-Do?" Zoey did her best to appear crabby, but the twinkle in her eyes gave her away and only succeeded in making Corri giggle again.

"India, could I have the glasses for a moment?" Nick asked.

"What do you see?" she asked as she handed them over.

"Looks like a great cormorant." Nick leaned back, sighting the glasses well into the sky before passing them back to India.

"You're right, it is." She nodded.

"Add that, Zoey," Nick told her. "One great cormorant."

"Is that with a *c* or a *k*?" Zoey paused, the pen in midair.

"A *c,* silly," Corri told her.

"Oh, of course. How silly of me. That's one great cormorant. With a *c."* Zoey tickled the child. "If you're so smart, I guess you know what that is over there on top of the porch."

Corri stood up to look, watching the brown bird as it lifted off in the direction of the marshes.

"It was a rail," she said. "A *clapper* rail."

"That's it, I give up!" Zoey tossed the pen over her shoulder and threw her hands in the air. "Having my nose rubbed in it by my big brother—who has, let's face it, made it his mission in life to harass his poor little sisters—is one thing. Being shown up by a six-year-old is something else all together."

"You can learn, Zoey," Corri told her earnestly. "I can teach you the birds I know."

"You are entirely too sweet, you know that?" Zoey patted the place next to her on the rock and pointed to the pen where it landed. "You grab that pen and come sit next to me and I'll try to be a good bird student."

"Get the pen ready, Zoey," Nick told her as a flock of birds landed in the trees behind the Light, and it seemed the count began in earnest.

Wrens of various species, songbirds and marsh birds, all gathered closely on the branches.

"Nick, there's a hawk," Corri whispered excitedly. "That's why they're all together like that. So he can't pick out one and eat it. Ry said it confused the hawks if the birds all sat real close."

"I guess it would be asking too much for me to just write 'hawk.'" Zoey tapped the pen on the back of the notebook.

"It's a red-tailed hawk," India told her. "It just landed on the railing at the top of the Light. Here, take a look."

Zoey traded the notebook for the glasses. "Oh!" she exclaimed. "Oh! Isn't he handsome? Oh, look at his eyes, they're so small and black and *beady*. And his beak! It looks so lethal. Oh, Nicky, he's perfectly *regal*."

Zoey watched the large bird turn this way and that on the railing, his head moving like that of a model in the camera's lens. When he finally lifted off, it was with a push from the rail and wings outspread to embrace the wind.

"And that's why people watch the birds." She smiled. "To see such sights. Are they rare, those, um, red-tailed hawks?"

"No, they're pretty much staples around here," India told her.

"Nicky, I want to see something rare." Zoey turned to him as if he had some control over what flew over the Light that day and what did not. "I thought that's why we were here. To look for something rare."

"You bird-*watch* to look for something rare," India teased her, "you bird-*count* to check populations, migrations, document species new to the area."

"Well, I'm going to see something *rare* before I leave here today," Zoey told them, "and then I'm going to make a wish on it."

"When you wish upon a *bird?*" India frowned. "And here, all these years, I thought it was *star.*"

"She's been spending entirely too much time with you," Zoey grumbled, glaring at her brother.

Nick laughed and returned to the job at hand. Ten kinds of sparrows, two kinds of blackbirds. Juncos. Black-capped chicadees. Cardinals, rufus-sided towhees and yellow-rumped warblers. Jays and crows, grackles and catbirds, nuthatches and even a few bluebirds. But nothing rare. Nothing exotic. Nothing worthy of being wished upon.

Nick looked at the sky and glanced at his watch. "I think we'd better get moving. It will be getting dark soon, and I don't like the thought of going across the inlet without lights. If any of the bigger boats are coming through, they won't be able to see us."

Zoey stuck out her bottom lip and pretended to pout.

"Sorry, sweetie. Maybe next year."

"Yeah." Zoey stood up and dusted off the back of her jeans and sighed.

"Corri, it's time to leave," India called to the child, who had gone to the end of the jetty.

"I'll get her," Nick told her.

"So, what did you think of your first day of birding?" India held out the glasses for Zoey to hold while she unzipped her jacket and slid the notebook into the inside pocket.

"It was fun." Zoey nodded, focusing the field glasses on something behind India. "I'd do it again next year. If I'm invited."

"Of course you're invited."

"Indy, what's kind of big, sort of light blue gray on the bottom and has black streaks on its face?" Zoey asked.

"I don't know, Zoey, what's kind of big, light blue gray on the bottom and has . . ." India stopped. "Do you see something that looks like that?"

"Umm-hmm." Zoey nodded. "It has yellow legs."

"You're making this up, right?" India asked.

"No. It's right there, on that low branch. Here, take a look."

"Damn!" India exclaimed, all but jumping up and down.

"I have never seen one out here this time of year. Never never *ever*."

"What?"

"It's a yellow-crowned night heron," India said, a touch of awe in her voice. "Nick, come see. Zoey found a yellow-crowned night heron."

"No way," he said, taking the proffered glasses from her hand. "I'll be damned. I never saw one here before."

"All right, you two." Zoey put an arm around each of their shoulders. "This is very sweet. You pretend to see something neat, I'll make a wish and we'll all go home happy."

Nick lowered the glasses. "You can wish for real on this baby." He winked and held the glasses out to Corri, saying, "Come look. You might be old before you see one of these again in December."

"Really?" Zoey asked. "Is it really like, uncommon?"

"Very." India grinned.

"Really." Zoey grinned back.

"Go 'head, little sister. Make your wish so that we can go home."

Zoey bit her lip and smiled, a big, glorious happy smile, wrapped her arms around herself and closed her eyes. When she opened them again she said, "Okay, Nicky, we can go now."

As he helped her into the boat, Nick asked, "So, what did you wish for on your wishing bird?"

"I wished for someone who would look at me the way you look at India," she said, patting his cheek fondly, "so that I could look at him the way she looks at you."

Nick kissed the top of her head. "Duchess, somewhere in this vast world there is a man who has spent the better part of his life wandering, just searching for you." He sighed. "And someday, heaven help him, he'll find you."

Walking to the boat with Corri, India felt Ry's presence as surely as she felt the wind rustling through her hair.

A shiver ran up her spine when Corri turned back to the Light and waved.

"Why did you do that?" India asked, knowing what the answer would be.

"I was saying goodbye to Ry," Corri said matter-of-factly as she swung her little legs over the side of the boat.

India glanced over her shoulder, just in time to see the sun's rays dip a fraction lower behind the lighthouse and spread soft beams through the second-floor windows. For a second she could almost imagine that the very structure had winked at her. "Bye, Ry," she whispered, and she followed Corri into the boat.

"I'll bet Georgia's here." Zoey hopped out of Nick's car and raced across August's front yard and up the steps like a shot.

"Yeah! Georgia!" Corri fled the backseat and raced behind Zoey.

"Are you going to hit the ground running and abandon me too?" Nick asked India.

"Never."

"Well, this might be our only quiet moment for the rest of the day," Nick said, reaching into his jacket pocket to withdraw a tiny box wrapped in gold foil, "so I should probably give you this now. Open it."

He sat back, watching for her reaction when she opened the box.

"Oh, Nick, they're beautiful." India held up the earrings to admire their color. "Are they amethysts?"

"Actually, they are violet sapphires," he told her. "I saw them in an antique store. They matched your eyes so perfectly I couldn't resist."

"They are wonderful." She leaned across the console to wrap her arms around his neck. "I love them."

"Good." He beamed, accepting her thanks and her kisses.

"I want to put them on." She slipped the slender gold hoops from her earlobes and replaced them with the big oval-shaped stones. Pulling the visor down to look into the mirror, she murmured, "They're the prettiest stones I ever saw. Gorgeous. Thank you, Nick."

"You are very welcome. Now let's go show Mother how perfect they look on you."

"Your mother already saw them?"

"She was with me when I found them in Baltimore, the weekend we went down to watch Georgia dance." He hopped out the driver's side and slammed the door, then waited for India at the end of the walk. "So were Georgia and Zoey. The consensus was that I would never again find stones such a perfect match to your eyes and that you had to have them. I almost think if I hadn't bought them for you, my mother would have."

India slipped her hand through his arm, thinking about all the Enrights gathered around the counter discussing the color of her eyes in a Baltimore antique store, and she smiled. She could see and feel the circle of her life expanding to hold them all, Nick and his sisters, his mother, and the smallest seed of joy began to expand slightly inside her chest.

"Where's my baby sister?" Nick asked from the hallway.

"We're all in here," Delia called from the dining room. "You're just in time. August and I have dinner just about ready to serve."

"Mother, you've been cooking again," Nick teased, knowing that his mother hadn't prepared an entire meal in fifteen years, having employed a full-time cook to do the honors for her. He swept Georgia off her feet, spinning the tiny elfinlike blonde around the room, before gently setting her down.

"Yes, I have been cooking, darling." Delia kissed his cheek. "And it's been fun. August and I have had a wonderful time. India, dear, let me see those earrings on you. Oh, yes, perfect with your eyes. Look, girls, India is wearing the sapphire earrings."

Swept up in the Enrights' descent upon her earlobes, India found herself laughing. The Enright women were filled with love and the warmth of the holiday spirit, and in seeing them all together, India thought perhaps she had found the genesis of Nick's sensitivity and gentleness, of his ease with women and his understanding of the opposite sex. He was, she knew, a man who without apology wore his heart on his sleeve. It was all there in the toast he offered at the dinner table.

"To the extraordinary women in my life." He stood, his glass of Christmas wine held aloft in a gold-rimmed goblet. "To Miss Corri Devlin"—he addressed the child who sat at his left—"who delights us all just by being Corri. To

August, a woman of great strength and wisdom, who shared her wonderful family with me and permitted me to feel a part of it. To Georgia, the iron butterfly, who looks so delicate but who we know is solid as a rock; and to Zoey, who brings spirit and life to everything she touches. And Mother, who is the glue who holds us all together, and who always inspired us to follow our hearts. . . . And to India"—his voice dropped just slightly—"who has filled all those tiny places in my life that I never even knew needed filling. . . . Thank you all for sharing this wonderful holiday season with me."

There was a silence as the women at the table sipped at their wine, all hoping to dislodge the lump in their throats.

"Thank you, Nick." August sniffed. "And if I may, I'd like to offer a blessing on our children, Delia." August looked to the opposite end of the table, where Delia occupied the head, and said, "Those who are with us, and those who are not."

Delia nodded slowly, then raised her glass to her lips. "To *all* of our children."

Delia and August exchanged a look of quiet sympathy.

"Well then, Delia, shall we feed the ones we have with us today?" August rose, motioning for India to help serve the many dishes that were lined up on the sideboard, waiting to become part of the holiday feast.

"That was lovely, Nicky." Zoey sighed. "Sometimes it's just so hard to believe that you're the same brutish beast who used to tie us up and leave us in the orchard and tell Mother that we ran away from home."

"I only did that once," he reminded her.

"No, it was more than once," Georgia corrected him. "It was at least three times that I remember."

"I think you have me confused with Ben," Nick replied innocently. "It was Ben who used to like to torture you."

"Nice try, Nicky. But as I recall, it was Ben who always saved us from you." Zoey sipped at her wine and peered at him across the long, low centerpiece of greens, pineapples and pomegranates that marched down the center of the antique dining table.

"I wonder where Ben is these days," Georgia mused.

"I've wondered that many times myself," Nick said as he

rose at the silent command from his mother to come into the kitchen.

"Me, too." Zoey swirled her wine slowly in the thin crystal goblet.

"You always had such a crush on him," Georgia recalled.

"Who is that, dear?" Delia entered the room ahead of her son, who carried the golden Christmas goose on an ornate silver tray.

"We were talking about Ben Pierce," Georgia told her, "and wondering whatever happened to him."

"I've gotten the occasional card from him over the years." Delia said, placing a silver serving bowl of mashed potatoes and leeks on the table.

"I didn't know that." Zoey turned to look at her mother. "Why didn't you ever tell me? When was the last time?"

Delia shrugged. "It didn't occur to me, I suppose. Or maybe you were on one of your little jaunts when it arrived, Zoey, I don't really recall. The last card was for my birthday, maybe two or three years ago. I believe I mentioned it to Nicky."

"I think that last one was posted in London," Nick added.

"Yes, that sounds right," Delia said over her shoulder as she returned to the kitchen.

"London?" Zoey looked at Nick. "I wonder what Ben would be doing in London."

"Same thing he could be doing anywhere," Nick said with a shrug, "since we don't know what he does for a living. Or maybe he was on vacation."

"Isn't it odd that he remembered Mother's birthday after all these years?" Zoey mused thoughtfully.

"Yes and no," Nick said. "I think Mother is his link to a *time* in his life. Maybe every once in a while, he thinks back to that time."

"And it just conveniently happens to be around Mother's birthday?" Zoey took the bowl of Brussels sprouts from India's hands and placed them on the table.

"Now, this is your childhood friend whose mother worked for your mother?" India placed the oyster, cornbread and sausage stuffing on the table near Corri, who had developed a real fondness for this old Devlin family special.

"Oh, Maureen was far more than an employee to me," Delia said, looking at the table to see if anything was missing. Satisfied that the appropriate dishes had made their way into the dining room, she nodded to August and the two women seated themselves at their respective ends of the table. "She was like that sister I never had. She ran my house, ran my life, so that I could work those first very important years while I was struggling to make my literary mark. Ben was like a second son to me. I loved that boy, I willingly admit it. I hated to see his grandfather take him after Maureen died, but he was his only living relative. He had every right to want to raise his grandson."

"And you just lost track of him after that?" August asked.

"I wrote to him several times over the years, but I never got an answer. I think maybe it hurt him too much to think back to those days when we were all together, when his mother was still alive," Nick said.

"I think you might be right, dear. It was terribly hard for Ben." Delia nodded. "I know he wasn't happy with his grandfather. I've always thought that someday our paths would cross his again, though."

"Maybe someday they will," Georgia said, then turned to Zoey and frowned. "Why are you putting food on my plate?"

"Because you haven't put anything there yourself," her sister snapped.

"I did so." Georgia speared an extra Brussels sprout and plopped it onto Zoey's plate.

"Two Brussels sprouts. One very small, very thin piece of goose. A tablespoon of stuffing. Six—make that seven— very tiny carrots." Zoey proceeded with a roll call of the contents of Georgia's plate.

"Zoey, may I remind you that I have a mother, and that she is, in fact, in this room? You might note that she is not giving me grief."

"Georgia, you are so thin you look like an afterthought," Zoey defended herself.

"Zoey, I dance for a living. It's sort of like doing aerobics all day long."

"That's why you need to eat. You need energy." Zoey spooned a heap of dressing onto Georgia's plate.

Georgia heaped it back onto Zoey's. "I am not dancing today. I don't need—"

"Girls, that's enough. Zoey, leave your sister alone. Georgia, Zoey's merely concerned about you, as we all are. It's obvious that over the past several months you've lost weight that you clearly can't afford to lose. And we'll discuss that later." Delia adeptly shelved the topic of her youngest child's weight.

"This is a very handsome room, Miss Devlin," Georgia ventured after a few moments of studied silence. "I feel like I'm sitting in a colonial museum."

August leaned over to pat Georgia's hand. "Thank you, dear. I feel that way myself some days. It's almost overwhelming to think how many generations of Devlins called this house home. Now, this room is the original keeping room—circa 1720, possibly a little earlier—which accounts for a fireplace of those proportions." She pointed to the opposite side of the spacious room.

"People used to cook in that fireplace because they didn't have a stove," Corri told Georgia, "and in the winter they slept in here because it would be warm."

"That used to fascinate me too when I was little," India told Corri. "I used to think of Eli and his wife and their children all huddled around the hearth at night, trying to stay warm while one of those fierce January storms pounded away outside."

"And all of the recipes August used today are family recipes," Delia told her children.

August chuckled. "The women in this family have been, through the ages, keepers of diaries, of journals, so we know what foods were served through the years. The corn and squash we have today was from a very early recipe—early 1700s—but the stuffing for the goose was handed down by Amanda Devlin, who married Eli's grandson Stephen and lived in this house in the late 1700s. She was the flower of the Tidewater, they say, and brought with her a cook from her parents' plantation, thus introducing a southern touch to family tradition. The sweet potatoes with bourbon were Amanda's contribution also, I believe—Georgia, you must try them. And of course, each successive generation has left its mark on the house, adding to it here and there, changing the facade occasionally as fashion dictated, while at the same time adding to the family menus."

"Which explains why there is a Victorian-style wraparound porch on this house that has roots that are almost three hundred years old," India added.

"Three hundred years," Georgia murmured.

"We'll give you the grand tour after dinner if you like," India told her.

After dinner things were less serene, the Enright sisters having volunteered for the predessert cleanup. After fifteen minutes of snipping at each other, Georgia slammed the door to the powder room and locked herself in, and India sought Nick's help to talk her out before Delia realized that her two daughters were at each other's throats.

"What were they arguing about?" an amused Nick asked as he followed India to the back of the house.

"I'm not really sure that I know," she replied. "I went into the kitchen to put coffee on for dessert, and Georgia sort of whooshed past me into the powder room."

"Zoey, where's Georgia?" he asked innocently.

Zoey shrugged. "I'm sure it's none of my business."

"Zoey." Nick leaned back against the counter and folded his arms across his chest. "What was it this time?"

"Georgia is hardheaded and intractable," Zoey announced.

Nick rolled his eyes. Turning to the powder-room door, he rapped softly with his knuckles. "Georgia, come out here and talk to me."

"No."

"Why not?"

"Not while *she's* there."

No question as to who "she" was. Nick sighed.

"What did she do?" he asked sympathetically.

"Oh, what did *she* do?" Zoey snorted. "Why do you always assume that it's something that *I* did? Why do you always take her side?"

"Georgia, open the door and talk to me."

There was silence for a long minute.

"Georgia?" Nick repeated. "Tell me what she did."

"Oh, that's the last straw!" Zoey took off her apron and flung it in the general direction of her brother's head, then she stomped into the front hallway and up the steps to the second floor.

"She's trying to make me eat, Nicky."

"What a fiendish thing to do." He smacked his fist into his open palm. "We'll send her away. Someplace where it's always cold and there's no Bloomingdale's or chocolate."

"Nicky, it's not funny." Georgia's voice raised an octave. "I'm a big girl. I do not need my siblings forcefeeding me."

"Georgia, we care about you. You don't look well and it worries us."

The latch slid softly and the door opened just wide enough to see Georgia's tiny porcelain-doll face, eyes reddened, peering out.

"That's a good girl." Nick took her hand through the door. "How 'bout if we get our jackets and take a little walk, you and I?"

Georgia nodded, and India took the cue to retrieve their outerwear from the front hall.

"Not too long, Nick," India told him, "unless you want your mother to come looking for you."

"No, I don't want that. See if you can stretch out the time till dessert. Tell them that the coffee's not ready or something." He kissed the tip of her nose on the way out the back door.

A somber Zoey joined India in the kitchen five minutes later and asked, "What can I do to help?"

"Here, you finish rinsing and I'll empty the dishwasher," India told her.

"Where's Nicky and the little princess?"

"They went for a walk."

Zoey *hummphed* and ran warm water over heirloom dinner plates absentmindedly.

"She makes me so angry, India." Zoey fought back stinging tears. "Something is wrong with her and she's shutting everyone out."

"Maybe whatever is bothering her is something that she wants to deal with on her own."

"I'll bet she weighs just over a hundred pounds," Zoey told her.

"I don't know that that's uncommon for a professional dancer."

"Three months ago she weighed a good ten pounds more. I know something's wrong, India."

India rubbed a gentle hand on Zoey's back. "Look, I never had a sister. I don't think I fully understand the dynamics of that relationship. But I think if something is seriously wrong, Nick will find out what it is and he'll help her deal with it."

"She never lets me do anything for her," Zoey said softly. "She'll take help from Nicky but never from me."

"Are we almost ready, dear?" Delia bustled in through the dining-room door. "I think Randall will be here . . ." She paused, observing. "Where are your sister and brother?"

"They stepped out for a bit of air," Zoey told her. "Nicky wanted to stretch his legs, so Georgia went with him."

Delia eyed her daughter suspiciously but did not challenge her. Instead, she turned to India and said, "August has told me about your little problem with that land-deal person. I hope you don't mind that we discussed it."

"You mean Lucien Byers?"

"Yes. She said his investigator has been unable to trace any of the parties who were at that so-called settlement." Delia lifted a truffle from a small crystal plate and bit into it.

"Well, I don't think it takes a genius to figure out that everyone put phony signatures to the documents."

"India, I happen to know an excellent private investigator. He's worked on a few things over the years. Would you mind if I asked him to look into this?" Delia asked.

"I don't know what he'll find that Lucien's man has missed, but sure, that would be fine. I was planning on calling Lucien this week anyway. I'll tell him."

"Let's not tell Mr. Byers just yet." Delia started back toward the front room, where Corri entertained her new kitten with a long strand of red wool ribbon. "The fewer who know and all that."

"Well, thank you, Delia, but . . ."

Delia had already left the room.

"You'd better get used to Mother if you plan to be around for any length of time." Zoey sighed. "And from the looks of things, that's a given."

"I think your mother's imagination is working overtime," India confided, and Zoey laughed for the first time since dinner.

"Always. That's what makes her the most popular mystery writer in the world." Zoey turned a puzzled face to India. "But you know, I can't help but wonder why my mother would need the services of a private investigator."

∽∾ ∽∾

Rosemary Potatoes
(makes 6 servings)

2½–3 pounds new potatoes, scrubbed, unpeeled, and quartered
6 tablespoons butter, melted
1/2 teaspoon salt
1–2 teaspoons crumbled dried rosemary

Arrange potatoes in a baking dish. Combine butter, salt, and rosemary, pour over potatoes and toss.

Bake at 350° for 40 minutes or until tender.

Chapter 25

"India, do you really think you should be going out tonight?" August stood in the doorway of India's bedroom, her hands on her hips, a worried look on her face.

"I'll be okay." India's slight frame was wracked by a sudden cough. "At least I think I will. Anyway, Nick said he has something very special planned for dinner, and I don't want to spoil it."

"You'll spoil a hell of a lot more than dinner if you come down with pneumonia," August said dryly.

"I won't. I promise." India stood up shakily and wrapped her robe around her a little more tightly. "But maybe, just in case, a little hot lemonade with honey probably wouldn't hurt."

"Ah! So you have a sore throat too."

And chills and a headache, but you don't have to know that.

"I thought I'd drink some on a precautionary basis." India suppressed another cough, hoping that her aunt would go to the kitchen to make her hot drink so that she could fall on the bed and cough her face off, which she did the minute August's footsteps could be heard trailing from the hallway to the back of the house.

A hot shower would help warm her up too, she told herself, but she found that the hot water and cool air in the bathroom only left her feeling more chilled. Common sense told her that she belonged in bed—alone—but it was New Year's Eve and Nick had planned a surprise for her that night. A black-tie evening, he had told her, though he refused to say where. Who could resist such temptation?

And she had a new, beautiful, long satin dress of midnight blue to wear and her Christmas earrings. Surely she could hold herself together until midnight.

She barely made it past nine o'clock.

Nick picked her up in a chauffeured limousine promptly at eight-fifteen. Seeing Randall, Delia's driver, India had assumed that they would be spending the night with Nick's family. So she was surprised when he turned into the lane leading to Nick's cabin. Thinking perhaps they were stopping to pick up something that Nick had forgotten, India offered to wait in the car.

"It will be a long, cold New Year's Eve for both of us if you do that." Nick held out his hand to assist her.

She shivered in her long black evening cape as they strolled the deck walkway to the front of the cabin. He held the door ajar for her to enter into the warmth of the big room, which was warmed by a blazing fire and the aroma of all manner of wonderful things.

"India, this is Mrs. Colson," he told her. "I borrowed her from mother. She is preparing an incredible dinner for us."

India smiled and said an uninspired hello to the short-haired woman with the wooden cooking spoon in her hand. Nick took her wrap and her teeth began to chatter. Perhaps if she stood a little closer to the fire.

"Sweetheart, I promise you this will be a New Year's Eve you'll never forget," Nick whispered in her ear.

She turned around in his arms—and passed out cold.

When India woke up, she was in his bed. Gone was her satin dress, replaced by flannel pajamas that must have been Zoey's, judging by their length. In spite of the flannel garments and the flannel sheets, the down comforter and the afghan, she shook unmercifully.

"India, why didn't you tell me you were so sick?" He leaned over her anxiously.

"I didn't want to spoil your surprise," she answered weakly.

"Dinner we can always have," he told her, then shook his head. "Why is it that women do not want to admit that they have a problem? First Georgia, now you."

"Did you ever find out what was troubling her?"

"More or less. I think the head ballet guy in her troupe has been stringing her along for a while," Nick made a fist with one hand and massaged it roughly with the fingers of the other. "He's been giving her a hard time, and now it appears he has replaced her with another dancer. But none of that has anything to do with the fact that you are one very sick lady." He pulled the covers up to her chin. "Which is why I called Bradshaw's Pharmacy. Luckily I caught Tom just as he was closing up for the night. He offered to send over some over-the-counter products that he thought might be helpful. He should be here in about ten minutes."

In less time than that, Mrs. Colson appeared in the doorway and held up the bag from the pharmacy. India greeted her with a cough.

"Fever, chills, headache, sore throat, hacking cough?" Mrs. Colson ventured.

"That pretty much sums it up." India nodded miserably.

"Tylenol. Juice. Stay in bed. More Tylenol. More juice." The cook nodded ruefully. "Forget the paté."

Nick popped the lid off the Tylenol bottle and handed two to India, which she washed down with the juice brought in by Mrs. Colson.

"How does some herbal tea sound?" he asked.

"It sounds good," India told him.

"Peppermint or chamomile?"

"Peppermint."

By the time Nick returned from the kitchen with her tea, India was sound asleep. He tucked Otto next to her on the pillow and went to call August to let her know that her niece would not be home that night, nor probably the next.

Fueled by fluids and aspirins, cool compresses to her forehead and warm blankets, India drifted in and out of consciousness for the next thirty-six hours. All she could later recall was that every time she opened her eyes, Nick was there. Morning, afternoon or the dead of night, he was there with a drink, cough medicine, or a book to read aloud to her. It was late afternoon on the third day that she realized that the book was *Gone with the Wind* and that he was well into the story.

"So, how am I?" she asked.

"You're coming around." Nick smiled and put the book down, lifting a hand to feel her forehead. "You're not nearly as warm as you were this morning. How's your throat?"

"It's still sore," she admitted.

"The headache?"

"Pretty much gone." She shifted to sit up a little and made a face. "I hope I look better than I must smell at this point."

"I'd say it's pretty much a toss-up." He grinned.

"Can I take a shower?"

"If you can stand up that long."

She sat up all the way. It seemed to take all of her strength.

"Hmm. Maybe not," he decided. "Are you hungry? How about some soup? I made some yesterday."

"What kind?"

"What kind?" He scoffed. "What do you think my mother told me to make as soon as she found out you were sick?"

"Chicken soup?" she ventured.

"Of course. It's the universal antidote. We have enough chicken soup to handle an epidemic. You game?"

"Sure." Her voice was still faint, her throat still weak.

"Here." He tossed her the remote control. "See if you can find anything to occupy yourself with while I heat up your soup."

The news disoriented, the talk shows irritated. The music videos were tasteless and the shopping channels were all showing electronics. India turned off the TV and pulled herself all the way up to a sitting position for the first time in days. It was an effort to hold herself there until Nick came back with a tray of golden chicken noodle soup and lightly buttered toast. He placed it gently on her lap, then sat next to her while she tasted small spoonfuls of the warm, fragrant broth.

"This is wonderful stuff, Nick. Are you having some?"

"I had some for lunch," he told her, "and am looking forward to something a little more substantial for dinner. Do you need help? Want me to hold the bowl?"

"No, I'm fine." India put the spoon down and sighed. "You are too good to me, Nick, taking care of me like this."

"Wouldn't you do the same for me?"

"Of course," she said without hesitation.

"I think that's what it's all about," he said softly, tucking an errant strand of stringy blond hair behind her ear.

"I guess I really blew your wonderful New Year's Eve surprise." She bit her bottom lip. "And I never even told you how handsome you looked in your tuxedo."

"You'll have other opportunities. And there's always next New Year's Eve." He traced small circles on the back of her left hand.

"It was such a totally lovely idea, having dinner here."

"You didn't last long enough to see the rest of it."

"What else was there?" She frowned, trying to recall.

"You missed the string quartet."

"You hired a string quartet?"

"Yup."

"Oh, Nick, I feel terrible." Her eyes pooled at the thought of all the trouble he had gone to, to make their first New Year's Eve together a wonderful, memorable night.

"Don't be silly, it's not something you had control over. And besides, I plan to let you make it up to me."

"How could I possibly do that?"

"Oh, I'm sure you'll think of something." He grinned. "Think along the lines of *love slave.*"

India laughed for what seemed to be the first time in weeks.

"I think I want to try that shower now."

"Let me help you." He offered her his hand. "And while you're in the shower, I'll find something for you to wear. Zoey and Georgia always have clothes here."

India tried to remember something that might have felt better than washing her hair after three days in bed but could not. The steamy warmth of the shower revived and relaxed her, and she felt better than she had in days. Not well, but better, and she said so when she had dried herself off and slipped into the flannel boxers and fleecy pullover Nick brought to her.

"I'm delighted to hear that, but let's not overdo it," he told her. "You're getting right back into bed."

He led her by the hand back to the king-sized bed, where fresh sheets awaited and plump pillows beckoned. Hot tea with lemon steamed from a cup placed on the bedside table, and the phone had been moved to within easy reach.

"I thought you might like to call August and Corri," he said as he helped her back into bed.

It was the last straw for weak and frazzled emotions. India burst into tears.

"What is it, India?" he asked, all concern and gentleness, which only made her cry all the harder. "What, sweetheart? Tell me what's wrong."

"You take care of me when I'm sick, nurse me around the clock. I look like a refugee and smell like a goat, but you feed me. You made me *chicken soup,* for God's sake." She cried into his shoulder.

"Whatever was I thinking?"

"You read to me when I was too sick to move. *Gone with the Wind.* My all-time favorite book." She grabbed hold of the front of his shirt. "You put fresh sheets on the bed and worry about Corri worrying about me."

"Clearly, I've been out of line." He ran his fingers through his hair and glanced toward the ceiling. "Can you ever forgive me?"

"You hired a string quartet to serenade me on New Year's Eve," she sobbed.

"I should be punished." He hung his head, pretending to appear contrite. "Would you like to beat me?"

She laughed in spite of herself and pulled him closer.

"You are so *right,"* she told him, wiping the tears from her face with the back of her hand. "How can I not fall in love with you, Nick, when you are so *right."*

"What have you got against falling in love with me?" He stroked the back of her head.

"If I fall in love with you I'll close the door on ever going back to Paloma."

"Explain to me why this might be a bad thing, when all

313

the people you love—the people who love you—the places you love, are all in Devlin's Light."

"It used to make sense to me," she said. "It really used to make sense to me. Now I don't even remember why. My work there was—*is*—important to me."

"The work will always be important to you, Indy, and it should be. You do a great job, you do what needs to be done. But you can do it anywhere you choose. You can have your cake and eat it too, as the saying goes. You don't have to go back to Paloma to fight bad guys. We have bad guys of our own down here. Come home and fight them, Indy."

"I think I have to give serious consideration to doing just that." She sighed. "It all seemed so easy before. There was so much going on in Paloma, so little going on here. Now I'm not so sure just how much that matters."

He gently eased her back onto the pillows, a twinkle in his eye. "It must have been the love potion I slipped into the chicken soup."

"Enright, you're the last man in the world who would need to resort to potions when it comes to getting women." She traced his jawline with the back of her hand.

"I don't want 'women,'" he told her. "I never wanted 'women.' I never wanted more than one woman in my life, and I knew if I waited long enough, I'd find her. And I have. The only woman I ever really wanted, the only one I can't do without, is you. I love you to distraction, India Devlin, and once you're all better, we'll discuss what I propose we do about that."

He kissed her forehead, then frowned. "But in the meantime, you're still warmer than you should be, and your eyes are getting a little bit of a sleepy glaze on them again. Why don't you call Corri and August now so you can talk to them while you're still lucid, then we'll watch a movie till you fall asleep."

"Okay." She reached for the phone and dialed the number. She *was* tired all of a sudden. "Aunt August? Hi, it's me. A little better, yes."

Nick opened the curtains behind the bed and let in the light from a stark gray morning.

"What time is it?" India stretched.

"Time for breakfast, if you're feeling up to it."

"I am. I'm almost hungry today."

"That's a good sign. How 'bout scrambled eggs and some toast made with homemade bread?"

"That's what I smelled." She smiled.

"I think there's some obscure law that says that on cold, snowy days in early January, it is mandatory to have a fire burning and homemade bread in the oven."

"It's snowing?"

"Like a blizzard. Are you strong enough to come into the other room to eat?"

"Yes. Let me just wash my face, then I'll be in."

She felt stronger, her legs less wobbly, and her head was not so foggy. She splashed water on her face and brushed her teeth with toothpaste on her finger. Feeling almost human, she followed the fresh-bread scent through the house.

Breakfast was set up in front of the fireplace, in which blazed a healthy log or two to warm and cheer the big room. Music floated from several speakers to seep through the silence and wrap around the room like a turban. It was cozy and intimate, and she knew in her bones that she would never want to be anywhere else, with anyone else.

"Come look out the window." Nick stood with his back to the room. "The snow is incredible. The bay has simply disappeared into a white blur."

India came up behind him and slipped her arms around his waist. He felt good and solid, wonderful and strong. He felt like no one else ever had, or ever would.

"Nick?" she said, her voice still raspy.

"Yes, Indy?"

"I love you, Nick." She rested her head against his back and rocked slightly.

"Are you sure it isn't the fever come back?"

"No fever. I'm feeling much better. I'm feeling well enough to *know*," she said. "And what I know is that I've never loved anyone else. I never will. I never want to be without you, Nick."

"That is one thing you will never have to worry about." He turned to her and took her in his arms. "I'll never be farther away than you want me to be."

They rocked slightly together in front of the big window.

"So, what was it that put you over the edge?" he asked, a trace of merriment in his voice. "It was the chicken soup, right?"

"It's everything," she said simply, "everything you did to show me that you cared. It's everything you do and everything you are."

He started to sway with the music, the sweet, poignant cry of Clapton's guitar. "Wonderful Tonight." The world outside was wrapped in a swirling blanket of white, the snow blocking out everything but the two of them and the music.

"How much better are you feeling?" he asked when the music had stopped.

"Much," she assured him. "Come over in front of the fire and you can see for yourself just how good I feel."

Chapter 26

"India, I really think this is unwise of you." August was trying her best not to lecture. After all, India was a grown woman. Still, her aunt felt compelled to state the obvious. "As sick as you have been, going to the Twelfth Night Ball is sheer folly. You'll have a relapse. You'll expose yourself to other people's germs, you'll—"

"Have a wonderful time in spite of all of those things." India sponged small dots of liquid foundation onto her nose, hoping to make the red go away. "It's no use, I look like Rudolph. Maybe I should wear a mask and keep it on all night and no one will notice."

"Well, perhaps Nick will have enough sense to bring you home early," August rationalized.

"Aunt August, I have not been to the Twelfth Night Ball in years. I have been looking forward to going with Nick and dancing my little feet off. And I'm going to do exactly that." India smiled to herself, thinking she sounded a little like Scarlet O'Hara. Any other time she would have bristled at the very thought that she, India Devlin, that straight-shooting, tough prosecutor, could have anything whatsoever in common with the little flirt from Tara, but on Twelfth Night it tickled her. She was determined to dance until she dropped and have a wonderful time.

She had hoped that they could attend the dance classes

317

the first week of January so that Nick could learn and she could brush up on the period dances that would be featured that night, but, given her recent illness, India knew that she was lucky to be going at all.

"I will be keeping an eye on you, miss," August reminded her.

"I know that you will, Aunt August." India laughed.

"Indy?" Darla called from the bottom of the steps.

"Up here, Dar, come on up," India called back.

"Wow! Look at you!" India exclaimed as Darla swept into the room in a blue satin gown that once belonged to one of India's twin great-great aunts.

"Is this too funny?" Darla laughed. "Just like prom night. Except this time we're going with the same man."

"Nick will have the time of his life," India assured her. "Here, help me get this dress over my head and then I'll put your hair up."

"And I'll do yours." Darla slid the gossamer satin over India's head and fastened the back with the little hooks that closed women's dresses a hundred years earlier.

"We could still pull it off," India said as she swept Darla's hair atop her head and secured it with bobby pins.

"You want to see if we can fool Nick?" Darla grinned.

"Of course we can fool Nick."

When India's hair had been identically swept up, they stood side by side in front of the mirror.

"Nah, we'll never get away with it." Darla shook her head wistfully. "Not after I've had two children. Your waist is much smaller, India."

"Not 'much,' maybe a little. And speaking of children, the baby-sitter should be here any minute. It was a great idea to share a sitter tonight, Dar."

"Well, you know, since Kenny's been taking the kids more often, they've settled down a bit. Jack was with him over the weekend and they spent all day Sunday out at the nature sanctuary."

"I'm glad that's working out a little better. I felt badly for Kenny, to tell you the truth, Darla. It must have been very difficult for him when you left."

"It was." Darla sat down on the edge of the bed, careful

not to wrinkle the borrowed ball gown, and crossed her legs. "I think I didn't give Kenny enough credit back then. All I knew was that I was unhappy and wanted out. No wonder he went a little crazy. I mean, I worked so hard for so long to be such a good little wife and mother, he never knew how unhappy I was. Then I just walked. I was so unfair to him."

"Dar, we can't change the past. The important thing is that Kenny has reconciled with his children and is spending more time with them. That's what matters." India heard a car door slam and flew to the window to look out. "It's Nick. I promised the dance master we would be there a little early so that he could put us through our paces for the grand march. Let's see what he thinks of our twin look."

Look alike they may have, but it was clear that Nick only had eyes for India, a fact that no one in the old Devlin mansion could have doubted.

August stood proudly to one side in the festively dressed ballroom and watched her beloved niece take her place at Nick's side just inside the doorway, where they awaited the music that would signal the start of the Devlin's Light Historic Society's Twelfth Night Ball. She was beautiful, her girl was, and she was *here,* poised to lead the grand march on the arm of the man that she was, judging by all indications, totally in love with. Just as she herself had once done, years ago, before the world called to her and lured her away with the promise of something better, more exotic. She had never found it, had never found anything better, anything more exotic than what she had felt on that night long ago when she had stood in exactly the spot where India was standing. Other nondancers began to filter into the room to spectate, and August moved slightly toward the bandstand to accommodate the crowd.

"Seems I might know that bonnie blue dress she's wearing," a voice rasped in her ear. "Seems I might have seen it before."

August turned to find Captain Pete dressed in his best naval uniform and leaning on his cane.

"You would remember such a thing," August said softly.

"There are some things a man never forgets," he said without looking at her. He moved his fingers slowly against the palm of his hand, as if feeling the cool of the satin between them, and for the first time in years, Augustina Devlin blushed.

Just as the music began, India closed her eyes and let it all soak in, just for the fun of it. Here she was, dressed in elegant satin with sparkling hairpins holding up her hair and a mile of pearls wrapped around her neck, holding the hand of the most handsome, wonderful man on the face of the earth. Nick's Christmas earrings caught the light and glittered. The music echoed of another time when other musicians played similar tunes in this very room, and other ladies, dressed in their finest, had lined up in the wide hallway to await the music's invitation to enter, to dance, and perhaps to fall in love.

The small orchestra, which specialized in period music, began to play, and at the signal from the dance master, India and Nick swept into the room, which was brilliantly lit with the tongues of a thousand candles, as tradition dictated. Once the grand march had ended, and the guests had all taken their places, the candles would be extinguished and the electric chandeliers turned on. But for now, the candles lent a romantic glow, and, combined with the strains of the expertly played music and the graceful dancing, the evening was off to a joyful start.

After the first two waltzes, India tugged on Nick's arm, trying to catch her breath. "I have to sit down."

"I keep forgetting that you've only been out of bed for two days. Let's find a chair for you and I'll get you a cup of punch."

"This seat right here will be fine." India sank into the first empty chair she saw.

Nick set off in search of the punch bowl while India watched the other dancers, their silks and the satins spinning like colored tops across the highly polished dance floor.

Nick divided his waltzes between India, Darla, and August, with a gallant turn now and then for others from August's circle, all of whom clucked knowingly and approvingly as they watched Nick swirl around the dance floor with India in his arms.

"I think I've had it." India sighed and sank back into the

amply padded chair. "My feet cannot dance another step.
But look, there's Darla over there with that bore Ted
Reynolds. Do you think you could rescue her?"

"I believe she did promise me this dance." He nodded.
"And then we might think about leaving."

"Oh, but it's early," she told him. "There are fireworks at
midnight, then a lovely supper, then the unmasking—"

"But there's also a lovely piece of moon over the bay," he
whispered in her ear, "and I'm not so sure I wouldn't rather
have a little *private* unmasking, if you get my drift."

"On the other hand"—she opened her white lace fan and
fluttered it coyly—"I suppose, having been ill, one should
take care of oneself and get to bed early."

"Hmmm." He looked in the direction of the stairwell
leading to the second floor and the room Captain Jon had
shared with his lady. "What are the chances that anyone
would miss us for an hour or two?"

She snapped the fan closed and smacked him on the
shoulder with it. "Don't even think about it. Good grief,
Nick, they're giving *tours* tonight. Could you imagine the
scandal?"

Nick laughed and went off on his mission to save Darla
from the clutches of Ted the Terminally Dull. India waved
to an old friend from high school who joined her to gossip
about who was wearing what, who was dancing with whom,
and who the few unknown dancers might be behind their
masks. When the music ended, the announcement was
made for all to assemble on the verandah overlooking the
gardens to watch the fireworks display, which marked the
midnight hour and the official end of the holiday season for
another year. Nick escorted both India and Darla, and with
an arm around both, the group *ooohed* and *ahhed* at the
brightly colored lights that dazzled the January sky.

"There are so many here this year, we've had to go to a
buffet rather than a seated dinner," August was telling a
short, dark-haired woman dressed in black velvet trimmed
in gold with a matching mask, "and we've easily seated over
a hundred here in past years."

"Well, the Twelfth Night Ball in Devlin's Light is becoming quite the thing." The woman nodded and allowed

August to lead her back into the ballroom through one of two open sets of French doors. "We heard about it all the way up in Parsippany and it sounded like such fun."

"Well, if you've enjoyed this, you'll have to come back for the Midsummer's Night Social," August told her.

"Really?" The woman's eyes sparkled. "Tell me all about it."

"What fun that all of those traditions are still being followed," India told Nick, "and that those that fell by the wayside over the years are now being revived. They stopped doing Midsummer's Night back when I was in high school."

"This must have been some place to live in, years ago," he said, turning his head to look across the expanse of lawn, which now lay in dark stillness, the fireworks display having ended for another year.

"It was. Someday you'll have to read the journals that some of my ancestors kept detailing the social life in Devlin's Light. Who wore what. Who danced with whom. Who flirted with whose husband."

"Much like the conversation here tonight," he pointed out.

"Precisely the same." India laughed. "Maybe I should start keeping a journal of my own."

"Shall we see if Darla wants to leave now or after supper?"

"Actually, since she did all the baking for tonight, I think it might send a poor message if she was to leave before dessert."

"We can stay another hour." Nick nodded. "I think we want to hang out a little with your aunt. Seems that low-cut green velvet has attracted more than a little attention, don't you think?"

"I did notice that Captain Pete appeared to be shadowing her a bit tonight, and she didn't seem to be grumbling at him for it. I told you I thought there was something there."

"You did indeed. Let's see if we can catch up with them and figure out exactly what." Nick held out his hand to her.

"Where did Darla disappear to?" India frowned and looked over her shoulder. "She was just right there."

"She probably fled to the kitchen to escape the clutches of Ted the Terrible."

"I guess." India took his hand and together they joined the crowd filtering toward the lavish buffet supper awaiting them in the grand dining room.

Hand-carved roast beef, pink and perfect, and scrumptious honey-baked ham, rosy and fragrant, were the crown jewels in the evening's feast, which started with oysters on the half shell, smoked bluefish with fresh dill dressing, and brie topped with raspberry pureé and wrapped in phyllo pastry; the repaste ended with a spectacular array especially prepared by Darla's Delectables.

"If I never see another poached pear again it'll be too soon," Nick groaned, and India laughed. "Or chocolate. I make a mean chocolate cake, India, I pride myself on that. But I have never experienced the likes of what Darla did with that soufflé."

"It was that incredible coconut cake that did it for me." India leaned against him. "And just how many of those tiny fruit tarts did you have, anyway?"

"One too many, obviously. At least one too many. But I think it was the truffles that finally put me over the edge."

The lights in the ballroom dimmed, and the music began to play. India and Nick looked at each other and groaned at the thought of a sprightly waltz.

"Maybe just a walk around the verandah," Nick suggested.

"I'll try," she told him, "though I feel more like rolling than walking."

The night air was still unseasonably balmy, and the warmth from the day combined with the slightly cooler evening air to form a mist across the side lawn. The lights from the ballroom spilled gently through the windows and spread a faint haze over all. It was timeless, the night and the mist and the music, and India could not help but say so.

"There are some things that do seem to endure," Nick said. "Nights like this must be one of those things. And you do feel it here, in this house, don't you?"

"I always have. This house was always a draw for me." India leaned back against the white wall that ran the length of the open porch. "I remember times when I was a child, before the restoration began in earnest and the house was open to the public for things like this, I would come here, thinking if I sat quietly enough, I would see one or another of my ancestors."

"Did you?"

"Frequently. At least I thought I did," she mused.

"You could have told me that there might have been an audience." He pointed to the windows on the second floor where Salem's lamp shone brightly. "I might have put a little more into my performance."

"If you had put anything more into your performance, you'd have had to carry me out of here," India whispered as another couple joined them to share the night air.

"Lovely evening, isn't it?" The man nodded.

"Lovely," Nick and India agreed in unison.

"Time to go, my sweet." Nick took hold of India's elbow. "I figure it will take us another hour to say all of our goodnights and get back to the cabin. You still owe me a dance on the deck in the moonlight—such as it is tonight—from New Year's Eve."

She grinned. "Well then, we should put the moonlight—such as it is—to good use. Let's find Aunt August and let her know that we are leaving."

August was easy to find, surrounded as always by her circle of friends and their spouses, with Captain Pete thrown into the mix for an added fillip this year. August fussed proudly over India for having danced too much on her first night out since having the flu, and she agreed that it was time for India to call it a night without asking where India would be spending the rest of it.

Darla, on the other hand, was nowhere to be seen.

India checked the kitchen but was told that she had not been in there since early in the evening, when she poked in to add a few small finishing touches to the desserts she had delivered that afternoon. Nick went through every room on the second floor, thinking perhaps she had wandered, but she was not there.

"I'll run outside," Nick told her. "Maybe she's out there."

"We just came in," India reminded him.

"Well, maybe she was on the front porch or the other side of the house."

India paced the long front hallway uneasily, a finger of fear chilling her back from her shoulders on down. "Maybe the garden," she suggested when Nick came back shaking his head. "Maybe she just went off to sit by herself. Maybe she was thinking back to last year, being here with Ry."

"I'll check in the garden," Nick told her.

Several others had quietly joined in the search. Taylor Anderson, one of the members of Chief Carpenter's staff who had attended the ball with his wife, along with one of Pete's sons who was attending his first Twelfth Night, followed Nick down the stone path to the garden. India stood on the back porch and watched the three men disappear into the darkness of the gardens that lay beyond the house.

"Call an ambulance!" Pete's boy raced through the night, shouting and waving his arms frantically. "Get the chief! Get an ambulance!"

The small crowd gathered at the back of the house seemed to freeze, not quite comprehending the meaning of the young man's words. Chief Carpenter stepped forward and asked, "Jake, what is it?"

"She's down there!" The boy pointed toward the garden. "There's blood! . . . I never saw so much blood!"

He leaned against the railing, and it was clear that he was about to be violently ill.

India's brain, at first unwilling to respond, finally sent a message to her feet and she took off down the steps.

"No, India, go back and call the ambulance," the chief called over his shoulder. He did not want her there, not knowing exactly what he was going to find.

Ignoring him, she kicked off the high heels, which were sinking into the soft ground, and ran past him, a lithe, frantic figure driven by fear and the need to protect someone she loved. In the distance she could see the white of Nick's tuxedo shirt gleaming in the dark, and she fled to him.

"Nick, what—"

"India, no . . . go back." Nick's voice was curt with alarm.

Behind her other footsteps followed, but she ceased to hear them as she neared Nick and the figure he was leaning over. Darla lay face down on the ground, her blond hair now crimson. Blood splattered her shoulders and the back of her dress. With a cry, India fell to the ground next to Nick and reached for her friend.

"Don't touch her," Chief Carpenter warned. "Wait for the ambulance." He turned to Nick and said, "It looks like she's lost a lot of blood. Did you find a pulse?"

"Yes, but it's weak." Nick backed away to make room for the chief.

"Dar?" India leaned over her. "Dar?"

"Come away, India," Nick tried to gently raise her, but she would not go. "The ambulance is here. Look, here come the EMTs with a stretcher."

"Darla?" India repeated as if she had not heard. Her tightly fisted hands dug into her gut and she cried without even knowing.

"Nick!" She sobbed in disbelief as the ambulance crew carefully and efficiently guided the still body onto the stretcher and gently secured it. "Why would someone do this to her? Why would anyone want to hurt Darla?"

Nick shook his head and gathered her into his arms and let her cry, asking himself the same question. He did not like the answer that was beginning to swim in his brain. He did not like it at all.

Chapter 27

"Can I stay with her?" a shaken India asked the young emergency-room doctor.

"Maybe later." He brushed past her as if she was invisible before seeming to evaporate before India's eyes as he moved behind the curtain where Darla lay on a gurney.

"Come wait out here with me, India." Nick tried to lead her toward the waiting room.

"I want to stay with her," she protested.

"Sweetheart, you'll be in the way," he told her gently. "Let the doctors take care of her, and then you can sit with her for as long as you want. Right now let them do their jobs so that they can help her."

India nodded numbly and followed Nick into the waiting room, where several rows of worn and faded orange-colored chairs were lined up with clinical precision across the length of the room. He guided her to a chair and pushed gently on her shoulders, indicating for her to sit, and she did so woodenly. He dropped some coins into a vending machine and handed her a paper cup of darkly questionable coffee, knowing she wouldn't drink it, but it would give her something to do with her hands. Chief Carpenter came in and spoke softly with Nick, but India was unable to comprehend the conversation. All India understood at that moment was that they had all lost too much. They could not lose Darla too.

She rose and paced, becoming nearly hypnotized by the simple process of putting one foot in front of another. At some point the doctor emerged to speak with the chief, who followed him down the hallway, speaking in hushed tones.

"What?" India asked Nick, wide-eyed.

"I don't know," he told her. "She's still unconscious, Carpenter said. They're moving her to a room."

"I want to go." India muttered.

"I know that. Let them get her settled and we'll see if we can arrange that."

Forty minutes later, India stood in the doorway of a dimly lit room. Darla lay on her stomach, black stitches running across the back of her head like train tracks where her hair had been cut. Several strands still held vestiges of blood, the dull brown red mixing obscenely with the pale gold. There seemed to be tubes and monitors everywhere.

"Are you a relative?" the doctor asked from the doorway.

"A friend," India whispered.

"Normally we only permit relatives to stay," the young woman told India as she made a note on the chart, "but since none have arrived yet, we'll let you take the first shift."

Nick moved a chair close to the bed for India to sit in, but she could not stay in it. She stood, rather, next to the bed, gently rubbing Darla's arm and talking her from kindergarten through to the present in a steady stream.

"Remember when we were about five and you got caught picking Mrs. Murdoch's prized marigolds?"

"Remember that summer we went to camp and we tried to sneak across the lake in a canoe?"

"Remember when we were sophomores and we got locked out of the house in our nightshirts at Candy Allen's sleepover party?"

On and on through the night, India kept up the dialogue, hoping for something as small as the flutter of an eyelash, but Darla's condition never changed.

"Remember when you and Lynnie and I got caught smoking in the back of the bus on the way back from a basketball game?"

"I remember that." A soft voice drew her attention to the

doorway. "Junior year. You were both grounded for a month and drew severe censure from the principal."

"Kenny." India held her arms out to the man who had once been Darla's husband.

He hugged her briefly before stepping past her, nodding absently to Nick and seating himself gingerly on the side of Darla's bed. With one tentative hand, he gently stroked her back and began to cry.

"You tell me why anyone would want to hurt her." Kenny drew a hand through his thick dark brown hair.

"I was thinking maybe you could do that." Chief Carpenter stood in the doorway.

"Chief, you have got to be kidding." Kenny shook his head in disbelief. "You couldn't possibly think I would do something like this."

"I'm looking for motive, son." The officer came into the room and leaned against the radiator, which fussed and hissed.

"You're going to have to look someplace else," Kenny told him.

"Chief, Kenny would never hurt Darla." India stepped forward to defend him.

"Well, India, let's take a good look at this thing." Carpenter sat in the chair opposite Nick's. "We have a woman who has been struck in the back of the head with a blunt object—possibly a baseball bat or piece of pipe, we're not sure—not once but several times. It appears that someone wanted to not just hurt her, but to kill her."

"Darla doesn't have an enemy in this world—"

"Now India, that's just exactly what we used to say about your brother," Carpenter argued. "And there are some folks in town who still aren't sure that Kenny ever forgave Ry for stealing his wife."

"Ry Devlin did not steal my wife, Chief," Kenny said as if very tired. "Ry had just married Maris when Darla and I separated."

"Well, there are some who think that there was hard feelings there just the same." Carpenter rubbed his chin while watching Kenny's face. It showed nothing.

"Chief, I love Darla. I never stopped loving her. Not when she left me, not when she decided she was going to marry Ry. I always knew she had feelings for him. When he came back to town a few years ago, I knew it was only a matter of time." Kenny sighed. "I just figured that Ry was an itch that Darla had to scratch. But I didn't kill him for it, and I didn't try to kill her."

"Can you tell me where you were tonight, Kenny?"

"I was home, Chief."

"Anyone with you?"

"Nope."

"Did you leave the house at any time?"

"No."

"Is there anyone who can confirm that you were there?"

"My son, Jack, called me just before midnight. I told him he could stay up late and call me. The baby-sitter would be able to tell you that."

"Who baby-sat for your kids tonight?"

"Jenny Adams." He nodded in India's direction. "The kids are at the Devlin house with Corri."

"That's right," India told him. "Darla and I shared a baby-sitter. And Jack did say he was calling his dad right at midnight."

"Well, unfortunately, we don't know what time Darla was attacked yet." He stood up and looked at Kenny for a long time, then sighed loudly. "Son, I am afraid that I would be remiss in my duties if I didn't ask you to come down to the station with me to answer a few more questions."

Kenny Kerns stood up slowly, looking not so very different than he had in high school, his hair curling over the collar of his plaid flannel shirt and his long athletic legs wrapped in jeans. His face, however, bore a look of resignation that aged him before India's very eyes.

"Tell her I was here if she wakes up," Kenny said to India. "Tell her that I . . ."

"I know," India told him. "I will."

India watched as the two men walked down the quiet hallway toward the elevator.

"Nick—" she turned to him—"Kenny Kerns did not do this. There was no reason for him to want to hurt her. Darla told me that they were getting comfortable with each other for the first time in years." India began to pace as she spoke. "That Kenny had stopped drinking, that he was seeing the kids on a regular basis. That they were spending more time talking. But for the life of me, I cannot think of any reason why anyone would want to hurt her."

"I'm beginning to wonder if anyone did," Nick said.

"What do you mean?" India paused in midstride.

"Maybe Darla wasn't the target," he said softly.

"Make sense, Nick."

"Maybe it was supposed to be you."

"Me? Who would want to kill me?"

"Maybe the same someone who killed Ry."

"Why?"

"If we knew why," he told her, "we'd know who. But think about it. You and Darla were dressed alike. You look so alike. In the dark, no one would have known it wasn't you."

He stood up and put his arms around her. "India, I think we need to have one more conversation with the chief tonight. There is a murderer in Devlin's Light, but I don't think it's Kenny Kerns."

"I'd feel better if you were in that car with them," Nick told Indy as Delia's silver Jaguar carefully negotiated the crunching stones that made up Nick's driveway. "Mother was perfectly willing to have you come with August and Corri to stay for the week. And I think there's a greater need to get you out of town than either of them."

"I couldn't bear it if anything happened to them." India crossed her arms and shook her head. "They'll have a great time with your mother—Corri has never been permitted to take time off from school before—and I'll have a great time here with you. Chief Carpenter and his officers will keep an eye on the house on Darien Road, and you will keep an eye on me."

"Well, I admit that the thought of having you here twenty-four hours a day, every day for a week, has a certain appeal."

"I would hope so." She looped an arm through his and pulled him up the step to the wooden walk on the side of the cabin. "And besides, I can't leave town while Darla is touch-and-go, Nick. I have to be there for her."

"I understand."

"It looks like we might get some snow." She pointed skyward as they reached the back of the cabin. The low-lying clouds were plump as feather beds and just as lofty.

"Maybe we'll get snowed in," he mused. "Maybe we should take a run to the grocery store and stock up."

"You could drop me off at the hospital for a while."

"Uh-uh." He shook his head. "You will not be out of my sight until this is over."

"Nick, you cannot possibly be with me every minute of every hour from now until whenever."

"Watch me." He grinned.

"I will." She poked him in the ribs as she went up the steps and into the house, leaving him leaning over the deck railing watching a ragged line of snow geese fly overhead.

She came back out with her pocketbook slung over her shoulder. "Drive me into town now and we'll do a little food shopping and we'll spend the rest of the afternoon with Darla." She wrapped her arms around him from behind and whispered, "I'll make it worth your while when we get back."

"A trip into town it is—" he grinned—"and I'll take you up on that little offer later."

There was no change in Darla's condition, though the doctors all said that she could regain consciousness at any time. India did not want her oldest friend to be alone when that happened, so she tried to spend every day there, leaving Darla to Kenny in the evening. No charges had been made against Darla's exhusband, his next-door neighbor having assured the police that she had heard Kenny moving around the apartment at different times throughout the night, but she never did hear him leave. Since her beagle barked at every noise, she was certain she would have heard him had he come down the steps that night. It had seemed that Chief Carpenter had mixed feelings about letting Kenny go home. On the one hand, it meant that Kenny was innocent, as the chief's gut told him the young man was. On the other hand, it meant that Nick Enright was probably right about there being a killer loose in Devlin's Light, a suspicion that sent Carpenter's ulcer reeling along with his blood pressure.

Under other circumstances, a week to spend alone with

Nick would have seemed like pure heaven, but under a threatening cloud, her stay at the cabin was marked by a lack of gaiety, a somberness that even Nick's warmth and love could not dispel. Only at night, in Nick's arms in the big bed they shared with Otto the Bear, did India forget that the same threat that had sent her brother to his grave and had put her best friend into a coma now appeared to hang over her.

On the third morning of her stay, India got out of the shower, dressed and went into the kitchen for the big breakfast Nick had promised her and found him on the phone.

"Thanks, Mom. I appreciate the information. No, I'm not sure what it means. Right, I will. Talk to you soon." He hung up the phone and stood looking out the kitchen window for a long minute.

"Okay," she said from the doorway. "Spill it."

"What's that?"

India made a face. "Don't be cute with me, Nick."

"My mother had a private investigator trying to track down the employee of Byer's World who had arranged for the supposed sale of your land."

"Will Shuman, his name was."

"Right. Well, this P.I. couldn't find a trace of him."

India raised an eyebrow. "Did he check with social security, voter registration?"

"He ran traces six ways to Sunday. It's as if this person never existed," Nick told her.

"That's odd." She frowned.

"Oh, it gets better," he said. "There is no record of the attorney, the settlement company or the person who notarized the papers that Lucien gave you."

"It's as if they all disappeared off the face of the earth."

"Or they never existed at all," he said.

"What are you getting at?"

"Look, it's clear that a massive scam was pulled off. But against whom?"

"Lucien Byers. Byers World."

He sighed and leaned back against the counter. "What do you know about Lucien Byers?"

"Only that he's the head of this real-estate development company that Maris scammed out of a quarter of a million dollars."

"But how do we know that?"

India's eyes narrowed and she studied him from across the room.

"We have only his word, this story that he told you, and copies of some phony papers that he gave you. How do we know that that isn't part of the scam?"

"You mean that Maris never sold him anything? What would he hope to gain from that?"

"Maybe some type of settlement from the Devlins."

"He didn't look like a man who was hurting for money, Nick. He was well dressed, carried one of those really good leather briefcases. Drove an expensive car."

"You know that none of that means anything," he reminded her, adding, "I'm surprised that you would take that attitude, knowing how many crooks you've sent up."

"You're right." She nodded. "I should know better than to assume. But I had no reason to suspect this man. And every reason to believe that Maris would have pulled something sneaky like that. Did your mother's investigator find out anything about Byers at all?"

"He is the head of Byers World. The company does exist. That much we know. Mother said she told him to look a little deeper and call her back. We'll see if anything develops over the next few days."

India rested her head against his chest and sighed. "I don't like all this. I don't like being on this side of the bad guys."

"No one does."

"Prosecuting is one thing. Being the victim puts a whole new spin on things. When it's your family that's involved, suddenly it isn't all so routine."

"We'll work it out, I promise." He kissed the top of her head and she stirred against him. "One way or another, we will get to the bottom of this. Hopefully before someone else gets hurt."

"Whoever it is, they've taken all they're getting from my family," she told him. "It's my turn now."

Chapter 28

*T*he front door slammed and India could not get there quickly enough.

"Indy, we're home!" Corri shouted.

"I see that you are." India held out her arms and the child bounced into them. "I missed you, Corri. I missed you every day."

"I missed you too. Wait till you see what Delia gave me!"

"Delia?"

"She said I could call her that 'cause 'Mrs. Enright' was too formal. Aunt August said just plain old 'Delia' was too familiar, but Delia said 'poppycock to that.'" Corri paused—barely—to take a breath. "Look! Look at what I got!"

Corri opened a box and held it up for India to peek inside. A small turtle scratched tiny claws onto the cardboard bottom.

"Ry used to have a turtle like that," India told her.

"That's what Aunt August said."

"Where did you find it?" Nick leaned against the doorway, eating an apple.

"The pond behind the barn."

"I used to find turtles there. Tadpoles in the spring, frogs and salamanders in the summer. Unusual to find a turtle out of hibernation this time of the year."

"One of the dogs dug it up, Mr. Emmons said," Corri explained. "Mr. Emmons had it in an aquarium, but he said he thought the turtle liked me better so I could take him home."

"Where is Aunt August?" India asked.

"She's outside talking to Mrs. Peterson." Corri pointed out to the sidewalk, where August was trying to extricate herself from a conversation.

"And Amber had fun too. Delia has a big old cat named Gracie who let Amber nap on the window ledge with her." Corri bent down to open the travel crate that served as a temporary home for her kitten.

"Well, that just shows how special Amber is." Nick laughed. "Gracie has never suffered other pets graciously."

"We told her that Amber wasn't staying," Corri explained, "so it was probably all right."

"I'm sure that must have had something to do with it." Nick nodded.

"Corri, why don't you take the turtle and the kitten into the kitchen. Later, we'll get an aquarium for him."

"Mr. Emmons gave me one. It's in the back of the car. See, Randall is getting it out." Corri pointed out the window.

"Hmm. Maybe I'll go out and give him a hand with the bags," Nick said.

"And I'll see if I can help Aunt August." India followed Nick through the front door.

"How was everything?" August hugged India after Janelle Peterson had satisfied herself that she had all the gossip she was going to get out of August Devlin that day and gone on about her business. "How is Darla?"

"Everything was quiet." India took the shopping bags from her aunt's hands. "And Darla is coming around. She opened her eyes on Wednesday. Kenny has taken some vacation time from his job and is spending the days at the hospital and has the kids at night. It's been hard on all of them."

"And I take it we're no closer to knowing who . . ."

"Not a clue, Aunt August." India paused at the top of the steps. "Chief Carpenter had a man here at the house twenty-four hours a day for the past week and says he's not heard or seen a thing."

"We could just have well stayed here then." August dropped a suitcase near the foot of the steps while she removed her heavy coat.

"Oh, but then you wouldn't have spent a week at Delia's." India's eyes danced. "So tell me, what was it like?"

"Great fun. And you're right, I wouldn't have missed it." August laughed. "I haven't been away in ages, and Delia has her own little resort right there in her home. Exercise room, indoor pool, an indoor track if you want to run, India! A spa. She had a masseur come in three times last week so that we could have a massage after we worked out with her trainer."

"Delia has her own trainer?"

"Oh my, yes. Every other day. She says it helps her stay in shape because she sits at her computer so much."

"Well, it sounds as if you had quite a week."

"We did, India, but I worried about you."

"You didn't have to." India draped an arm around her aunt's shoulders. "Nick took care of me, and the police were watching the cabin as well as the house."

"Well, I just wish we could get to the bottom of this." August slammed the closet door. "We've had enough, India. First Ry, then this attack on Darla that was probably meant for you. What is at the bottom of it all?"

"I wish I knew." India took August's arm and led her into the kitchen. "Has Delia's private investigator come up with anything new on the phony land sale?"

"I don't know." Grateful to be back in her own kitchen, August went on automatic pilot and ran water for the coffee maker.

"Did she happen to mention why she has a private investigator on call?" Nick sat down at the table and folded his hands in front of him.

"What?" August asked.

"My mother. Did she say why she just happens to have a private investigator who seems to be at her beck and call?" Nick frowned.

August shrugged. "Your mother is very well known, Nick. She probably gets a lot of crank mail. I guess in her position, it would be a good idea to have someone you can trust checking into such things."

"Hmmm." He rubbed his chin. "I think she was getting some pretty funky mail there for a while."

"Then she would want to have someone available to check people out, if she had to. It makes sense."

"I guess so." Nick leaned back into the old wooden seat.

"Indy, can you help me carry the aquarium upstairs?" Corri called from the hallway.

"I'll get it," Nick told India, rising from his chair. "It'll give me a chance to check out this turtle."

"It's so good to be home." August sighed. "As merry a time as we had, there really is no place like Devlin's Light."

"I know what you mean."

"Do you, now?" August's eyebrows raised.

"Yes, I do," India told her pointedly.

"Well. It's about time." August unceremoniously poured the water into the top of the coffee maker, a small smile of satisfaction on her lips. Maybe, she thought to herself, things might just work out after all. "Now then, bring me up to date on everything that happened in town while I was away."

"I'll miss you tonight." Nick stood in front of India, running his hands up and down her arms. "I was just starting to get used to having you at the cabin all the time. I'm not ready for you to go back to Darien Road."

"Ummm. Me too." She stood on tiptoe and kissed his mouth. "But I think I need to be with Corri tonight, and I think I need to stay close to Aunt August till this is over."

"I feel better knowing that the chief is keeping a man on watch here," Nick told her. "But if anything doesn't seem right, I want you to call me, hear?"

"I hear. And I will," India promised him.

"India," August called from inside, "Corri is ready to be tucked in."

"I'm coming," India told her.

"Lock up," Nick reminded her.

"I will." She kissed him again before sending him on his way back to the cabin alone.

"And call me in the morning." Nick lingered for a second.

"I will."

"And don't open the door for anyone."

"Don't worry so much. We have a police guard. He has a gun. We'll be fine." She blew him a kiss.

She watched him as he walked to his car, then waved as he pulled away from the front of the house. Crossing her arms, she went to the end of the porch and studied the night sky, searching in the dark for a wishing star. She found one, blinking high behind the choppy clouds. *I wish that Darla would be all right. I wish that we could find whoever it was who hurt her.*

A rustle in the leaves to her right caught her attention. She stepped back toward the house, instinctively moving into the shadows.

"Oh, Taylor!" She placed her hand over her fluttering heart as the young police officer rounded the corner. "You gave me a start. I didn't see the patrol car. Are you early?"

"I'm sorry, India," he said. "I didn't mean to. My car has a flat, so I walked over from the station. And it's already eight o'clock—that's my shift."

"Aren't you going to be cold out here?" India frowned.

"Maybe, by the time we get towards midnight." He shrugged.

"Let me get you a key," she told him, disappearing into the house momentarily. "If you get really cold, just come in for a while. You can watch as good from inside as you can from outside, I guess."

"I probably won't use it, but thanks anyway. My instructions were to patrol the outside."

He held the key out to her, but India shook her head, telling him, "Keep it, just in case."

"Well, I should probably run it past the chief," Taylor noted.

"Tell him I said thanks for keeping you here."

"I'll do that." The officer touched the brim of his hat as he must have seen the sheriffs in old Westerns do.

India took the steps two at a time and all but skipped down the hall to Corri's room.

"Now," she told the child, "I want a full report on everything you did last week."

"Oh, Indy, it was so fun." Corri yawned. "Did you know that Delia has a swimming pool in her house?"

"No! Now, where in her house was it? In the living room?" India sat on the side of the bed and pulled her feet up, settling in for a chat.

"Of course not, silly." Corri giggled. "It was in a room off her big sunroom. Delia has two sunrooms. One is real big and has fancy tiles and big fans in the ceiling and lots of plants and white furniture. The other is small and has a little chair with a sort of stool to put your feet on and it's all white and green and has trellises on the wallpaper."

India could almost picture it, a small, serene private retreat for the world's most popular writer of mysteries.

"And the pool is very big and has lots of pretty tiles on the bottom and there are even trees in there."

"Trees in the pool?"

"No, in the pool room." Corri laughed, then her face grew very serious. "But guess what else she has, India."

"I can't."

"Delia has ponies," Corri confided, clearly awed.

"Ponies?"

"And horses. They all live in a big barn. They even have a big circle in the barn to ride in. And"—she held her breath—"she said I could ride any pony I wanted."

"So, which one did you ride?"

"All of them."

"All of them?" India fought to bury a laugh.

"I couldn't decide, and I didn't want any of the ponies to think I didn't like them, so I took turns and rode all of them." Corri nodded, sinking back onto her pillow. "But not the horses. They were all too big. I told them that someday I'd be bigger, and I'd come back and ride them too."

India tucked the soft pale pink blanket under Corri's chin.

"Do you think I will, Indy?" Corri's eyes were at half mast. "Go back someday?"

"I feel certain of it, sweetie."

"Good. I liked it there. It's different from Devlin's Light.

There's no bay. But there's a pond. It was so fun." She sighed, and her eyes closed just a teensy bit more.

"What was the best part?" India asked, sliding her legs to the side of the bed, knowing that, within seconds, Corri would be fast asleep.

"The ghost couldn't find me there." Corri smiled into her pillow.

"What?" Startled, India froze at the side of the bed.

"The ghost couldn't find me," Corri repeated.

"Corri, honey, there's no such thing as ghosts."

"There is, Indy, there is."

"Tell me what it looks like, sweetie," India said gently, anticipating Corri's description of a white-sheeted thing, or perhaps a vaporous specter that floated above the floor. What had this child been watching on TV? "Describe your ghost to me."

"Mommy." Corri yawned into her pillow.

"The ghost looks like your mommy?" India whispered to the child, who was all but fast asleep.

"Umm-hmm."

India sat motionless for a very long moment. Maris had been such a painful thorn in the side of the Devlins that she had forgotten there was one in the house who might view her in a totally different way. Whatever she may have been as a person, she was still Corri's mother. And Corri must have missed her so much that she had herself convinced that she still saw her.

Quietly turning off the bedroom light, India leaned back over the sleeping child to kiss her goodnight. *No matter how much we love her,* India acknowledged, *I guess she will always be Maris's daughter.* How, India wondered, had one such as Maris given life to a child so loving, so good as Corri?

And how to convince Corri that there was no ghost?

Tomorrow, she told herself as she tip-toed from the room, *I'll talk to Aunt August and see if she has any thoughts on how to deal with the situation.*

But when India awoke the next day, her aunt had already left the house to run errands, and the ghost was forgotten for a while.

"Corri seemed to really enjoy staying at my mom's,"

Nick told India when he came in through the back door later that afternoon. Not trusting the school bus to get Corri home safely, he had insisted on picking her up himself after school. "She got to ride the ponies."

"All of them." India nodded. "Did she tell you?"

"So that none of them would have hurt feelings."

"It boggles my mind that Maris Steele could have given birth to a child who is so sensitive to the feelings of others. Even if those others are ponies."

"Well, I'd say that this time the apple fell far from the tree. You hate to say it of anyone, Indy, but Corri is better off without her mother in her life. A woman who schemes, steals . . ."

"And yet Corri misses her so much she even thinks she sees her." India thought back to the bedtime conversation of the previous evening.

"What do you mean, she thinks she sees her?" Nick frowned.

"Corri thinks she sees Maris's ghost. She is adamant about it. She told me last night that the best thing about being at your mother's was that the ghost couldn't find her."

"That doesn't sound like a child who misses her mother. That sounds more like a child who is *relieved.*"

"I don't think it's a simple thing, Nick. From all accounts, all of Corri's memories of Maris may not be good ones, but the fact remains that she was still her mother, and I'm sure that Corri loved her all the same."

"Maybe we should talk to her, help her to understand that there are no ghosts."

"I tried to do that. She insists she sees her."

"Look, I have an idea." Nick pulled India onto his lap. "Why don't we take Corri out to the cemetery and show her Maris's grave again. We'll explain to her that that is where her mother's body is buried, and that once you are dead and buried, you can't—Indy, what's that look for?"

"That's not exactly Maris's grave." India squirmed uncomfortably.

"Indy, she's either buried there or she's not."

"She's not."

"She's not?" he repeated. "Then who is?"

"No one. Maris's body was never recovered. Ry erected that marker as a memorial, for Corri's sake."

They looked at each other for a very long, hard minute.

"Are you thinking what I'm thinking?" Nick asked.

"I don't know what I'm thinking. It's too bizarre," India whispered. "Do you think Maris could be . . . I mean, why would she pretend to be . . . If she really wasn't . . ."

"Maybe she faked the whole thing."

"Why? Why would she do that?"

"Probably for the same reason she pushed Ry down the lighthouse steps. Which would have been the same reason she tried to kill you last week. But she's not going to get you, Indy." Nick's jaw squared. "She'll have to get through me first. And I'm not budging."

"It has to be money." India began to pace. "I *knew* she never loved him. It was never in her eyes. She married him for money. She killed him for *money*."

"Lucien Byers," Nick said softly. "My mother said that her private investigator—who is former secret service with major league connections—can't find a lead on any of the people who were supposedly at the settlement where Maris sold this parcel of land to Byers." Nick frowned. "What if *none* of these other people ever existed? What if it was all a scam?"

"You mean Maris didn't sell land to Lucien? That he made it all up?" India crossed her arms over her chest and sat on the arm of the sofa. "Why would he have pretended to have bought land from Maris? Why would he have come here at all? It doesn't make any sense, Nick."

"Supposing there was something that he wanted, something he could only get from Ry, and he used Maris to get it . . ."

"Then Maris got what they wanted, then pretended to drown?" India frowned. "If she had what she wanted, why go to the trouble of faking her own death? Why didn't she just divorce Ry?"

"And why did she come back and kill him? And why would she come back now?" Nick's eyebrows knitted together.

"And why would Byers come here and tell me he'd bought land he hadn't bought?"

"I think I'd like to talk to Mother's detective. Now's a good time for a more thorough background check on Lucien Byers. And after that, I think we need to call Chief Carpenter and let him in on what we're thinking."

"Do you think we should tell Aunt August?" India stood in the middle of the room, her fisted hands shoved into the pockets of her jacket.

Nick rubbed his chin thoughtfully before answering. "Not yet. I think we need to get all the facts and discuss it with the chief first."

"I will gladly, happily kill Maris with my bare hands." India's eyes glowed at the very thought of it.

"First we have to find her," Nick reminded her, "and that may be the hard part. Don't forget, Indy, if she is really still alive, she has managed to avoid being seen for two and a half years."

"Except by Corri."

"Corri only saw Maris because Maris wanted her to."

India repeated the comment to Chief Carpenter later, down at the police station.

"Then maybe we need for Maris to want Corri to see her again," the chief suggested.

"No way." India shook her head curtly. "You are not going to use her as bait. We believe that this woman killed my brother, that she almost killed Darla. I don't want her near Corri, not ever again."

"Then we'll have to figure out some other way to smoke her out." Carpenter tapped his pen on the top of his desk.

"She wants something. She's impatient enough now to get it that she tried to kill a second time," Nick said. "She'll come out of the woodwork on her own. And I don't think we'll have to wait all that long before she does."

"I hope you're right, Nick." India stood up, filled with impatience of her own.

"India, I want to warn you not to do anything you'll regret," the chief told her sternly.

"Don't worry," she told him as she opened the door to leave. "If I find her before you do, I won't be the least bit sorry."

Chapter 29

"What are you thinking?" Nick asked, watching India's face change expression as she pored over the front page of the newspaper. "Your face has taken on a very serious look, but you have a sort of gleam in your eye."

"Hmmm?" She glanced up. "Oh. I was just reading about this case that the county D.A. is trying next week."

"And . . ." He gestured for her to continue.

"And"—she grinned—"I was thinking about how I would handle a case like this."

"What is it?"

"Two nine-year-olds have accused their basketball coach of sexually abusing them. The coach is a pillar of the community. Well known. Well regarded."

"And the kids?"

"Both from the low end of the economic spectrum. The parents of one of the boys weren't even going to pursue it." She spoke thoughtfully, as if from another place.

"Why not?"

"Because they know that the coach will have the best lawyer money can buy representing him. Which he does." She tapped the paper. "Howard Branneman."

"You know him?"

"Our paths have crossed." She grinned. "Very similar paths, I might add, to this very scenario."

"Who won?"

"Let's just say that Mr. Branneman has made it known he'd like a second shot at me." India laughed.

"You won the first round?"

"Twenty-five years without parole." She nodded. "That's what his client got."

"Twenty-five years," Nick repeated. "It could have been worse."

"His client will be eighty-seven years old by the time he's released. If he lives that long," she said dryly.

"Why don't you give Branneman what he wants?" Nick tossed the paper back to her.

"What's that?"

"Another shot at India Devlin."

"The case is being tried here, in the county . . . Oh, I get it." She nodded. "You're trying to say that if I went to work for the county, I could take on Branneman again." She shook her head. "I'm sure the case has been assigned already. It would be a good one to try, though."

She rested her chin in her upraised palm and stared out the window.

Behind her, Nick grinned. This time there had been no protests about Paloma and being needed there, no mention of the work she'd left behind. It was, he thought, a very good sign.

Five feet away, the phone began to ring. He was whistling when he went to answer it.

"India, it's August." He handed her the receiver.

"Hi. Oh? How long ago did she call?" India bit her bottom lip. "Really? I'll call her right back. Is she at the office? Okay. Thanks for letting me know."

She hung up the receiver but kept her hand on it, asking Nick, "Do you mind if I call my office?"

My office. Still. So much for reading the signs.

"Go on," he told her, and he turned away, trying to ignore the light in her eyes.

"Roxie . . . hi. My aunt said you called . . . what's up?" She leaned against the wall, her eyes focused on the bay outside the kitchen window. "I thought that case wasn't on the calendar till the spring. Yes, I remember it well. Did you find my notes?"

India began to pace back and forth, slowly, deliberately, as he had seen her do in court. The phone was propped on her right shoulder.

"I'm sure they're in the file, Roxie. . . . I put them there myself." India frowned. "I probably have them on a disk somewhere. Check the computer in my office and . . . Are you serious? What fool would have erased all my files?" Her foot tapped out her agitation. "I know I have a copy of the disk, probably in the box of things that's been sitting on my dining-room table for the past six weeks. How soon do you need the information?"

India sighed. "I'll drive up tomorrow. We can have lunch and you can bring me up to date on 'All My Children.'"

She hung up the phone and turned to see Nick watching her.

"I didn't know you watched soap operas," he said.

"What? Oh. That's how I refer to my caseload," she told him. "'All My Children.'"

He nodded. Suddenly it was *her* caseload again.

"I don't think this is a good time for you to take off for Paloma. Not with a killer on your heels."

"Maris won't even know I'm gone. And I'll only be in Paloma for one day."

"Are you sure?"

"I'm certain." She nodded. "I'm going to go to my house, I'll get the disk, I'll go to the office and have lunch with Roxie."

"I think I want to go with you."

"Don't be silly."

"I don't think you should go anywhere alone."

"I'll be fine," she insisted. "Would it make you feel better if I called Paloma's finest and asked someone to meet me at the townhouse?"

"Yes, it would."

"Nick, it's unnecessary."

"Humor me."

She shrugged and picked up the phone. "Yes, I'd like to speak with Detective Brown, please. . . . Yes, it's India Devlin. Yes. I'm fine, thank you. Yes, I'll hold."

"Done," she said when she had hung up the phone. "Are you happy now?"

"Yes," he said, though he didn't look very happy at all.

It was too soon for her to go back, he thought as he looked out over the water. It wasn't out of her system yet. She would sit down and spread that file out and that would be the end of her staying in Devlin's Light.

He watched her toss bread crumbs off the deck to the ducks and wondered if he had already lost her.

"I'll be a little later than I thought," India was telling him at one o'clock the following afternoon.

"What's the problem?" Nick felt the little trickle of apprehension bite at the back of his neck.

"No problem. But my boss asked me to stop in around four."

"So he can make a pitch for you to come back?"

"Probably. And I figured as long as I'm here, I might as well have dinner with the gang."

"India, I don't think you should do that. I think you should be home before it gets dark."

"Excuse me?" she said quietly.

He could *hear* her eyebrows rising all the way to the top of her forehead.

"India, you seem to forget that there's a killer after you."

"I haven't forgotten anything, Nick. But I'll be damned if I'm going to hide in that house on Darien Road until Maris comes looking for me."

"Just the same, I think you should be home."

"Nick, stop it. You're not my parent."

"What am I, India?"

"You're the love of my life, Nicky." She sighed. "I'll be home when I'm finished here, and I'll be fine."

"I'll be at the house when you get back."

"Look, it might be late. Why don't you ask Aunt August to let you sleep in Ry's old room?"

"I'd rather sleep in your room."

"We'll see what we can work out. Look, I have to go. Roxie's waiting for me. I'll see you later."

It was much later—almost midnight—when India pulled into the drive. She parked the car closer to the house than she normally did and looked around for the police officer who was supposed to be watching the house. In the shadow of the back porch, she saw Taylor and waved to him. She felt reassured, knowing that he had been waiting for her, that he watched her as she unlocked the door and slipped quietly into the kitchen.

"India?"

Her name, whispered, hung in the air.

"Where are you, Nick?"

"In the sitting room."

He was alone in the dark; she could not see his face and so did not see the look of total relief that she had come back, that no harm had befallen her. He opened his arms and she slid into them.

"You were worried," she said.

"Yes."

"I told you I'd be fine," she reminded him.

"I guess I was afraid . . ."

"Don't be." She placed a finger against his lips to silence him. "When did everyone else go to bed?"

"Around ten."

"Really?" She toyed with the hair that curled over his collar. "Then I guess Aunt August and Corri are sound asleep by now."

"Most likely." He nodded. "Indy, there's something we need to talk about. Something I need to tell you."

"Later, Nicky. Right now I'm very tired from the trip, and I want to go to bed." She stood up and took him by the hand, leading him to the back of the house. "If we were very, very quiet . . ." She started up the back steps.

"I can do quiet," he assured her. "I can do *very* quiet."

"I never showed you my collection of perfume bottles," she whispered softly.

"Tonight would be a good night for that," he agreed. "It would be a very good night."

"Nick, you can't fall asleep here," India told him. "If Corri comes in in the morning and finds you in my bed, it would not be a good thing."

Nick grunted a soft protest, knowing she was right but not liking it.

"The day will come when I won't be sneaking in and out of your bed."

"No doubt," she said, smiling, "but since it's not here yet, you have to get up and go on down the hall to Ry's room."

Reluctantly, Nick swung his legs over the side of the bed, stood up and quietly gathered his clothes. He bent down to kiss her one more time, and she asked, "Are you sure you know where Ry's room is?"

"Ummm-hmmm," he murmured sleepily. "We have to talk, India. Something you need to know."

"And tomorrow you will tell me," she said. "Nicky?"

"Hmm?" He turned in the doorway.

"I love you."

"Thank you, sweetheart, for telling me that even as you kick me out of your bed in the middle of a very cold night. I love you too."

"Goodnight, Nick." India grinned and got cozy under her blankets, reluctant to see him go. She wanted his warmth, needed to sleep curled up in the circle of his arms.

From downstairs, the clock on the mantel chimed two o'clock. India turned over and smooshed her pillow under her head. An hour later, she was smooshing it in the opposite direction. There was just too much on her mind. The case that she and Roxie had discussed was one that had been of particular interest to India. She was certain it could be won. Certain that if questioned the right way, the defendant would break on the stand, in spite of his protestations of innocence. It had been hard to turn it over back in December, harder still today to walk away from it. And then there had been the meeting with her boss.

A subtle sound at the end of the hall caught her attention, and she held her breath, listening, as the faintest footsteps seemed to echo at the foot of the stairs. Had Nick gone downstairs for a snack?

Maybe she would join him, she thought, thinking back to the dinner she had only toyed with earlier. She had felt torn, as she had known she would, and it had been difficult to be the odd man out. She had sat in the crowded bar and picked at the fajitas that had been placed before her, while her former colleagues tossed the familiar and easy banter back and forth. Now, at almost three-thirty in the morning, she was starving. Maybe, if she asked very nicely, she could talk Nick into making waffles.

Swinging her feet over the side of the bed, she stood up and, with quietly measured steps, made her way down the hall. From the time she had been in high school, she had known which stairs creaked and which could be trusted to permit her to come and go without detection. The house lay still and cold around her, and she wished she'd had the sense to put on her robe over her nightshirt.

An indistinct sound caused her to freeze in midstride.

It wasn't coming from the kitchen, and it wasn't Nick.

India sank back into the shadows of the front hall and listened. Someone was in Ry's study shuffling papers. It didn't take much imagination to figure out who that someone might be. India paused to consider her options. She could try to get back upstairs and wake Nick. She could try to get to the door to find Taylor. Either way, she ran the risk of alerting Maris, who could so easily flee.

Or she could take Maris herself.

There really wasn't a choice, as far as India was concerned. On the tips of her toes, she crept into the sitting room and, with nimble fingers, sought the fireplace poker.

Without thought of the consequences, she slid along the wall toward the study. The door moved almost imperceptibly, but she caught the motion. Still against the wall, she raised the wrought-iron poker over her head and swung as the dark figure emerged from the unlit room. One smack sent the figure to the floor.

With a *whoosh* of an exhalation, India dropped the weapon on the floor and knelt to turn the figure over.

"Oh, my God!" she cried. "Taylor! I forgot all about Taylor!"

"So it would seem," said a voice from behind her in the darkened hall.

India turned to face her former sister-in-law.

"Thanks, India," Maris said. "I was wondering how I was going to get rid of him. Guns are so noisy, and knives are so messy. You know how I detest a mess."

"You bitch," India hissed, every muscle tensing with the effort to remain still, to determine if her adversary was armed and, if so, with what sort of weapon.

"Now, is that any way to greet long-lost family?"

"You were never family. What trick did you use to get my brother to marry you?"

"Why India, you know that the oldest trick still works best." Maris laughed derisively.

"You told him you were pregnant?"

"Can you believe he fell for it? 'Ry, what will I do? Who will take care of my baby and my sweet young daughter?' Of course, three weeks after the wedding, I had a 'miscarriage' . . . but, well, Ry was such a sucker for that little brat, I could probably have gotten him to marry me anyway."

In the dark, India could all but see Maris's mouth twisted unpleasantly. There was no touch of Corri's sweetness anywhere in the face that stepped into the dim light that flooded in from the streetlamp outside the front window.

"She's not yours," India stated flatly. "Corri's not yours."

"Of *course* she's not mine. Do I strike you as the maternal type?"

"Whose, then?"

"It seems my cousin Angela had a real wide streak of bad luck a few years back. Got herself knocked up and run over by a car inside of eleven months. Corri was two months old when she died. My mother took care of the baby. Not that it matters."

"It matters," India said softly.

"Oh, don't tell me. Let me guess. Now *you* want to adopt her. This whole family suffers from severe white-knight syndrome, you know that? You're every bit as sappy as your brother was, India. And almost as annoying. I'll tell you, it was worth 'drowning' to get away from him."

"Why did you marry him, then?"

"India, have you been gone so long that you don't know that the Devlin family owns the largest section of privately owned beach on this side of the Delaware Bay?"

"It's not exactly the French Riviera, Maris. That stretch of beach couldn't be worth that much."

Maris laughed. "You are very short-sighted, India. I'm surprised you haven't been able to figure it out."

"Why don't you explain it to me?"

"Well, you're right about that stretch of beach not being the Riviera. The sand is coarse and it's always got dead, smelly things on it. Most notably those big, disgusting horseshoe crabs."

Maris looked at India meaningfully.

"You still don't get it? Let me give you another clue. India, what is the only thing that horseshoe crabs are good for? Other than covering the beach with all of those disgusting, slimy eggs." Maris laughed derisively.

"I don't have the faintest idea."

"You know, Ry always bragged about how smart you are. I was so sick of hearing your name. India this and India that. I couldn't stand you. Everyone thinks you walk on water. It'll be such fun to watch you sink."

India's fists clenched tightly.

Maris sighed with studied exasperation. "I can see I have to explain this to you. India, do you know what LAL is?"

India frowned, trying to recall. "Some substance from horseshoe-crab blood. Nick mentioned it once."

"Limulus amoebocyte lysate. LAL. It's the standard agent used internationally to test medical drugs for contamination by bacteria. It sells for three hundred dollars an ounce. It's also being tested as a cancer inhibitor. The government regulates how much blood can be taken from a crab—can you imagine?—but if you owned access to a steady supply of crabs, if you owned a large enough section of beach, the government would never know how many crabs were bled or how much blood was taken from each."

"A laboratory that had an unlimited amount of blood could control the market," India said flatly.

"Bingo."

"You married my brother with the intention of killing him for the beach . . ."

"And can you imagine my horror when I found out that I would have to share it with you?" Maris rolled her eyes. "Of course, I didn't realize that at first. My mistake—I should have investigated better."

"Why didn't you just kill him early on and get it over with?"

"Now, how obvious would that have been? Man marries penniless woman, three weeks later is found dead? *Duh.*" Maris rolled her eyes. "The spouse is always the most logical suspect, India, you of all people should know that.

No, I had to put some distance between me and the event, if you will."

"So you pretended to be dead for two years? How did you plan on resurrecting yourself?"

"It's all so simple, India. You want to hear the story that I'm going to tell when I come back? It's such a heartbreaker." Maris leaned back against the wall, her left hand on her hip, the right hand still out of sight in her jacket pocket. "When the storm came up, my little boat was tossed about like a toy. The current took me miles from Devlin's Light. Then, as the storm intensified, poor little me was tossed out of that tiny rowboat like a rag doll and into the bay, where I was struck on the head by my boat. Fortunately, a passing boat saw me fall out and rescued me. Sadly, when I awoke, I had no recollection of my name or anything else, for that matter. It's taken two years of therapy for me to regain my memory. And here, now, I return to Devlin's Light, only to find that, in my absence, my beloved husband has been killed." Maris raised her left hand to her face in a motion of sheer melodrama.

"You will not get away with this. There will be an investigation."

"And they'll speak with the person who 'rescued' me, and with my 'therapist.'" Maris waved her hand as if all were immaterial. "You'd be surprised what you can buy with enough cash, India."

"Where would you have gotten so much cash?" India said aloud, then she knew. "From Lucien Byers. His two hundred and fifty thousand dollars."

Maris laughed. "Well, of course, it was Lucien's money."

"I can't believe you thought you could get away with this."

"India, the only thing that's keeping us from getting away with it is *you*. Don't you see? If the land had passed to me, as Ry's widow, none of this would be necessary now. I would just take what was legally mine and leave Devlin's Light as a bereaved widow. After selling off all the land, of course."

"And I suppose you had a buyer already lined up?"

"Now, was that *pun* intended?" Maris started to pull her right hand from her jacket pocket.

At that same instant, the hall light flashed on. Maris was startled, and in that split second, India's best right hook connected neatly with Maris's jaw with a force sufficient to lift the smaller woman off the floor and send her crashing backward against the wall, from which she slid into a quiet heap on the floor.

"Nicely done, sweetheart." Nick nodded appreciatively from the doorway. *"Very* nicely done."

"Thank you." India bent over Maris to search for the gun India feared might be there. She was relieved to find empty pockets. "Did you hear?"

"I heard everything." Nick opened the front door as Chief Carpenter's patrol car pulled up in front of the house.

"So did I." Taylor sat up, rubbing the back of his head.

"Oh, Taylor, I am so sorry." India leaned down to help him up.

"I'm okay. I was only out for a minute or two. But once she started, I thought I'd let her go ahead and finish her confession." The young officer stood up on knees that wobbled just a bit. "I knew you were in no danger, India. I had my gun, which I would have used if I had had to, but I could see Nick in the hallway behind you two. I knew you weren't in any real danger."

"So, look what we have here." Chief Carpenter strolled into the front hallway, his hands on his hips.

"Did you pick up the other half of the duo?" Nick asked.

"He's in custody. Thanks for the tip, Nick. That was pretty clever, you putting it all together like that." Carpenter patted Nick on the back.

"Who's in custody?" India asked.

"Lucien Byers."

"I don't get it." She shook her head.

"That's because you don't have the benefit of the information I got this morning from my mother's P.I. The information I waited up to tell you, but you, er"—he glanced at the chief and back at India, then dropped his voice to add—"you thought it could wait till tomorrow."

"And what information was that?"

"That about three years ago, Lucien Byers purchased a medical laboratory that had been instrumental in developing the techniques of extracting LAL."

"Byers was behind this?"

Nick nodded.

"Why did he come to the house with those phony documents?"

"Once they realized that the trust provided for joint ownership of the property, he knew he had to get around you to get to the beach. He figured if he had access to even a small portion of the beach, it would be as good as having the whole thing. With you in Paloma, you'd never know what was going on."

"What would be going on?"

"He'd be raiding the beaches for horseshoe crabs."

"And taking them to his lab to extract the LAL."

"Right. But he was afraid that killing you would focus too much attention on the whole matter. He preferred conning you to killing you. He figured he could get you to negotiate a settlement to keep the Devlin name out of a lawsuit."

"So there never was a land sale? That was part of the scam?"

"Which explains why my mother's P.I. could not locate any of the alleged players. The attorney, the settlement clerk, the title company—none of them existed."

"All that, for a few miles of beach." India sat down on the bottom step. "My brother was killed over a few miles of beach."

"Which, in the long run, would be worth millions of dollars," Chief Carpenter reminded her.

"If you were willing to exploit it," India said sharply.

"There are many who wouldn't hesitate a second to do just that very thing."

From behind India, a robed August appeared at the top of the steps and slowly descended. Her eyes darted around to take in the tableau in the front hallway: India, seated as if weary on the bottom step, Nick standing protectively nearby, the chief of police standing over a sullen Maris Steele Devlin. August stared at the young woman who had been presumed drowned for the past two years.

"It was Maris, Aunt August. She faked her drowning. She's not dead," India told her.

"Hmmph, I'm not surprised in the least," August pronounced from the third step, her arms folded crisply across her chest. *"Malum vas non frangitur."*

India looked up over one shoulder to where her aunt stood glaring at the crumpled heap that was Maris. "I'm sorry, Aunt August. It's been a long night. You'll have to help me with that one."

"A bad vase doesn't break."

Chapter 30

*M*aris sat against the wall, one hand rubbing the back of her head, the other holding her chin. With sullen eyes she watched the crowd that seemed to sprout in the front hall of the Devlin home.

"My lip is split," she whined, casting malevolent glances at India from across the wide hall.

"Be grateful it isn't your skull," India replied coldly.

"Where'd you learn to throw a punch like that?" Chief Carpenter was clearly impressed.

"Boxing lessons," India told him.

"I'd say they were worth every penny." Nick sat down next to her on the step and put an arm around her. "That's one hell of a right hook you've got."

"I get a phone call." Maris pointed to the chief as if instructing him. "I want to call Lucien Byers. He'll get me a lawyer."

"Well now, I don't know that I'd waste my one call on him, since in about twenty minutes or so you'll have a cell-to-cell connection, so to speak," the chief told Maris pointedly. "And come to think of it, he may not be real quick to help you obtain counsel. No, if I were you, I don't know that I'd be counting on Mr. Byers right now."

"What are you talking about?" Maris glared at him.

"Mr. Byers was picked up about an hour ago, on a tip from Mr. Enright. Good work, by the way, on the part of that investigator of yours, Nick." Carpenter tipped the brim of his hat in Nick's direction. "Anyway, Mr. Byers sure had a lot to say. Why, he was still talking when I left to come over here, and he told me what you were up to tonight. The bottom line is, I suspect that he is going to distance himself as much as possible from you, him being our star witness against you and all that."

Maris laughed harshly.

"You must think I am incredibly stupid."

"That's probably the nicest thing we'd say about you," India muttered.

Ignoring India, Maris scowled and told the chief, "I know this routine. I've seen it a hundred—a *thousand*—times on TV. The cops separate the suspects, they tell each of them that the other blamed the whole thing on them. . . . I'm not falling for it. Lucien would never—"

"He already has. We have his statement describing how you lured Ry to the Lighthouse that—"

"How?" India's head shot up.

"Well, Lucien tossed some little pebbles to Ry's window to awaken him. When Ry got up to look out, the first thing he saw was the light at the top of the tower. Of course, he went to investigate, just as Maris knew he would do. When he reached the top of the steps, Maris was waiting for him." Chief Carpenter recited the story as Byers had related it to him. "Maris flashed the light directly into his eyes, blinding him, so that she could push him over the railing. I'm sorry, August, India." He nodded to the Devlin women, then added, "Byers says he had no idea that Maris was going to kill Ry."

"That's a lie!" Maris all but spat at him. "I told him that was what it would take to get Ry out of the picture. It was her"—she pointed to India—"that he didn't want to kill."

She snapped her jaws shut, realizing that what she said was tantamount to a confession.

"I want a lawyer. I am not saying another word until I have a lawyer."

Carpenter turned to the young officer who had accompanied him to the house. "Help her up, Sergeant. Easy now with those cuffs. We don't want a lawsuit for excessive force."

"You were right," India told Nick, "that whole land-scam thing was a fraud."

"I don't understand." August sighed deeply and sank to the steps.

"Byers thought it was too risky to kill India after having killed Ry," Nick explained. "But he needed access to the beach if he was going to be able to get around the restrictions on the number of horseshoe crabs he needed to get his hands on. The only way to get to the beach was through India."

"Horseshoe crabs?" August exclaimed. "Why on earth did Lucien Byers want a supply of horseshoe crabs?"

India related the importance of the ugly crustaceans to her aunt, then added, "I guess he knew I'd never willingly sell off the beach, and so he had to find a way to get me to turn some portion of it over to him."

"Right. He was betting that you'd eventually offer him a settlement before you would let the Devlin name be touched by scandal."

"I can't say that it wouldn't have worked." India sighed.

"Except that Maris got antsy," the chief told them. "It was taking too long. She decided to go ahead with her own plan and kill India. The Twelfth Night Ball presented the perfect opportunity. She hid on the grounds, watching for a chance. She thought she'd found it, there in the gardens."

"Except that it wasn't India," Nick said softly.

"Poor Dar." India's eyes filed with tears.

Carpenter motioned to the officer to take Maris out to the waiting police car.

"You were here in the house one night when I was here alone," India called to Maris. "It was you that I heard on the steps."

"More than one night. I even left you a little calling card once."

India frowned, trying to recall.

"I left one of Ry's records on your bed," Maris told her.

"Weren't you afraid of being seen by someone who, unlike Corri, would know that you weren't a ghost?"

"I just couldn't resist." Maris shrugged. "It was all part of the game."

"Was terrifying Corri just part of the game too?" India's eyes began to blaze.

"I needed a source of information from within the family." Maris shrugged indifferently. "I still had a key to the house, so I used it."

"You frightened her." India stood up, her fists clenching, and Nick took her arm, protecting her from the possible consequences of taking one more swing at Maris. "You let her believe that she was your daughter."

"You mean she isn't?" Nick and August asked in unison.

Before India could answer, a tiny, trembling voice from the top step asked, "She's not my mommy?"

"Corri, sweetheart, come here," India said gently, holding her arms out to the child who stood wide-eyed, surveying the scene below: two police officers, Maris in the doorway with her hands cuffed behind her back, everyone else in nightclothes.

"She's not my mommy?" Corri repeated.

"Sorry, kid, I know what a disappointment it must be, but no, I'm not," Maris said, cocky even now.

"Who is my mommy?" a confused Corri asked.

"A cousin of Maris'," India told her. "She died when you were very small. That is, assuming that that wasn't a lie too."

"That wasn't a lie," Maris told her.

"So I don't have a mommy at all." Corri's tiny face darkened as she pondered this latest bit of news.

"I'm sorry, sweetie, that you had to find out this way." India sat down and pulled the little girl onto her lap. "But it doesn't change things. You are a part of this family, now and always."

"Oh, please!" Maris rolled her eyes. "You Devlins are all alike." To the sergeant she said, "Get me out of here before the music begins to swell in the background. I can't take another minute under this roof. I'd rather be in jail."

"Well then, we'll be more than happy to accommodate you." The chief pointed to the door.

Without a backward glance, Maris was gone.

"Corri, I know this must come as a big shock," India told her. "I know it must be hard to find out that the person you thought was your mother isn't really."

"No." The word was muffled somewhere in the area of India's shoulder.

"No, what, sweetie?" India asked the child.

"No, it's not hard, that she's not my mommy."

India looked from August to Nick.

"You're not upset to find out she's not?"

"I'm *glad* that she's not. She was scary." Corri raised her head to look into India's eyes. "Mommies are not supposed to be scary."

"Did she scare you when she came into your room at night?"

"She didn't!" August exclaimed.

India met her aunt's eyes over the top of Corri's head and nodded that it was, in fact, true.

"It scared me because she said if I told you that she was there, that she would make people come and take me away." Corri lifted a teary face, and India's heart nearly broke.

"Corri, no one can take you away. You belong to us. Ry adopted you, remember?" India cradled the child in her arms.

"But Ry died. She said they would take me and give me to someone else."

"You are not going anywhere, Corri Devlin. I promise you that." India kissed the top of her head and rocked the girl slowly in an ageless, maternal motion.

"Indy." Corri sat up suddenly, as if something of great import had just occurred to her. "Little girls need to have a mommy."

"This is very true." India bit her lip, watching the old light begin to return to Corri's face.

"You could be my mommy." Corri twisted one of the buttons on the front of Indy's nightshirt.

"I suppose I could." India nodded, as if contemplating the possibility.

"And *you*"—Corri turned and pointed at Nick—"could be my daddy. Ollie said it's better to have both."

"Hmmmph." Nick sat down next to them on the step, rubbed his chin thoughtfully and winked at her. "Ollie just might be on to something."

"Corri, I think that we should—" India began.

"That we should all give this some thought and talk about it tomorrow." Nick spoke as much to India as to Corri. "But right now, I think we should all go back to sleep. It's been a very busy night for all of us."

"Indy, would you tuck me in?" Corri asked.

"You betcha." India held out her hand to the child.

"'Night, Nick." Corri pressed a kiss to his cheek and started up the steps. "'Night, Aunt August." Corri covered a yawn with a small fist.

August patted the tangle of strawberry-blond curls as they passed her on the steps.

"Oh, the havoc that that woman caused in this family," August said angrily as she went the rest of the way down the steps. "To think of what she did to my boy . . . what she did to that precious child . . . to Darla . . ."

"Well, there's some consolation, somehow, in knowing that she's not Corri's mother." Nick watched August pick up the fireplace poker and return it to its place in the sitting room.

"Hmmmmph," August snorted. "No surprise there. *Non generant aquilae columas.*"

August locked the front door, then went to the back of the house to check the back door, leaving Nick standing in the hallway to translate on his own.

He smiled as the meaning became clear.

Eagles do not bear doves.

"I thought you might be down here." Nick's long legs covered the short distance from the top of the dune to India's spot at its base in two strides.

She patted the space beside her on the sand and he sat down.

"I love it here this time of the year." She sat with her elbows resting on her upraised knees. "I love all of it—the bay, the marshes, the tiny islands out in the inlet, the lighthouse. I love all of it, all of the time."

A slight breeze bent over a broken stalk of goldenrod that had, in late summer, graced the dune with color. Its flowers long dried and browned, the grayed wand waved along the sand, leaving a trail of tiny swirls to mark where it had been. India picked at the dried seed head.

"It won't be long before the dune will be all greened up again." She pointed to the yellow clumps of beach grass, the ragged little stand of bayberry with their scrawny limbs, the sea rocket that the breeze rustled along the sand like tumbleweed.

He watched her face but did not offer comment. He liked watching that soft glow come over her eyes.

"It's so peaceful here," she went on, in a contented, lazy voice. "But in another month or so, the birds will be back to nest and to breed. It's such a vital place." She pointed in the direction of his cabin, but he knew she meant the salt marshes that lay next to it and behind. "Man has messed with the marshes in every conceivable way over the years. We've drained them, dredged them, redirected them, polluted them. But it always comes back. It has to. It's too important a link in the food chain. It's taken us hundreds of years to recognize what the Indians who lived here knew. Every tiny organism has its place. Every worm and every crustacean. They're all part of the whole. And I love every bit of it."

A lone gull swept down, low over the water, searching for a last meal in the late afternoon. The sky was just beginning to turn slightly darker, the palest blue easing deeper, the lavender light just taking the first steps toward fading to purple. In the distance, the lighthouse rose majestically, casting a serene shadow on the waters.

"I spoke with Chief Carpenter about an hour ago," Nick told her. "It seems that even Maris's marriage to Ry was a fake. They arranged for a phony justice of the peace to perform the ceremony. After she 'drowned,' she lived with Byers."

"That's the only bit of good news that's come out of this mess." India looked back toward the bay where the whitecaps chased each other to the shore. "That, and the fact that Maris is not Corri's mother."

"The worst of it's over now." Nick stroked the back of her hand with gentle fingers.

"It'll never be over," she told him. "Ry will always be dead."

"We can't change that, Indy. We can only move on."

He desperately wanted to ask her about that, about where they'd be moving on to, and *when,* but he feared the answer. If she was to leave him soon, did he really want to know today, when her hair smelled of salt and the winter sun and her eyes looked like dusty lilacs just after a summer rain? Right now he wasn't sure that he wanted to talk about the future and the hole she would leave inside him when she left.

"When I went into the office yesterday morning, I found an interesting bulletin on my desk." She turned to him.

Nick's stomach twisted, but he refused to blink.

"What was that?"

"A memo from the FBI. They picked up a man in Utah a few weeks back. He was living in a cabin in the mountains. They were led to him by a ten-year-old girl whom he had abducted. She got away." India's voice dropped to almost a whisper. "She found her way back to town. She was able to tell the police where the cabin was."

Nick waited, wondering the significance.

"His name was Russell Tanner." She swallowed hard.

"Russell Tanner?" Nick frowned, trying to recall if he had heard the name before. It was unfamiliar.

"He was a drifter. He drifted through Devlin's Light once, back in 1979."

"The man who killed your friend?" he asked.

India nodded. "Sooner or later, they all get careless. They take one victim too many, and they get caught. I'm only sorry that he was so careful for so very long. My heart breaks for all the pain he's caused over the years." She paused and took a deep breath. "There were bodies buried around the cabin. Five bodies. Five more girls like Lizzie who will never grow up."

Nick massaged her shoulders, and she exhaled.

The drone of a boat's engine disturbed the silence. Out across the bay, a Boston whaler headed toward the inlet and the marina on the other side.

"But there is some consolation." She turned his face up to his.

"That he was finally caught?"

"That he was caught in Utah." She smiled wryly. "Utah is the only state left that still uses a firing squad. Of course, legally they have to give him a choice between that and lethal injection. But we can always hope that he'll be perverse and will opt for the firing squad. I've heard it happens sometimes."

"What happens?" Nick continued the slow, easy kneading of the muscles on the back of her neck.

"That the convicted will choose the nastier means of dying, thinking that he's making it more difficult for the executioners. Not that it would be hard to pull the trigger on him." India dug absentmindedly in the sand with a broken piece of shell. "It wouldn't bother me in the least to watch them put the hood over his head. Watch them pin the X on his chest to mark where his heart is. If in fact he has a heart."

She watched a wild cat stalk an errant piece of sea grass that had blown toward the water. Nick sighed, wondering if the news from Utah had put to rest the demons that had stalked her for so many years. He took her hand and traced the outline of her fingernails with the tip of his index finger, asking nothing else from what was left of the day than to sit on the hard, cold sand, wrapped in winter clothes, watching the last traces of the day dip into the bay.

Finally, when he knew he had to, he asked, "What will you do now?"

"What do you mean?"

"Now that Ry's killer has been caught . . ."

"It doesn't change my plans." She shrugged.

He exhaled sharply, his heart seeming to escape his body along with his breath.

"When will you be leaving?"

"Leaving?" She frowned.

"To go back to Paloma."

India looked into his eyes and saw such sadness there. *Poor Nicky,* she thought. *He hasn't figured it out yet.*

"Your three months are almost up," he reminded her.

"True." She nodded and tried to look solemn.

"And Ry's killer has been caught. And that's why you took the leave, isn't it? To find out who killed Ry?"

"In the beginning, yes." She smiled. "But I've found so much more than that."

"Such as . . ."

"I found myself." India snuggled into his woolen jacket. "I found Corri. I found you, Nick. I'd have to leave far too much of myself here if I went back to Paloma."

Nick kept silent, not trusting his voice.

"And besides, how could I leave Darla? The doctors said she needs weeks of rehabilitation. She would be there for me, Nick. I have to be here for her. How can I help her if I'm in Paloma?"

"That *would* be a problem."

"Then there's the matter of the lighthouse. I have to finish the renovations. For Darla. Just like Ry planned. I promised him that I would see it through. And just think how much faster she will recover if she knows that she has the opening of her little tea room to look forward to. How could I make that happen from Paloma?"

"Well, I suppose that would be difficult."

"And Corri." India's eyes began to dance. "How can I be a proper mommy if we live three hours apart? There's no question of taking her to Paloma—I simply couldn't separate her from Aunt August."

"No question, that simply wouldn't do."

"So it seems that the best thing for me . . . the best thing for everyone . . . would be for me to stay here. In Devlin's Light. Like you said, Nick, I can always get a job."

"Well, it's tough to argue with that kind of logic." Nick was trying hard to pretend that they were discussing something no more important than the weather, but they both knew the implications of her decision went far beyond anything that had been spoken aloud.

"As a matter of fact, I've already spoken to the county district attorney. I have an interview next Tuesday," she continued. "It might be a nice change, you know?"

"What's that?"

"The *pace* is slower. The number of violent crimes in the county is nowhere near what we had in Paloma. When I spoke with him—Jake Marshall, his name is—he said that it was unusual for anyone in his department to work past six o'clock at night. Fancy that, Nick."

Nick smiled.

"I figure I could use the time at night to help Corri with her homework. Maybe even volunteer to coach her soccer team next year."

"Sorry, that job is filled," he told her. "I already signed up. We might have an opening for someone to run the snack bar, though."

"Whatever." She grinned. "I just want to be there every step of the way from now on."

India sifted a handful of sand through her fingers and watched the light breeze carry the small grains away.

"Nick, you don't think I'm copping out, do you?" Her brows knit together pensively.

"What, by not going back to Paloma, where you went from one nightmare to another?" He scowled, then realized what she meant. "You've more than paid your dues, babe. Whatever you felt you owed—to Lizzie, to whomever—you've paid it in spades. It's time for you to come home and have a life, Indy."

India stretched her legs out in front of her, making blue denim lines in the sand. She leaned back on her elbows, watching his face.

It was all too good to be true. All too perfect. India held on tightly to the well of joy that was building inside her, almost afraid that if she moved too suddenly, it would shatter and be lost.

Know where you belong, and with whom.

Oh, I do. I do. She smiled to herself.

"Well, then." Nick cleared his throat. "I think we should celebrate this momentous decision with dinner tomorrow night."

"That would be fun."

He leaned over and kissed her gently, fighting the urge to cover her body with his.

All in good time, he reminded himself.

"I suppose I should get back to the cabin. I have some things to take care of." He lingered just briefly over her lips. "I'll pick you up tomorrow night at eight o'clock."

"Great." She smiled.

He stood up and brushed the sand from the back of his pants, prepared to walk away.

"Oh, and Indy?"

"Hmmm?"

"Wear your blue satin dress."

Chapter 31

The moon hung low over the bay to shed a glow over the water. Another unseasonably warm night, soft as April. A long limousine drove slowly up the drive leading to Nick's cabin.

"Madam." Nick offered his arm to India and assisted her from the back of the car. He winked at Randall, who stood alongside the handsome vehicle as the couple emerged. "Thank Mother for me."

Randall winked back.

"Randall drove all the way to Devlin's Light just to pick me up on Darien Road and drive me out here?" India frowned.

Nick grinned and took her elbow, leading her toward the front of the cabin. "Isn't it a magnificent night?"

"Ummm," she agreed. "The best."

"The best is yet to come," he whispered in her ear and took her hand.

"Nick, what are you up to?"

He merely smiled and opened the back door, sweeping low with one hand in a courtly gesture, motioning for her to enter. A steady fire blazed in the fireplace, lending its warmth to the big room. Nearby stood a table for two, set with delicate, pure white bone china and tall white candles, proud in silver candleholders, all on a snowy white damask cloth. A round crystal bowl held creamy white roses and fragrant white lilies, which filled the air with their scent. Above all, a hundred white and silver balloons—all pronouncing "Happy New Year!"—floated and bobbed toward the ceiling.

"Nick!" India clapped her hands in delight. "It's wonderful! Magical!"

"Well, I thought perhaps we should try one more time to celebrate the new year together."

In the kitchen, an aproned cook bustled.

"You're looking so much better than you did the last time I saw you." Mrs. Colson turned and smiled. "And you are just in time. Everything is ready."

Mrs. Colson pointed to a silver tray upon which sat perfect paté surrounded by small melba crackers that looked homemade. A magnum of champagne, braced in ice, stood nearby in a silver cooler.

"You brought Mrs. Colson all the way down here again?" Indy whispered.

"How do you think I got Randall back with the limo?" He winked mischievously.

"You mean, Randall and Mrs. Colson . . ."

"He's a confirmed bachelor, she's an attractive widow. Who knows what could happen?"

With one hand, Nick swung India's cape from her shoulders onto the arm of the sofa. With the other, he took her elbow and led her to the table.

"This is all so beautiful." She looked into his eyes as he held the chair for her. "Nick . . ."

"Sit down, sweetheart." His eyes glowed with love and anticipation as he poured the golden, bubbly liquid into the tall, fluted champagne glasses. He handed one to her, saying, "We have to drink a toast to the new year, India. Our first whole year together. But not our last."

From somewhere outside, the sweet sound of music drifted through the windows, filling the room with enchantment.

"Violins?" she asked, wide-eyed.

"Left over from New Year's Eve." He grinned. "They wouldn't leave till I let them play."

India bit her bottom lip as she raised her glass to touch

the fragile rim to his, her throat constricting with emotion as she looked into the eyes of the man she had come to love so deeply.

"I love you, India Devlin. I want to live with you and be a part of your life, from now until always. I want to watch the sun rise over the bay with you every morning, and dance in the moonlight with you at night. I want to raise Corri with you. I want to play with our children on the beach and teach them how to count the birds on Christmas Day. What do you want, India?"

"All of those things," she told him. "And you, Nick. I want you."

"My mother always says that life is a journey. Will you share your journey with me, India?"

"Yes," she whispered, mesmerized by his voice, by the vision he had shown her.

"Well then." He raised her fingertips to his lips and kissed them, just before he slid a circle of gold, upon which sat a large sapphire the color of violets, onto her ring finger. "Let the journey begin."

**POCKET BOOKS
PROUDLY PRESENTS**

WONDERFUL YOU
Mariah Stewart

**Available
from
Pocket Books**

**The following is a preview of
Wonderful You. . . .**

A discordant sound from somewhere in the big and rambling house rattled the silence that wrapped around the sleeping child like a Band-Aid and shook her forcefully from her slumber. Pulling the covers up over her head to shield her from any stray Night Things that might be lurking about, she opened one eye to sneak a drowsy peek, just to make certain that nothing of questionable intent had, as yet, invaded the sanctuary of her room.

All appeared well.

A slow sigh of relief hissed from between her lips and she slowly inched the blanket away from her face. Drawing confidence from that small but brave act, she sat up quietly and leaned her back against the tall, carved wooden headboard, careful, for all her bravado, not to make the bed squeak and perhaps invite attention to herself. Not that *she* believed in Night Things. Her little sister did, but, of course, her sister was only eight, and *she* was already eleven.

A sudden, nameless *thud* from the front of the

house sent her scurrying back under the sheltering wing of her blankets, where she huddled in the cavelike warmth for a long moment, holding her breath to quiet herself as she strained to acclimate her ears to the sounds the house made at night.

Cautiously she slid to the edge of the bed until her head and shoulders hung over the side.

From somewhere in the night she heard voices.

She forced herself to remain there, suspended between the floor and the side of the bed, between fear and curiosity.

Curiosity, as always, won out.

Easing herself onto her feet without making a sound, she picked careful steps across the thickly carpeted floor, her feet making hollow wells in the deep blue wool pile. A deliberate finger pushed aside the bedroom door and she peered into the hallway, hoping neither to startle nor be startled. A glance up the long corridor to her right assured her that the door to her sister's room was closed over. Employing great stealth, she crept into the hall, her destination the balcony that overlooked the dimly lit grand foyer below, from which the faint sound of muffled voices could be heard.

Someone was downstairs with her mother.

She paused at her brother's bedroom door, briefly considering whether to wake him. Her brother always treated her like a baby, even though he was only three and a half years older than she was. If she woke him up, he would think it was because she was afraid. Taking a deep breath, she crept past his door and continued alone down the hall.

Once at the railing she lowered herself onto the floor—oh, so quietly—and leaned slightly into the space between the balusters, seeking the best view of the scene below.

Her mother, wrapped in her dark green chenille bathrobe, stood facing a white-haired man in a dark-colored overcoat. Between them stood the boy, who was facing her mother, and it was to him that she spoke, her low voice but a whisper in the night. The girl wished she could hear what was being said.

No one looked happy, least of all the boy.

As her mother spoke, she brushed the hair back from his face with both hands, but he appeared not to be looking at her, but rather at the floor of black-and-white-checkered marble. The man never spoke at all.

Finally the boy nodded, just the tiniest tilt of his head, and as her mother turned toward the study, the grandfather clock chimed a rude and sudden four bells. Trying to follow the drama and caught up in it, the girl leaned a bit too far to the left and banged her forehead upon the wooden railing. The soft *bump* echoed, floating downward like carelessly tossed confetti through the darkness to the foyer below. The man and the boy both looked upward with eyes that seemed to tell the same story from vastly different points of view. The eyes of the boy burned dark and fierce, while the eyes of the old man held little else but sorrow. Both of them, she would someday realize, had appeared equally lost.

Her mother returned with the boy's jacket and held it open to him, helping him to ease arms heavy with reluctance into the sleeves. She hugged him then, holding him only long enough not to cause him embarrassment. The boy was almost as tall as her mother, and the girl wondered why she hadn't noticed before.

She froze at the sound approaching from behind, a soft footfall on the plump carpet. Light fingers touched her shoulder to reassure. Without turning around, she knew that her brother, too, had felt, rather than heard, the disturbance. Together they watched, in silence, as the drama below played out.

Finally, her brother pointed at the old man in the foyer and whispered, *"That's* his grandfather. He's taking him back."

The girl bit her lip. As if she didn't know who the man in the dark raincoat was. "He doesn't want to go, Nicky. He wants to stay here. Can't we do something?"

"Mom said Ben belonged with his grandfather, Zoey. It's what his mother wanted."

"I wish she hadn't died, Nicky. I wish everything could be just the way it was." The girl's bottom lip began to quiver in earnest. Her hero was leaving, and there was nothing she could do about it.

A nod from her mother seemed to imply a hesitant consent, and the man opened the front door. Before the girl could so much as blink, the man and the boy had disappeared. Her mother stood alone in the open doorway, wrapping her arms around herself against the chill of the night air, and there she had remained long after the sound of tires crunching on stone had ceased.

A sense of overwhelming sadness drifted to the second floor and the girl leaned back upon her haunches to ponder it all. The boy—who, unlike her brother, had never treated her like a baby, and had never been too busy to teach her how to climb trees and throw a fast ball and catch frogs down near the pond—had vanished into the night, and there was, about all, a dense air of finality she did not comprehend.

"Nicky, do you think we'll ever see him again?"

He wanted to reassure her, to tell her yes, of course, Ben would be back. But having already learned that children were, after all, pretty much at the whim of adults, he merely shook his head and said, "I don't know."

∽∾ ∽∾

Zoey Enright leaned against the window and watched as, for the third day in a row, fat drops of water smacked and spattered against the wooden steps leading to the entrance of My Favorite Things, the shop she had opened but seven months earlier. April showers were one thing, she grumbled as she let the lace curtain fall back against the glass, but this was ridiculous.

Unconsciously she straightened a stack of hand-knit sweaters for the fifth time in half as many hours. Like all of the merchandise in her shop, the sweaters were exquisite things, handmade of hand-woven wool, one of a kind, and pricey.

Maybe a bit too pricey for this rural Pennsylvania two-mule town, her sister Georgia had ventured to suggest.

At the time, Zoey had brushed off Georgia's concern with a wave of her hand. What did she know, anyway? She's a *dancer,* Zoey had pointed out, not a shopkeeper, and Georgia had shrugged that she'd only been voicing a concern.

Zoey had been convinced that her unique little shop would be the talk of Chester County, located, as it was, in a honey of a tiny renovated barn midway between Wilmington, Delaware, and Lancaster, Pennsylvania, just a pleasant drive from the country chic of Chadds Ford and all those new upscale housing developments. The nearest shopping was a strip mall that was under renovation and wasn't scheduled for completion until next year. By that time, Zoey had hoped to have her clientele all firmly locked up, and there would be a steady stream of repeat shoppers beating a path to her door to find all those very special goodies they could not buy elsewhere.

Shelves laden with baskets of sweaters, wooden toys and dolls, pottery and jewelry, hats and afghans, painted boxes of papier mâché and stained-glass windows lined the shop and competed for the attention of the customer's eye. From old-fashioned clothes racks, satin hangers displayed dresses from the turn of the century, some antiques, some reproductions. Authentic Victorian boots of softest black leather trimmed with jet beads sat next to nineties-style granny boots. Marcasite bracelets from the twenties and thirties shared case space with new pieces styled by up-and-coming contemporary designers.

A glance at the calendar reminded Zoey that she had been open for business for exactly seven months today. With backing from her mother, internationally renowned mystery writer Delia Enright, Zoey had spent the entire summer preparing for her grand opening back in September. Georgia had driven up from Baltimore, where, as a member of the famed Inner Harbor Dance Troupe, she worked hard to make a name for herself in the world of ballet. Early in the morning of opening day, Georgia had knocked on the front door and waited patiently for Zoey to admit her as the very first customer of My Favorite Things.

"So," Zoey had said, after she ushered her sister into the shop, "what do you think of my little venture?"

Georgia had stood drop-jawed in the middle of the colorful, hand-made rag rug that covered the center of the floor.

"Zoey, it's awesome. It's like . . ."—Georgia had sought to do justice to Zoey's displays—"Like a tiny mall full of perfect little boutiques."

"Exactly." Looking pleased and somewhat smug, Zoey folded her arms across her chest, watching with pleasure as her sister lifted item after item and marveled at the variety.

"Where did all this stuff come from?" Georgia held aloft a small hand-blown glass perfume bottle to admire the workmanship.

"Here, there, and everywhere." Zoey grinned.

"Well, it's all wonderful." Georgia had lifted a black beaded shawl and draped it over her shoulders to cover the river of thick, straight blond hair which ran the length of her back.

"That's the real thing." Zoey's blue eyes sparkled with pride as she straightened out the back of the shawl. "Circa 1920. Those are real glass beads, by the way, hand-sewn on silk."

Georgia glanced at the price tag.

"Ouch!" she exclaimed. "Are you kidding?"

"Nope." Zoey leaned back against the counter.

"Zoey, this is one pricey item."

"Georgia, that shawl is hand-made. It's eighty years old and it's in mint condition. I don't know where you're likely to find another like it. And the price, I might add, is barely marked up over what I had to pay to get it."

"It is gorgeous. There's no question that anyone would love to have it. I just hope that you'll be able to find a buyer for it. I'd feel a little more confident if you were a bit closer to Philadelphia, or Wilmington—even closer in toward West Chester would help—but as far out as you are into the country, well, I just hope that you haven't priced yourself out of a sale."

"I'd be lying if I said that the thought hadn't occurred to me," Zoey admitted, "but that shawl was so perfect that I had to have it. It's like these sweaters." She held up a dark green woolen tunic. "The lady who makes them wanted an arm and a leg for them, but they're clearly worth it."

"Zoey, I'm not the financial whiz in the family, but I don't think you'll make much money if you don't mark up what you buy."

"I know, but I thought that in the beginning, at least, it would be a good idea to have some really eye-catching things."

"Well, you've certainly accomplished that." Georgia removed the shawl gently and carefully refolded it, placing it back on the shelf. "I just hope that the locals appreciate your style and that they shop here frequently enough to keep you in business. I'd buy this"—she patted the shawl—"in a heartbeat if I had a few extra hundred dollars I didn't know what to do with. You must have spent a bloody fortune on your inventory."

"Actually, the bloody fortune was Mom's," Zoey admitted. "She was as excited about this venture as I was, and you know how Mom is when she gets excited about something. Besides putting up the cash, she really got into scouting out the most unusual, the most exquisite things—that collection of Victorian mourning pins, for example . . ."

Zoey opened the case and removed a tray of pins that looked, Georgia noted, strangely like hair.

"They're made out of hair," Zoey said with a grin, "and human hair, at that. A hundred or so years ago, it was a popular custom to cut off some of the locks of a deceased loved one and twist them into rings or bracelets or pins, depending, I guess, on how long the hair was."

"Ugh! That's disgusting." Georgia handed the tray back with a groan. "None for me, thanks."

"They're not exactly to my taste, either, but they

are kind of interesting. Mom was kind of drawn to them. She's probably thinking about how to use them in her next book. Besides, she thought that if we were aiming for an eclectic stock of merchandise, we should really go all out and find some things that probably wouldn't be available anywhere else locally."

Delia Enright had totally backed the efforts of her daughter. Zoey was her middle child and the only one of the three who hadn't—as Delia delicately put it—*landed* yet. Nick, her oldest child and only son, was a doctoral candidate who had found a contented life studying marine species in the Delaware Bay. He had met a wonderful young woman, and before the year was out, India Devlin would become his bride. Georgia, Delia's youngest, had never wanted anything but to dance. Pursuing her goal with a single-minded drive, Georgia had, at sixteen, been invited to join the prestigious Berwyn Troupe. Three years later, she had been asked to become a charter member of the newly formed Inner Harbor Dance Troupe, where she had, for the past six years, worked hard and performed with blissful zeal. It was only Zoey who had yet to find her place.

It wasn't for lack of effort or desire on her part. Over the past several years, Zoey had tried her hand at any number of occupations, all of which she had mastered, none of which had fed her soul and promised her the kind of long-term gratification she craved. The joy that Georgia had found in dance, the satisfaction her brother had found in identifying and studying marine life, the pleasure experienced by her mother in crafting her novels, had eluded Zoey all her life. *Many are called, few are chosen* aptly described Zoey's quest for a career she could sink her teeth into.

As a child, when asked what she would be when she

grew up, Zoey would answer, "A teacher. And an astronaut. And a newslady on TV. And a fashion designer . . ."

And so on, and so on. There were few things that hadn't caught Zoey's imagination. Over the years, she had, in fact, tried her hand at all of those things—except for being an astronaut, but she hadn't completely given up on that.

The problem was that, for all the things that caught her fancy, and all the things she did well, nothing had sustained her for long.

"Zoey is a bit of a late bloomer," Delia would explain matter-of-factly when questioned about her middle child's current status. "One of these days, she will find her place, and she'll be an outrageous success and live happily ever after." Delia would then pause and add, "It's just taking her a little longer to get there, that's all."

Zoey had on many occasions silently offered thanks that she had been blessed with a mother who understood *perfectly*. It had been Delia who, recognizing her daughter's sense of style, encouraged her to open the shop and fill it with all manner of wonderful things. Delia had had every bit as much fun as Zoey had, shopping for all those one-of-a-kind items that overflowed from every nook and cranny of My Favorite Things—all of those wonderful things that were *not* beating a path out of the store under the arms of the droves of those happy shoppers who were all, alas, happily shopping elsewhere.

"Charming, Zoey." Georgia laughed as she entered the shop through the back door and shook off the rain. "Absolutely charming."

"Is this hat great with these amber beads around the brim?" Zoey turned to greet her sister with a wide grin as she pushed her long black curls behind her ears and plopped a wide-brimmed hat of brown felt upon her head.

Georgia dropped a heavy purse of dark green leather onto the floor.

"Umm, I think it's the red rose that makes it." Georgia raised her hand to touch the huge red silk blossom pinned to the underside of the brim. "But there are probably only a handful of women on the planet who could get away with actually wearing such a thing. You just happen to be one of them."

"Nonsense. Just about anyone with some imagination could wear this." With a swoop, Zoey plunked the chocolate brown creation on her sister's head.

"Zoey, I look ridiculous." Georgia sought to remove the oversized hat from her undersized head.

"Silly." Zoey readjusted the brim, tilting it slightly to one side. "It's all in the attitude. There. See?"

"It's too extreme for me."

"It's extraordinary."

"It's too exotic." Georgia laughed and fell into the word game they had played with each other for years.

"Well, it is an extravagance." Zoey grinned. "But then again, it's an exclusive."

"It is an excellent hat." Georgia concluded the banter. "But I look like a female impersonator doing Bette Midler—and doing her badly, I might add."

Removing the hat with its glittering beads and huge floppy rose, Georgia replaced it on its stand.

"I'll admit that the hat is a kick, Zoey, but it may be a bit avant garde for the territory. It's a shame there isn't more traffic out here. You really have the most delightful things." Georgia picked the hat back off the stand and preened in front of a small mirror. "It does sort of grow on you after a while, doesn't it?"

"It looks great on you, Georgy."

"You know, you probably could sell ice to the Eskimos." Georgia told her. "I'll take the hat."

"It's yours."

"Zoey, you can not hope to establish a business by giving away your stock."

"Consider it an early birthday gift. It looks too wonderful on you for you not to have it. And that hat won't make or break this shop." Zoey wrapped the hat in tissue before sliding it into a plastic bag with *My Favorite Things* in purple script.

"The lack of traffic, as you noted, is the problem." Zoey straightened a basket of colorful scarves, hand-knitted by a woman from Chester Springs who loomed and dyed her own wool. "That strip mall down the road just in from the highway is killing me. It wasn't supposed to be opened till this coming summer. When was the last time you heard about a construction project running six months *ahead* of schedule?"

"That was a tough break." Georgia nodded.

"And having those outlet shops open up out on Route One sure helped a lot, too." Zoey sat down on a little white wicker settee.

"Maybe you should consider taking some things on consignment for a while," Georgia suggested, "and give your cash flow a chance to build."

"The cash is flowing mighty slowly these days," Zoey admitted glumly.

"What does Mom say?"

"I haven't had much of an opportunity to discuss it with her. She's been sort of holed up with her computer. You know how she is when she starts a new book. . . ."

"Underground" was the term Delia's children used to describe her single-minded drive to write.

"Well, if you need a loan . . ."

"Thanks, Georgy, but Mom's been pretty generous."

"As always." Georgia smiled, knowing that Delia had always maintained an open checkbook where her children were concerned. She had, over the past few years, purchased and decorated a charming condo for Georgia outside Baltimore when she had joined the troupe. And two years ago, she had completely renovated the old crabber's cabin that Nick had purchased on the Delaware Bay. "Well, you know that if you need anything at all, I'm here."

"Thanks, Georgia."

"Look, if we're all going to have dinner together tonight, I'd better get back to the house and start now to blast Mom out of her office." Georgia slipped into her dark green down jacket.

From a nearby basket, Zoey grabbed a plum-colored scarf and drapped it around her sister's neck.

"Thanks, Zoey, but I think you've given away all the merchandise you can afford to for one day."

"It goes great with that glorious mane of hair, and the purple plays up the green of your eyes." Zoey hugged her sister in the doorway and straightened the scarf around her neck. "I'll just take a few minutes to close up here. Then I'll meet you at the house."

Zoey watched Georgia dodge the raindrops on the way to her car, then closed the door and locked the deadbolt with the key. On the floor beside the counter she spied the plastic bag that held the brown felt hat that Georgia had left behind. It *had* looked great on her sister, Zoey nodded to herself.

Turning to flick on the switch that would turn off the outside lights on the front of the shop, Zoey paused to peer through the windows at the cars that flew past on their way to the newly reopened shopping center a half-mile down the road, and she sighed. She grabbed the bag holding her sister's hat and closed up shop for the night.

Look for
Wonderful You
Wherever Paperback Books Are Sold